A Noteworthy Courtship

by

Laura Sanchez

Chapter 1

Fitzwilliam Darcy paced his bedchamber, finally coming to rest in a large armchair by the fire. His mind was in turmoil. For eight and twenty years he had survived on the foundation of duty and honor under society's dictates. Each hardship cast his way had been conquered by maintaining a standard set by duty to his family. The death of his mother followed by the death of his father, running the family estate and supporting his young sister – he had held his head high through them all. He was renowned for his superior estate management and greatly respected for the fair and honest treatment of his tenants. He was fully prepared to seek a bride of wealth and connection, a woman who would further his own position in society and that of his young sister. All of these things ruled his existence, gave him purpose and direction – until he met her. Elizabeth.

She had driven him to distraction. With every moment, he thought of her sharp wit and playful manner. He saw her eyes sparkling with merriment, questioning the very rules of society with which he had been ingrained since infancy. She challenged him and teased him without pause or regard for his position in society. Images of her from hours earlier as they danced at the Netherfield ball replayed over and over in his mind. Oh, how he loved to hear her laugh, even if he was merely hearing it from across the room. His eyes had never left her throughout the evening, so entranced was he by her lively disposition – so opposite from his own. Even her confrontation about Wickham during their dance enticed him. In the moment, she had sparked his ire; yet now he was haunted by the fire in her eyes, revealing a passionate nature never displayed by women of his circle. In short, she was the polar opposite of the society women clamoring to be the next Mistress of Pemberley.

"How is this possible?" he muttered to himself, "Of all the circumstances I have endured, is this...is she to distract me? It cannot be!"

He needed advice. Confident he may be with estate matters, affairs of the heart were different. He longed for his father's advice, knowing that with his support, he would have the strength to either forget her or face society's approbation with his father by his side. But which path would his father advise? His parent's marriage did not seem to be one of convenience, but his mother's family was of no comparison to the Bennets. He needed someone to help him clear his mind, to justify the conflict he felt. At this point he simply needed assurance he hadn't gone mad! Bingley's advice, though easily accessible, would be highly predictable. How could Bingley object to his friend's pursuit when he was also clearly besotted by a Bennet? His cousin, Colonel Fitzwilliam's advice was equally objectionable, unless of course he wished to be ridiculed until the end of his days because "*staid and fastidious Darcy*" had gone completely soft over a woman. Being a reserved man with a small circle of friends, and an even smaller circle he could rely upon, he decided to fall into old habits and rely upon himself. Darcy rose from his chair and paced along the foot of his bed.

"Get a hold of yourself man!" he chastised himself, "You are a Darcy! At this rate you are no better than Beaumont!"

Andrew Beaumont, son of the Earl of Norfolk, had been a great friend to Mr. Darcy and Mr. Bingley during their Cambridge years. He had impressed Mr. Darcy with his logic until he did the completely illogical. After spending the summer months after Cambridge in Essex, he announced his engagement to Miss Evelyn Howard, an acquaintance of his younger sister. Though the Howard family had some favorable connections, most were through Miss Howard's friendship with Miss Beaumont. The Howards had recently lost what little fortune they had and Miss Howard would have been forced to seek employment. It was rumored amongst the ton that she had joined the Beaumont siblings in Essex as Miss Beaumont's companion. The Earl had refused his consent and adamantly demanded that his son give up the connection. Upon Andrew's persistence with the match, the Earl disinherited him in favor of his younger brother. Fortunately, Andrew had already inherited a small estate from his maternal grandfather, allowing the new Mr. and Mrs. Beaumont to live comfortably. Mr. Darcy, along with the rest of London society, had dropped the acquaintance with little remorse.

Mr. Darcy resolved to uphold the standards he had been taught since infancy. His cousin, the eldest son of Lord Matlock, had done his duty by marrying the well dowried daughter of a Duke, and he would do the same. There was no hurry for him to wed, but he must avoid the senselessness of making a poor match while on holiday in a remote country town. Mr. Darcy devised a course of action to avoid weakening his determination. The first and most necessary step would be to avoid meeting with Miss Elizabeth. Second would be to limit his interaction with Miss Bingley as far as civility would allow. A reminder of what type of wife he could expect to find amongst the ton would hardly be helpful. Third, he would attempt to keep himself as busy as possible. If delving head-first into estate business had proven ample distraction to overcome the grief of losing his father, it should in turn distract him from thinking of Elizabeth.

Finally satisfied with his resolve, he retired for the night, thinking of his father and all of the Darcys and Fitzwilliams that had gone before him. As he slept, however, his mind was no longer able to suppress the visions of the woman he truly desired – Elizabeth.

به‌به‌به

The next morning dawned clear and bright. As Mr. Darcy awoke, he banished any lingering memories of the night's alluring dreams and strode to his writing desk. He seated himself and dipped a fresh quill into the inkwell. Lifting his pen, he squared his shoulders and committed a few short words to paper, the words he had repeated to himself as he drifted off to sleep the night before. His determination had not diminished overnight and the finality of these words on paper would reflect the finality of his decision. He would not allow infatuation to overcome him, and he would not dare to describe this infatuation as love.

Mr. Darcy rang for his valet and prepared for the day ahead. Glancing towards his desk, he walked over and placed the note into his coat pocket. As one component of his plan was to keep himself occupied, he decided to lengthen his morning ride. He would head into town and peruse the local bookshop. Surely their selection would be inferior to that of any bookseller in London or his own collection in town or at Pemberley, however Netherfield's library shelves were sparsely filled and surely anything available in Meryton would be an improvement. As an added incentive, he may even chance upon some of the younger Bennet sisters in town. What better way to strengthen his resolve than to encounter the extraordinary lack of propriety displayed by her squealing and flirtatious sisters?

At Longbourn, Miss Elizabeth rose later than was her usual custom. She and Jane had stayed up after arriving home from the ball discussing Mr. Bingley. Elizabeth was thrilled to see her sister feeling all the happiness she rightly deserved. If only Mr. Bingley would propose, perhaps Mrs. Bennet would see some semblance of reason and give up her constant attempts to match Elizabeth with Mr. Collins. She knew she could hardly accept such a man as her husband, but her mother's encouragement of her suitor continued unabated.

Miss Elizabeth threw a wistful glance out the window, sorry to have missed the chance to walk out and enjoy the serenity of such a beautiful day before breakfast. As she descended the stairs, she became increasingly aware of her mother's voice, and then alarmed as she overheard the words being spoken to Mr. Collins. "She will be honored sir, to be the next mistress of Longbourn! Of course you and Elizabeth shall take care of us after the two of you inherit!"

As unfortunate as it was to be the intended recipient of Mr. Collins' imminent proposal, she was lucky enough to escape the house through the still room before her presence was known. As she darted through the back gardens, she could hear a shrill voice calling from her bedroom. "Lizzy! Lizzy?! Where is that girl? Jane, Jane! You assured me Lizzy was here preparing herself, and of course she should prepare with Mr. Collins awaiting her! Oh, if she could have but the slightest compassion for my nerves! Oh, Hill, Hill!" Elizabeth could not help feeling remorseful at leaving the rest of the household to bear the brunt of her mother's frustrations; however, staying home to reject a most unwanted proposal from Mr. Collins would only increase her mother's vexation.

Mr. Darcy spent the early morning exploring the countryside before turning his horse towards Meryton. After leaving his mount to be cooled down and watered, he headed through the village square, thankful that few of the gentry were in town at this hour, given the late closing of the ball the night before. Upon reaching the bookshop, he leisurely searched for familiar titles he might enjoy during the remainder of his stay in Hertfordshire. Finding a section of the shop containing used copies and many first editions, he decided to peruse these books more thoroughly. He was impressed to find *A Political Romance* and pulled the book from its shelf for closer inspection. He had read Sterne at Cambridge, but not since, as satire was not one of his favorite genres. He quickly thumbed through the first section, thinking that Miss Elizabeth Bennet would be able to appreciate Sterne's mockery of upper-class squabbling. He rolled his eyes at his own turn of thought and pulled the note from his pocket, laying it across the open pages.

"Be strong, man," Mr. Darcy muttered under his breath. Embarrassed that someone may have overheard him, he glanced over his shoulder to see the shopkeeper approaching him. Snapping the book closed, he turned around to receive his greeting.

"Mr. Awdry at your service sir, may I be of assistance?"

"Thank you, sir. I was just browsing after making my selections here," answered Mr. Darcy, gesturing to the books he had selected.

"Excellent choices, sir. If there is nothing else you need, would you allow me to package those for you?"

After taking the three titles handed to him, Mr. Awdry hesitated. "And the Sterne, sir?"

"Not today, thank you," answered Mr. Darcy as he returned *A Political Romance* to its place on the shelf. Reaching for his money clip as he walked to the counter, he looked up to observe a breathtaking yet horrifying sight.

Elizabeth Bennet had entered the village square and was meandering past shop windows across the street. She turned into the bakery just as Mr. Awdry handed Mr. Darcy a brown parcel containing his purchases. Thankful for the opportunity to escape without greeting Miss Bennet, Mr. Darcy left the bookshop and headed directly to the stables. Thanking the stable boy and handing him a sixpence, he mounted his horse and urged the stallion into a quick trot.

Just as Netherfield Park came into sight, he straightened in his saddle as a startling thought came to mind.

"Blast!"

Placing his hand over the empty pocket of his jacket, he remembered the note so carelessly left behind. *"I really have gone distracted,"* he grumbled as he turned his horse and galloped back towards Meryton.

Miss Elizabeth left the bakery in good spirits, allowing the pleasant taste of Mr. Harland's sweet rolls to ease the morning's troubles from her mind. She decided to visit Mr. Awdry's shop and inquire as to whether he had received any new merchandise from town. Hearing Mr. Awdry reply to the negative, but that he expected a small shipment the next day, she wandered through his collection of used books. Mr. Bennet's birthday was nearly three months away, but Elizabeth enjoyed seeking out unusual titles for her father. Noticing a book that was slightly askew, she reached to push it into place when the title caught her eye. She smiled softly as she pulled Sterne's book from the shelf. She recalled her father's pride in owning one of very few original copies of the work. Her grandfather had acquired the copy before the book was edited by the publisher to half its original length. Gently leafing through the yellowing pages, she was surprised to find a small fresh sheet folded and tucked within. Never one to deprive her curiosity of its satisfaction, she discreetly removed the sheet and unfolded it. In admirably neat and distinctly masculine handwriting, she read the following:

*November 27, 18_*
Be warned heart, my mind shall conquer you!

Miss Elizabeth stifled a scoff at the absurdity of the words before her. She did not doubt that many people made decisions that followed their minds and not their hearts; however, if a man needed a written note to convince himself not to follow his heart, surely he was fighting a losing battle! Glancing over her shoulder and seeing no one to observe her actions, she pocketed the note. While she knew not the author of the pilfered note, being dated – *quite fastidiously she might add, who would date a note to themselves?* – as written today, there was a fair chance he may return for it. Sharing her father's amusement in exploiting the follies of others, she could not resist the temptation to replace the note as soon as possible with a response of her own. She returned the old book to its shelf and bid Mr. Awdry good day, promising to return on the morrow in case the shipment from London had arrived.

As she made her way to the door, she narrowly avoided colliding with a tall figure practically running into the shop.

"Mr. Darcy," she curtsied, vainly attempting to restrain her smile at his decidedly flustered countenance.

"I....." he faltered slightly. Then with a curt bow, he replied evenly, "Miss Bennet....I beg your pardon, I was not attending."

"Do not trouble yourself sir, I was able to perceive your stampeding approach and prevented the inevitable. I hope there is no unfortunate matter causing your haste."

"Nothing of import, excuse me." With that, Mr. Darcy turned on his heel and continued into the shop.

Not surprised in the least at such a lack of civility from Mr. Darcy, Elizabeth merely shrugged and continued on her way. She headed home, wondering who had written the note now hidden in her pocket. Perhaps young Mr. Goulding or one of the Lucas boys would be the recipient of her teasing. After all, it could not possibly be Mr. Bingley, as he seemed perfectly happy to allow his heart to lead him to Jane. As for Mr. Darcy, that gentleman would first need to be in possession of a heart in order to lose his control over it.

Relieved to have his encounter with Miss Elizabeth at an end, Mr. Darcy turned his attention to the same shelf he had perused only an hour earlier. Taking Sterne's title, he quickly opened it to remove the note he had so carelessly misplaced. Looking at two unaltered pages of text where his note should have been, he furrowed his brow and returned to the front page of the book to search more carefully. A less-than-manly gasp was heard from the back corner of the Meryton bookshop as Mr. Darcy reached the last page of the book. The note was gone.

Leaving the shop nearly as quickly as he had entered it, Mr. Darcy mounted his horse and headed back towards Netherfield Park. If he had hoped to be calmed by the monotony of time spent with Miss Bingley and the Hursts, he was sorely mistaken.

Chapter 2

Though the acclamation was typically used to describe another house in the neighborhood, on the twenty-seventh of November, Netherfield Park was in uproar. After the astonishing behavior she had witnessed at the previous night's ball, Miss Bingley was determined to quit Hertfordshire as soon as may be. Mr. Bingley had positively mooned over Miss Jane Bennet the entire evening while the remainder of the Bennet family made a complete spectacle of themselves. She had planned to enlist Mr. Darcy's aid in confronting her brother during breakfast, but that gentleman had yet to return from his morning ride.

In the breakfast room with Miss Bingley and the Hursts, Mr. Bingley had announced that he would postpone his trip to London in favor of paying a call at Longbourn. Try as she may, Miss Bingley was unable to dissuade him. She had bemoaned the unsuitability of mixing with the inferior local gentry each day since their arrival, and to her brother, the rant sounded no different than it had each day previous. Mrs. Hurst did point out the impropriety of calling so shortly after the ball, but her brother simply responded that propriety be hanged – he wanted to see Miss Bennet, and he could not imagine the Bennets would object to his company. Mr. Bingley left the breakfast room and headed for the stables, wishing he had been wise enough to leave the house before breakfast as Darcy had.

Naturally this turn of events threw Miss Bingley into a vengeful fit of nerves. Her bitter monologue was immediately audible as Mr. Darcy entered the house before luncheon. Seeing that she was addressing the Hursts as they all moved away from him, he lightened his steps, hoping to reach the staircase unnoticed.

Unfortunately it was at this moment that Mr. Hurst turned around and bellowed, "Ah, Darcy, there you are. My wife and sister have been lamenting your absence. Do join us for luncheon!"

Having no means of politely excusing himself, Mr. Darcy fell into step behind the group, pondering how convenient it was that Mr. Hurst chose this particular day to be sober and sociable.

❦❦❦

"Surely you see the danger in this, Mr. Darcy?" implored Miss Bingley from across the dining table. "To be paying call the morning immediately following the ball. Such a thing would never be attempted in town. The country manners here in Hertfordshire are such a poor influence on Charles!"

"I doubt the likelihood that anyone will begrudge your brother's attentions, though it may be a slight breach of propriety," Mr. Darcy replied evenly, reaching for his glass.

"Begrudge him!" Miss Bingley scoffed, "Certainly not, they rejoice at having caught him. The expectations he has already invited have surely been increased by his marked attention last evening. You must assist us, dear Mr. Darcy, in helping Charles to recognize the mistake he is making."

At this moment, Mr. Bingley entered the room with a beaming smile, which only diminished upon hearing his sister's words. Fortunately for Mr. Darcy, his attention was caught by Mr. Bingley's entrance before he could make an offensive reply.

"And what mistake have I made this time, Caroline?" her brother asked warily.

Miss Bingley started slightly, but with little shame at being overheard, immediately repeated her objections to her brother's interest in Miss Bennet.

"As much as I appreciate your concern, I see little use in attempting to dissuade me from the woman I love. On that note, I cannot abide your company if you insist on disparaging someone so faultless as Miss Jane Bennet. I shall retire for the remainder of the afternoon and return to you at dinner." With that, Mr. Bingley quit the room as quickly as he had entered it.

❦❦❦

Miss Elizabeth arrived home from the bookshop and found Jane in the garden clipping lavender stems and collecting them in a basket.

"Lizzy! There you are. We were beginning to be concerned at your absence, so I decided to work here in the garden and watch for you."

"I see, and your attending the garden had nothing to do with escaping our mother, Jane?" she asked teasingly. Jane smiled broadly in response as she continued, "Do not trouble yourself, dear sister, for if this is the secret behind your love of horticulture I will not be the one to tell Mama. Simply allow me the use of some blooms for a new batch of lavender water and you shall be assured of my silence on the subject."

"Of course Lizzy," replied Jane, giving her younger sister a sideways glance with a modest version of their father's twinkle in her eye. "I must admit Mama did become rather exuberant when Mr. Bingley called on us."

"Oh Jane," giggled Elizabeth, "That certainly does account for your cheery mood, you seem almost giddy!"

"Yes Lizzy, surely you can understand my happiness! Mr. Bingley was perfectly charming as he declared that his thoughts were so fixated on all of his friends at Longbourn this morning that he could not help but visit."

"Yes, surely he was all anticipation for a good chat with Mr. Collins, discussing dance partners with Lydia, and finishing out his morning looking at Mama's new Irish lace! How kind of him to say that he looked forward to seeing us all, though I am sure your Mr. Bingley only had eyes for you as he said it."

At the last, Jane blushed and changed the subject to avoid further doses of her sister's teasing. "Mama was quite concerned for Mr. Collins, Lizzy. The two of them searched the house for a quarter of an hour looking for you this morning. Mr. Collins spent much of his time this morning asking after your return, but I believe he has now gone to visit Mr. Martin at the church. Mama was indeed quite beside herself until she spied Mr. Bingley coming up the drive."

Elizabeth knew her sister well enough to translate Jane's restrained comments as meaning her mother had been frantic and Mr. Collins had spent the morning lying in wait to stalk her as prey. She could very well imagine her mother's erratic behavior, calling for smelling salts to relieve her distress over Elizabeth's disappearance, only to be instantly cured when Mr. Bingley arrived. She entered the house, grateful for the empty hallway that allowed her to sneak upstairs to her room unnoticed. With a mischievous smile, she tossed her bonnet aside and sat down to pen the teasing response she had thought up during her walk home.

Elizabeth came down for luncheon only to be scolded by Mrs. Bennet for running off again and missing Mr. Bingley's call.

"Of course what should your company mean to Mr. Bingley!" lamented Mrs. Bennet, "Except that you may provide yourself as a convenient chaperone. He should have proposed today if you had been home instead of sticking your nose in every book in the county!"

"Surely Mama, Jane's beauty is such that Mr. Bingley will be unable to restrain himself from calling again regardless of my absence today. In fact, if Mr. Darcy were to have accompanied him, my tolerable appearance may have proved so little tempting as to drive the man away with Mr. Bingley in tow."

"Oh, hang Mr. Darcy! What is he to you, pray? You, Lizzy would do better to concern yourself with how you are depriving Mr. Collins of your company. You disappeared this morning before any of us were down for breakfast, only to return so late that now Mr. Collins has gone to pay his respects to the rector. You know how Mr. Martin's wife likes to carry on, and of course she will invite him to dine. Now one of their daughters will snatch him up and then what shall become of us!"

"Perhaps it is as you say, Mama. If he should betroth himself to one of the Miss Martins, we would hardly hear the end of his favorable opinion on the subject. However, should he return this evening unattached, I am sure Mr. Collins will happily continue to regale us with tales of the superior society of Lady Catherine deBourgh."

"Oh child, your impertinence shall be the death of me!" spat a flustered Mrs. Bennet, "You are determined to leave us starving in the hedgerows! You have already lost your chance today with Mr. Collins, although I doubt manners such as these will improve your ability to catch him tomorrow!"

"Mama," interrupted Jane, "Perhaps you would care for us to call on our Aunt Philips this afternoon? It may be a bit early to discuss the Netherfield Ball, but I believe she would enjoy our company."

"Yes! Oh Jane, you must tell her of your call from Mr. Bingley! We must not tarry and wait to call on her until tomorrow. It shall all go just as I have planned! Tomorrow you shall be at home, for Mr. Bingley shall call upon you again, and surely he will propose!"

Elizabeth gave Jane a grateful smile for once again diffusing their mother's displeasure. If only she had been able to do so without bringing up the topic of her expected union with Mr. Bingley, but subjects that did not drive Mrs. Bennet's thoughts to matrimony were few and far between.

Not typically one to enjoy the society of this particular aunt, on this occasion Elizabeth was delighted to visit their Aunt Philips, and she obediently joined her sisters above stairs to retrieve her bonnet and pelisse. Certainly Mary would be agreeable to stopping at the bookshop along the way to the Philips' home. After Jane had left the room, she pocketed a small note that would soon find itself lodged within the old, yet recently well-aired pages of a certain novel.

Netherfield Park was no longer in uproar as dinner was a decidedly subdued affair. Miss Bingley was still at a loss for handling her brother's new-found confidence. She infinitely preferred his typical cheery and bendable manner, as it was far easier to manipulate. As soon as the meal was finished, Mr. Bingley excused himself, asking if Mr. Darcy would care to join him in the library.

"Are you planning on escaping the house at an ungodly hour again tomorrow?" Mr. Bingley asked while pouring a glass of port for each of them.

"Forgive me, I meant no slight to your hospitality by being absent for so long, but yes, I was planning to ride into Meryton in the morning."

"No apologies necessary. I have always understood your desire to avoid my sister's company, and given her behavior since we arrived in Hertfordshire, I am inclined to avoid her myself. There is some business I have in town as well, might I join you?"

"Certainly, Bingley. I would never be averse to your company."

"I may not be prepared to leave at first light, as I do enjoy a good breakfast before leaving the house, but if you do not mind waiting for me, I promise to be ready to depart before my sisters make an appearance."

A Noteworthy Courtship

Mr. Bingley and Mr. Darcy rode away from Netherfield Park the following morning. Mr. Bingley wore his usual contented grin and Mr. Darcy tried to mask his apprehension, silently cursing himself for not thinking to simply purchase the copy of *A Political Romance* the day before. On their way towards Meryton, Mr. Darcy enquired as to the time of Mr. Bingley's appointment in town.

"Appointment? No, my 'business' is nothing of a serious nature. I actually just wished to visit a few shops and see if anything catches my eye. Miss Bennet was truly angelic at the ball, her hair adorned with the tiniest sparkling hairpins. I complimented her on them, and she mentioned that they were a particular favorite of hers, an heirloom from her grandmother. It put me in mind to give her a gift of equal beauty that she might have a treasure to remind her of myself as well. Would you care to accompany me?"

Mr. Darcy expression hardened as he replied, "Join you in a shop full of ladies' frippery? I think not. And besides – a gift, Bingley? I doubt that would be appropriate given your current situation with the lady."

"Not you too Darcy!" Mr. Bingley laughed, "You have already heard my sisters voice their concerns on that score. I am perfectly aware that my admiration of Miss Bennet has been plain for the neighborhood to see, but as my intentions are honorable, I see no reason to dampen my displays of affection."

"Bingley, I would be the last person to doubt your honor, but for Miss Bennet to receive a gift from a gentleman who is not her betrothed...surely you see the risk to her reputation?"

"I say Darcy, I had not thought of it in those terms. I shall simply have to rectify the situation before I present any gifts to my lovely Jane! Certainly there would be no impropriety in my lavishing her with all the finery she deserves after I propose!" Observing his friend's startled countenance he added, "Come man, surely you know I cannot go much longer without asking Jane to become my wife. I simply need the opportunity!"

With that, Mr. Bingley grinned and raised a playful brow at Mr. Darcy before urging his horse into a gallop. The two gentlemen raced across the fields until the village of Meryton came into sight. Mr. Bingley tipped his hat to his friend as he headed towards the goldsmith's shop while Mr. Darcy continued on to pay another visit to Mr. Awdry's back shelves.

Mr. Darcy was the first patron to enter Mr. Awdry's bookshop that morning. Certainly it appeared unusual that he should require any additional books after coming in twice the previous day, but Mr. Awdry merely shrugged his shoulders at the idea. As long as this rich gentleman continued to purchase a few titles each time, he was welcome to enter the shop as often as he liked.

After making a good show of perusing the shelves and selecting a few books, Mr. Darcy moved to back corner of the store, removing the book he had cursed all the way back to Netherfield Park the day before. He carefully thumbed the pages. Irrational as it may be, he hoped somehow his note had been overlooked the previous day and could now be retrieved. His breath caught in his chest as he found a folded sheet of paper, tucked in the same location, but definitely not the sheet he had left the morning before. Too shocked to dare opening the inexplicable note, Mr. Darcy discreetly moved it to his pocket and paid for his purchases. The mysterious paper burned in his pocket as he left the shop. As much as he had intended to read the note in the privacy of his room at Netherfield, he was not half a mile from Meryton before he sought out a secluded grove to satisfy his curiosity. He took a deep restorative breath as he pulled the note from his pocket and unfolded it to read the following:

While I cannot pretend to be an expert on great battles nor minor skirmishes within one's own person, I must say that after defeating the heart, the mind shall miss its counterpart exceedingly.

Mr. Darcy's countenance took a sour turn as he read the teasing words before him. Though he had not known what to expect, he certainly had not anticipated such a mocking response. Surely there were very few people aside from Colonel Fitzwilliam with the gall to tease him in the face of his imperious nature. All the more disturbing was the truth made evident by the writer's elegant script, it was clearly written in a feminine hand. As he read the note again, his serious mien was broken by a slight twisting of his lips. The note was impertinent, but certainly she, whoever she may be, could not have known the identity of her recipient. That this woman would not only remove his note, but replace it with a response showed a very singular type of wit. He could not but find some amusement in the way his own words had been intentionally misconstrued. Mr. Darcy shook his head and chuckled, placing the note back into his pocket as he leisurely returned to Netherfield Park.

The rest of Mr. Darcy's day was as peaceful as he could have expected. Miss Bingley's agitation was only increasing with each day their party remained in Hertfordshire. She was further incensed when Mr. Darcy returned alone, stating that her brother would again be spending the day at Longbourn. When Mr. Bingley did return to Netherfield, he was greeted by a stream of complaints, which he completely ignored as he went above stairs to dress for dinner.

That evening, Mr. Darcy resigned himself to spending the following day catching up on his business affairs, which would include writing to his steward and London housekeeper that he would stay on in Hertfordshire for some time. After requesting use of Mr. Bingley's study on the morrow, he retired to his rooms. Before he rang for his valet, he remembered the note still tucked into the pocket of his waistcoat. He had already determined while riding back to Netherfield that leaving a response in the morning was absolutely essential. The mocking words he had read challenged and intrigued him. Though it would occur under rather odd circumstances, this written debate would certainly prove to be much more of an entertainment than the drawing room conversation available at Netherfield. Sitting at his writing desk, Mr. Darcy readied his pen and quietly declared, "Very well, madam – let the games begin!"

No one was surprised to see Mr. Bingley riding up the drive at Longbourn before the youngest Bennets had even dressed for company the next day. He was all smiles and friendliness as he joined the family for breakfast and took what was now generally thought of as his seat, which was of course beside Jane. Mr. Bennet was quite amused by the gentleman known in his mind as Jane's barnacle, but took no offense at his undeclared intentions. He much preferred to watch this charade of a courtship come to its natural conclusion and teased that it would be most economical for all those involved if Mr. Bingley simply took a room at Longbourn. At first, this had alarmed Mr. Bingley, and fearing he had offended Mr. Bennet, he stuttered his apologies for calling so frequently. A glance at the mirth misting over the older man's eyes and a gentle smile from Jane were all it took for Mr. Bingley to know all was well.

After the meal, Mrs. Bennet suggested a stroll in the garden to her two oldest daughters and the men she considered to be their future husbands. Mr. Bingley inquired about a meadow he had seen on his rides from Netherfield. Elizabeth was quick to comment on the beauty of the location, explaining that she and Jane had often walked there as children and she could still remember looking up at her older sister as she made daisy chains to adorn their hair. Not being a man of great stamina, Mr. Collins begged off and headed towards the library. Mrs. Bennet narrowed her eyes at her second daughter as the walking party left the house, unable to understand her most ungrateful child. Try as she would to arrange an opportunity for Mr. Collins to propose, Elizabeth thwarted her plans at every turn. It was as though the unfeeling girl had no desire to catch Mr. Collins at all!

Again Mr. Bingley returned to Netherfield in the late afternoon, not joining company until they were to dine. After dinner, Mr. Bingley again excused himself to retire to his rooms, much preferring to daydream of Miss Bennet than to observe his sister's harsh countenance. No sooner had he left the room than Miss Bingley addressed Mr. Darcy, imploring him to convince Mr. Bingley to return to town at once.

"I apologize madam, but that I shall not do."

Miss Bingley paled as Mr. Darcy continued. "I agree her connections are less than ideal, and I have already related to him as much. However, I abhor deceit of any kind and will not lure him to town under the pretense of a short trip with the premeditated intent of persuading him never to return to Hertfordshire."

"But surely, Mr. Darcy, you would not wish to see your friend continue with the false conviction that she returns his affections?"

He did question Miss Bennet's feelings for Mr. Bingley, and pitied his friend for the embarrassment he was sure to face through a connection to the inferior Bennet family. However Mr. Bingley was set on his course, and after all, this unofficial courtship had been taken too far for him to abandon Miss Bennet without exposing himself to censure. Seeing no reason for his friend to leave and harboring his own desire to stay in the neighborhood, Mr. Darcy replied, "I cannot detect a regard for him in her manner, but would require further observation of her countenance to be truly convinced of her indifference. As he seems determined to spend a great deal of time in company with Miss Bennet, I see no harm in my accompanying him on one of his future visits."

This statement earned the response Mr. Darcy had intended. Miss Bingley blanched and clearly struggled to form a suitable reply. Unwilling to disagree with the object of her aspirations, yet unable to agree with a visit to Longbourn, Miss Bingley quietly made her excuses to retire for the evening.

Chapter 3

Miss Elizabeth was becoming quite vigilant in her morning ritual of walking out early to avoid Mr. Collins. Normally she did not take quite such early walks in such cold weather, but even if she did catch a cold, she would be grateful for the excuse to remain above stairs in a room which propriety would not allow Mr. Collins to enter. Though often frustrated by her mother's lack of understanding, she was glad Mrs. Bennet was not resourceful enough to conjure up the notion of rising early and preventing her from making her escape. Her efforts became worthwhile when she reached the bookshop and opened *A Political Romance* to find another note tucked within its pages. She had not been certain of finding another note, but many of her acquaintance were drawn to her sharp wit and playful manner, and she considered it possible that this gentleman would be as well. She hoped this unknown gentleman had wit enough to attempt a verbal sparring match with her and would be equally intrigued by the oddity of their means of communication. She was delighted to see he had attempted to rise to the challenge, and was unable to restrain a large smile and the tiniest of giggles. Unfortunately her outburst did not go entirely unnoticed, and as she turned away from the bookshelf, she found herself under the scrutiny of Mr. Awdry's questioning glance. She blushed lightly and moved over to a rack of fashion plates in a poor attempt of showing them to be the reason for her excitement. Mr. Awdry merely shook his head, wondering at Miss Bennet's uncharacteristic behavior and frequent visits.

As she returned to Longbourn, Elizabeth strolled slowly along the path, already formulating her reply as she read the following:

*November 29, 18_*

A person can hardly allow their heart to run reckless, with its emotionally driven and changeable desires. Indeed it shows a great strength of character to only act on carefully considered, logical conclusions. Forgive me if this concept is less exciting than the romantic notion that one should forsake everything else they hold dear in the name of following their heart?

Elizabeth made sure the note was concealed before the Longbourn came into view. She quietly entered the house and spent a few moments refreshing herself in her room before joining the family for breakfast.

‿‿‿

Though his intent to visit was only expressed to vex Miss Bingley, Mr. Darcy reluctantly joined Mr. Bingley in calling on Longbourn. He could not yet disagree with Miss Bingley's opinion of the Bennets, however he acknowledged that his friend's honor was engaged, and there was little choice but to accept the inescapable match. Mr. Bingley was as determined to see Miss Bennet as ever, and the two men arrived scarcely a quarter hour after breakfast. As the gentlemen were announced, Miss Elizabeth said a silent prayer of gratitude for Mr. Bingley's early arrival, as it would again shield her from Mr. Collins' attentions. Elizabeth knew Mrs. Bennet would be so focused on devising an opportunity for Mr. Bingley to propose that she would be distracted from providing the same service to Mr. Collins. So engrossed was she in these musings that Elizabeth scarcely noticed Mr. Darcy entering the room behind Mr. Bingley. Catching his intent stare in her direction, she released a sigh. She may have to spend the morning in

Mr. Darcy's disdainful company, but at least his presence would be an additional buffer between herself and Mr. Collins. Foolish as her cousin may be, he could hardly propose marriage in a room full of guests.

Mrs. Bennet immediately signaled for Mr. Bingley to be seated beside Jane. Before her mother could direct an unwelcome companion to the seat beside her, Elizabeth stood and moved to speak with Jane and Mr. Bingley.

Mr. Darcy stood behind the sofa upon which Jane and Mr. Bingley were seated, ostensibly admiring the view of Longbourn's gardens from a nearby window. His intention had been to observe Miss Bennet, but at present he was overwhelmed with emotions that justified his resolve to limit his time in Miss Elizabeth's company. He realized how mistaken he had been in presuming that he could meet her with indifference and feared his admiration would be evident in his features. He replayed his decisions from the night of the Netherfield Ball and all the reasons he could not allow her to tempt him.

Mr. Darcy's thoughts were interrupted by Mr. Bingley's voice.

"Wouldn't you agree, Darcy?"

Mr. Darcy cleared his throat. "Yes, I suppose I would," he answered carefully, having not the slightest idea what he had agreed to.

"Wonderful. Miss Bennet, perhaps you might suggest where we shall walk today? I particularly enjoyed your meadow yesterday; the stories of your childhood memories there were truly enchanting."

Jane blushed and answered softly, "Thompson's pond was another favorite of our youth, particularly for Lizzy. It may be too muddy to approach the bank with all the rain we have had this past week, but there is a nice wooded path circling it, and it is a relatively short distance from here, not more than a mile."

Mrs. Bennet was quick to arrange the walking party. "Yes, that will do very well Jane, you always have such elegant taste." Mrs. Bennet scanned the room, formulating the best way to arrange the three single men in her drawing room for a walk with her daughters. Obviously Mr. Bingley should walk out with Jane, she thought, but what of Mr. Darcy? Proud and disagreeable he may be, but he had chosen to come with his friend, and the opportunity must not to be overlooked. He is rather bookish, she thought, alike to Lizzy and Mary, but Lizzy is for Mr. Collins and Mary would never catch the eye of such a man. Lydia deserves such a rich man, if only she were not already engaged to spend the morning with Mrs. Forster. Oh well, she would not look at a man without a red coat in any case. Hmm, Mrs. Bennet pondered, that leaves Kitty – she is nothing to Lydia's liveliness or Jane's beauty, but yes, I believe she shall do rather nicely.

"Mr. Darcy," said Mrs. Bennet, "I am sure Kitty would be glad to accompany you, and Lizzy, of course you should like to walk with Mr. Collins." With a nod of her head, Mrs. Bennet waved her handkerchief, dismissing them to retrieve their wraps and considering the matter settled.

Startled expressions were clear on the faces of two members of the proposed group upon hearing Mrs. Bennet's arrangements, but neither Mr. Darcy nor Elizabeth would have thought to commiserate with the other. Once the party exited the house, Mr. Collins hastened to Elizabeth's side and offering his arm, placing her hand upon his elbow before she had a chance to refuse. Kitty only took the briefest glance at Mr. Darcy's stern countenance before turning to walk with Elizabeth and Mr. Collins, leaving the intimidating man to follow them at his leisure.

Mr. Darcy was well suited to his position at the rear of the group, as no conversation was required of him and he had ample opportunity to survey the others. Upon observing Miss Bennet, he was surprised to see resemblances of the gentle manner in which his mother used to address his father. His mother had always spoken softly, a reflection of her calm disposition, and as his sister had inherited this trait, he could not but see the same in Miss Bennet. The lady did seem more open with Mr. Bingley away from her mother. He now suspected her conduct was parallel to his behavior amongst society mamas. Many of his acquaintances from Cambridge had younger sisters, and he could scarcely speak a civil word to the young ladies out of respect for their brothers without raising expectations. Miss Bingley was a prime example, and unfortunately she was one of many.

Mr. Darcy also observed the interaction between Mr. Collins and Miss Elizabeth. Mr. Collins did not seem to be a dangerous man, he was simply irritating, but he was completely oblivious to the exasperation clearly written on Miss Elizabeth's face. Mr. Darcy had observed a similar reaction at the ball, and Mr. Collins' overtures had not diminished. His intentions were clear and there could be no impediment to a marriage between the two, considering his position as the heir to Longbourn. He could not but feel sympathy upon seeing her endure Mr. Collins' company, regardless of the fact that she would soon be bound to him for the rest of her days.

Finally the walking party reached a knoll overlooking the pond, and seeing the small bench situated at its crest, Mr. Bingley offered Jane the opportunity to sit and rest. Mr. Bingley then turned to converse with Mr. Darcy as Mr. Collins rambled on to no one in particular about the surrounding flora and how such specimens would thrive at his parsonage under the advice of Lady Catherine. Elizabeth gladly took the opportunity to quit her cousin's company and seated herself beside Jane. Unfortunately, upon witnessing her movement, Mr. Collins moved to stand beside her, and his comments alternated between courting his cousin and displaying reverence to the nephew of his patroness.

As Mr. Collins' monologue continued, Mr. Darcy turned his head away from the rest of the party and stared into the horizon. Elizabeth grew angry that he would willingly arrive at Longbourn only to stalk off as though they were unworthy of his attention. He was under no obligation to mix with the local populace if he found their company insufferable. If only she could have read his thoughts, she would have known it was only Mr. Collins he found insufferable, and on that subject, they were in perfect agreement.

Observing that he had lost Mr. Darcy's attention, Mr. Collins finally ended his speech. Sensing the awkwardness of the moment, Mr. Bingley attempted to dissolve the tension.

"Well then, shall we return?"

Closing her eyes, Elizabeth lowered her head and breathed a small sigh of relief as Mr. Bingley offered his arm to Jane and the couple moved away from the bench.

"Miss Elizabeth?"

Elizabeth opened her eyes and was surprised to see not a pale and clammy hand, but a firm masculine one reaching to assist her. Looking up to see Mr. Darcy's stern countenance, she took his hand and murmured her thanks. Seeing that the rest of the party was walking towards the path, Elizabeth removed her hand from Mr. Darcy's and turned to follow. Mr. Darcy hesitated, clearing his throat before moving to walk beside her.

After a few moments of silence, Elizabeth addressed her companion. "I am surprised to see you visiting at Longbourn, sir."

"Indeed."

"I had not thought you approved of your friend's intimacy with certain families in the neighborhood."

"If you refer to your own family and more particularly to your sister, Mr. Bingley's honor is now engaged and I see little option for recourse that would not damage his reputation as well as hers." replied Mr. Darcy, clearly showing that he was reluctant in his acceptance of the match.

Elizabeth turned to look at him sharply, "Yes, I suppose he is now among the gentlemen in the neighborhood who deserve our pity for their bad fortune."

"I would not think a man ought blame bad fortune for result of his own actions."

"And what of those whose lives have been influenced by the actions of other men? Are they also unworthy of regard?"

Mr. Darcy's countenance darkened as he replied, "I gather you no longer refer to Mr. Bingley, but rather a member of the militia."

"How very astute of you, sir. I refer to the very one. Or are there so many men you have cast off that it is difficult for you to keep track of them all?"

Ignoring the latter portion of her remark, he replied in a measured tone, "I could hardly consider myself a gentleman if I had not severed all acquaintance with that......rogue." He turned away as he practically spat the last word, unwilling to pass Wickham's name from his lips.

"Yes, as the son of a steward, he must be devoid of honor and integrity, even after receiving the same education as any gentleman. It is quite interesting sir, that I have heard several remarks from yourself and Miss Bingley implying a disreputable nature in Mr. Wickham's character, yet I have drawn no evidence to support such claims from his manner or his history with your family."

"And yet you have reached your conclusion so decidedly while only considering that scoundrel's estimation of his own worth?" he retorted quickly, his face alight with agitation. "A villain of the worst kind can acquit himself where there is no testament of the truth to refute him."

"And who better to provide such a testimony than yourself, Mr. Darcy?" Elizabeth glared into his eyes, daring him to further vilify himself.

Mr. Darcy paused and glanced back and forth, seeming to gather himself before he continued walking, and stated evenly, "I have no desire to discuss his dealings with my family, and am under no obligation to relinquish my privacy. Mr. Wickham's character is displayed well enough through his disreputable habits, leaving debt and disappointment everywhere he goes."

Elizabeth was mollified slightly by this display. At least he showed a good deal of concern over the matter, where she had believed him to have cast the man off as nonchalantly as a pebble in his shoe. "Certainly you have a right to keep your privacy, sir, but as to your reasoning for doing so, I must point out one major flaw. If he were so dishonorable a man as you claim him to be, the traits you describe would hardly make themselves known until the damage has been done, leaving little opportunity for recourse to those he had used ill. Does that not place a gentleman with your knowledge of his character under some obligation to expose him for the protection of those who unknowingly cross his path?"

Mr. Darcy widened his eyes in exasperation. "Would you have me follow him everywhere he goes, from Devonshire to Scotland, warning the general populace away from placing their trust in him?"

Elizabeth observed that he seemed rather frustrated by her implications. She turned away to hide her amusement as an image of "Sir Darcy, Defender of the Innocent" riding from county to county appeared in her head.

"No sir, I would hardly expect you to play the part of a knight in shining armor. However," she continued seriously, "if Mr. Bingley knew of a true threat to my family or the neighborhood in general, I imagine he would at least concern himself enough to warn my father of it."

Both fell silent at this, and continued on until Longbourn came into sight. Elizabeth felt exhausted from first dealing with her cousin's senseless conversation and then arguing with the most disdainful man she had ever met. So absorbed was she in her anger at Mr. Darcy, that she neglected to think on how his choosing to accompany her had kept Mr. Collins from her side. Mr. Darcy continued to silently berate himself for multiplying his folly by not only agreeing to the excursion, but walking beside Miss Elizabeth on their return. Not only had she been infuriating, she had been right, and he was left feeling obligated to address Mr. Bennet regarding the scoundrel befriending his daughters.

Upon returning to the house, the party had only reassembled in the drawing room for a few minutes before Mr. Darcy announced that he would be taking his leave. Mr. Bingley bid farewell to Mr. Darcy, asking him if he would be so kind as to inform Miss Bingley that he would be dining at Longbourn. He then returned his attention back toward Jane. As Mr. Darcy left the room, Elizabeth moved to take a chair very near the sofa where Jane was seated with Mr. Bingley at her side. She was sorry to ingratiate herself into their conversation, but would not risk being seated alone in Mr. Collins' presence. Mrs. Bennet called to Elizabeth, accusing her of interrupting a private conversation, but Mr. Bingley was kind enough to dissolve the situation. He declared that Miss Elizabeth was no interruption at all, and he would be pleased to hear another delightful story of Jane's childhood days.

When the ladies retired to dress for dinner, Elizabeth was pleased to remember the note she had retrieved earlier in the day. Never being one to take long in her preparations, particularly for a family dinner at home, she quickly changed her gown and straightened her hair before pulling out her writing supplies.

Chapter 4

The following day was Sunday, and while two persons currently residing in Hertfordshire were disappointed to have the locked doors of Mr. Awdry's bookshop separating them from a certain book, the rest of the populace prepared for church.

Mr. Bennet escorted his wife and his five daughters to their family pew, greeting friends and neighbors along the way. The Netherfield party had already arrived, Mr. Darcy and the Hursts were already seated, and Mr. Bingley was standing in the aisle conversing with Mr. Long.

"Good morning Mr. Long, Mr. Bingley," greeted Mr. Bennet.

"Yes, a pleasure to see you this morning, Mr. Bennet, Mrs. Bennet." replied Mr. Bingley. Turning to their daughters he added, "Ladies, I trust you are all well this morning."

As the Miss Bennets rose from their curtsied replies, Mrs. Bennet gave her eldest daughter a slight nudge, unaware that her daughter hardly needed encouragement to address the handsomely smiling gentleman before them.

"We are all quite well, sir, thank you," Jane answered demurely. "The weather has continued to be rather fine, and we all enjoyed the opportunity to walk to the service this morning."

"I also observed that is quite pleasant out," Mr. Bingley smiled broadly in return, "Perhaps you would allow me to escort you home, Miss Bennet?"

"I believe I can answer for my daughter that she could enjoy your company, and if you would be so kind as to remain with us for luncheon, she could wish for little else," Mr. Bennet cut in, "But if you will excuse us, I believe Mr. Martin is ready to begin."

Mr. Bingley nodded his agreement as the Bennets moved towards their pew.

Mr. Collins had left for the church earlier than the Bennet family, but his brief separation from the family did not save Elizabeth from finding him seated beside her during the service. As they rose to sing the first hymn, she was pleasantly surprised to hear that he did not sing off-key, however the inflection in his voice as he gave his own importance to the words prevented any enjoyment of his performance.

After the service, Mr. Bingley joined the Bennet family as they spoke to their acquaintances. As the crowd thinned, Mrs. Bennet began her usual orders to arrange the party for the walk home. Jane was already on the arm of Mr. Bingley, and the two were wandering towards the parish garden.

"Oh, Lizzy dear," cooed Mrs. Bennet, the tone of her voice forewarning Elizabeth that something was afoot, "I believe Mr. Collins is still in the sanctuary speaking with Mr. Martin, go in and let him know the family is preparing to walk home. Be sure to collect Jane and Mr. Bingley on your way out." She gave her daughter a large wink, and taking her husband's arm, walked in the direction of Longbourn with her three youngest daughters in tow. Elizabeth knew her father too well to doubt that he was aware of Mrs. Bennet's scheme, however she also knew him well enough to know that he would prefer to hasten his steps to his library than attempt to dissuade his wife.

Not long after the eldest Miss Bennets and their admirers had left the church, Elizabeth observed a certain nervousness in Mr. Bingley's countenance. Noting the frequency with which he placed his hand over his breast pocket, she recalled that this was his first opportunity for a moment alone with Jane. She discounted the times her mother had ushered everyone from the room left the two alone as a pair of goldfish in a teacup. She could easily understand his reluctance to propose under such strained circumstances, knowing Mrs. Bennet was listening at the door, ready to burst in at any moment. Elizabeth summoned her courage, and soon allowed Mr. Bingley and Jane to trail behind.

Conversation between the two had been very stilted since leaving the church, and Jane's concern was mounting, until suddenly Mr. Bingley stopped short and turned to face her.

"Miss Bennet, I am sure you are aware of my regard, but I have longed for the opportunity to speak freely of my feelings for you. May I?"

"You may," Jane answered in little more than a whisper.

"Oh, my dear Jane," he replied, taking her hands in his, "From the moment I first saw you at the assembly, I was enchanted. You are truly the most beautiful woman of my acquaintance and I have never known a tenderness or compassion such as I have found in you. I have long since been unable to think of my future without your comforting presence and I long to know that I shall never again face a day without you by my side." He dropped down on one knee, pulling an elegantly crafted ring from his pocket, "Miss Jane Bennet, please tell me you will fill my days with pure joy and consent to be my wife."

At that moment, Mr. Bingley knew no amount of teasing would ever cause him to hide his well-known smile again, as he saw its equal in his beloved's face. Upon hearing her soft "yes", he slid the ring into its rightful place on her finger. Looking again at her brilliant smile, he could no longer restrain himself, rising from his knee to catch his beloved Jane about the waist, lifting her as he spun in a circle, laughing with elation over finding pure bliss.

Still chuckling, he placed her back on her feet, and returned her hands to his. "Forgive me Jane, you have made me so happy, I seem to have forgotten myself."

"Believe me, Mr. Bingley," she met his gaze, displaying her emotions as boldly as she would dare, "there is nothing to forgive."

"Jane, if it is agreeable to you, I would love to hear you call me Charles."

"I would like that...Charles."

Jane could not keep a smile from her face as she said his name. She had thought of him as Charles for so long, but had not dared to speak so aloud, even to Elizabeth.

"Jane," he said softly, placing a hand on her rosy cheek, "Do I ask too much...I would very much like to kiss you."

Embarrassed, Jane nodded slightly in response, and so it was that she received a very gentle first kiss.

They gazed into one another's eyes, their trance being broken as Mr. Bingley once again laughed with overwhelming happiness and she laughed softly in return. Turning again towards Longbourn, they spoke of the joy they found in one another, and Mr. Bingley asked when he might speak to her father.

"I am sure Papa would be happy for you to speak to him as soon as you wish, I simply cannot wait to tell Lizzy."

"Let us speak to her now if it pleases you, we should catch up to them sho.....I say, Collins!!" Mr. Bingley shouted. He was quite alarmed to look down the road and see two familiar figures walking rather close together. With a backwards glance at Jane, he ran towards the pair, observing the odious man holding Elizabeth on his arm rather closely to himself, leaning in as he spoke to her. A horrified expression was evident on Elizabeth's face when she turned her head at the sound of Bingley's voice. Within moments, Mr. Bingley reached the couple, with Jane gracefully hurrying herself along in his wake.

"I say, Collins," said Mr. Bingley, looking sharply at his future cousin, "we did not realize we had lost sight of you." As Mr. Collins remained oddly silent, but kept himself leeched to the lady beside him, Mr. Bingley turned to address his future sister. "Is everything alright?"

"It is, Mr. Bingley," she replied, finally managing to loosen her captor's grasp, though not able to remove herself completely. "I was just telling Mr. Collins we should have slowed our pace or turned to find you."

"I apologize for neglecting you, Miss Elizabeth."

At this moment Jane arrived, and Mr. Bingley smiled lightly at his new fiancé as he continued, "I am sure Jane would enjoy your company on the short remainder of our walk home."

Jane had already moved to her sister's side, and as she took Elizabeth's free arm in hers, Mr. Collins finally relinquished the other.

"Thank you, Mr. Bingley," Elizabeth said earnestly, and turned with her sister to walk briskly in the direction of Longbourn. When they had obtained a reasonable distance from the men, Jane gently questioned her sister.

"Lizzy, I certainly hope nothing grievous occurred before Charles reached you? We should never have allowed you to be left alone with our cousin. I do not know how I could have been so absentminded."

Elizabeth relaxed as she let out a frustrated sigh, "Truly it was nothing of consequence, I cannot forget it soon enough and I am merely grateful no one bore witness to it but yourself and *'Charles'*." Elizabeth raised her eyebrows as she spoke Mr. Bingley's new appellation. "And may I ask how it is that now you are to be called 'Jane' and he is 'Charles'?"

A broad smile again crossed Jane's features as she replied, "Lizzy, I am so happy to tell you! Charles has just proposed! He said he was sure I had long been aware of his feelings and that he could not go on without knowing I would be by his side. It was everything I could have possibly imagined. But oh Lizzy, what you must have endured in my absence, I shall never forgive myself."

"Nonsense, Jane. Any discomfort I experienced while having another ridiculous conversation with our equally ridiculous cousin was well worth its trouble to see you so happy!"

Meanwhile a less pleasant conversation was had between the two gentlemen still standing halfway between the church and Longbourn.

"Mr. Collins, I must ask that you tell me what was occurring between yourself and Miss Elizabeth while Miss Bennet and I were separated from you."

Mr. Collins stood up straight, and raising his chin slightly, stated, "I was simply flattering my betrothed with those little delicate compliments which are always acceptable to ladies."

"If I am not mistaken, sir, Miss Elizabeth is not your betrothed, nor does she consider your *'compliments'* to be acceptable."

"Oh, but surely you see, sir, that my cousin and I have been designed for each other. Mrs. Bennet has readily given her blessing, and I am sure as Miss Elizabeth becomes more accustomed to the manners which are appropriate between engaged persons, she will no longer feel the need to demure, as is the habit of elegant females."

"I would not use a mother's blessing as reason to consider yourself formally engaged. I would also advise you to refrain from offending Miss Elizabeth, and let your behavior towards her be reflective of propriety."

As Mr. Collins seemed unable to recognize any great difference in their opinions of his conduct, Mr. Bingley turned towards Longbourn and resolved to speak with Mr. Bennet on matters concerning not one of his daughters, but two.

❧❧❧

Immediately following the midday meal, Mr. Bennet retired to his library. A few moments later a loud shriek was heard from the front parlor, signaling that Mrs. Bennet had noticed her eldest daughter's engagement ring. Mr. Bingley took this as his cue to address Mr. Bennet, and a knock at the library door soon followed. Mr. Bennet bade his visitor to enter, and was not surprised in the least to see Mr. Bingley stride into the room, closing the door behind him. Before Mr. Bingley could be seated, Mr. Bennet began to speak.

"Ah, here you are, Mr. Bingley. Given the racket emanating from my parlor, I imagine you have finally asked for Jane's hand and are now here to request my blessing. I gladly give it."

Though stunned by Mr. Bennet's bluntness, Mr. Bingley was quick to acknowledge his consent. "You assume correctly, Miss Bennet was gracious enough to accept me during our walk from the church. I thank you for your blessing sir. I promise I will provide for your daughter well, and I love her very deeply."

"Yes, yes, very well then, I will not keep you from her." Mr. Bennet reached for his book as he spoke, subtly dismissing his future son from the room.

"I beg your pardon, sir, but there is another matter I would speak to you about." Mr. Bingley replied rather seriously as he seated himself across from Mr. Bennet.

Noting the serious tone of the ever-jovial man's voice, Mr. Bennet jerked his eyes up and nodded for him to continue.

"I am afraid the walk from the church was more eventful than you realize. Shortly after Miss Bennet accepted my suit, we bore witness to a rather disturbing scene between Mr. Collins and Miss Elizabeth."

"What?! Do not tell me that oaf has worked up the audacity to overstep his place. I demand to know exactly what occurred."

"Nothing of a compromising nature from what I observed, I only saw them walking rather closely to each other, which seemed to be as pleasing to him as it was disturbing to her, and he leaned closer in a familiar manner as he spoke. Of course as soon as I witnessed this, I moved to assist her. Miss Elizabeth was visibly distressed by his conversation and seemed very relieved by my interruption."

"Yes, well," Mr. Bennet visibly relaxed as he spoke, "I believe we are all *distressed* by conversation of any length with my cousin."

Concerned that Mr. Bennet did not appear to think the matter a serious one, Mr. Bingley continued, "I am sure you will be glad to know I reproved Mr. Collins quite thoroughly, pointing out the evils of his conduct. I fear, however, that he was not as receptive to my admonishments as perhaps he should have been."

"Thank you, sir. That will save me the trouble of a most unpleasant and nonsensical conversation with my cousin. If you will send Elizabeth to me, I will speak with her to confirm the details of her walk home and ascertain that all is well."

"As you wish, sir," Mr. Bingley said with a twinge of resignation seeping into his voice. He attempted to mask his frustration in light of his newly found understanding with this gentleman's daughter. It seemed men of the Bennet line had a propensity for dismissing his opinions. Perhaps a few too many years yielding to his domineering sisters had weakened his ability to express himself forcefully. He had allowed his sisters to make his decisions when he lacked a strong opinion on the subject at hand, but as he would soon have a wife and four new sisters, this was a matter of importance.

A few moments later, Elizabeth occupied the seat Mr. Bingley had just vacated. She sat quietly waiting for her father to speak, apprehensive of how he would react the information Mr. Bingley had imparted. He may be offended enough to send Mr. Collin's away, she thought, but if he believed her to be compromised, he may demand that she marry the odious man.

Seeing that his daughter would not offer her story without being prompted, Mr. Bennet broke the silence. "Well Lizzy, I have had an interesting account of your walk from church this morning. Mr. Bingley has expressed concern that Mr. Collins may have harmed you in some way, and saw him behaving very familiarly towards you. Though I find Mr. Bingley to be a rather trustworthy gentleman, I have doubts that my silly cousin would be foolhardy enough to accost you. Do be so kind as to enlighten me as to the details of your latest escapade with our outlandish relative."

"Oh Papa, please believe me he has not violated propriety in any extreme way. It is true that he held my arm closer than necessary, but it was his conversation that caused me distress."

"Yes, our distress at conversing with the man is a popular subject today, but I fail to see how this aspect has changed since the day of his arrival. I am glad to hear he has not disrespected you; Jane's young man was quite incensed at the display and gave Collins quite a lecture on his behavior. In the future, I suspect his overtures will be subdued in Mr. Bingley's presence. However, he shall leave us as planned at the end of the week; I cannot imagine that he would not heed the calling of the illustrious Lady Catherine deBourgh. Whatever notions he currently entertains regarding you will dissipate when he receives no invitation to return to Longbourn. Then, my dear, you shall be as rid of him as the rest of us."

"But Papa, he talks of nothing but how I shall like to be mistress of Hunsford Parsonage, and how he is certain Lady Catherine will approve of me! He speaks to me as though I am his betrothed, and none of my arguments to the contrary have dissuaded him."

"Come, come, Lizzy. Mr. Collins has not asked you for your hand nor approached me for his consent, and I am confident that if he were to trouble himself on either count, he would be soundly refused. Any person with half a wit would not take a word of his nonsense seriously. I advise you to see the humor in our cousin's harmless folly and give you leave to make as much sport of him as you like." With an amused smile, Mr. Bennet reopened his book and did not look up from it as he continued to speak. "I believe you have now spent more time in a stuffy library with an old man than is your wont on a sunny afternoon. Go on and join your sisters now, as I imagine Jane would like to take Mr. Bingley into the garden. I am sure the poor gentleman has heard his fill of pin money and fine carriages by now."

The rest of the afternoon passed quickly. Mr. Bingley was happy to escort Jane into the garden, and Elizabeth was kind in her duties as chaperone, giving the couple relative privacy to relish in their new understanding. Mr. Collins spent the afternoon indoors, writing to his curate and going over passages for the sermon he would be giving in the Hunsford parish the following Sunday.

When all members of the house had retired for the evening, Jane looked at Lizzy's face in the mirror as she brushed out her sister's hair. They discussed the events of the day, Jane beaming at every mention of her beloved Mr. Bingley. She still felt a little awkward referring to him as Charles outside of her private thoughts, but whenever she let his Christian name slip out, she could not stop herself from sighing contentedly and gazing at the ring on her finger. At long last, the topic of Mr. Bingley had been nearly exhausted, and Jane reluctantly brought up her intended's conversation with Mr. Collins.

"Mr. Bingley was kind enough to relate to me the majority of his conversation with Mr. Collins, Lizzy. I am still very sorry you were placed in such an uncomfortable situation, but I was greatly comforted by Charles' assurances that we shall do our best to shield you from him. He is quite determined to be of use to his future sisters, and I admire him so greatly for his compassion."

"Jane, I shall be very glad to have your Mr. Bingley as my brother."

Chapter 5

After the unpleasantness of her last walk, Elizabeth was glad to once again enjoy the outdoors in solitude. When Jane had left her room the previous evening, it had proved rather difficult to keep the events of the day from her mind. Her thoughts leapt between overwhelming happiness for Jane, and astonishment at Mr. Collins' persistence and her

A Noteworthy Courtship

father's complete refusal to assist her at present. She had finally found distraction in lighting an extra candle and penning a response to the second note she kept hidden in the bottom of a small trunk. She now ambled along one of her favorite wooded paths, carrying her latest piece of teasing wit to deliver as soon as she was ready to turn towards Meryton. Little did she know that at the same moment, Mr. Darcy was turning his horse as far from Meryton as possible, knowing there was no use for venturing into Mr. Awdry's shop until the morrow.

Mr. Darcy was glad to ride directly into Meryton the following morning. He had spent the previous day once again in Mr. Bingley's study, going over his business correspondence. His steward was capable of handling nearly every aspect of the estate, as he had done out of necessity immediately following old Mr. Darcy's death, but he still preferred to be as involved as possible. Citing the necessity of a few texts on agriculture for use with Mr. Bingley, Mr. Darcy once again entered the Meryton bookshop with an ulterior motive in mind. He exited the shop with a parcel in his hand and a folded paper in his pocket, and leisurely rode in the direction of Netherfield Park. Once privacy had been gained on a sheltered path, he drew the missive from his coat and read the following.

> *Your comment on "romantic notions" puts me in mind to a current novel, which you most likely have never read as it is written by "a lady", wherein a Mr. Ferrars does not find happiness until he walks away from his fortune and chooses to live modestly, married to the woman he loves. If you doubt that a character who acts in such a way could exist as a hero in a published and well circulated work, the novel is entitled Sense and Sensibility.*

Mr. Darcy had actually read the book, as Georgiana had been very eager to read it, and he preferred to be familiar with a text before it was permitted to her. He was reluctant to admit he had enjoyed it, and for more than the delightful conversation it provided with his sister. He was not immune to the positive aspects of a marriage based on affection; he simply did not believe such extreme differences of situation could result in happiness outside of the realm of fiction. A novel would hardly be romantic if it expounded the difficulties that would inevitably befall its characters in the real world.

❧❧❧

The next morning, Mr. Darcy could be seen leaving Mr. Awdry's establishment with yet another parcel of books. He had again arrived early to avoid meeting any of the local gentry while he attended his clandestine correspondence, and made a few more purchases to justify his presence in the eyes of the shopkeeper. At least the sparse library shelves of Netherfield Park provided ample excuse for his frequent need to purchase a few titles. Mr. Darcy returned to Netherfield to find the front rooms quiet and empty. He merely shrugged, assuming Mr. Bingley had departed for Longbourn the moment the last bite of his breakfast passed his lips, and the hour was still early for the rest of the household to descend the stairs. He made himself comfortable in the library, requesting that the footman inform any who would inquire that he was attending to his business affairs and was not to be disturbed for the remainder of the day.

The two single gentlemen residing at Netherfield Park deemed to join the ladies and Mr. Hurst as the evening meal commenced. The ladies kept conversation light and civil, having learned to keep any biting remarks regarding the local populace to be made out of their brother's hearing. As the dessert course was being served, Mr. Bingley addressed his sisters.

"Louisa, Caroline, as you have both been kind enough to extend your congratulations on my recent engagement, I am sure you are anxious to become further acquainted with your future sister. It is unfortunate that you have been unable to accompany me on my recent visits to Longbourn, but you will soon have the opportunity to meet together, as I have scheduled a dinner for the entire Bennet family here on Friday evening."

Mrs. Hurst grimaced slightly, and was formulating a civil response when Miss Bingley addressed her brother. "Now Charles, that is but two days hence, we cannot possibly entertain on such short notice. I would suggest next week, but Louisa and I were planning a brief trip to town for our holiday shopping, were we not, dear sister?" Mrs. Hurst feigned awareness of this plan excellently, to which Miss Bingley nodded smugly as she continued. "When we return, we may examine our schedules and see if this dinner might be accomplished before the holidays."

Mr. Bingley's expression hardened as he replied in a firm tone, "I extended our invitation this afternoon, Caroline. The dinner will be held on the date I have already selected. If you are concerned, I am sure our housekeeper would be happy to assist you. Better yet, Mrs. Bennet is renowned throughout the neighborhood for her excellent dinner parties, and I am certain she and Jane would be delighted to coordinate the dinner with you. We can dispatch a note to Longbourn straightaway requesting for them to call on you in the morning."

"Oh Charles, none of that will be necessary! Why, after hosting the ball, certainly I can arrange a small dinner without assistance," Miss Bingley replied. Mr. Bingley listened to his sister with a placid smile, concealing his amusement as she dissembled, contradicting her previous statement as she continued, "It may not be a lavish affair, but I doubt the Bennet family will notice if it lacks the extravagance one would expect in town."

Satisfied with their conversation, and seeing that the meal was complete, Mr. Bingley suggested that the gentlemen might retire to the library. Mr. Hurst declined, reaching for the brandy bottle on the sideboard, while Mr. Darcy rose and bowed to the ladies before exiting the room with Mr. Bingley in his wake.

ふふふ

"So the Bennets shall be dining at Netherfield," commented Mr. Darcy once the gentlemen had gained the privacy of the library. "One might wonder if you will be able to keep yourself from Longbourn's door long enough for the family to prepare for the evening."

Mr. Bingley chuckled as he poured a glass for each of them. "Come, Darcy. You know as well as I it is only appropriate for me to invite them to dine, particularly in light of my sisters' reluctance to pay a congratulatory call on Miss Bennet. I recognize your distaste for her family, but I am confident even you can survive their company for one evening."

"And have you invited the riveting Mr. Collins to join the party?" Mr. Darcy asked his friend as he accepted the proffered glass.

Mr. Bingley grimaced at the thought of dining with the loathsome clergyman. "I admit I did not mention him specifically, but as he is a guest in their home, I imagine the Bennets will have little choice but to allow him to accompany them."

"At least you will see less of your future brother once he returns to Kent. I, however, will have two persons triggering my desire to avoid Rosings."

"Brother?" Mr. Bingley asked with confusion, "Do you not mean cousin?"

Mr. Darcy rolled his eyes at his friend's naivety. "I realize nothing has been announced, but surely you see that Mr. Collins will marry Miss Elizabeth. I would not be surprised if Miss Bennet hopes the four of you might share a wedding day."

"Good heavens!" Mr. Bingley sputtered, nearly spitting out his drink. "Mr. Collins has certainly not been discreet regarding his intentions, but you cannot believe that Miss Elizabeth would subject herself to be shackled to such a man!"

"I can very well believe it. Granted the man is tedious company, but that is of little matter considering the eligibility of the match."

"I see, Darcy. I suppose then there could be no objection to your marrying my sister as her 20,000 pounds make her an eligible match, unless of course you would prefer to add the value of Rosings Park to your holdings by marrying your cousin."

The disgusted look on Mr. Darcy's face assured Mr. Bingley he had made his point, and he returned to the subject of Elizabeth Bennet. "I see that you understand Miss Elizabeth has much to consider aside from Mr. Collins' status as heir to Longbourn. The poor girl has tried to avoid his advances."

"What on earth do you mean, Bingley?" Mr. Darcy asked with concern.

Mr. Bingley eyed his friend, not oblivious to his strong reaction. "As I said, Miss Elizabeth has never welcomed his attentions, and though I understand Collins has yet to propose, she would soundly refuse him. I observed him behaving in an overly familiar manner and she was quite clearly distressed. I am glad Jane and I were able to intervene, and of course I tried to speak to Mr. Collins regarding his treatment of my future sister."

"That moronic clergyman imposed himself upon her? What else has been done? Why did you not speak to her father that he might order that snake of a man out of his house?" Mr. Darcy was nearly shouting as he spoke the last, quite clearly incensed at the idea of Mr. Collins in close proximity to Miss Elizabeth.

Mr. Bingley was now fairly certain of the meaning behind Mr. Darcy's heated response, whether or not the gentleman was prepared to admit it. "Easy there, Darcy. According to Miss Elizabeth, he did nothing more than hold her arm rather close and spout the same courting chatter while refusing to hear her entreaties that his attentions were unwelcome. I did speak with Mr. Bennet, and while I agree he should intercede, I could not convince him that the gravity of the situation merits such action. My daily presence at Longbourn shall go a long way in deflecting the man."

Mr. Bingley attempted to hide a smirk as he added, "I must say you are conducting yourself rather protectively towards Miss Elizabeth, dare I suspect you of jealousy towards Mr. Collins? If you are harboring tender feelings I would be most surprised indeed, however that would certainly explain your behavior on our last visit." He dared not mention how well it would explain Mr. Darcy's behavior at that very moment.

Mr. Darcy turned away, returning his glass to the serving tray, and paused there, keeping his back to the room.

"I assure you I feel nothing of the kind, Bingley." he answered through gritted teeth. "If you would excuse me, I believe it is time I retire for the evening." Mr. Darcy left the room without a backward glance.

That night, Mr. Darcy was unable to keep his conversation with Mr. Bingley from his mind. The ball was now eight days past, and he thought he had since been moderately successful in driving Elizabeth from his mind. He had felt resentment towards the idea of her being married to Mr. Collins, but was able to push it aside as merely the lot any woman of her low station could expect in life. Assuming she would be happy to accept Mr. Collins made her just like any other mercenary woman of the ton. Knowing now that she would refuse such a man emphasized the independent spirit which had so thoroughly captivated him. Even if he could not consider her for his own wife, she did not deserve to continue to be chased by Mr. Collins.

On Thursday morning, Miss Elizabeth was prevented from leaving the house, but not by the parent whose interference she feared most.

"Will you not join me in the library, Lizzy?" Mr. Bennet asked his favorite daughter.

Once they entered the library, Mr. Bennet sat behind his desk and leaned back, gazing at his daughter quizzically. Unaware of the reason for her summons, and anxious to search for another note, Elizabeth broke the silence.

"Is there some matter of import you wished to discuss with me Papa? I was just about to go into the village, and I would be happy to fetch something if it would save you the trouble of venturing forth."

"Into the village, eh, Lizzy? For a girl who professes her love of ambling through the countryside to any person willing to listen, you certainly have taken a fancy to the beauties found along the road to Meryton as of late."

Not knowing how to respond without revealing her true motivation, Elizabeth looked down at her hands. Mr. Bennet observed his daughter and raised his brow before he continued.

"I happened to stop into the bookshop yesterday afternoon, and had a most interesting conversation with Mr. Awdry. He was rather reluctant to discuss it, but nonetheless he related that you have come in rather frequently this past week, seeming very interested in his first editions, yet on each occasion, you have left empty-handed. You have never been a girl prone to overspending; tell me, has your mother insisted on spending all of your allowance on lace, or are the muddy conditions out of doors obliging you to spend your every farthing on a vast supply of fresh petticoats? Then again, I recall hearing that Mr. Awdry's nephew has recently come to help him, perhaps he has caught your eye? I must say you could do far better, but should you declare yourself hopelessly in love with the lad I suppose I may be willing to consent."

Elizabeth's eyes went wide at her father's jest. "Oh Papa, I can hardly be enamored when I have yet to meet the young man. Besides, I have heard he cannot be a day over eighteen!"

"Never fear Lizzy," Mr. Bennet laughed, "I realize a girl must have her secrets, and I am sure yours are far less scandalous than those of your younger sisters. However, I should warn you that as I am now aware of your affinity for the bookshop – or perhaps the company found within – I shall take you up on your offer to fetch something for me. In fact, I am finding my library's selection rather dull and may send you to Mr. Awdry quite frequently in the near future."

Elizabeth and her father smiled at each other in silent understanding. As much as he would find amusement in hearing her story, he would not press her for information or prevent her from continuing this peculiar behavior.

Upon exiting the library, Elizabeth discovered that Mr. Bingley had arrived. Another delightful morning was spent in conversation with Jane's future husband, occasionally interrupted by Mr. Collins' commentary on the delights of finding one's future mate. The gazes cast in Elizabeth's direction after these comments were disturbing in more than one fashion to at least three parties forced to witness them. Jane and Mr. Bingley were quick to change the subject, and with very little effort, encouraged Mrs. Bennet to dominate the conversation with discussion of their wedding details.

After luncheon, Mrs. Bennet announced that her daughters and their young gentlemen would like nothing better than a walk in the garden. Once they had all quit the house, Jane asked Elizabeth to take a turn with her, and with a loving gaze at Mr. Bingley, released his arm and took up her sister's. Mr. Collins moved to follow them, but Mr. Bingley casually stepped into his path with a raised brow and stern expression. Mr. Collins' babbled about the delicate conversations which young ladies must be allowed to hold privately, and declared that he would spend his afternoon counting the windows and surveying their glazing. Longbourn was to be his future home after all, though it was nothing to Rosings Park. As Mr. Collins trotted off, Mr. Bingley shook his head and turned to rejoin Miss Bennet and her sister. Elizabeth took the opportunity to thank Mr. Bingley for his actions, and the trio enjoyed the gardens for a little over an hour before Mr. Bingley departed for Netherfield.

Not ten minutes after Mr. Bingley left Longbourn, Elizabeth smiled as her father called her into his library to suggest that she visit the bookshop in Meryton. If questioned, she was to inform her mother that he had given her explicit instructions for a purchase of import, and she was not to be waylaid for any reason, even if said reason was waiting for Mr. Collins to make ready to escort her.

۽۽۽

As it was, her father did indeed have business with Mr. Awdry, for the moment she mentioned she had come in at Mr. Bennet's request; Mr. Awdry called for his nephew to bring out a crate that had just arrived from London. After a few minutes, the young man appeared, and Elizabeth hid her mouth behind her hand, so as not to reveal the smile that came forth in remembrance of her father's teasing. If she were of a flirtatious nature, perhaps her father would have been more accurate in his jest than he would have liked. Matthew Awdry's current situation would prevent him from being marriageable for a gentleman's daughter, but he was definitely an attractive young man. If only he would have joined the militia instead of working for his uncle, her youngest sisters would be in raptures. While the Mr. Awdrys were preparing the package for her father, Elizabeth was able to achieve her primary objective.

The introduction to young Mr. Awdry in addition to awaiting her father's parcel caused Elizabeth to remain in the shop longer than she had intended. She arrived home just as her sisters retired to dress for dinner, and was unable to find a moment alone to read the note. The evening meal could not move fast enough for Elizabeth's curiosity, and at the earliest moment, she pled fatigue. With a few reassurances to Jane that she was well, Elizabeth climbed the stairs and locked her door before opening the missive.

December 4, 18__

Mock me if you dare, but I have read Sense and Sensibility, and while I enjoyed the lady's style, I believe her story supports my point. Your Mr. Ferrars, champion of contentedness found in nothing more than his true love at his side, is also a man who does the honorable in the name Miss Steele only to be made a pauper, and find his brother in receipt of his fortune. The next we hear of him, his brother has gained the hand of Miss Steele, but Edward is glad to be free of the fiancé for whom he abandoned his fortune and declares his love for Miss Dashwood. Does this not show the error of following the fickle whims of the heart?

To hear that this man had read and even admitted to enjoying *Sense and Sensibility* took a few moments to absorb. When she had first read the book and recommended it to her father, he laughingly replied that never in his days would he read such drivel, but if he were ever so inclined to read of the heartache of others, the gossip columns of his newspaper would suffice. Granted this undisclosed gentleman had a rather cynical view, but nevertheless his expressing one at all was enough to elicit her teasing.

Chapter 6

Before the sun rose on the day of Jane's engagement dinner at Netherfield Park, Mrs. Bennet was aflutter in making preparations for her daughters. Though the dinner would only consist of the family party, she was determined to show her daughters at their best. She had always believed one daughter connected well would raise their social standing, and this was her first opportunity to exhibit her daughters' elevated status. Mrs. Bennet had petitioned for new gowns from the moment the engagement had been announced, and the appeal was repeated daily, but Mr. Bennet had steadfastly refused. Mrs. Bennet was glad she had absolutely insisted on a new evening gown for Jane, and found solace in knowing that the dress would be picked up within the hour. As she merrily pointed out to Mr. Bennet, his refusal had not been extended to lace and ribbons, and therefore all of her daughters would accompany Jane to the milliners that they might accentuate their existing gowns. She gave strict instructions for their purchases and insisted they be allowed use of the carriage. Elizabeth was grateful for her mother's absence, as Jane would be amenable to selecting a few hair ribbons for her while she ventured into the bookshop instead.

ళళళ

Dinner at Netherfield Park was an enjoyable affair for some, and a rather trying affair for others. Mr. Bingley and Miss Bennet were inseparable for the entire evening, happily displaying their affections more openly as was now within the bounds of propriety. While most of the party looked upon the engaged couple's behavior with satisfaction, two did not.

Miss Bingley had managed to avoid the subject of her brother's engagement since its formal announcement, no difficult feat as his frequent trips to Longbourn left them in each other's company but rarely. But however much she wished to forget that Jane Bennet would soon be her sister, she was unable to ignore a truth so openly displayed before her.

Outwardly, Mr. Darcy appeared to be as aloof and disapproving as ever. In reality, he had observed that Miss Elizabeth was as beautiful as she had been at the ball, and his inability to repress his emotions troubled him greatly. As to Mr. Bingley's engagement, he was resigned to the match, and even happy to see the mutual affection so evident between the two. However, his disgust at the behavior of Mrs. Bennet and her youngest daughters, combined with his still seething anger towards Mr. Collins, covered his face with a haughty expression which many in attendance mistook for disapproval akin to Miss Bingley's. Fortunately, both unhappy parties were not inclined to voice their grievances, and the gaiety amongst the rest of the party continued as the dinner was announced.

Mr. Bingley had personally chosen the seating arrangements to ensure that Jane was by his side and his remaining guests were as comfortable as possible. As mistress of the house, he had placed his sister at the opposite end of the table, and placed Mr. and Mrs. Hurst to either side. Mr. Collins and Mrs. Bennet were placed near the Hursts, along with Lydia and Kitty. Mr. Bennet was seated next to Jane, leaving Mr. Darcy seated beside Elizabeth.

Elizabeth was very happy to celebrate her sister's engagement, and between herself and Mr. Bennet, the company was entertained with many charming tales of her youth. With each story, Elizabeth pointed out that while she might have been inclined towards mischief, Jane seemed to have been born an angel and remained as such. Mr. Bingley joined in with anecdotes of his own younger days, and though Mr. Darcy contributed not a word, as he was trying desperately not to lose himself in the charms of his dinner partner, the entire head of the table was grateful for their light and peaceful conversation.

The pleasant interaction could not survive the entire meal, however, as Mrs. Bennet addressed Mr. Collins, speaking loudly enough to overshadow all other conversation at the table.

"Mr. Collins, I am sure you have noticed how delightfully well in looks our Lizzy is this evening. I have always instructed her on how ribbons best accentuate her curls, and I am sure, sir, that you appreciate the extra effort she has taken this evening."

At this, many eyes darted towards Elizabeth while she turned away with apparent interest in a painting hanging behind Mr. Bingley. Mr. Darcy's eyes lingered longer than most as he stared openly into the intricate weaving of ribbons in Elizabeth's hair.

"Yes, my dear Mrs. Bennet. I daresay all of my fair cousins are in good looks this evening, and it is a comfort to see that cousin Elizabeth shall know how to properly present herself at Rosings Park, where we are sure to be invited to dine with Lady Catherine deBourgh."

Mr. Darcy was still lost in Miss Elizabeth's curls, but snapped out of his reverie at Mr. Collins' mention of his aunt. He scowled and reached for his glass, wondering at the amused expression on Mr. Bennet's face. Little did he know that his emotions had been written clearly on his face as he gazed at Miss Elizabeth. Nor did he realize how fortunate he was that the only person in the room to notice, Mr. Bennet, found not alarm, but entertainment in the scene. The confused look on Mr. Darcy's face only increased Mr. Bennet's amusement. Mr. Darcy looked away, and seeing that Mr. Bennet was not to offer any explanation for his merriment, his mind turned to speculation. His reflections were interrupted anew as Lydia spoke up and addressed Mr. Bingley.

"Oh Mr. Bingley, I do wish you would have invited some of the regiment. This would have been such a merry party if Denny and Saunderson were present."

Mr. Bingley had opened his mouth to respond, but before he uttered a word, Mrs. Bennet asserted, "Yes, a few more men at the table would rounded out the seating arrangements quite nicely, though I must say my girls can attract the attention of men above the station of an officer."

Mrs. Bennet proceeded to look pointedly at Kitty, and then smile eagerly at Mr. Darcy, as though expecting a rejoinder. Mr. Darcy was obviously appalled and took a large gulp of wine. Again Mr. Bennet was amused. If only his wife were not so engrossed in matching Elizabeth with Mr. Collins, she would see just which of her daughters could attract Mr. Darcy's attention.

The uncomfortable pause did not last long as Lydia loudly exclaimed, "Oh mama, you know how we all adore a man in his regimentals. I would particularly love to dine with Mr. Wickham, what cheery company he would be, and of course he is most handsome." Lydia's mention of her particular desire to dine with Wickham was all the fuel needed for Mr. Darcy to firmly resolve to speak with Mr. Bennet.

Dinner finally drew to a close, and Mr. Bingley reluctantly suggested a brief separation from the ladies. After a few minutes of Mr. Bingley's forlorn glances at the door, Mr. Darcy told him to go ahead and join the ladies, and asked Mr. Bennet if he might spare a few moments to have a word with him. Mr. Bennet was rather surprised to be addressed by the serious young man, but allowed Mr. Darcy to lead him to the library as their host quickly disappeared into the drawing room with a lumbering Mr. Hurst in his wake.

৵৵৵

"I appreciate your complaisance in speaking with me, Mr. Bennet. I assure you this matter should not take up much of your time."

"Well I hope it is nothing too serious, as it has already led you to speak far more words than I have ever heard you string together," Mr. Bennet chuckled. The look on Mr. Darcy's face made evident that he was not accustomed to teasing, so Mr. Bennet continued in effort to placate him. "I do appreciate your taking the time to address me with whatever this may concern. How may I be of service to you, sir?"

Clasping his hands behind his back, and looking slightly perturbed, Mr. Darcy began, "Actually, sir, it is I who am in need of providing a service to you that is long overdue. I believe the neighborhood in general is aware of my prior connection with one of the officers in the militia, though perhaps I have been too reluctant to speak of my history with the man."

"Yes, we have all been subjected to Mr. Wickham's tales of woe, and I must tell you he casts a rather dark shade on your character, though you hardly need concern yourself with the opinions held of you in this small society. I for one will assume you to be no more a villain than the average rich man."

"Mr. Bennet, I feel I must rectify some of the false impressions Mr. Wickham has undoubtedly given you. He has been generously given far more opportunities than he deserved, regardless of his origin. You may have wondered at a man of his age only just now joining the militia? Many men of humbler beginnings have accomplished far more."

Mr. Bennet was glad to hear his concerns regarding Mr. Wickham voiced, as he was beginning to wonder if he was the only person in the neighborhood not charmed by the fellow. "I believe you have stated my opinion precisely, not all young men are blessed with assistance in the church."

"Nor with 3,000 pounds in lieu of it," Mr. Darcy scoffed.

"Oh ho! Now I truly see the justice of your resentment. I suppose like many men, your pride does not tolerate such a wastrel blackening your name."

"On the contrary sir, if it were merely this, I would have remained silent. However, if you consider that a few short years after receiving 3,000 pounds he now has no better prospect than to join the militia, you may guess at my primary concerns. Mr. Wickham was correct that we were close companions as boys, but since then I have become all too aware of his dissolute ways."

"Are you suggesting concern for those who would extend him credit?"

"I am sir, as well as a certain danger to young ladies in the neighborhood."

Mr. Bennet's expression became stern as he finally realized the gravity of the situation. "I assume by your addressing me that you are concerned not only for tradesmen's daughters, but mine as well. I hope you have now imparted the worst of your knowledge of Mr. Wickham?" seeing Mr. Darcy nod his agreement, he continued, "I thank you for sharing this information as it was certainly in the best interest of my family for me to hear it. I know your friend's marriage to a Bennet will expose you to a rather silly lot, but I will endeavor to be one of a few to make this circumstance tolerable for you."

"There is no need to thank me sir. I have been silent on this distasteful subject for too long, and it eases my conscience to know that you are privy to his true nature and can safeguard your daughters accordingly." He was tempted to also warn Mr. Bennet to guard Elizabeth from Mr. Collins, but given the suspicions such conversation had arisen in Mr. Bingley, he did not dare.

ৡৡৡ

Mr. Darcy considered himself fortunate that Mr. Bennet entered the drawing room ahead of him and therefore did not see his reaction to Elizabeth. He had just spent an entire hour seated beside her at dinner, but he had made extreme efforts to keep his eyes on his plate. He was not prepared to enter the drawing room to the sight of her laughing merrily with Miss Jane and Mr. Bingley, looking just as elegant as she had in his dreams. For a few moments, the scene before him unfolded in slow motion and he imagined that as she turned and smiled, her affection was directed at him rather than her father. In that moment, he knew he was in grave danger of losing his resolve and was on the verge of telling himself he did not care, when an unpleasantly familiar voice addressed him.

"Mr. Darcy, allow me to tell you how honored I am to again receive the great privilege of dining with the nephew of my noble patroness."

Mr. Darcy stared at Mr. Collins, unable to give even a curt nod in response. However the clergyman needed no encouragement to continue speaking.

"It gives me great honor, though I would not claim to rise above my station to consider myself well acquainted with so illustrious a person, that your presence provides a member of so esteemed a family to oversee the great step I take towards my future life, of course under the commission of Lady Catherine deBourgh. As you may already know, your noble aunt has bid me to seek a wife, and I am forever grateful to have the opportunity to seek your superior discernment regarding my actions on this course. I might only hope your approval of my intended shall reflect a similar opinion from my patroness. As I have told cousin Elizabeth many times, it would be a most supreme honor if we are fortunate enough to have our blessed union take place with the nephew of Lady Catherine deBourgh in attendance. Perhaps you would advise me to notify Lady Catherine of my progress in this endeavor, as she would be most pleased to know I have taken her words to heart."

"I am not aware of any formal engagement having been announced by Mr. Bennet, and as such I do not believe it is proper to broach such a topic in company."

Mr. Collins smiled knowingly and moved to pay his compliments to Miss Bingley on hosting such an excellent dinner. Mr. Darcy wondered at the ease in which he rid himself of Mr. Collins' presence, and the odd smile on the gentleman's face as he bowed. He would never have guessed that in his own mind, Mr. Collins had interpreted his reprimand regarding the inappropriate nature of his discourse to mean that he would prefer to address the topic in private. The poor man would not soon realize this anticipated conversation would never come.

Miss Elizabeth had overheard Mr. Collins' speech, along with most of the room, and was stunned to hear Mr. Darcy's subtle reproach in her defense. She could not imagine why he would trouble himself to respond to the ridiculous little man, especially for the sake of a woman of so little consequence to himself.

Across the room, Miss Bingley was aghast to be approached by Mr. Collins. She struggled for a response that would dismiss him from her company, and shot a pleading glance to her sister, Mrs. Hurst. Elizabeth thought she observed a small smile of amusement on Mr. Darcy's face as he observed the scene.

Miss Bingley finally found refuge from Mr. Collins when Mr. Bingley suggested they might like some music. He was rather glad Jane did not play, as it allowed him to keep her by his side with her hand in his.

Unfortunately for Mr. Darcy, he had wandered too close to Miss Bingley to avoid her entreaty for him to turn the pages for her as she played. His expression hinged on the verge of a scowl as Miss Bingley repeatedly brushed her elbow against his arm while she played, much to the continued amusement of Mr. Bennet. It had always been obvious to him that with regard to Mr. Darcy, she was a huntress of the first order, and wondered if perhaps the forces driving Mr. Bingley's barnacle-like behavior were hereditary. How anyone could mistake the man for proud, he did not understand. All he saw was a young man desperately trying to remain civil in the face of those who wished to stable him like a prized stallion. Mr. Bennet found too much hilarity in the young man's predicament to let him escape, and devised a method of prolonging the scene.

After Miss Bingley completed her concertos, Mr. Bennet paid her the appropriate compliments and requested that Elizabeth might play, innocently suggesting that Mr. Darcy continue his excellent work at turning the pages. Mr. Darcy graced Mr. Bennet with a cold stare and raised brow, but remained beside the pianoforte, seating himself once Miss Elizabeth had selected her music.

As she settled herself, Miss Elizabeth spoke in a low voice, "Forgive my father, Mr. Darcy, I believe he is just having some merriment at our expense. I know this piece rather well, so you need not trouble yourself with the onerous task of turning pages for the daughter of such a man."

She could not determine the meaning of the look he gave her, but after he did not rise from the bench, she began to play. She assumed he was gazing intently at her fingers in order to properly turn the pages, as his hand seemed to tremble slightly each time he reached to turn them. She furrowed her brow as she observed her father, mirth beginning to water his eyes as he chuckled silently behind his hand. After her performance, Mr. Darcy paid her an appropriate compliment on her playing and offered his arm to guide her to a seat beside her father.

The rest of the evening passed congenially for all. Mr. Collins finally found a receptive ear in Mrs. Bennet, and the two loudly extolled the virtues of Netherfield Park and the future weddings of the eldest Miss Bennets. Miss Bingley, unable to garnish Mr. Darcy's attention, found solace in the company of her sister. Mr. Bingley enjoyed a lively conversation with the remainder of the party, with the exception of Mr. Darcy, who kept silently to himself. When the clock struck the latest hour deemed appropriate, Mr. Bennet called for the carriage and the dinner party came to an end.

Late into the night, Mr. Darcy replayed his actions during the evening's gathering. In some moments, he was proud of his restraint, yet he was concerned with regard to Mr. Bennet's actions. He suspected Mr. Bennet must be aware of his regard for Elizabeth in order for him to act in such a peculiar manner. As he thought of Mr. Bennet's orchestrating their time at the pianoforte, he drew sickening parallels to the behavior of so many other parents who thrust their daughters into his company. If this were Mr. Bennet's motivation,

Elizabeth may even dare to expect his addresses. Upon further reflection, it was of little consequence, as it would simply indicate them to be of like mind to the rest of society.

Chapter 7

Saturday morning dawned clear and still, the silence broken only by the rhythmic beating of hooves upon the earth, which was suddenly interrupted by the rustle of upset leaves. Startled by the contact of passing branches, Mr. Darcy straightened his upset hat, cursing himself for allowing his thoughts to be entrapped in reminiscence of the previous evening. Forcing Elizabeth's enchanting image from his mind, he ruefully thanked his horse for staying to the familiar path, despite the lack of guidance from so inattentive a rider. He reminded himself of his purpose for riding into town, and thought of the note he anticipated in response to his opinion of *Sense and Sensibility*. Elizabeth had refused to discuss books in a ballroom, and most likely had yet to read— *stop thinking of her!* With a flick of his heel, he urged his mount into a gallop, and with a determined expression, focused on the route ahead.

The bookshop appeared to be empty upon his arrival, muffled voices and occasional shuffling sounds indicating that Mr. Awdry and his nephew were working in the back room. Pleased with the opportunity to avoid their notice, Mr. Darcy quickly removed the expected missive and escaped undetected.

Now that his more pleasurable errand had been completed, Mr. Darcy rode determinedly to speak with Colonel Forster. He loathed the necessity of revealing his history with Mr. Wickham. Experiencing it had been sufficient exposure to the scoundrel, much less reliving it through discussion with a stranger. However he could not shake the conviction that irreparable damage would come if he did not expose Mr. Wickham in at least some way. If his duty to the common good of the people of Meryton was not motivation enough, his closest friend was now tied to the neighborhood's most prominent family.

Mr. Darcy entered the house taken by Colonel Forster and his wife, and was led to meet with the Colonel in his study.

"I must say, Mr. Darcy, I am surprised that you would desire to speak with me."

Mr. Darcy resisted the urge to groan at this statement. He had heard this opinion voiced all too frequently as of late. He had always thought his silence and reserve left him open to far less ridicule than men with looser tongues, but perhaps the opposite was true.

"My honor as a gentleman requires that I reveal to you my history with one of your lieutenants. It is incumbent that I advise you of the inherent liabilities his connection brings to your regiment..."

࢛࢛࢛

Mr. Darcy rode hard across the countryside; he could not forget the details of his conversation with Colonel Forster fast enough. Nothing had been said of his most personal dealings with Mr. Wickham, yet simply listing the dissolute habits of his father's godson was never a pleasant experience. Mr. Wickham was a thorn in his side; and no less so at present than in his boyhood days. After the wretched affair in Ramsgate, he had thought himself finally rid of the man's plaguing existence, but now wished he had followed Colonel Fitzwilliam's advice and shipped the miscreant to the West Indies on the first available boat. Eventually his anger cooled, and with a sigh he reined in his mount, allowing the horse to move leisurely towards a stream along the border of Netherfield Park. Jumping down from the saddle, he led his horse to the water and sat along the bank, reaching to his pocket for the pleasant distraction he surely needed.

Though I cannot agree with your statements, and might offer many sound rebuttals to your cynical view, I shall instead address a much more pressing concern. I must say that without some credible explanation, I will be forced to completely rethink my concept of your character, given that you are far too familiar with silly romance novels typically read to fulfill the romantic daydreams of young ladies. What say you sir, has heartbreak led you to heal your wounds and renew your hope in such a fashion?

A Noteworthy Courtship

Mr. Darcy laughed softly as he folded up the teasing note he should have seen coming. While he had expected a heated rebuttal to his opinion, as he had received from his sister, he was not disappointed. She had clearly indicated herself to be capable of such, yet the witty repartee she had chosen in its stead was quite enjoyable. The few sentences she committed to paper had lightened his mood, and he was compelled to attempt an equally playful response.

Saturday also brought the scheduled departure of Mr. Collins, an event which could not come soon enough for all members of the Bennet family, save one. From the very day of his arrival, Mrs. Bennet had considered Elizabeth destined to wed her cousin, and she was rather vexed to see him leave before the event took place. Mrs. Bennet had pressed her husband daily to assure Mr. Collins of their good will towards the match, but to no avail. Mr. Bennet was not desirous of a confrontation regarding that gentleman's intentions towards his favorite daughter, and as an invitation to return to Longbourn would not be issued, Mr. Bennet assumed the matter would settle itself. The length of time that would be necessary for his cousin's aspirations to dissipate he knew not, but as Mr. Collins would be passing the required time in Kent, he did not overly concern himself. So it was that Mr. Collins prepared to leave Hertfordshire, still under the delusion that he was engaged to Elizabeth Bennet.

Mrs. Bennet contrived a moment alone between Mr. Collins and his presumed fiancée, requesting that Elizabeth provide her company while he oversaw the loading of his trunks. The two went into the hall for their wraps, and as Mr. Collins handed Elizabeth her coat, he also slipped a small letter into her hands. For a moment her skin crawled, and she was horrified that he may be the nameless man with whom she had been exchanging notes. She dismissed the idea as ridiculous, but paled as she realized the dilemma brought upon her by the letter in her hand. Mr. Collins was now exiting the house, and she immediately followed him, forcefully holding out the letter in his direction.

"Mr. Collins, you know very well I cannot accept a letter from you," she said through tight lips.

Mr. Collins smiled at her affectionately, causing her to pale even further, "Of course, my dear cousin, you are concerned that we have yet to formalize our engagement, and I am certain her Ladyship will admire your sense of propriety. No one has observed our exchange, and given the long separation we are about to endure, I am sure your amiable parents would be understanding if you chose to show them my missive. I am glad you have accepted my token of affection and will say no more on the subject if such a course would be pleasing to your delicate sensibilities."

Before Elizabeth was given any further chance to object and insist he take back the letter, the rest of her family emerged from the house to bid their cousin farewell. Fearful of her mother seeing the letter, she reluctantly placed the distasteful paper in her pocket.

Finally Mr. Collins' equipage disappeared down the drive, and the family returned to the house, Elizabeth lingering outside. She was disgusted to have something from Mr. Collins so close to her person. She felt it would be most suitable to feed his note to the pigs, but out of morbid curiosity, walked to a private section of the garden to open it. After reading the first few lines, she found many of his phrases to be the same ridiculous flattery he had spouted during his stay. Not wishing to devote another moment to his misplaced affections, she balled the letter in her hand before entering the house and threw it into the nearest fire without any further examination.

❧❧❧

With the absence of Mr. Collins, life at Longbourn took a joyful turn. The Christmas season was approaching with all of its festivities, and Mrs. Bennet engrossed herself in Jane's wedding plans and engagement celebrations. The family attended church, and Mrs. Bennet smiled proudly as the first of the banns were read. Certainly all of Meryton had already been supplied with her good information, but she reveled in the opportunity to lord her good fortune over her neighbors. At the close of the service, Mr. Bingley was soon to be found at Miss Bennet's side, and the two gracefully accepted the well wishes of their friends and neighbors.

Miss Bingley and Mrs. Hurst received acknowledgement of the brother's good fortune as insincerely as would be expected, while Mr. Darcy stood off to the side, responding with no more than a curt nod when directly addressed. Miss Elizabeth could not but look upon the glowering party with contempt, and would have continued to do so, if not for her desire to avoid Mr. Darcy's stare. She instead cast her eyes upon her serenely happy sister and a cheerful Mr. Bingley. A long string of invitations for parties in honor of Jane's engagement could be overheard, promising a very festive Christmas season indeed.

❧❧❧

The next morning, Mr. Darcy deposited another note into its hiding place with an amused smile struggling to break free from his lips. After having spent the better part of Sunday afternoon mulling over his choice of words, the phrases he eventually committed to paper were playful and reflected a side of him rarely seen since his boyhood days. Many of his closer acquaintances and relations would describe him in a more amiable light than he was viewed in Hertfordshire, but few would describe him as lively or exuberant. He had always endeavored to show strength of character through his seriousness, but the anonymity of this correspondence gave him a welcome opportunity to lower his guard.

Mr. Darcy mounted his horse after leaving the bookshop, and was assaulted by the boisterous voices emanating from a carriage driving through the village. With no great amount of surprise, he recognized the Bennet carriage and immediately deduced the occupants to be Mrs. Bennet and her youngest daughters. Though he was unable to distinguish the exact words being spoken, he cared not, and rode in the opposite direction before he might be recognized and called into a frightfully taxing conversation.

❧❧❧

"Mr. Bennet! You will not believe the news we have heard from my sister Philips. Why, it is all that is being discussed in Meryton!"

Mr. Bennet sighed as he resignedly folded his newspaper and looked at his wife. "I assume you would like to share with me this riveting bit of gossip that has overshadowed even the importance of Jane's engagement in the eyes of the good people of Meryton."

"More important than Jane's engagement? What nonsense!" Mrs. Bennet paused and stared at her husband dramatically before sharing her news. "It seems Mr. Wickham has left the regiment, and so suddenly that he had not even the opportunity to bid a proper farewell to his general acquaintance. No one seems to know why he left, but we have heard it from Mrs. Forster herself that he is definitely not expected to return."

Mr. Bennet presumed his reason for leaving would no longer be a mystery once the sordid details of his time spent in the area were revealed. He wondered if perhaps Mr. Darcy had troubled himself to speak with the commanding officer of the regiment, which pleased him greatly, as it would save him the trouble of barring the man from his home.

"I think it dreadfully inconvenient that he left before Christmas," cried Miss Lydia, "Oh, how I wished to dance with him at all the balls and parties! It is wickedly unfair that he has been sent away!"

"There, there, Lydia," Mrs. Bennet patted her daughter's arm consolingly, "I am sure there shall be plenty of other officers for you to dance with, and besides, with Jane's connection to Mr. Bingley, surely you can do much better for yourself. I daresay the only officer who might have been worthy of you was Colonel Forster, if he had not found that wife of his. Yes, he would have been much better off with you!"

"Oh mama, as if I could care for so droll a man as Colonel Forster! I had such hopes that I might catch Mr. Wickham. He would make such a fine and dashing husband, and to think we might have even married before Jane! I am sure he shall miss me dreadfully, wherever he has gone."

"And I!" Kitty cried petulantly, "I am sure he shall miss me just as much as you!"

"Oh Kitty, what do you care of Mr. Wickham?" cried Mrs. Bennet. "You would do better to apply yourself to Mr. Darcy! Why, if only you would show more interest in him to Mr. Bingley, he would surely bring Mr. Darcy along when he visits Jane. You must be certain to ask after him directly when Mr. Bingley calls this afternoon. Now that I think on it, he may even bring Mr. Darcy along with him as he did last week, and we cannot allow the opportunity to go to waste. Now go upstairs and put on your green muslin." Kitty left obediently to heed her mother's command as Mrs. Bennet turned to address her husband.

"Oh Mr. Bennet, what a fine thing for our girls! First Jane shall marry Mr. Bingley, and if Kitty would only exert herself, she may have a chance at Mr. Darcy. He is a cold, silent sort of gentleman, and there is

Miss Bingley to consider, but even if she should not catch him, think of all the other young men that she will meet at the wedding!"

"Yes Mrs. Bennet, I am sure there are plenty of young gentlemen of great fortune and little sense among Mr. Bingley's acquaintance who would like nothing better than a silly young wife of little means or importance, and who better than our girls. Yes, I daresay they will be lurking in the hedgerows, hoping for an introduction."

The first winter storm began in the early afternoon and continued through the night, bringing with it a bitter wind and a light snow. After enjoying another morning free of Mr. Collins' attentions, Elizabeth donned her winter coat, informing her father that she would spend her afternoon enjoying the beauties provided by the snow that had fallen overnight. He smiled knowingly and gave her an errand in the village. Elizabeth left the house and dutifully selected a path that wandered through the woods towards Meryton.

In the bookshop, Elizabeth purchased the newspapers her father had requested and waited until Mr. Awdry was distracted by another patron before opening a certain novel and tucking its unbound contents away amongst her parcels. After delivering the requested items to her father, Elizabeth went up to her room and anxiously read the following.

*December 9, 18_*

You wound me madam! By this description you would have me as a simpering dandy with said novel preciously tucked into the pocket at my breast. I assure you that such is not the man behind this pen. Is it too much to imagine that I may know a young lady who professed her interest in this work such so energetically that I read it to appease her?

Elizabeth laughed aloud, imagining a peculiar little man with a plume in his cap, expounding his distress over Marianne's illness. She was startled from her merriment by a sharp knock at her door, and before she could compose herself or hide the note, her father appeared in the doorway.

"I had come to assure myself that my errand was not too taxing on you, as you retired to your room immediately upon your return, but I am glad to see the exercise has not kept you from your usual good spirits."

Spotting the note in her hands, Mr. Bennet's tone took on a bit of seriousness. "Now Lizzy, I have never been one to press your confidence, but you have always given it freely, and my curiosity has grown such that it is now getting the better of me. Would you care to share with me the truth behind your frequent visits to Mr. Awdry's establishment?"

"Oh Papa, I fear you will be very angry with me. Please do not imagine what I relate to be indicative of anything untoward, it has really been a simple form of amusement, through rather unconventional means."

"Your explanation thus far seems to create more questions than it answers. I suggest you answer me a bit more directly. I would prefer not to drag you down to Mr. Awdry for an explanation as I did when you were ten years of age and arrived home with your new coat used as a satchel, full of cookies pilfered from the village bakery."

Elizabeth sighed, and seeing no means of escape, proceeded to explain the events that led her so frequently to the bookshop. It was rather fortunate that her impulsiveness and sense of humor were reminiscent of her father's, as he was much more amenable to such actions simply for amusement than her mother would be. Mr. Bennet laughed and advised Elizabeth that while he prided himself in having a daughter able to best any gentleman in the neighborhood with her wit, she ought proceed with caution, as any note that fell into the hands of her mother would definitely lead to a forced marriage to Mrs. Long's widowed brother, or whoever else the poor man might be. However the young lady mentioned in the most recent note may turn out to be the gentleman's wife, in which case she would be subject to her mother's ire, as surely having such actions revealed would drive away Mr. Collins and leave them all ruined. Considering his daughter thoroughly teased on the subject, Mr. Bennet gave Elizabeth a smile to assure her of his good humor, and left the room.

Elizabeth was relieved to have once again benefited from her father's lenient parenting, and acknowledged the truth of his warning that she be cautious. She could not help but wonder about the identity of the young lady her writing companion had mentioned. For a moment she felt something akin to jealousy before chiding herself that she had no idea of the man's identity. Just as her father had teased, he could very well be a stuffy old man of fifty years, and the young lady could then easily be his daughter. A small part of her insisted that he must be an eligible young man, considering the tone and manner of address in his letters. While she might like to believe he was a handsome young man, her rationale insisted that this was only wishful thinking.

Mr. Bennet returned to his library. Only his Lizzy would dig up a scrap of paper amongst the dusty old books of Mr. Awdry's back shelves and use it as a channel for merciless teasing. He wondered if perhaps he should not allow such a breach of propriety to continue, yet considering the storms of complaint and rebellion that accompanied such attempts to control his wife and daughters, he decided not to raise the ire of his favorite, that he may at least have peace with one member of the family when Jane moved to Netherfield.

Chapter 8

The following day brought the official invitation for the much anticipated Yuletide Ball at Lucas Lodge. In previous years, the Yuletide Ball had been the event of the annum, and once discussion of the Netherfield Ball had died down, it had been the central topic of conversation over tea for ladies between twelve and sixty.

"Oh girls! There is so much to do!" cried Mrs. Bennet, "Thank goodness Mr. Bingley has anticipated us and will kindly bring his carriage to escort us into the village. Now we shall all get new gowns for the Lucas' ball, after all it is being given for Jane, in honor of her engagement."

Elizabeth whispered to Jane that the ball was rumored to be in honor of the season, but they best not remind their mother of so gross a falsehood.

Mr. Bingley arrived as promised, riding alongside his carriage to escort the ladies of the house into Meryton. Mrs. Bennet, Kitty and Lydia would not be satisfied until they had scoured through every good in the milliner's shop, while Jane and Elizabeth spent a few moments making their selections before returning to Mr. Bingley. The gentleman suggested they walk to the bakery, and seeing the eager twinkle in his eye as he expressed his desire for some holiday sweets, the ladies smiled and readily agreed. As they basked in the delightful scent of snickerdoodles and gingerbread cookies, Elizabeth excused herself to make a quick detour into the bookshop while Mr. Bingley made his selections.

಴಴಴

The following morning, Mr. Darcy awoke with a smile, and left the house in eager anticipation. He had settled into a routine of knowing when to expect a note, and was astonished by how keenly he looked forward to reading *her* words. He found it difficult to comprehend the manner in which she had inspired him to expose himself and tease in such a light-hearted fashion. He had never thought himself capable of finding amusement at his own expense, and was anxious to read her response.

You would do well to learn, sir, not to make an open invitation for mockery if you are not thoroughly prepared to receive it. As to your defense, I would prefer the term sentimental ninny to simpering dandy, but I am glad to know that you are neither. I hope this "young lady" under your influence is encouraged towards reading on more serious topics as well.

Mr. Darcy chuckled as read the first portion of the note, impressed by her ability to invent an appellation even worse than he had. He also appreciated her comment towards his sister's reading habits. Though extensive reading was not generally an esteemable pastime for accomplished young ladies, he had in fact greatly encouraged her to become familiar with as many of the books in his library as possible. He had also never heard a lady express an opinion on his care over Georgiana except to praise him. That this woman would be bold enough to offer constructive criticism was quite refreshing. He released a contented sigh as he urged his horse on towards Netherfield, already plotting the words he would leave in response, knowing the following day's activities would include another visit to Mr. Awdry's establishment.

✍✍✍

Two days later, the weather proved rather cold, and reluctantly Elizabeth stayed indoors during the morning hours. Mr. Bingley had admitted the previous day that it would behoove him to spend some time going over estate matters with Mr. Darcy, and was not expected until dinner. Jane and Elizabeth had escaped their mother's constant prattle regarding wedding clothes and were preparing the last bundles of winter foliage and herbs to be dried. Mrs. Hill entered, informing Elizabeth that Mr. Bennet had requested her presence in the library at her earliest convenience. With a smile to Jane, Elizabeth tied off a bundle of rosemary and headed towards the library, assuming her father desired her company to read together or to play a game of chess.

"Lizzy, my dear, you should be glad to know that although you have yet to make her acquaintance, you have been fortunate enough to receive the approval of Lady Catherine deBourgh."

Mr. Bennet chuckled, and showed a long letter from Mr. Collins to his confused daughter.

"I will spare you the details of his raptures, but I must tell you it was rather comical to read his explanation of how the great lady was at first rather put out to hear that you were a witty, lively sort of girl, and was greatly mollified when he explained how your respect for her station would be sure to quiet you, and you would gladly consult her advice on improving your comportment. I can just imagine your response to such condescension would be quite the opposite, and there is a conversation I would like to witness, it if did not require my giving you away to such a ridiculous man."

Mr. Bennet looked upon his daughter's face, and seeing little amusement, but a great deal of unease, he came to the point and held up an additional letter, seal unbroken.

"Mr. Collins has also enclosed a letter which he implores me to pass on to his 'fiancée', but as we both know that such a woman does not reside in this house, I will not trouble you with it." Mr. Bennet gave Elizabeth a comforting smile and tossed the letter into the fire.

"Now, on to a more pleasant topic. With the Christmas season approaching, I do have some shopping to do, and I am sure this cold weather has kept you from leaving the house this morning." Mr. Bennet gave his daughter a knowing look, indicating himself to be perfectly aware of why being kept indoors on this particular day was more distressing than would normally be expected. "Let me call the carriage and what say you join me on a ride into Meryton? Perhaps you will find a gift for your dear old father in the bookshop while I brave the shelves of ladies' frippery for your mother."

Elizabeth was indeed successful in finding a gift for her father, as well as some sheet music for Mary. Her father teased that she must be exchanging quite extensive letters if she required two packages for their conveyance to Longbourn. Elizabeth sighed and lifted the top parcel, revealing a small white sheet that had been tucked between the packages. Before he was able to inquire further, she teased her father in turn, noting that he had survived the perils of shopping for her mother tolerably well. Mr. Bennet replied that he had indeed found something suitable, and perhaps if he were quite lucky, she would declare it to be a splendid surprise and be cured of her nerves for a fortnight at least.

Upon their return to Longbourn, Elizabeth excused herself to deposit the gifts she had purchased into her room. She removed the small sheet of paper she had hidden and read the following:

December 13, 18__

The "young lady" is my sister, and while I would not wish her to adopt reading habits as dull and stuffy as mine, I have encouraged her to read many of the classics. She has not my penchant for reading, preferring to spend her time painting or practicing at the pianoforte, but her talents in these areas lead me to believe that her time is well spent.

Elizabeth had apparently reached the limit of his ability to reply with a witty rejoinder, which was just as well, as she could carry on forever in such a way. She was immediately impressed by the obvious devotion this man had towards his sister. Though she had no brother to whom she could compare, she had never seen such a bond between siblings of the opposite sex amongst her acquaintance. Young boys and girls were raised so differently, and once childhood playmates were taught to become genteel young ladies and dutiful young gentlemen, brothers seemed to become more protective than affectionate. She saw that this man spoke highly of her talents, and hoped the young lady was not stifled under the pursuit of being an accomplished woman. Not one to keep an opinion to herself, Elizabeth resolved to enquire further.

Once again, Elizabeth prepared to depart from Longbourn and tuck a note between the pages of a once inconsequential book. As she passed the open door to the library, she was about to notify her father that she would be out for a walk when he motioned for her to approach him.

"Off with another letter for Mrs. Long's brother, eh?" Mr. Bennet chuckled, "I had thought you would abandon the idea once you discovered him to be an old widower, but then you may prefer being a stepmother to his girls, as they are far less silly than your sisters."

"Papa, you should not tease so! I have it on good authority that one of my sisters is a veritable angel. Besides, you know me well enough to suspect that I possess the intellect to discreetly inquire about the lady in question, and you may care to know that she is his sister."

"Aha! Well then, I humbly retract my previous statement, and wish you all the luck with young John Lucas. I am sure one day the neighborhood will forget that you are more than a twelve-month his senior!"

Elizabeth smiled and rolled her eyes in mock frustration. Mr. Bennet waved his daughter off, so as not to further delay her from her *walk*, as she had called it. Retrieving his newspaper, he found difficulty focusing on its printed words as his mind tallied the number of young men in the neighborhood with sisters, and found the spectrum of possible identities rather slim indeed.

The next day was rather pleasant for December. Though still a bit cool in light of the season, it was at least dry. Thus Mr. Darcy found himself perched atop his horse, paused in a grove he had first found weeks before, with a similar note unfolded in his hands.

By your description, she is all that is accomplished. I have once heard it described that in addition to the talents your sister has already developed, a woman must possess a certain something in her air and manner of walking, the tone of her voice, her address and expressions to be deemed truly accomplished. For your sake, I hope she is all that is open and artless, allowing her natural talent and pleasant qualities to speak for themselves, a display which is certain to terrify persons of high society.

Mr. Darcy felt a sinking feeling in the pit of his stomach as he read an exact quotation of Miss Bingley's haughty turn of phrase. He paled and forced himself to acknowledge what was now painfully clear. It was her – *Elizabeth.* He had been foolish enough to believe he was corresponding with some mysterious well-bred woman, but deep down he should have known. He had rallied himself so completely against Elizabeth, such that he did not see the obvious fact that of any woman in the neighborhood, it would be her. He had instead used thoughts of this enigmatic woman to support the notion that Miss Elizabeth was not as special as his heart wished her to be. He had been desperate to believe there were witty and intelligent women in his sphere, and that he had yet to meet them because he simply had not applied himself to seeking them out. His carefully constructed defenses had all gone to rot. Elizabeth was unique, and he found himself wanting her even more.

Mr. Darcy forced the letter back into his pocket and galloped his horse towards Netherfield in a foul mood. He chastised himself for his foolishness, questioning how he had let such lovesick delusions lead him to that wretched bookshop nearly every day for the past fortnight. If only he had had the sense to leave immediately after the Netherfield ball, perhaps he would have been able to keep his infatuation in check.

Before long, his sagacity finally overcame his ire, and he slowed his horse as he considered the situation before him. As reality continued to wash away the haze the last weeks had created, he realized the alarming degree of danger in which his actions had placed him. They had not seemed problematic at the time, but the notes he had left were concrete evidence of the impropriety he had committed. If the notes were ever revealed to another party, and if she were able to deduce his identity, surely Mr. Bennet would demand that he marry her. As much as he wished to return to Pemberley and leave the events of the last months to be forgotten, he would have to proceed with caution. He would find a way to continue their correspondence into the new year before breaking it. He could not take the inherent risk of timing his departure with the end of their exchanges.

He consoled himself with the knowledge that she may not yet be aware of his identity, and he desperately hoped she was not. He would require an opportunity to speak to her and gauge her reaction to him. Though he detested the activity, he admitted dancing with her at the upcoming ball would be the best way of obtaining a private conversation without attracting attention. After all, propriety required that he also dance with Miss Bennet in light of her recent engagement to his close friend. Perhaps if he timed these dances well, he would be able to avoid obliging Miss Bingley with a set. Most difficult of all, he reminded himself, he would need to leave another note, and without any indication that her words had impacted him so profoundly.

Longbourn was a flurry of activity in preparation for the ball. Her mother did not object when Elizabeth insisted her ensemble was well prepared as Mr. Collins was not expected to return for the event. However Elizabeth soon discovered that this complaisance regarding her own wardrobe simply reflected her mother's opinion that she should make herself available to aid her sisters. So it was that she had nearly given up hope of reaching the bookshop on the appropriate day, and was relieved to escape and retrieve the following missive.

*December 18, 18_*

Though I would consider my sister to be quite accomplished, she is rather too shy to be open amongst any but her closest acquaintance. I would consider artlessness to be a positive attribute, and though this trait is not common in higher circles, I am no less inclined to appreciate it.

Elizabeth was glad to know he would never esteem the practiced airs of women such as Miss Bingley and Mrs. Hurst. She did not look forward to meeting with them the next evening at the Lucas' Ball, and hoped they would not be too unkind in their treatment of Jane. However they were Jane's future sisters, and even she could not remain ignorant of their true natures for long.

Elizabeth awoke before dawn on the day of the Yuletide Ball, and left the house just as the first rays of sun glowed behind the distant hills, lest she be kept from her errand by her mother. Mrs. Bennet had insisted the previous evening that all of the girls retire early, that their complexions would be fresh and vibrant for the evening's festivities, and she would hardly be amenable to Elizabeth exerting herself on this occasion. Fortunately, she arrived home just as Mrs. Bennet's first calls were heard from above stairs, and was able to sneak into the kitchen for refreshment. She rested easily, knowing that her errand had been accomplished, and could not but wonder if her innominate correspondent might be in attendance at the ball.

Chapter 9

The evening of the Yuletide Ball finally arrived, much to the excitement of the people of Meryton. Mr. Bingley had ordered his carriage to be readied early, that he might first travel to Longbourn to convey his fiancée and her family in his own larger equipage. Thus Mr. Darcy was left to escort the Hursts and Miss Bingley in his own carriage, and reunited with his friend at the ball.

As Mr. Darcy entered Lucas Lodge, with the unfortunate necessity of offering his arm to Miss Bingley, he observed the scene with a distaste equal to that which he felt at each previous gathering. The general company displayed the lack of fashion and want of decorum he had come to expect from his social inferiors. He observed Mr. Bingley and Miss Bennet joining the first set of the evening, and wondered how his friend could feel at ease in such ill-mannered company. Yet there was nothing to be done for it, and knowing this was the last time he would be subjected to such company, he sighed and set about accomplishing the task at hand. Mrs. Hurst and Miss Bingley had been trapped into conversation with some of the local matrons, and Mr. Darcy took the opportunity to excuse himself, approaching Mr. Bingley as he led Miss Bennet from the dance.

"Bingley, Miss Bennet." Mr. Darcy bowed as he greeted the couple, "As this is the first public event in honor of your engagement, allow me to again offer my congratulations."

"No need for formalities, old man," Mr. Bingley laughed, "I know you have long recognized Jane for the angel that she is."

Mr. Darcy gave a slight nod to Mr. Bingley and turned to Miss Bennet as she thanked him politely.

"Miss Bennet, would you allow me to deprive your fiancé of your company by dancing the next with me?"

"Certainly, Mr. Darcy."

Upon her positive reply, Mr. Darcy offered his hand to escort Miss Bennet to the floor, leaving a shocked Elizabeth in their wake.

"I see you are surprised by Mr. Darcy's inviting your sister to dance, Miss Elizabeth, but he is ever conscious of paying respect where it is due, and he is a very loyal friend." Mr. Bingley smiled and indicated towards the dancing area as he extended his hand, "Would you do me the honor?"

"Why yes, Mr. Bingley. Propriety calls for nothing less, and our dancing now will keep you from the necessity of giving up a later dance with our dear Jane." Elizabeth returned Mr. Bingley's smile, belying the sterile nature of her words.

Mr. Bingley was quick to reunite with Jane after her dance with Mr. Darcy, and offered to bring her refreshment. Mr. Darcy joined him without a word, and upon their return, Mr. Bingley offered a glass of punch to Jane while Mr. Darcy did the same for Elizabeth.

"Thank you, Mr. Darcy." Elizabeth struggled to keep a curious expression from her features as she reached to accept the refreshment she had not requested.

Elizabeth took a sip of punch before adding, "I see you have now filled your obligation to your friend."

Mr. Darcy furrowed his brow at the twinge of bitterness in her tone, but before he could consider a response, his companion turned towards the excited approach of Mrs. Bennet and Miss Catherine.

"There you are Jane! Oh, what a wonderful affair this has turned out to be, and all in the honor of yourself and Mr. Bingley."

"Yes Mama, we are all glad to gather together and celebrate the season with our friends and neighbors," Jane replied softly.

Ignoring the majority of her daughter's demure response, Mrs. Bennet turned an eager eye upon the eligible gentleman in the group, who then realized with horror that he was the primary reason for her approach. "Mr. Darcy sir, I noticed your dancing with Jane, how kind of you to compliment her thus."

"It is expected that I honor the intended bride of so close a friend," the gentleman replied stiffly.

"Why yes, being such a good friend as you are to Mr. Bingley, we shall all be nearly family once he is married to Jane. And gentlemanly as you are, I am sure you would enjoy giving a dance to one of his future sisters as well." If Mr. Darcy had not already deduced the meaning of her words, Mrs. Bennet made all clear with a nod and pointed look towards Miss Catherine before turning back to him expectantly.

Mr. Darcy cleared his throat in futile attempt to break the matron's gaze before replying. "Indeed Mrs. Bennet, I was just about to ask Miss Elizabeth if she might dance the next with me."

Turning to Miss Elizabeth, he asked sedately, "Would you do me the honor?"

Not unconscious of the glare being sent her direction by her mother, but oblivious to any means of polite refusal, Elizabeth assented. Mr. Darcy offered his hand to escort her, and without another word, led her to their place in the next set.

Ever skillful at diffusing social tension, Mr. Bingley promptly addressed his future sister, "Miss Catherine, I would be delighted if you might dance the next with me."

Mr. Bingley then escorted her to the floor as well, leaving Mrs. Bennet and her eldest daughter to each other's company.

"Well Jane, can you believe the nerve of her!" Mrs. Bennet huffed. "First, Lizzy allows her fiancé to leave for Kent without so much as a formal announcement to the neighborhood, and now she is dancing with Mr. Darcy, who we all know finds her only tolerable. I dare say I cannot blame him, what with the impertinent remarks always flying from her mouth, but how is Kitty to catch his eye if Lizzy wastes his time so?" Jane could only smile politely and turn her eyes towards the couples taking their places for the next dance.

As the dance began, Elizabeth addressed Mr. Darcy.

"It seems I am to apologize for my mother's behavior Mr. Darcy, as she goaded you into this dance."

"Do not apologize for conduct that is not your own."

The emotionless tone of his voice convinced Elizabeth that Mr. Darcy had spoken more with politeness than sincerity, and both parties continued the dance in silence.

Mr. Darcy was torn. His every sense was overwhelmed by the enchanting lady before him, yet he was determined to exhibit nothing but indifference for fear of revealing himself. His thoughts churned at an alarming rate, and he determined to break the silence before he became lost in his musings.

"Do you have any particular plans for the holiday season?" he inquired.

"Mr. Bingley has been kind enough to invite us to spend Christmas Day at Netherfield," Miss Elizabeth replied.

"I see."

Elizabeth huffed as the movement of the dance turned her away from Mr. Darcy, frustrated by his meager attempt at forwarding the conversation.

"And yourself, sir?" she entreated.

"I shall be leaving shortly to spend the holiday with my sister."

"Yes, it must be preferable to spend the season with your closest relative as opposed to insignificant strangers. I am sure she will be glad to have you arrive before Christmas."

Elizabeth made no attempt to disguise the icy tone that flowed so naturally into her voice. Christmas was less than a se'en-night hence, and that his young sister was deprived of his company at such a time riled her. She thought of the devotion another gentleman felt towards his own sister, and was confident that *he* would never conduct himself in such a manner.

As their dance ended, Mr. Darcy led Elizabeth off the floor and silently walked away. She had little concern for where he might be headed and went to speak with Charlotte Lucas. Elizabeth spent the rest of the evening observing Jane's glowing happiness and scrutinizing the young men in attendance – for she knew her correspondent was likely to be among them. Thankfully most were privy to her impertinent nature, and were not taken aback by her inquiries regarding their current reading habits, or their opinion of their sister's accomplishments.

Mr. Darcy spent the remainder of the evening in his own company, slowly pacing the rooms. If his first dance with Elizabeth those few weeks ago at Netherfield had enchanted him, this evening's set had rendered him breathless. Though he had told himself he remained in Hertfordshire only for his intriguing correspondence, which he had thought to use in aid of conquering his feelings for Elizabeth, he also had to admit that his heart relished in the pleasure he found in gazing at her, though bittersweet in light of the torment it brought to his mind, knowing he could never have any serious designs on her. To now know his inducement to remain was not two women, but one, overwhelmed him. He watched her laugh and tease, observing her playful manner from across the room, while overhearing the insipid conversation of the women around him, and reminded himself of what a fool he had been to think those precious notes could have been written by anyone else. He had lingered in Hertfordshire, oblivious to the tide rising around him, and was in grave danger of finding himself in over his head. He would have to leave immediately before he lost control and exposed his identity, as he could hardly hold a civil conversation with her, now that he knew. He had already planned to leave shortly to spend the holidays with Georgiana, but in light of the insignificant girl taking an increasing hold of every piece of his heart, he could not leave soon enough.

When Mr. Bingley and his guests finally returned to Netherfield Park, all were soon enveloped in slumber, save one. Within hours of the close of the ball, Mr. Darcy had sent an express rider to London, and written a note to Mr. Bingley, explaining his departure at first light, which was sure to take place before his missive would be received. He only hoped his express would arrive in time, else all would be for naught.

Chapter 10

It is a truth universally acknowledged that a rich man in possession of sufficient funds is wont to spend a portion of his income quite frivolously. As such, Mr. Darcy's removal from Netherfield Park did not necessitate an end to his notes being placed in wait for a certain lady of the neighborhood. So it was that as the Darcy coach moved through Meryton, a stop was made in the village before continuing on towards the high road to London. Mr. Darcy collected the expected letter, leaving in its place a small blue ribbon, taking care to leave the ribbon slightly visible as it hung over the spine of Sterne's book. He then re-entered his carriage, and after signaling the coachmen to drive on, opened the note.

It pleases me to know that you are not affronted by persons who do not practice the art of putting on airs, for I admit that is one skill in which I may be found severely lacking. I cannot hide my true opinions, and those who wish I might demure politely in favor of popular opinions will find themselves disappointed. But such is the life of us country savages. Perhaps if I had been educated in town, my comportment might be more socially acceptable, yet my partiality for the country forbids me from wishing it had been so.

He smiled wistfully, and began to think of his reply, having already planned to write his response while his horses were changed at the next posting inn. If his express had reached London as planned, Thompson would be waiting there to collect his letter, letting a ribbon of sapphire hue be his guide for its placement.

December 21, 18__

Bingley,

As you read this missive, you are likely aware of my departure this morning. I ask that you forgive the impropriety of my quitting your hospitality without a proper farewell. Rest assured all is well, and please accept my fondest wishes for your holiday season.

Yours etc,

Fitzwilliam Darcy

Mr. Bingley sat confused, wondering at the odd note as he set it down on the table before him. He had rung for his valet after finally willing himself from his bed and its pleasant dreams of dancing with his beloved Jane. He was surprised to see Hawkins enter his dressing room bearing a note addressed to him in Mr. Darcy's familiar hand. He had hoped to speak with Mr. Darcy regarding the events of the previous evening. No sooner had he been relieved to see his friend loosen his reserve by dancing with Jane, and then Elizabeth, than he saw Mr. Darcy's countenance harden as he kept to the perimeter of the room, silent and taciturn as he had been at their first assembly in Meryton. He first concluded that Mr. Darcy must have had business to attend, or been anxious to begin his holiday with Georgiana, yet neither warranted so hasty a departure with so little explanation. Not one to worry excessively, he resolved to speak of the matter with Jane to gain her opinion, as he had promised himself for luncheon at Longbourn.

Over luncheon, Mrs. Bennet enquired after Mr. Darcy's absence, and expressed her hope that he was not unwell, as she had been unable to locate him the latter half of the ball last evening.

"I believe he was quite well last evening, he simply has never welcomed large gatherings as eagerly as myself."

"I see. Well he is most welcome to join you more frequently when you come to call, Mr. Bingley, as we are certainly no large party here."

"Actually ma'am, he left quite early this morning, and is most likely en route to Pemberley to celebrate the season."

"Indeed! We are so sorry to see him go. I had thought he would remain at Netherfield and celebrate with us. He had not the opportunity to stand up with Kitty at the ball, which I am certain he would have found pleasurable."

Though none of the other occupants of the room appeared to notice, Jane observed her fiancé's unease with regard to the discussion of Mr. Darcy. She was not taken by surprise when, after the meal, he requested she accompany him out into the gardens, and readily assented.

As the engaged couple left the room, the rest of the family retired to the drawing room where Mrs. Bennet openly lamented the loss of Mr. Darcy. Reluctant she may have been to abuse his closest friend in Mr. Bingley's presence; she had no such scruples towards doing so in his absence.

"Oh, it vexes me greatly, Mr. Bennet, to think of what we shall be deprived by Mr. Darcy's absence."

"Yes, my dear, I am certain we all feel greatly the loss of his company. Perhaps if you had considered my advice in the fall that he may not have been such a villain as the neighborhood assumed, you might be arranging two wedding breakfasts." Mr. Bennet spoke sarcastically, reluctant to admit that he did regret the gentleman's departure, as it left the neighborhood containing one less person of any sense. As the remaining young gentleman had now left the room, Mr. Bennet excused himself to the comfort of his library. He had observed Mr. Darcy's countenance at the ball, and was not surprised to hear that he had quit the neighborhood. He considered the possibility that perhaps his daughter's correspondence would end without his interference after all.

Mr. Bingley offered Jane his arm upon quitting the house, and the two soon found themselves seated on a garden bench. Mr. Bingley kissed her hand and kept it firmly enclosed in his, turning his head away in evident distraction. Jane rested her free hand upon their joined ones, encouraging Mr. Bingley to look upon her face and graced him with an assuring smile.

"I admit, Jane, that I am rather surprised at Darcy's departure. I did not relate the whole of it in the presence of your family, but he departed before dawn this morning, and my delay in arriving here was actually due to this." He pulled a folded letter from his pocket and held it in his lap.

Withdrawing his hand from hers to open the letter, he handed it to Jane, and nodded gently for her to read it. She accepted the letter and upon finishing it, looked up at Mr. Bingley with a calm expression, waiting for him to explain his distress over the apparently normal letter.

"Forgive me, Jane. Perhaps I my concern is unwarranted, but I cannot shake the feeling that he is concealing something. At first, I thought he had a pressing matter of business, but Darcy and I have discussed our business dealings with each other since Cambridge, and he had not planned to leave for London until tomorrow."

"Perhaps the holiday festivities of last evening made him realize the extent to which he misses his sister's company, and he resolved to be near her as soon as may be. I imagine he must be anxious to see her, and she equally anxious to see him. I am certain a letter inquiring after his journey would be returned with a positive response that all is truly well."

Mr. Bennet gazed out upon the garden from his library window. He observed with pride Jane's manner of supporting Mr. Bingley, she truly would make him an excellent wife, and as much as he liked to tease about it, he did could not doubt that Mr. Bingley's attachment was equally sincere. He very much did doubt, however, that Mr. Darcy was as anxious to see his sister as Jane supposed, as he had a strong suspicion as to the real reason behind the gentleman's departure. Mr. Bennet sighed. Though he had never allowed thoughts of matchmaking to enter his mind, he could not but think the young man would have made a sensible addition to the family.

The next day brought several ladies of the neighborhood calling on the ladies of Longbourn to discuss the Yuletide Ball. Mrs. Bennet held court in the drawing room, and amid the discussions of gowns and dance partners, and exclamations of how uniformly Jane and Mr. Bingley were admired, Elizabeth was able to leave the house unnoticed.

A Noteworthy Courtship

As she walked a circuitous route towards Meryton, Elizabeth thoughts turned unbidden to Mr. Darcy. Though she had sworn to loathe the man, and quite often found little difficulty in doing so, she could not deny that he was quite intelligent and well-educated, rare traits amongst gentlemen in vicinity. Further detrimental to her loathing was her reluctant admittance that he was rather handsome, and had been the most favorable of her partners at the ball with his skillful movement and fine figure.

Knowledge of his departure left her feeling a strange sense of trepidation towards entering the bookshop, and as she reached the back shelves, she could not shake her apprehension that the binding of *A Political Romance* would contain no more than Sterne's original text. The anticipated note was present, however, and she chastised herself for her foolishness in suspecting the writer to be Mr. Darcy. What an insensible notion indeed that he would be secretly charming beneath his disdainful exterior. If she could imagine this to be true, she may as well believe him to be Robin Hood and herself Maid Marian.

Exiting the bookshop, Elizabeth refused to feel any disappointment over eliminating the arrogant man from her list of possible correspondents, and paused along the path to Longbourn to read the following.

December 22, 18__

I cannot condemn your freedom of expression with regard to your opinions, nor can I deny my similar preference for the country over town. There is a certain tranquility found in nature that cannot be duplicated in the bustle of London. That is not to say, however that London does not have its advantages in refinement. Entertainments such as concerts and art galleries cannot be discredited, though the theatre is a personal favorite.

Elizabeth was pleased to find such continued accord between their views. Though she rarely had the opportunity to attend the theatre, she had greatly enjoyed the performances she had seen, and looked forward to reading accounts of his experiences in further detail.

The afternoon brought the arrival of the Gardiner family for the blessed holiday celebration two days hence. The children were eager to reunite with their elder cousins, and Mr. and Mrs. Gardiner warmly extended their congratulations to Jane. Mrs. Bennet rushed to her brother and his wife, well into expressing her raptures over Mr. Bingley and the grandeur of Netherfield Park before they had entered the house.

The hours before dinner passed quickly. The Gardiner girls relished in Jane's elegant company as she complimented their dolls and dressed their hair, while the boys begged Elizabeth for tales of pirates, knights, and any other mischief upon which their cousin was the resident expert. Mrs. Bennet and her youngest daughters probed Mrs. Gardiner for information on the latest fashions in town. The hectic atmosphere seemed all that the Gardiners expected upon their arrival. It was not until dinner that Mrs. Bennet had finally extinguished all subject matter related to fashion and Jane's wedding that her discourse turned to a subject which caused Mr. and Mrs. Gardiner no little concern.

"We must not forget Lizzy's good fortune, for though she may not have pin money equal to Jane's, she is quite fortunate indeed to have secured Mr. Collins. If only she could have kept him from leaving the neighborhood before a wedding date could be set, I would be very happy indeed."

Mrs. Gardiner cast a questioning glance in her niece's direction, as Elizabeth's letters had reflected a rather disfavorable opinion of Mr. Collins.

"Mama, again I would ask that you not speak so. I have not 'secured' him and there is no connection between Mr. Collins and myself, aside from his being our cousin."

All at the table noted Elizabeth's discomfort, save her mother, who continued to extol the relief that would be brought her nerves by having a daughter married to Longbourn's heir. Mr. and Mrs. Gardiner looked upon their niece with compassion, and were disappointed to observe more amusement than concern in Mr. Bennet's countenance.

Elizabeth pled fatigue and excused herself to retire soon after the family joined in the drawing room after dinner. Mrs. Gardiner offered to accompany her niece, as travelling had left her feeling rather weary as well, and excused herself with a knowing look to her husband, who soon suggested to Mr. Bennet that the gentlemen retire to the library.

"Brother Bennet, I must admit I find myself baffled by the scene I witnessed at the dinner table this evening," Mr. Gardiner began, "I have always known my sister to be exuberant with her notions, and I understand your reluctance to correct them, as their sheer volume would leave you little time for anything else, however I am surprised you have not felt the need to intercede in this case."

Mr. Bennet laughed, "Yes, I do feel for my dear Lizzy being subjected to such nonsense, but she defended herself quite well, and once the topic of Mr. Collins passes from my wife's favor, the matter will be forgotten."

"I am not sure I would take Elizabeth's distress so lightly, but more importantly, what of her reputation? From what I have heard of Mr. Collins, I doubt he is handling the situation with any circumspection, despite his lack of formal arrangement."

"Do not be so concerned Edward. No man of sense would believe a word Mr. Collins says, and as to her reputation, I doubt my girls will come into contact with any young gentlemen from Kent. Any young man interested in my daughters would have to overcome their mother; if a man is capable of that, and by off chance he had been in that part of the country, hearing Mr. Collins' unfounded rumor could be of no consequence to them. I am sure this will all blow over soon enough."

"Let us hope you are correct," Mr. Gardiner replied reluctantly.

৵৵৵

Christmas at Netherfield enveloped all the merriment the season should entail. The addition of the Gardiner children reminded many in attendance of the holidays of their youth. Even Mr. Bingley's sisters were able to enjoy the occasion tolerably well, as they could not but look fondly upon a scene so similar to that of their own childhoods. That is not to say either Miss Bingley or Mrs. Hurst mixed with the Bennets and Gardiners any more than necessary, but their brother's resolve had begun to influence them, and their behavior need not be so guarded in the absence of Mr. Darcy and their desire to impress him.

৵৵৵

Christmas in London, though celebrated in the same fashion as years previous, felt rather dull in the eyes of Mr. Darcy. While he greatly enjoyed Georgiana's Christmas carols, and occasionally joined her in song, every family gathering with the Fitzwilliams felt cold and sterile. Each member of the party was jovial in their own way, yet each exhibited a formality and reserve that he would have once called civility, but now simply seemed detached and empty. It was as though each person knew, rather that felt it was a season to be joyful. He envisioned the Christmas party at Netherfield, loud and boisterous, yet full of the gaiety and laughter associated with the idyllic holiday scene of family gathering together and children opening their packages. The image of Elizabeth seated on the floor surrounded by her own brood of children, laughing and smiling amidst their squeals of glee upon opening each delicately packaged gift, played in his mind. He could not envision any woman of his circle in such a scene, and still mourned the loss of seeing his sister thus with his own mother, as his father said she had done with him.

ھھھ

The month of January passed in a hectic blur for the occupants of Longbourn. Mrs. Bennet would allow her daughter's wedding to be nothing less than the finest affair the neighborhood had ever seen. Every aspect was discussed and planned to the smallest detail. Fortunately for Elizabeth, Mrs. Bennet primarily sought the opinion of Jane and Mr. Bingley when deciding these matters, though the input of others affected her decisions but rarely. Mrs. Bennet much preferred to make the most fashionable selections and report to her acquaintance every new detail scheduled for this most elegant event.

Elizabeth was therefore at liberty to continue a regular exchange of notes with her unknown correspondent. Their discussions turned to literature, and she was pleased to find his tastes similar to hers. Though not always of like mind, she found her equal in wit and logic, and their discussions often reached a level that could have easily been unintelligible to many.

Chapter 11

Mr. Darcy looked over the letter before him. Well more than a fortnight had passed since he last laid eyes upon Elizabeth. He had hoped distancing himself and keeping busy would quell his interest, but to no avail. Though he knew the chances to be slim, he had determinedly attended several dinner parties in search of a witty, intelligent young lady of suitable social standing. Yet each attempt at conversation was clouded by comparisons to Elizabeth. She haunted his every dream at night, and by day he began to acknowledge that since his mother's death, he had rarely been happier than those few months spent at Netherfield. He was still unable to envision a life without her, and began to acknowledge that he had struggled in vain, and should return to Netherfield to reconsider her for his wife. With a resigned sigh, he sealed the letter, went into the hall and approached the nearest footman, requesting that he have the letter posted directly.

A few days later, a servant entered the drawing room at Netherfield Park to deliver the post, completely unaware of the significance a certain letter would hold for the master of the house.

*January 10, 18_*

Charles,

Thank you for your letter and the concern expressed therein regarding my departure. Please forgive any unintentional concern I had caused, as well as the delay in this response. Your missive had to be forwarded from its original destination at Pemberley, as I decided to spend the entirety of the holiday in London. I am sure you had a very joyful holiday; which you may avoid describing with missed words and inkblots as Georgiana and I will accept your invitation to Netherfield, arriving in three weeks time to attend your marriage to Miss Bennet.

Yours etc,

Fitzwilliam Darcy

Mr. Bingley was relieved to finally hear from Mr. Darcy, and just as Jane had predicted, the letter confirmed that nothing was amiss. His sisters inquired as to the contents of the letter that caused such a ridiculous grin on his face, but wishing to avoid their effusions over the Darcys arrival for as long as possible, he instead left the room for a private conference with his housekeeper regarding the preparation of two guest suites.

ৡৡৡ

At long last, the Darcy carriage pulled into the drive at Netherfield. The journey had gone smoothly, and the half-day's travel was completed in the last minutes of the afternoon light. Mr. Darcy handed Georgiana out of the carriage, and the pair were instantly greeted by Mr. Bingley. Warm welcomes and heartfelt congratulations were exchanged as the trio entered the house. Mr. Darcy inquired after his sister's comfort, and when she expressed her desire to rest before the evening meal, Mr. Bingley invited Mr. Darcy to join him in the library.

"It is good to have you back at Netherfield, Darcy."

"Thank you Bingley. Again, I must apologize for the manner in which I left you. I cannot think upon it without regretting my rudeness."

"Nonsense, I hope you would expect to find some measure of understanding between friends. Besides, if you feel there is any debt to be repaid, I am certain it will be repaid in full once you have tolerated all of the dinner parties and other gatherings in the upcoming weeks – that is unless you would prefer me to make your excuses."

"No, that will not be necessary, as I am rather looking forward to attending," Mr. Darcy replied nonchalantly.

Mr. Bingley was shocked by such an uncharacteristic declaration, until he realized the most likely cause of it. Combined with his early arrival for the wedding, Bingley was now further convinced that though the truth was well-hidden by reserve, he was witnessing the anomaly of a besotted Darcy. With a quivering lip the only evidence of his valiantly concealed mirth, he shot his friend a meaningful raised brow.

Mr. Darcy cleared his throat and quickly added, "For Georgiana's sake that is. She will be coming out next season, and the small, welcoming society here will be much less intimidating for her as she accustoms herself to the idea."

Neither gentleman felt this reason explained the matter sufficiently, but fortunately for Mr. Darcy, Mr. Bingley was kind enough not to acknowledge the fact openly.

As the sun rose over the first day of Mr. Darcy's return to Hertfordshire, he rode out across the property of Netherfield in the direction of Meryton. He was relieved to once again be able to tend the bookshop correspondence personally. He bid good morning to Mr. Awdry, and explaining that his sister had arrived with him from London, selected a few books of a more feminine appeal before disappearing amongst the back shelves. As he had done so often before, he reined in his horse just outside of the village for a brief respite in which to read the following.

I can well believe that as a young lad, you must have loathed time spent at school rather than in the country, but I must admit I have always been envious of a gentleman's right to attend universities and delight in their expansive resources. As a child, I spent many hours in my father's library, at first relishing in his reading of Perrault's tales, though I am sure in light of our discussions you will believe that my literary tastes have long since matured. I believe I am fortunate that my love of nature conflicts with remaining indoors, else my mother would be forever disgraced by gossip of her recluse daughter who never exposes herself to the light of day.

Her playful words lightened his mood, as they most always did, and he grew more confident in choosing her for his own benefit rather than seeking a socially acceptable bride.

❧❧❧

That evening at the home of Mr. and Mrs. Philips, the Netherfield party were among the last guests to arrive, as Mrs. Hurst and Miss Bingley had reportedly neglected to remember the engagement for dinner. Thus their departure had been delayed until an exasperated Mr. Bingley left with the Darcys, suggesting his sisters use the Bingley carriage when they were prepared to depart, knowing full well they would be unlikely to attend. Mr. Bingley was quick to find Jane among the other guests, and Mr. Darcy began to look for Elizabeth, yet Mrs. Bennet was quicker and gathered her daughters to greet the new arrivals.

"Mr. Bingley, there you are!" Mrs. Bennet effused, "We had begun to despair for you. And Mr. Darcy, you are very welcome, sir. We are all glad you have returned." In her own sense of subtlety, Mrs. Bennet glanced in Kitty's direction, allowing her gaze to linger before turning back to Mr. Darcy.

If any of the contentment Mr. Darcy felt in anticipation of seeing Elizabeth had been visible in his countenance, Mrs. Bennet's words and manners were its stone death. In a formal and disinterested tone, he performed the introductions between his sister and the Miss Bennets. While he was resigned to accept them, he still could not be pleased with allowing these women to enter his sister's sphere of influence, and made excuses on their behalf to go and seek refreshment. Elizabeth had observed the gentle expression in Miss Darcy's eyes, and had hoped to draw her into conversation, but was unable as the two quit their company.

Throughout the evening, Elizabeth's ire on behalf of Miss Darcy grew. Few of her neighbors were bold enough to approach Mr. Darcy, and though she was never near enough to hear what was said, each seemed to leave their company after only a few words had been exchanged. As was typically their wont, Kitty and Lydia suggested an impromptu dance. Young Mr. Lucas had been bold enough to approach Miss Darcy while her brother refilled her punch, presumably to ask if she might like to join the set. Having observed the scene, Mr. Darcy returned hastily, and Elizabeth knew Mr. Lucas must have been soundly refused as he walked away immediately and Mr. Darcy proceeded to guard his sister like a hawk.

Elizabeth was prone to forming her opinions expeditiously, and was not one to restrain herself from acting upon them. Determined that Miss Darcy was in need of rescue, she approached Jane and Mr. Bingley, and at the first pause in their current conversation, suggested that they join his friend.

"Miss Darcy," Elizabeth began, "Allow me to say it is a pleasure to have met you at last. Forgive me for not approaching you sooner to welcome you properly."

Miss Darcy murmured her response such that Elizabeth felt as likely to understand by lip reading as by hearing her.

Perceiving Miss Darcy's shyness, Jane added, "I am so glad you shall be able to attend our wedding, as you are such a valued acquaintance to Charles and his sisters. Miss Bingley has been quite complimentary of your abilities at the pianoforte."

Miss Darcy looked stricken, and Mr. Darcy seemed about to speak in her defense.

"Do not concern yourself, Miss Darcy," Elizabeth interjected with a smile, "if you are not fond of playing in company, for you find a kindred soul in me, and therefore I shall not allow anyone to force you into playing if you are averse to the idea. Though I must confess, having my sister Mary to compete with, you may rarely find the opportunity to play, even if you wished it."

"Thank you, Miss Elizabeth," Miss Darcy smiled shyly as she continued, "I admit I do not frequently play in company. I prefer a smaller audience."

"Aye, as do I. In fact, I must say sometimes the best audience is non-existent!"

Elizabeth laughed gaily, and was soon joined in her merriment by Miss Darcy and the engaged couple. Mr. Darcy looked on in growing admiration, pleased by her gentle and reassuring manner towards his sister. Elizabeth looked at Mr. Darcy, daring him to express his disapproval of their company, before turning away and leaving the gentleman to mistake her glance in his direction for understanding of his sentiments.

ﻉﻉﻉ

Upon returning to Netherfield, Mr. Darcy suggested Georgiana retire for the evening, while he and Mr. Bingley absconded to the library, not wishing to attract the attention of the Hursts and Miss Bingley. Mr. Darcy thought his first meeting with Elizabeth passed as tolerably as could be expected. Though once again immersed in tedious company, he had not embarrassed or revealed himself, and Georgiana had not been overwhelmed. That is to say she had not been uncomfortable expressing herself to new acquaintances, though Mr. Darcy felt she had been overwhelmed with attention from the young gentlemen of the neighborhood.

"Well Bingley, I believe the evening went very well. I should not have been so concerned that Georgiana would be intimidated."

"Yes, I am glad she felt so comfortable in Jane and Miss Elizabeth's company. You on the other hand..."

As Mr. Bingley trailed off, Mr. Darcy responded with an inquiring glance.

"Come, Darcy, I realize you are of a reserved nature, and that is a respectable quality, yet I once said I would not be as fastidious as you are for a kingdom, and the statement stands."

Mr. Darcy frowned at the reference to the assembly in the fall and dissembled, "Yes, but your manners have always been easier than mine, and as by some miracle my behavior has thwarted the hopes of all but one of the local matrons, I have no desire to change the neighborhood's opinion of me."

Mr. Bingley threw his head back and laughed. "Well said, Darcy! Considering the excitement that welcomed me to the neighborhood, imagine how they might respond to an easy mannered gentleman of more than twice my consequence!" Mr. Bingley had intended a very different conversation with regard to his friend's behavior, but Mr. Darcy had deflected his attempt at broaching the subject, and he knew the gentleman's confidence could not be forced, particularly on the subject of his affections.

Chapter 12

After completing a certain errand in town, Mr. Darcy returned to Netherfield to spend the day with Georgiana. As neither sibling was desirous of spending much time in company with Miss Bingley, the pair excused themselves after luncheon and retreated to the library. The afternoon passed quietly as Georgiana completed her studies while Mr. Darcy addressed a few business matters, and then challenged her to a few games of chess. Before long, Mr. Bingley arrived home and joined his guests in the library. Georgiana excused herself soon after to dress for dinner at the Longs', leaving the gentlemen to talk in peace.

"Well Darcy, as you are my groomsman, I suppose it is high time I sought your counsel regarding whatever pearls of wisdom you might have to offer for my entering the shackles of marriage."

"I hardly know what you expect me to impart, as I am equally inexperienced in the realm of matrimony. Perhaps Mr. Hurst ought be your advisor?"

Mr. Bingley recoiled in mock horror at the suggestion, and both gentlemen shared a good laugh at the absurdity of the idea.

"All I can say Bingley, is that I am truly happy for your having found a woman to marry with mutual affection. I realize there are some amongst our acquaintance who will not approve of your choice of wife, but do not allow the naysayers to cause you to withdraw from society."

"If people find Jane half as delightful as I do, I cannot imagine her entrance into higher society to be any cause for concern. I doubt there will be much objection to her connections, as my acquaintances have accepted me despite my family's fortune coming from trade. Besides, I am sure true friends will come round, just as they have for Beaumont."

Mr. Darcy was unable to maintain eye contact through Mr. Bingley's last remark, and turned towards the sideboard to refill his glass.

"Do not tell me you have not been in contact with Beaumont since he announced his engagement to the former Miss Howard?"

Mr. Bingley's eyes widened as Mr. Darcy's silence confirmed the truth of his supposition.

"For goodness sake man, he was one of our closest friends!" Mr. Bingley cried in shock mingled with exasperation. "Forgive the harsh nature of my outburst, but I admit I expected more of you, Darcy. If I did not know better, I would be concerned that you might intend to drop my acquaintance as well once I am married to Jane."

"Of course not Bingley, but the situation is not the same. While some may believe you could have married better, it will not be nearly as offensive as the gross difference in situation between Beaumont and his wife. If I did not see the difference between your case and his, I might have warned you against Miss Bennet, so that you would not come to regret your marriage as Andrew Beaumont surely does."

Mr. Bingley had always been of a forgiving nature towards the ton, particularly as many of his high society acquaintances from Cambridge had never held his familial origin in trade against him. However, Mr. Darcy's haughty attitude offended him and he retaliated, "What makes you think he regrets marrying a woman he loves? Do you suppose his love so shallow that other persons' ill-placed judgment would cause him to resent his wife? You surprise me by holding the opinion of society in such high esteem, as I had always assumed your distaste for London would lead you to disappear in the wilds of Derbyshire once you are married."

"Yes, just as my parents did." Mr. Darcy said quietly, almost to himself. He then turned to speak directly to Mr. Bingley, "You raise a fair point. Perhaps the three of us gentlemen shall enjoy the company that accepts us without remorse over those who do not."

Dinner at the Longs' was as distasteful to those of elite sensibilities as could be expected, with a very small redemption in the reduced size of the party and thereby smaller number of undignified persons to endure. As the group transitioned to the dining room, Mr. Darcy found he was seated next to his sister, but unfortunately also seated near Miss Bingley and far from Miss Elizabeth. As the meal commenced, he discovered the unfamiliar couple across from him to be Mr. and Mrs. Gardiner, the Bennets' relations in trade. Miss Bingley spoke to the Gardiners in a manner both elegantly phrased and decidedly insulting.

If Mr. Darcy concurred with her sentiments, he was too polite to reveal the truth of it, and merely listened as Mrs. Gardiner responded to Miss Bingley's comments with equal elegance and a great deal of tact. While he was reluctant to associate with persons in trade, he admitted that at least the Gardiners seemed to have better manners than Miss Elizabeth's closer relations.

The remainder of the evening passed in great frustration for Mr. Darcy, as he endured the unpleasantness of country society without the benefit of Miss Elizabeth's company. He was continually accompanied by Miss Bingley, and Miss Elizabeth made no attempt to approach him. He could not comprehend her motives for sending his sister an occasional smile across the room, while refusing to meet his eye. He could only assume that Miss Bingley's inescapable presence was a deterrent, and looked forward to calling at Longbourn the next afternoon.

The next morning at breakfast, Elizabeth looked upon her father with a discreetly inquisitive glance, and smiled mischievously as he responded with a wink. Shortly after this exchange, she declared her intention to walk into the village on an errand for her father, and was about to rise from the table when her mother accosted her.

"Lizzy! I demand that you stay home. There is no need for you to go traipsing off, and though your father delights in vexing me and refuses to tell me when Mr. Collins is expected, he is sure to come any day, and I will not have you absent from this house when he arrives. Let one of the servants assist your father for heaven's sake!"

Elizabeth shot her father a glance of mingled pleading and frustration. Her father had yet to correct her mother regarding the true state of affairs with respect to Mr. Collins, and while she had never found amusement in the predicament she faced, her father's seemed endless. Mr. Gardiner observed his niece, and dismayed by the scene before him, cleared his throat and looked pointedly at Mr. Bennet. Swaying under the increasing vexation of his most sensible relations, Mr. Bennet sighed and addressed his wife.

"I regret to inform you, Mrs. Bennet, that there is no need to anticipate the arrival of Mr. Collins, as he will be unable to attend the wedding. Apparently his curate has recently left him, and Mr. Collins has been unable to find a replacement. Thus he will be unable to absent himself from Kent, and I believe Elizabeth may conduct the use of her time as she chooses."

Mrs. Bennet's lamentations in response to this news only hastened Elizabeth's departure. Unfortunately for the remaining members of the household, the disgruntled matron's exclamations did not subside, despite the absence of their primary target, and continued even as her least favorite daughter returned to Longbourn. Elizabeth heard the racket upon her approach, and entered the house through the kitchen that she might reach her room without her mother's knowledge. With a contented sigh at her success, she closed to door and retrieved the fruit of her excursion.

February 5, 18__

Surely you realize I need no assurance that your literary tastes go beyond fairy tales from the nursery, though in future years you may have reason to revisit them. Do not think, however, that your exclusion from our nation's universities has severely hindered your quest for knowledge, as our discussions have shown you more knowledgeable of literature than several of my former classmates. A library can be a retreat where the world is logical, respectable, and free of insipid and frivolous concerns.

Suddenly the noise from below stairs was subdued, and Elizabeth strained to hear the cause of such uncharacteristic restraint. Mrs. Bennet's tirade had finally been silenced by the arrival of Mr. Bingley in company with Mr. Darcy and Miss Darcy. As Elizabeth heard the announcement of their guests, she hid the note and dutifully went downstairs to join her family in attending them. Once Mrs. Bennet had sufficiently welcomed her future son, she turned her attention to the gentleman she hoped would soon bear the same title. Mr. Darcy soon found himself on a sofa near Mrs. Bennet, across from Mr. Bingley and Miss Bennet, and seated next to none other than Miss Catherine. As Mr. Darcy remained silent, struggling for a means of extricating himself, Elizabeth approached Miss Darcy, suggesting they sit together and indicating towards a sofa away from the rest of the group.

"I hope you do not mind being separated from your own party, Miss Darcy. I sometimes find the atmosphere at Longbourn to be rather overpowering and would prefer quiet conversation at present."

Miss Darcy gave Elizabeth an appreciative smile for so politely claiming this preference as her own. She then glanced towards Mr. Darcy, and noticing her brother looking intently in her direction, gave him a smile as well.

Do not worry, Mr. Darcy, objectionable though I may be, I doubt I can corrupt your sister beyond redemption in just one private conversation. Elizabeth forced these spiteful thoughts from her mind and returned her focus to the shy young lady seated beside her.

"Now that you have passed a few days here, I hope you have enjoyed Hertfordshire thus far."

"I... have been comfortable at Netherfield. Mrs. Hurst and Miss Bingley have been quite attentive."

"I imagine they have! I will not embarrass you by repeating their sentiments, but they speak of you in only the most complimentary of terms." Observing that her gentle teasing had indeed embarrassed Miss Darcy, she continued, "I hope you have found the weather suitable for exploring the grounds about Netherfield, for they are some of the finest in the area."

"The weather has been pleasant, though I admit I have not had much chance to view the gardens." Concerned that Elizabeth may have misunderstood, she added hastily, "That is, I do very much enjoy the outdoors and have thought to ask my brother if he might accompany me about the grounds."

"I am glad to learn that nature is something for which we share a mutual appreciation, and though I cannot claim our garden to be comparable to that of Netherfield, I would be happy to show it to you now if the idea is agreeable to you."

Miss Darcy readily agreed, and Elizabeth rose to address her mother.

"Mama, Miss Darcy has expressed a wish to see the gardens. I thought perhaps the rest of the party might like to join us."

Mr. Darcy was quick to join Elizabeth and Georgiana, taking his sister's arm to escort her out of doors. Refusing to be dismissed by the imposing man, Elizabeth remained and conversed with Miss Darcy on many subjects, pleased to gradually draw her young guest into a greater sense of ease.

The conversation naturally turned towards the north country and Georgiana's fondness for Derbyshire, and she inquired as to whether Elizabeth had ever occasioned to visit there.

"I regret my traveling adventures have been far simpler than you might imagine. I have only gone as far as London with my aunt and uncle Gardiner, though I have heard of the beauties of Derbyshire as my aunt hails from a small town there, Lambton."

"Why that is but five miles from Pemberley!" Georgiana replied with more animation than Elizabeth had yet seen. "Is it not, brother?"

"Yes, I believe it is." Mr. Darcy replied abruptly.

Elizabeth furrowed her brow, surprised that her young companion was not put off by such a short reply from her brother, yet Georgiana continued without pause, "Then perhaps one day you will see the peaks and wilderness of which I speak, I am sure you would enjoy them."

Mr. Darcy then spoke with much more civility than he had moments earlier, "I am sure when Miss Elizabeth comes to Derbyshire, she will have plenty of time to enjoy the vistas."

Unsure of an appropriate response, and slightly unnerved by the gentleman's choice of words, Elizabeth changed the subject and asked Georgiana if she had an enjoyable garden in town, as she had mentioned spending a great deal of time in London for her studies.

The ladies' discourse continued, and was interspersed with rare contributions from Mr. Darcy, most of which were responses to direct questions from his sister. Elizabeth was unable to discern his motives for visiting Longbourn only to show himself unwilling to fully join the conversation. She assumed perhaps he wished to prove himself better mannered than Mr. Bingley's sisters, who had dined at Longbourn but once and uniformly declined invitations to tea. She considered it equally plausible that Miss Darcy had expressed a desire to become better acquainted with her family, and Mr. Darcy would not permit her attendance without his protection from such inferior manners. If only she had known his true reasons were quite the opposite of any negative suppositions she might have made.

When thinking over their conversation late into the evening, Elizabeth still wondered whether Mr. Darcy had intentionally spoken in terms of *when* and not *if* she would venture north. Surely he thought badly enough of her family to realize they had not the means for extensive traveling. The only other explanation she could imagine was that he assumed she would one day be a guest of his sister, but she did not think that likely, and dismissed the idea entirely, leaving her no less confused than she had been when his words were spoken.

Chapter 13

Knowing full well that the confrontation at the breakfast table the previous day had been caused by Elizabeth's desire to leave a missive amongst Mr. Awdry's books, Mr. Bennet found himself entering the same establishment the next morning. His suspicions and concerns had only increased with time, and noting his daughter's increased preoccupation with these communications, his patience had reached its limit. Though he was not fond of taking such trouble, he would not see his favorite daughter hurt at the hands of this gentleman, whom he had begun to fear would never reveal himself. Though he lacked knowledge of when this nameless fellow might visit the shop, he suspected it was the same gentleman who had recently arrived in town. Mr. Bennet had ridden from Longbourn under the pretense of estate business that would last the majority of the day, hoping the gentleman traveled to the bookshop as impatiently as his most favored daughter.

Mr. Awdry needed but a glance at Mr. Bennet's countenance to guess the motive behind his appearance, and rather wondered why he had not come on such an errand sooner. Mr. Bennet approached the counter and raised his eyebrow. Mr. Awdry merely nodded, silently indicating his assent, and led Mr. Bennet to the far corner of shop where used merchandise was kept. He paused for a moment, drew one book from the shelf, and silently handed it to Mr. Bennet before turning away. Mr. Bennet opened the book and thumbed through the pages, sighing as reached a small fresh sheet tucked within. He turned and seated himself at a nearby table, hoping the gentleman he was about to encounter was a man worthy of his daughter's trust.

Mr. Darcy entered and moved to the back of the store, anxiously anticipating Elizabeth's words, when he was shocked to see Mr. Bennet sitting at a small table nearby. If the older gentleman was equally shocked to find it was indeed a tall gentleman from Derbyshire glancing nervously at a certain shelf, he disguised the sentiment admirably.

"Mr. Darcy, sir, I must say I am surprised to see you here this morning, but not nearly as surprised as you appear to be at seeing me."

Mr. Darcy's shock grew ten-fold as he noticed the familiar title of the book placed on the table before Elizabeth's father.

"Mr. Bennet." Mr. Darcy greeted cautiously.

Seeing the younger gentleman's distress, Mr. Bennet teased, "You may have guessed that I have some rather interesting business here this morning, which is rather closely related to your reason for coming here. Would you care to take a seat, sir?"

"With all due respect, sir, I would prefer to speak with you in a more private setting."

"Come, come, Mr. Darcy. I would not be here this morning if it were not for Mr. Awdry informing me of the odd popularity of his shop with a certain member of my family. I assure you he only spoke to me of the person under my care, but if you have come just as often, he would not need much imagination to connect the two. Given the early hour, and the manner in which he left for the back room the moment you arrived, I believe this shall be private enough."

Mr. Darcy nodded as he sat down. He knew any father would insist he marry their daughter under the circumstances, and a part of him rejoiced in it. He thought surprise would never end, however, once Mr. Bennet began to express his opinion on the subject.

"Now before we discuss the matter at hand, I would know if I assume correctly that you are knowledgeable as to the identity of the young lady with whom you have been communicating?"

"I am, sir."

Mr. Bennet nodded his concurrence and began, "I will explain the situation from my perspective. I find it quite comical that while my daughter thought she might be sporting with one of the Lucas boys, she was in fact teasing a rather serious man in possession of a great estate. That you would continue in this farce was more difficult to reconcile, but given my gradually increasing suspicions of you, I have had some time to think on the matter. I have not been blind to your interest in my favorite daughter, and I commend your taste in appreciating her disposition, but I also have seen your reserve and realize you must believe in some nonsense that you are duty bound to make a great match in the eyes of society."

Affronted by the older man's light-hearted banter and mockery of himself, Mr. Darcy's composure faltered and he blurt out much harsher than he intended, "How long have you known?"

"Long enough, sir. I wonder at your ability to keep up this correspondence over the past month when to my understanding you were far from Hertfordshire, but curious though I may be, that is quite beside the point. As I said, I have known long enough, and I believe that you have a decision to make."

"I have already come to a decision, sir, and I would understand if you were to demand that I accompany you to Longbourn."

Mr. Bennet cleared his throat and fought to restrain a smile. He was pleasantly surprised that this serious young gentleman was finally willing to admit himself lost to Elizabeth. "I am sure you have something more romantic in mind than my exposing your improprieties and forcing you to marry. I doubt my Lizzy would take kindly to an obligatory offer of marriage in the aftermath of her suitor being called onto the carpet by her father. All I ask at present is that you continue to treat my daughter with the utmost respect. I would suggest that you resolve this in a timely manner; however, I also strongly suggest that you proceed with caution. As you know, your friend is marrying my eldest daughter, and you may often find yourself in company with Elizabeth in the future, no matter the outcome of this correspondence."

Mr. Darcy declined to comment, as he considered himself quite knowledgeable of the outcome, and cared little for the older gentleman's teasing. Mr. Bennet rose, leaving Mr. Darcy and Sterne's book at the table, and bid Mr. Awdry farewell. Once he heard Mr. Bennet pass through the door, Mr. Darcy slowly reached for the book in front of him. He removed Elizabeth's note, and without opening it, pulled a folded sheet from his pocket and replaced her note with his own, his intentions the same as they had been before seeing Mr. Bennet.

Upon leaving the shop, Mr. Bennet felt some concern regarding his daughter's reaction. After all, he had long been conscious of Mr. Darcy's interest, where his daughter had not, and he had never shared Elizabeth's violent distaste for the gentleman. However having heard excerpts from the letters Elizabeth received, and having observed her delight in their exchanges, he was confident that all would be well once Mr. Darcy revealed himself, though perhaps a good deal of explanation would be required. Elizabeth had made her dislike clear enough, and Mr. Darcy must have devised a plan to overcome it.

Chapter 14

After leaving the bookshop, Mr. Darcy was so focused on imagining Elizabeth's reaction to his most recent note that he all but forgot his anticipation towards reading her own. Recollecting its place in his pocket, he reached for the note and read the following.

I must bow to your superior dedication and reverence towards literature, as I will now reveal, much to the detriment of the studious reputation I may have established with you, that I have often read solely for my own entertainment, and though many novels lack sophistication or profound lessons to be learned, I have found them excessively diverting.

Mr. Darcy chuckled to himself, as her response embodied all the playfulness he had come to depend on. Excessively diverting indeed, and he was very much looking forward a time when she would daily invade his serious life with more of such diversion.

Miss Elizabeth left Longbourn before the rest of the house had risen and once again journeyed to the village to retrieve the expected missive. On her way back to Longbourn, she sat upon a fallen log, and anxiously opened the note, gasping at its contents.

February 8, 18__

You must know how I have enjoyed our exchanges, and I find I would enjoy conversing with you through more than just paper. Would I be too bold to request a meeting with you this coming Saturday? There is a very fine tree where the road from Meryton meets the lane to Lucas Lodge, and if it is agreeable to you I will be waiting at the hour of three.

Miss Elizabeth rose and turned off to one of her favorite paths in the opposite direction of Longbourn. After overcoming her initial shock, she was a bit disappointed to have been unable to discover his identity before he chose to reveal it, thus giving him greater advantage upon their meeting. Yet she would finally learn the truth, and might be allowed an open friendship, which would be quite welcome given the small size of her community. She smiled mischievously with anticipation. *So, after all these months, he is finally ready to reveal himself. The day after Jane's wedding of all times!*

Though he had no reason to feel nervous, as he was positive she would be amenable to their meeting, Mr. Darcy admitted he had been distracted since leaving the bookshop two days prior. After his confrontation with Mr. Bennet, he knew there was a reasonable possibility that she was already aware of his identity. He thought it a bit odd that Mr. Bennet would request he continue this odd form of courtship, yet he was willing to make this small concession if it would please his future wife. After all, he had chosen her for her liveliness and her wit, so it would be fitting for her to have an interesting tale for their future children.

I am all anticipation of the opportunity to put a face to my most diligent correspondent, and look forward to making your proper acquaintance.

He was pleased by her eagerness towards their meeting, and rode back to Netherfield, where he would have to put his future aside for a day as he prepared to stand up with Bingley.

ཚ ཚ ཚ

The wedding of Charles Bingley and Jane Bennet fulfilled every expectation of those in attendance. The Longbourn church had been meticulously decorated with the season's finest, and several blooms gave evidence of Mrs. Bennet's access to the greenhouse at Netherfield Park. As the wedding party gathered at the altar in anticipation of the bride, two persons studiously avoided each other's gaze. Mr. Darcy refused to show any undue attention under the scrutiny of all in attendance, while Elizabeth refused to allow such a taciturn and sour man take away from the happiest day in her beloved sister's life.

The ceremony transpired in much the same way as all wedding ceremonies do, and soon the bride and groom were greeting guests and accepting congratulations outside the church. For a fleeting moment, Elizabeth believed she may have seen a smile gracing Mr. Darcy's lips, but on second glance, it had disappeared.

Before long, all in attendance reconvened at Netherfield Park, decorated in extravagance equal to the church, with the addition of fine food and talented musicians.

After welcoming all of the guests to his home, Mr. Bingley led his new wife to lead the first dance. Knowing it to be expected of him to follow suit with the maid of honor, Mr. Darcy approached Miss Elizabeth. With a small upturn of his lips that would not constitute a smile in the face of a more amiable man, he held out his hand towards her.

"Shall we?" he said more in form of a statement than a request.

Having prepared herself for such an inevitable event, Elizabeth placed her hand in his and allowed him to lead her across the ballroom floor. Elizabeth had no desire to initiate conversation during their dance, as she much preferred to observe her sister. Thus Mr. Darcy was left perfectly content to dance in silence, beholding the woman in front of him, memorizing every aspect of her appearance. Elizabeth tried to avoid his unreadable gaze and sighed, thinking she had endured far too many dances with this man, but at least this was the last occasion on which they would be obliged to dance together for some time.

After parting with Mr. Darcy at the end of their dance, Miss Elizabeth relished in the joyful celebration of her sister's union. Even her mother's effusions were tolerable, as most of the company shared similar opinions regarding the blissful couple. So it was that Miss Elizabeth was laughing delightedly with Charlotte Lucas, and did not notice a certain gentleman's approach until his voice could be heard beside her.

"Miss Bennet, if you are not otherwise engaged, I believe we would enjoy dancing the last together."

Equally surprised by his appearance as his request, Elizabeth stumbled in her reply. At her strange look, Mr. Darcy, confused by her hesitation, added, "Forgive me, is the set already taken?"

"It is not, sir," Elizabeth answered, regaining a semblance of her composure.

Mr. Darcy nodded, presuming her acceptance. "Then I shall return to collect you at the proper time."

Mr. Darcy gave a small bow and retreated from her company as quickly as he had entered it. Elizabeth stared after his withdrawing figure in frustration. Endeavoring to control her anger over his presumption, she linked her arm to Charlotte's and moved to leave the incident behind her and allow herself to enjoy the remainder of the celebration. Her ire could not be suppressed as Mr. Darcy approaching for the last set, for her disappointment was twofold; soon her dear Jane would depart, and she would spend the last minutes of her sister's presence in company with Mr. Darcy.

As the first steps of their dance passed in a manner identical to their previous set, Elizabeth could not refrain from commenting, "Though I was courteous enough to allow one dance in silence, I believe I have previously stated my opinion that it is best if we have some conversation, Mr. Darcy."

"Indeed Miss Bennet, and as I have previously stated that by no means would I suspend any pleasure of yours, I should not hesitate to oblige you, though as the topic of books has previously been disallowed, I will solicit your opinion for a more acceptable subject."

"A simpler task I could not imagine, as the room is abuzz with discussion of the happy couple."

"As it should be, in light of the day's events."

Mr. Darcy and Elizabeth continued their dance in conversation that was interpreted as amiable by one, and merely civil by the other. Soon after, a crowd of well-wishers covered the front steps of Netherfield Park, as Mr. Bingley handed his bride into a carriage bound for their townhouse in London, and the onward for their wedding trip.

Chapter 15

Miss Elizabeth allowed herself the luxury of sleeping late the morning following her sister's wedding to Mr. Bingley, knowing a late start would only decrease the number of hours spent in anxiety over her plans for the afternoon. After luncheon, Elizabeth's anticipation grew such that she did not trust herself to keep her countenance under her father's watchful eye. She decided to call on Charlotte Lucas and professed her intention to make frequent calls at Lucas Lodge, for surely she could not spend too many hours at Longbourn without the inducement of her dearest sister's company.

At half past two, Mr. Darcy rode towards the location he had specified to Elizabeth, his pulse racing as he crested the last hill and spotted her coming up the lane from Lucas Lodge. He slowed his horse such that she reached the road from Meryton just as he approached a certain tree.

Observing the approaching horse and rider, Elizabeth could not believe her ill luck at having Mr. Darcy of all people disrupt such a momentous occasion. He could not have chosen a worse time to be riding into Meryton, and considering that many of the wedding guests had already departed for London, she had sincerely wished he would no longer be in the neighborhood at all. Her agitation grew as she perceived that he did not intend to acknowledge her and continue on his course, but was at that very moment dismounting his horse and walking in her direction. Rather than dwelling on discerning his motives for such uncharacteristic actions, she determined to be rid of him as quickly as possible.

"Mr. Darcy!" she exclaimed, giving evidence to her surprise.

"Miss Bennet, I see you have anticipated me," he greeted smilingly.

The gentleman moved to tether his horse to a certain tree over which she felt rather possessive, though it was by no means her own, and she addressed him as he secured the reins.

"Forgive me, sir, but anticipated you I most certainly have not, for I had no notion of encountering you. I..." she added nervously, frustrated by the unsteadiness she found creeping into her voice as she dissembled, "I am just returned from calling on Charlotte Lucas."

Charmed by her discomposure, he kept his eyes on his horse as he smiled smugly and shook his head, her misinterpretation of this action raising her ire. Though she was by no means surprised that he was not impressed by her inability to remain as staid and stoic as he, he had never openly mocked her for it. His expression remained the same as he turned to approach her, and she could not but attempt to remove the satisfied smile from his face.

"I am surprised you have yet to quit our unsightly neighborhood, now that the wedding has passed and you are not obligated to stay. I am sure Miss Bingley is pleased to have such a devoted guest."

Taken aback by her incivility, Mr. Darcy stopped his progress and answered with a hint of disconcertion in his voice, "I expected to be invited to Longbourn this evening, though I admit I am looking forward to being elsewhere."

"Yes, I suppose there is very little to be considered worthwhile in this provincial quarter. I wonder that you would anticipate such hospitality when you have accepted it so begrudgingly in the past, but it comes as no surprise to me that you are anxious to be away."

Mr. Darcy met her eyes before replying in a serious tone, "Forgive me if my natural reserve has led you to mistake my reticence in company for rudeness. Your comments at the Netherfield Ball led me to believe that you understood my disinclination for speaking elaborately in the performance of mundane civilities."

Mr. Darcy's anger began to swell as he observed that rather than being softened by his confession, Elizabeth's countenance showed mounting irritation.

"I have apologized for my aloof behavior, Miss Bennet," Mr. Darcy asserted brusquely, "Does that not mollify you?"

"Mollify me?" Elizabeth cried incredulously before she could attempt to curb her tongue. She glanced away in mild embarrassment over her outburst. Upon returning her eyes to the gentleman, however, she noted his intense and demanding gaze was still fixed on her and she added as calmly as she could manage, "I am afraid it does not, sir."

"I might, perhaps, wish to be informed why my endeavor at civility is thus rejected? But it is of small importance." *She cannot be serious! But we have crossed verbal swords before, go ahead Miss Bennet, profess those opinions which we know are not your own.*

Elizabeth sighed with frustration as she spoke in a controlled tone, "You apologize for the actions, but say nothing of the sentiments behind them. That is," she added with a touch of sarcasm equal to the last of his previous remark, "unless I mistake your meaning, sir."

"I fail to understand which sentiments you infer me to possess which would be considered improper."

"Your pride and arrogance have been displayed with hauteur from your first days in Hertfordshire, and you have evidenced your opinion even further by returning with your sister only to shield her from our influence. Even as you apologize for displaying it, your distaste for our country manners is quite clear."

"You are undoubtedly cognizant of the improprieties so frequently exhibited amongst your current acquaintance. But I wonder at your concern over the matter, as you will leave this society once you marry, and need feel no remorse." A hint of bewilderment crept into his voice as Mr. Darcy struggled to understand how their conversation had turned into such a heated argument. He had not given much thought to what she might say, as he had planned to communicate his desires immediately once they had acknowledged each other, but he certainly had not expected this.

"I do not see how quitting the neighborhood indicates by default that I will no longer care for my friends and neighbors."

Mr. Darcy smiled a little at this evidence of her goodness. "No, I suppose you would not, and it does you credit, but surely you realize the importance of establishing yourself in your current sphere, rather than focusing on the one you have left behind, as your sister must do in London. Though she may never be a predominate figure in society, I believe your sister will be accepted tolerably well. I am sure she is glad to be moving up in importance."

"I doubt very much that my sister will aspire towards a position in society reserved for persons such as yourself, she is too kind and humble. She may never be remembered or spoken of in London, but they speak very well of her here. She is renowned for her caring and amiable nature, and there are many in this community who love her for her good deeds, and will continue to love her, no matter how grand she becomes as mistress of Netherfield, because they know she will not forsake them. You, on the other hand, may reach the highest rung of our social strata, only to be known for the monetary value of your estate and the lineage of your parents. Your manners, or lack there-of, are rendered insignificant, and you will be nothing but a cold portrait hanging in an extravagant gallery full of men long forgotten in everything but in terms of their consequence."

For a long moment, Mr. Darcy stood silent, staring at Elizabeth in what she saw to be much the same disapproving manner he had frequently employed, unaware of the rapid movement of his thoughts as he deduced the reason behind her continued incivility. *Good god, she hates me with such ferocity that she does not realize I am the gentleman she came to meet with today. She does not even consider it possible that I could have penned those notes.*

Finally, he broke the silence, speaking in a low voice so opposite of his usually commandeering manner, that she almost thought him affected by the harshness of her words. "Excuse me, madam. You make it quite clear that you have long desired my absence, and I must return to my sister."

His countenance a rigid facade, Mr. Darcy turned from her and walked determinedly towards his horse, tipping his hat curtly as he urged the stallion into a canter with a flick of his heels. Once certain he was out of her view, he turned his horse off of the road and galloped across the fields. Even if he had been ready to love her despite his old objections, it was meaningless if she did not return his affections. Mr. Darcy rode back to Netherfield, and informed Georgiana that they would depart for London at first light. Leaving his sister to summon her maid and make the necessary preparations, he retired to his room to write a letter, as he had realized its necessity after he and Elizabeth parted company.

Soon after a lone rider could be seen traveling in the fading light of the afternoon, retracing his path after making an important deposit in Mr. Awdry's bookshop.

This scene could have been observed by Miss Elizabeth were she any closer to the village than she had been earlier that afternoon. As it was, she was oblivious to the rider, but noticed that the sun was beginning to set, and realized that if she did not return home now, the sky would be as dark as her hopes of meeting her mysterious friend.

Chapter 16

Miss Elizabeth returned to the house just before dinner and retired soon after, claiming fatigue from her afternoon walk. Her father had hoped to speak with her regarding a matter of some importance, but reasoned that the following day she would venture into Meryton, and he might waylay her in order to provide his daughter with more assistance than simply an excuse for going into town.

As Elizabeth headed towards the front door the next morning, Mr. Bennet observed that her agitation from the previous evening did not seem to have diminished overnight, and called her into the library.

"I was about request that you save your papa from making a trip into the village, but judging by your countenance, I will delay my request in favor of a more pressing matter." Mr. Bennet dropped his teasing smile and light-hearted tone of voice, "I hope there is nothing troubling you Lizzy?"

"No Papa, I believe I am just feeling weary in the aftermath of the wedding. Now that the busyness and excitement have passed, I realize how much I shall miss Jane."

"Never fear Lizzy, you sister shall be a scant three miles away, and I think you shall have plenty of opportunities to see her, as I have it on good authority that your mother plans to visit quite regularly once the Bingleys return from the coast."

Both laughed congenially as they envisioned Mrs. Bennet scurrying to her carriage to socialize with her neighbors in the finest house of the neighborhood, now her own daughter's home. Neither needed an opportunity to witness the scene to know with certainty how Mrs. Bennet would revel in expounding her good fortune, holding court at Netherfield just as she did in her own home.

"I am sure you are right, Papa," Elizabeth said gaily as her mirth began to subside. "The house just seems so quiet now that all the hustle and bustle is over, and somehow I do not believe life at Longbourn shall be quite the same."

Mr. Bennet thought carefully of how to phrase his response. "Yes, but things are not always as we are wont to believe them to be. If I am not mistaken, you have found an amiable companion in Miss Darcy these last weeks, though by the testimony of a certain gentleman, you might have expected to find her disposition to be quite the opposite."

"I admit she was not at all proud, and I did enjoy making her acquaintance, but I do not see how it shall be continued."

Mr. Bennet looked at his daughter inquisitively, wondering at the melancholy air behind her statement. "I would imagine you will renew your acquaintance from time to time with your mutual connection to the Bingleys. Did you not invite her to correspond with you in the meantime?"

"I doubt her brother would allow his sister to correspond with a young lady such as myself." Elizabeth looked down at her hands. *My unladylike speech yesterday certainly saw to that, though I stood little chance of meeting his approval beforehand.*

Now that the conversation had reached Mr. Bennet's intended juncture, he endeavored to carry a point he did not expect his daughter to take easily. "I would be wary of holding that opinion, my Lizzy, as I believe your dislike of Mr. Darcy was largely fueled by a gentleman whose information we have just deemed unreliable."

Elizabeth let out a frustrated huff. "While I cannot reconcile the impression of Miss Darcy professed by Mr. Wickham to my own experience with the same young lady, I do not see that as cause to completely disavow everything he has spoken of Mr. Darcy. There was truth in his looks, and I cannot believe such an intricate past to have been fabricated."

"Sometimes the most believable lies are those which are interwoven with bits of truth, Lizzy. A particular example comes to mind of a young girl, quite to your resemblance, who ran into this very home with hot tears and a dirty frock, proclaiming the injustice of having been pushed into the mud by one of the young boys in the neighborhood. While this event did occur, the truth of it was quite misconstrued, given the omission that she had first led him down a bank on some pretense or another, only to push him into the lake, and that the offense over which she had been so vocal was committed as a retaliatory measure."

A rather sheepish Elizabeth chuckled lightly with her father, remembering the incident quite clearly, and beginning to suspect her father's objective in regaling her with the childhood memory.

"If that boy's father and I had not related to each other the dissimilar explanations we each heard from our children, I doubt we would ever have learned the right of it. I believe you know who might be able to relate Mr. Wickham's story from another point of view, and I suggest you not pass final judgment or assume the two versions to be identical without hearing both of them."

Elizabeth sighed, "Mr. Wickham's accusations aside, there has still been plenty of evidence laid by Mr. Darcy himself towards his true nature."

"Yes Lizzy, but understand that Mr. Wickham led you to view Mr. Darcy's actions through a very cynical eye. I would not be so determined against the possibility that had he not insulted you to the offense of your vanity, you might have seen him in a different light."

"Perhaps you are right, Papa, but if you will excuse me, at the moment I prefer to lighten my mood by enjoying the fresh air."

"Very well, child." Mr. Bennet smiled, "Just be sure not to disappear until dusk, as lord knows what I will suffer at the hands of your mother's nerves if you are missed."

Though she truly did wish to lose herself in the joys of nature, dwelling on her father's words and the previous day's events seemed to be inevitable. Her father had been correct with regard to Miss Darcy, and though aloud she had protested, inwardly she began to question her assessment of Mr. Darcy. She could not but regret the harshness of the words she had spoken to him, no matter how strongly she had felt

A Noteworthy Courtship

the truth of them. He had obviously been stunned that she would dare to speak to him in such a way, yet when in the last of her tirade she spoke of his lack of personal significance, he had clearly been pained by her words, a feeling which she did not feel justified to inflict on anyone. Paltry though it was, the only excuse she could give for her wretched behavior was that she had allowed his words to infuriate her beyond reason and spoken unthinkingly while blinded by her fury. Not for the first time did she wonder if the expected gentleman had witnessed the scene of her long argument with Mr. Darcy, and been dissuaded from approaching her. She was loathe to acknowledge that during their heated discourse, she had paid little attention to her surroundings. Having nearly reached Meryton by this time, she resolved not to think on the matter any further until she had explored the possibility of finding a note to explain *his* absence the previous day.

*February 15, 18_*

I know you must be gravely disappointed by the circumstances of this afternoon, as I am sure its passing was not to your liking. Please allow me to sincerely apologize that I was unable to provide you the pleasant company we had anticipated. I regret to inform you that urgent business calls me away for the next fortnight, but please accept my assurances that our correspondence does not mean so little to me that I would wish to end it, and that a note will await you on the third of March.

His words seemed sincere and apologetic, and though still disappointed, Elizabeth tried to be placated by them. The extreme highs and lows of the previous two days had left her emotionally drained. She decided to take at least some portion of her father's advice regarding hasty judgments and, difficult as it may be, bide her time until the anticipated date before forming a set opinion.

Little did her father know that as he had been advising her to rethink her opinion of Mr. Darcy, the gentleman in question was on the road to Pemberley, planning a course of action not entirely dissimilar from that which was practiced after his departure following the Yuletide Ball. In the following days, it became common knowledge that the Darcys had indeed left the neighborhood. Mr. Bennet knew not whether to wish he had dragged Mr. Darcy to Longbourn like an errant child, or be glad that his favorite daughter would no longer be imposed upon by such a man.

Chapter 17

Mr. and Miss Darcy left Hertfordshire in what the latter may have considered undue haste, but she accepted her brother's reasoning that he was anxious to return to Pemberley. Even if she suspected this not to be his true motivation, escaping the roof under which Miss Bingley resided seemed incentive enough. What Georgiana dared not consider was to enquire as to the reason behind her brother's dark mood. While he did not exude the fury she had witnessed the previous summer, he was certainly despondent and rather pensive. After a week spent at Pemberley, Mr. Darcy announced that business called him to London. He suggested that as she had remained in London through the holiday season, Georgiana was welcome to stay at Pemberley in company with Mrs. Annesley and continue her studies there.

As the last days of February came to pass, the pensive state which had entranced Mr. Darcy finally bore fruit. Though he had initially been dumbfounded by Elizabeth's hostility, review of their interactions, along with remembrances of a few comments from Mr. Bingley, forced him to admit that he had left much to be desired. Though he now claimed to have overcome them, he had previously displayed his objections abominably. He could not deny the vast discrepancy between the gentleman he had been on paper and the man he had been in her presence, and understood her inability to make the connection. He called Thompson to his study with instructions that he would depart for Hertfordshire the next morning on an errand much the same as those he had completed several times before.

ৡৡৡ

The days had not passed quickly for Miss Elizabeth, but at long last the third of March arrived. She had not dared discuss her planned meeting with her father, and therefore had not shared the contents of her last note with him either. She had expected some form of questioning from him when she did not mention her notes or require his excuses for venturing into town, but simply accepted his apathetic approach gratefully. She had left the house under the pretense of a walk, her expressed desire to rediscover her favorite haunts in the gradually warming weather leaving none the wiser.

*March 2, 18_*

These weeks I have thought of little else but what your feelings must be regarding the events of that fateful day, and I cannot look upon my behavior without abhorrence. You had placed your trust in me only to be bitterly disappointed, and I fear apologies cannot acquit me of the injustice I have committed against you. All I request is that while I do not deserve such kindness, you would allow us to begin again and that I may show you the error of my ways has been attended.

Elizabeth's reluctance to form an opinion before reading this missive had dissipated much of the vexation she had felt after their missed meeting. The guilt weighing on her mind over her treatment of Mr. Darcy made it difficult for her to condemn the actions of anyone but herself from that afternoon. She thought it most fitting to clear his conscience with a confession of her own.

Elizabeth spirits were much improved by the words she had chosen to commit to paper, and could not but be heightened further by the Bingleys' return from their wedding trip. Her mother was quick to make good on her commitment to visit her married daughter frequently, and it would be quite some time before a single day would pass without Mrs. Bennet and her daughters calling at Netherfield Park. The Bingleys had traveled an easy distance to the coast of Essex, and thankfully the journey had not been too exhausting for Jane to answer many questions from her mother and sisters about the fashions she had seen and what fine accommodations they must have had. Though Elizabeth had scarce been given the opportunity to utter a word to her sister, Mrs. Bennet soon announced their departure. It was with great pleasure over her resourcefulness that Elizabeth managed to excuse herself from accompanying her mother, that she might enjoy more of her sister's company.

Without the overshadowing presence of Mrs. Bennet, conversation flowed more freely between the three who remained. Not wishing to address the topic so thoroughly exhausted by the recently departed guests, and equally desirous of allowing Jane a respite from conversation, Elizabeth turned to the gentleman in the room. With a jovial smile to belie any impression of ill-will, she asked after the current state of his library and teasingly commented on his good fortune in that if Jane were desirous of a larger collection, she would be too kind to begrudge him. It was then a broad smiling Mr. Bingley who announced he had something to show Elizabeth that would equally shock and please her, and left the room with a mischievous grin and the two ladies in his wake.

Throwing open a pair of heavy wooden doors, Mr. Bingley stepped aside and with his arm gestured for Jane and Elizabeth to precede him into the room. "May I present the new and improved library of Netherfield Park. Though it shall never compare to that of Longbourn, I hope, dear sister, you now find it more respectable, and will be able to lose yourself in its contents for many an afternoon."

Noting the substantial increase of books occupying the shelves, Elizabeth turned to her new brother with a great smile before moving to peruse the added selections. "Mr. Bingley I commend you for your great improvements, and you may one day rue the invitation, as I will take up your offer to occupy this room quite frequently."

"I doubt Jane would wish you to do any less, and therefore neither would I. But I cannot take credit that is not due me, and must inform you that it was Mr. Darcy who expanded my collection so."

"How very kind of him." Such simple words Elizabeth would never have imagined speaking in reference to that particular gentleman, and she paused momentarily before adding, "I suppose I should not be surprised, as we all know Mr. Darcy is rather fond of books."

"Yes, I daresay he may not have survived were there not a bookshop established in Meryton to save him from my meager collection! Though I believe he sent to London for many of the titles as well, and Georgiana was kind enough to send a few of his favorites from their townhouse."

༺༺༺

At the Darcys' home in London, the master of the house attempted to plan the solution for a tenant issue, pacing agitatedly as he fought against his distracted state of mind. He had been anticipating Thompson's return all morning, and had been able to keep his mind on little else. At long last, heavy footsteps could be heard approaching the study, and the long awaited man passed through the door. The dusty and ragged appearance of Mr. Darcy's trusted servant was excused as the heaving of his chest gave evidence to the direct route he had taken to his master. Accepting the expected packet, Mr. Darcy thanked him and suggested that he see the kitchen staff for a cold refreshment and hearty meal in appreciation of his efforts. As the awaiting footman followed Mr. Thompson through the doorway and closed the door, Mr. Darcy immediately removed the expected letter and read the following.

I admit I had looked forward to the chance to meet with you, but any disappointment was overshadowed by an unpleasant scene that occurred recently. Though I have often written to you in light-hearted and sarcastic tones, please be assured of my seriousness when I relate that I am equally guilty of greatly mistreating an acquaintance. While at the time I believed myself to be speaking words that were truly deserved, I now see my statements as scathing remarks spoken in false indignation.

It is in our making of amends that we can find relief from our feelings of regret. Therefore please consider yourself forgiven, as I do not share your opinion that such kindness is undeserved, and let us move on to subjects more pleasurable to both parties.

Her feelings of guilt regarding their confrontation were palpable as he read her note, and Mr. Darcy was relieved to be given a means to defend her actions in hope of alleviating her remorse. After writing his response, he reflected again on her words, and could not but feel a glimmer of hope that as she had written to forgive her correspondent, she might be amenable to reforming her opinion of him as well. He rang for Thompson and bade him to return to Hertfordshire the following day, supplying him with the sealed missive.

His own conscience had not been completely cleared however, another issue being brought to light as her words rang through his head, emphasizing the importance of making amends. He took up the long delayed task of writing to his friend Andrew Beaumont and his wife, offering his deepest congratulations on their marriage, arrival of their first child, and a sincere request that the friendship begin anew.

❧❧❧

Mr. and Mrs. Bingley's return to Hertfordshire brought the beginning of many dinner parties between Longbourn and Netherfield. A few days after their return, all were gathered to dine at Netherfield, when Mr. Bingley excitedly approached his wife and favorite sister in law.

"Elizabeth, we have some news for you which I hope you shall approve. I may have mentioned an old school friend of mine, Andrew Beaumont. He was unable to attend the wedding, as he and his wife were recently blessed with their first child, but as he resides in Essex, Jane and I..." here Mr. Bingley paused and smiled at Jane. Elizabeth had long observed that he could not speak his wife's name without gazing in her direction, and found it endearing that the habit had not been dissolved in the comfort of their marriage. Mr. Bingley continued, "We were able to visit the Beaumonts before returning to Hertfordshire, and they invited us to return for an extended visit as soon as we are able."

"Would you enjoy taking a holiday with us, Lizzy?" Jane asked her sister cheerfully.

"Indeed I would Jane, but I would not wish to be invading your privacy, and would take no offense should you and Mr. Bingley prefer to travel alone."

At this moment, Mrs. Bennet interrupted and inquired as to the subject of their discourse, to which Mr. Bingley responded cautiously.

"We are speaking with Miss Elizabeth about our planning a return visit to the Beaumonts, ma'am, who reside in Essex. We occasioned to dine at their estate near Hadleigh during our wedding trip, and were invited to return for a lengthier visit. As Mrs. Beaumont would enjoy the female companionship, Andrew suggested they would have room to host one of Mrs. Bingley's sisters as well. I was just in the process of persuading Elizabeth to join us."

"Oh, but why should Lizzy go?" Mrs. Bennet exclaimed, "She has no need of exposure in society when she already secured Mr. Collins. You would do much better to take Lydia, she would surely make a merry companion for you all."

With all the expertise of two and twenty years' practice, Jane answered her mother in a placating tone, "While I am sure Lydia would be an amiable companion, and Mrs. Beaumont spoke of her hope to one day make all of your acquaintance, she did express that perhaps Lizzy might join us. I believe it would only be fitting to comply with her wishes, as she will be welcoming us into her home."

"Well there you have it, Mrs. Bennet. It would seem our Lizzy is for Essex," Mr. Bennet stated, considering the subject closed, "Bingley, do tell us more about your friend, and when you intend to travel to Hadleigh."

Chapter 18

Over the course of the evening, the Bingleys determined to return to Essex in the third week of March, allowing time to appease their neighbors by paying calls and accepting dinner invitations. In conjunction with Mr. Bennet and Elizabeth, it was agreed that the traveling party, consisting of only the three originally proposed members, would remain through the month of April, a plan to which Mr. Bennet would brook no opposition, even from Mrs. Bennet. Once their plans had been settled, the evening at Netherfield came to a close. The following carriage ride to Longbourn was highlighted by Kitty and Lydia's exclamations that they deserved a holiday just as much as their older sister, and that their father ought find lodgings for them, as the Bingleys had not been so inclined. Throughout the whole, Mr. Bennet remained silent, and any rolling of his eyes did not reach the notice of his youngest daughters. It was not until all of the ladies had stepped down into the drive and headed towards the house that Mr. Bennet requested that his eldest unmarried daughter accompany him into the library.

"You do realize, Lizzy, why I have taken the trouble to be such a staunch supporter of this scheme, do you not?"

There were a number of reasons Elizabeth thought warranted her father's assistance in distancing herself from Hertfordshire, but unknowing of the particular situation to which her father referred, she smiled and said, "Whatever the reason, if it has led you to bear Mama's effusions on my behalf, I am thankful for it." She paused and met her father's eyes with a mischievous expression creeping into her features. "I trust it is not that you have succumbed to her protestations and will be conveying the entire family to the coast."

"Good heavens!" Mr. Bennet balked, "And commit myself to nearly fifty miles on the road confined in a carriage filled with talk of sea bathing and speculation over every wealthy gentleman residing near the coast? I have half a mind to be offended that you think me so insensible as to subject myself to it."

"Yes Papa, we shall have to pray for good weather, that you not be soaked through while escaping to share the driver's box despite a heavy downpour."

Father and daughter enjoyed a good chuckle over the image of Mr. Bennet scampering up to the driver's box, determinedly turning up his collar and hugging it to his face amid sheets of pouring rain.

"But in earnest Lizzy, I do believe some time away from our small society here would be beneficial to you. I realize we have not discussed you affinity for Mr. Awdry's bookshelves in some time, but I had hoped that by now you have expended your amusement on that score and will invest yourself in diversion of a more conventional sort. I realize we enjoy our country civilities, as they can be more lenient with regard to the bounds of propriety, but that does leave a dangerous opportunity for situations to go beyond the bounds of good sense."

The next morning found Elizabeth once again ambling along wooded paths in the direction of Meryton. Though she endeavored to take them lightly, she could not but acknowledge the sensibility of her father's words. She had intended nothing more than a single note to tease a young boy in the neighborhood, and the situation had gradually grown increasingly serious as she was reluctant to end the correspondence without deducing his identity, which proved to be no hardship as their exchanges had become rather enjoyable. She seemed to be scratching more men off of her list of probable candidates than existed in the vicinity, making the whole scenario most troubling. She had long since begun to rethink men and boys she thought she had ruled out. Mr. Bingley's comments in his library had initially sent her reeling, but upon further reflection, she determined Mr. Darcy to be no more likely than any other patron of the Meryton bookshop, of which there must be several for Mr. Awdry to earn a livable income from his establishment. In fact, he was even less so because of his frequent absences, which for all practical purposes eliminated him entirely, and by this estimation, he could be ruled out before taking into account his contrary disposition. An encampment of militia men did not help matters either, as with them she had a strong disadvantage when compared to local residents she had known all of her life. Perhaps her father was right; this was getting a little out of hand.

*March 6, 18_*

Though I will shortly abide by your request to leave the subject behind us, I must relate that my acquaintance with you leads me to believe any harsh words of which you are capable would be spoken under provocation, and spoken in defense rather than intent to harm. I cannot imagine you as one to speak with malicious purposes.

Now madam, I believe you have requested that this missive address at least one subject to be found mutually pleasing, and I shall gallantly comply. I have yet to mention to you anything about my dog. I should rather call it my sister's dog, as it was on her behalf that the animal came into residence here, yet as Jemma seems perfectly content to follow me about the house, we rarely think of her as such. As to the breed of this dog so frequently at my heel or atop my feet, we know its maternal origins to be a golden retriever, though she much resembles a smaller version of a Newfoundland. I had originally allowed my sister to bring her new puppy into her room for the night, but after Jemma managed to turn the knob of the door to my sister's chamber and come to scratch at mine, she has since slept on a rug beside my window. Rest assured my sister found the incident quite amusing.

P.S. I will reiterate that both name and gender of this animal were my sister's doing, for fear that without such information you will subject me to an endless stream of witticisms reserved for gentlemen whose dogs are not male and bear such unique appellations.

Miss Elizabeth's guilt was only lightly assuaged by his assurances, as she had come to believe that any provocation did not justify her words, but he had successfully diverted her with his next topic. She had nearly laughed aloud as she imagined the domestic scene he portrayed. Perhaps, she thought, there would be no harm in waiting until her departure to heed her father's advice to end this correspondence.

Mr. Beaumont was surprised to find the Darcy crest amongst his post, for he had long given up the expectation of receiving such a letter. Thankfully he was akin to Mr. Bingley in affability, and though he had not seen or heard from Mr. Darcy during the course of his marriage, he felt little reserve in allowing his old friend a second chance. An amiable correspondence ensued, filled with a happy mix of occurrences from the past three years, news of common acquaintances, and estate business. Despite their lack of direct communication, Mr. Beaumont had never ceased to hear of Mr. Darcy's assistance to Mr. Bingley, and he enjoyed the opportunity to provide a reunion that he assumed would be amenable to all. Thus, Mr. Darcy received a letter relaying information he found both exciting and distressing.

*March 16, 18_*

Darcy,

I am glad to hear our renewed acquaintance is as pleasurable to yourself as it is to me. I have taken the liberty of reading your letters to my dear Evelyn. She much appreciated your anecdotes, particularly those in regard to our friend Bingley, which put her in mind that we ought extend an invitation to you. I believe I have mentioned that Mr. Bingley and his wife were kind enough to visit with us one evening during their wedding trip, and I have just received a letter from him, accepting our invitation to return for an extended visit. Forgive us the short notice, but Mr. Bingley and his wife, in company with one of Mrs. Bingley's sisters, will arrive Monday week, and we would be honored for you to join us here at Ashingdon at your earliest convenience.

Yours etc,

Andrew Beaumont

Mr. Darcy immediately penned a reply with an affirmative response. In light of his recent correspondence with Mr. Beaumont, he had realized how great a friendship he had given up, and was thankful for the honor of their invitation. If not for their young child, the Beaumonts would have already received an invitation to Pemberley, which he would now be able to extend in person, suggesting that they would be welcomed at the earliest time they were amenable to traveling such a distance.

If only Beaumont had specified which sister would be joining the Bingleys. Certainly of all her sisters, Mrs. Bingley seemed closest to Miss Elizabeth, yet he could not allow himself to dwell on this possibility without confirmation. Despite the strong temptation to write to Mr. Bingley, he could not consider such an inquiry to be entirely proper, and it would definitely raise his friend's suspicions. In the end, he decided not to write, acknowledging that there was little chance of receiving a timely reply. Within the week the Bingleys would depart from Hertfordshire and he himself would be departing for Kent.

Just as Miss Elizabeth had begun to settle into a renewed series of agreeable exchanges with her correspondent, the time for her departure to Essex came near. Undecided as to how far she wished to comply with her father's advice, she determined not to make the severance her father seemed to prefer until after her trip. So it was that

Miss Elizabeth deposited a note between Sterne's now sentimental pages, without the intent of returning for six weeks at the least.

I must inform you that after this missive, I shall not be returning to Mr. Awdry's establishment until May's flowers are blooming in the fields. Even as I write, I am preparing for my imminent departure, for I am pleasure bound. As of yet, my plans are to return the first week of May, but as ladies so frequently are, I am dependent upon the whims of my traveling companions.

A grin effused over Mr. Darcy's face as her words gifted him with the information he most wanted to hear. She would indeed be the sister invited to join the Bingleys in traveling to the coast, and if he were desirous of uncovering her current opinion of him, he would now have the perfect opportunity. Though he would have been happy to travel to Essex solely for the company of his friend, he was very glad he had accepted the Beaumonts' invitation after all. His regard for Elizabeth had not diminished, and he had determined to pursue her in earnest, a task he would much prefer to accomplish in the relative privacy of Hadleigh as opposed to the venus flytrap Mrs. Bennet set for eligible gentlemen who passed through the gates of Longbourn.

కుకుకు

On the morning of their departure, the Bingleys arrived at Longbourn for an early breakfast before their journey to the coast. Fortunately, Mr. Bennet and Miss Elizabeth were the only members of the household prone to rising early, and much of the morning meal passed with only four at the table. At long last, the remaining Bennets had appeared, Elizabeth's trunks had been loaded, and Mr. Bingley announced that they had best depart in order to reach Ashingdon in due time. After sufficient farewells had been exchanged, Mr. Bingley handed his wife and her sister into the carriage, and they smiled and waved their last goodbyes to the group assembled on Longbourn's steps.

Once the carriage was well underway and the three passengers had settled in comfortably, Elizabeth addressed her hosts. "I must thank the two of you again for inviting me along. I believe I will much enjoy a respite from home."

"I can see how Mama grates on your nerves, Lizzy," Jane replied kindly, "I am sorry I cannot be more frequently in your company to dissuade her from speaking of our cousin."

"Now Jane," Elizabeth said, with a conspiratorial glance at Mr. Bingley, "I believe we all know that Mama cannot be dissuaded once she sets her mind upon a topic of conversation, but that is neither here nor there, as I would not have you under the impression that I have only joined you for such evasive purposes. I have been all anticipation of pleasant company and ocean vistas since you first suggested the trip. Tell me, how did you like the coast, Jane?"

"It was quite lovely. The breeze coming across the ocean is quite refreshing, and I feel quite indebted to Charles for our accommodations as the view from our rooms was breathtaking." Jane graced her husband with a loving smile and quickly turned back to Elizabeth, still growing accustomed to displays of affection towards her newly-wedded husband, and not wishing to embarrass her sister.

"With such a smile as a reward," Mr. Bingley rejoined, "I am sorry to admit I had little to do with their selection, and owe a great deal to Andrew Beaumont. He was very sorry not to attend the wedding, but once I relayed our intent to travel to Southend, he insisted on examining lodgings for us."

Jane added, "Mr. and Mrs. Beaumont were so kind to invite us to dine with them during our holiday. I found a delightful companion in Mrs. Beaumont, there is something very natural and welcoming in her mode of expression, and her adoration of their little Alexander is simply charming. I do believe you will like her very much, Lizzy."

The Bingleys and their guest traveled on in companionable discourse regarding the country diversions of Hadleigh and the entertainments to be found in Southend. Little did they know that at that same time, a large carriage was traveling en route to Kent, its passenger wishing to be headed in the same direction as they.

Chapter 19

In the late afternoon, the Bingley carriage approached Ashingdon. Over the last few miles, Elizabeth had enjoyed the local scenery and the fresh crisp air blowing the faintest salty aroma of the sea into the coach. As Mr. Bingley handed the ladies down from the carriage, the Beaumonts' housekeeper greeted them, directing a manservant to their luggage and inviting the newly arrived party into the drawing room, where the Beaumonts eagerly awaited them.

"Bingley, old friend, so glad you were able to join us!" Andrew Beaumont beamed. "Mrs. Bingley, I judge by your countenance that married life remains as agreeable to you as when we last met. Miss Bennet, welcome to Ashingdon, we are delighted to make your acquaintance."

Miss Elizabeth was then introduced to Evelyn Beaumont, who was seated aside, cradling a very small Alexander Beaumont who was just drifting off to sleep. Mrs. Beaumont greeted her guests with enthusiasm nearly equal her husband's, though definitely in a softer tone so as not to disturb her peaceful babe. She explained that she had hoped Alexander might be awake when they arrived, and apologized for not coming out into the drive to greet them. She then excused herself to settle the infant into the nursery, and invited her guests to enjoy some refreshments until her return, at which point she would be happy to show them to their rooms if they desired some time to rest before dinner.

৵৵৵

"Well Bingley," Mr. Beaumont spoke as his guests enjoyed the various dishes served at his table, "I dare say the jovial spirit of your nuptials must have been catching, for you will not guess who I heard from not long after."

"And who might that be?" Mr. Bingley inquired complacently, though he had gathered a strong supposition as to whom Mr. Beaumont referred before he had uttered his response.

"You can imagine my surprise at receiving word from Darcy after all these years, but he has apologized, and I am satisfied to allow that he has acquitted himself admirably through our recent correspondence. After all, Darcy always said you and I were too yielding by nature, and thereby incapable of holding a grudge, though I admit I do not interpret this as quite the negative attribute he claims to consider it. He expressed a desire to acknowledge Evelyn properly, and while we could not accept his invitation to Pemberley with Alexander being so young, Darcy has accepted our invitation and should arrive here just after Easter, as he is obliged to fulfill a prior commitment to his aunt."

Mrs. Beaumont was not blind to Elizabeth's reaction when Mr. Darcy was mentioned, nor that the young lady scarcely touched the food on her plate during the remainder of the meal once his upcoming arrival had been announced. She had rarely occasioned to meet Mr. Darcy before her marriage, and spoken to him infrequently on those few occasions. Her husband's portrayal, which due to her felicitous marriage she considered rather trustworthy, rendered the gentleman in a much softer light, and she was curious to learn how Miss Bennet had perceived him.

‫ى ى ى‬

The week preceding Easter passed very pleasantly for those in residence at Ashingdon. Though Miss Elizabeth knew her sister incapable of giving anything but praise, she found Evelyn Beaumont much as Jane had described her to be. It was no hardship for Elizabeth to be separated from Jane whenever Mr. Bingley suggested he take his wife for a curricle ride along the coast or into Southend for tea, as she hoped the newlyweds could consider this sojourn in Hadleigh as an extension of their wedding trip, and the hours of their absence were spent affably with Mrs. Beaumont. The two got along quite well, the vivacity of one complementing the easy manners of the other, and Elizabeth was pleased to find in her hostess a common affinity for nature. Mrs. Beaumont was more an accomplished woman than her guest in the traditional sense, such that Elizabeth passed a few afternoons in the gardens, enjoying the fresh air and holding baby

Alexander as his mother painted a miniature of his likeness, all the while chatting amiably with Evelyn and eliciting coos and smiles from Alexander.

The entire party reunited for dinner in the evenings, and Elizabeth was pleased to witness the gladsome exchanges between the gentlemen. Many anecdotes were shared from their Cambridge days, regarding all subjects from eccentric professors and library tomfoolery to holiday visits and dormitory pranks. The stories most unsettling to Elizabeth's composure, however, were those that included Mr. Darcy, and as he had been a close friend at Cambridge to both gentlemen present, his name was mentioned quite frequently. That Mr. Darcy had been known for his fastidious study habits or excellent marks was expected, but remembrances of his goodwill interspersed with occasional tales of exploits – albeit in retaliation – were most puzzling, as Elizabeth could not reconcile the young man described in such humorous stories to her own impression of the gentleman.

٭٭٭

Mr. Darcy's arrival in Kent was a fairly uncomfortable experience, but no more so than he had expected it to be. As she had for years previous, Lady Catherine crowed over her nephew's presence, taking every opportunity to praise her daughter Anne for the few accomplishments she did possess, and many that she undoubtedly would have developed had her health allowed. Colonel Fitzwilliam had accompanied Mr. Darcy, and made many attempts to turn their aunt's conversation to more neutral topics, much to the appreciation of at least one of his cousins.

Mr. Darcy had feared meeting with Mr. Collins, as the ridiculous parson had so ingratiatingly introduced himself in Hertfordshire, and frequently boasted of the invitations he received from his patroness. Thankfully Lady Catherine saw fit to host her nephews to the exclusion of all others, and as Mr. Collins was not seen aside from Sunday services, it was not until the time for Mr. Darcy's early departure drew near that unpleasant scenes arose.

"Darcy, I absolutely insist that you remain at Rosings, in accord with your normal custom of residing for a fortnight at least. If you remain another month complete, we can arrange for Georgiana's transportation from Pemberley. It is far too long since she was last in company with Anne."

"I thank you for the generous invitation, Lady Catherine, but as I have already explained, I cannot accept."

"Nonsense, Darcy. These trifling acquaintances you plan to visit are beneath you, and you need not pay them undue attention. What of your family? Have you no concern for the company of your closest relations? Your sense of honor should compel you to remember your duty to us."

"I am sure my father would be most pleased to welcome you to Matlock, Aunt Catherine; that is if you are desirous of strengthening the familial bonds amongst your relations," Colonel Fitzwilliam interjected cheekily, "I imagine the Earl would hope to be remembered in a discussion of your nearest relations, as few are closer related than a brother."

"Anne's health would not allow it," Lady Catherine retorted before turning her attention back to her more favored nephew.

"Darcy, I demand that you oblige me."

"Forgive me, Aunt, but my commitment has already been made to the Beaumonts, and there are matters of business to be addressed as well. Surely you understand that I cannot neglect matters beneficial to the increase of my estate."

This last comment finally struck the right cord with Lady Catherine and she relented, but not without eliciting further instruction. "I still consider you indebted to me for a proper visit. Perhaps you shall bring Georgiana to me come Michaelmas."

Each person in the room knew this to be a summons, not to be confused with an invitation, and though he had little intention of complying, Mr. Darcy did not consider this an advantageous time to refute his aunt's demand.

꼭꼭꼭

On the thirtieth of March, just one day after the Easter holiday, the Darcy carriage traveled north along the road from Kent, stopping only for the intermittent change of horses en route to Essex. As the sun began to lower in the western sky, the sound of an approaching carriage could be heard growing ever louder, before ceasing as the coach and four arrived at Ashingdon.

Miss Elizabeth knew this moment would come, and prudent though it may have been to use this forewarning to prepare herself, all attempts at doing so seemed to be in vain. She had long regretted the words spoken the day following her sister's wedding, and would now face the gentleman who would certainly agree that they had been completely inappropriate, and in all likelihood strongly resent her for speaking them. She could only resolve to conduct herself with civility and hope that any aversion Mr. Darcy felt towards her would have no ill effect on the general company.

Seated in the parlor with her sister and Mrs. Beaumont, Miss Elizabeth awaited the inevitable as the gentlemen could be heard exiting the study to greet their friend. She was barely able to contain her astonishment at hearing not two, but three jovial voices emanating from the hall. She wondered for no short moment if Mr. Darcy was not the gentleman lately arrived, as the voices she overheard gave every impression that greetings were being exchanged in much the same cheery manner as they had been with Mr. Bingley upon their own arrival.

The ladies rose from their seats as the gentlemen entered the parlor. Elizabeth trained her eye towards anything but the familiar tall form passing through the doorway. Mr. Beaumont then proceeded with the introductions.

"Mr. Darcy, I understand you are well acquainted with Mrs. Bingley, and her sister, Miss Bennet."

"A pleasure, Mrs. Bingley, Miss Bennet."

"And may I present my wife, Mrs. Evelyn Beaumont."

"Mrs. Beaumont," Mr. Darcy bowed, "I thank you for welcoming me into your home."

After a few minutes of conversation and refreshments, Mr. Darcy retired to settle into his rooms and divest himself of his traveling clothes. The ladies soon followed to prepare for dinner, and much too soon for Elizabeth's liking, the ladies reconvened in the parlor. Fortunately, the gentlemen did not emerge from Mr. Beaumont's study until just moments before dinner was announced. Elizabeth's comfort was short-lived however, as she recognized the party of six adults not only meant she would be seated next to or directly across from Mr. Darcy, but he would most likely escort her to the dining room. Her ruminations were interrupted by the very gentleman approaching, proving the truth of her latter supposition.

"Miss Bennet, may I say how pleasant it is to meet with you again," Mr. Darcy said, a soft smile tugging at his lips, "May I escort you?"

Elizabeth was surprised not only by the lack of severity in his tone, but also the earnest expression in his eyes.

"You may, sir," she softly replied.

Once in the dining room, Miss Elizabeth found herself seated beside Mr. Darcy, and soon discovered this to be the preferable arrangement as while he may have been closer in proximity, he could not easily observe her countenance throughout the meal. Though he did not speak as often as Mr. Bingley or Mr. Beaumont, the comments he did contribute were polite and unaffected. He seemed to take eager interest in friend's estate, and despite its smaller size, he did not speak with condescension.

The party broke up soon after dinner, as Mrs. Beaumont excused herself to tend the baby, and not long after Mr. Darcy expressed his intent to retire, having spent a full day traveling.

As Miss Elizabeth prepared for bed in her room, she was surprised by a gentle knocking at her door, which she immediately recognized as Jane, who had used that particular rhythm each night at Longbourn when she desired a sisterly chat. The sisters grinned impishly at the stolen opportunity for another late-night conference, before Jane addressed her sister.

"You were very quiet this evening, Lizzy."

Elizabeth let out a long sigh. "Oh Jane, I simply cannot make sense of Mr. Darcy. I thought I had sketched his character so faithfully, and until this evening I had been given little reason to doubt the veracity of my opinion."

"Perhaps there was a reason behind his reticence in Hertfordshire. I still believe he improves on further acquaintance."

"Though I had once questioned the validity of that statement Jane, I must bow to your superior understanding, as it appears you may be correct."

Chapter 20

The following day, Miss Elizabeth dressed early and headed towards the breakfast room, in hopes that she might refresh herself with a quick cup of tea and a muffin before heading out for a solitary walk. She had yet to make sense of the confusion brought upon her by the previous evening's events, and the addition of her talk with Jane combined with her continued embarrassment over her previous conduct were hardly conducive to her attempts at discernment.

Her plan was not to be, however, as upon entering the breakfast room, she observed a lone figure seated at the head of the table, almost completely hidden behind an open newspaper, his presence only distinguishable by the fingertips supporting the printed pages and a steaming cup of coffee on the table. Wishing rather than believing the gentleman to be Mr. Beaumont or Mr. Bingley, Miss Elizabeth averted her eyes and moved quietly towards the sideboard. As her figure passed the window, temporarily obstructing the morning light and casting a shadow upon her silent companion, the newspaper was folded down, and its reader blessed his good luck at finding one of his ambitions for the day already accomplished.

"Good morning, Miss Bennet."

Elizabeth could no longer ignore the other occupant of the room, as any guise of remaining silent for the polite purpose of allowing him to read undisturbed was rendered inapplicable by his address, and would now be considered rudeness.

"Good morning, Mr. Darcy."

As Elizabeth turned to greet the gentleman, revealing the full plate and fresh cup of tea she had now prepared herself, he rose and pulled out the chair beside him, and gesturing with his hand, invited her to be seated. As she reached the table, he silently took her plate, placing on the table, and allowed her to seat herself as he pushed in her chair. His wordless manner of conduct she may have found officious or at the very least a reluctant sacrifice to civility, if not for the subtly gentle expression in his eyes, which upon reflection she would admit was not entirely unfamiliar.

Mr. Darcy then poured himself a fresh cup of coffee and resumed his seat, but left the newspaper aside as he addressed Elizabeth.

"I trust you are enjoying your stay at Ashingdon?"

"Yes," Elizabeth smiled weakly, "the Beaumonts have made for excellent company, and I cannot be averse to witnessing my sister's felicity with her new husband."

Mr. Darcy did not immediately reply, instead fidgeting with his cup for a few moments before inquiring further. "And do you find the environs here to your liking?"

Elizabeth could not comprehend why he would make such an effort towards amiable conversation, especially in light of unpleasantness of their last discourse, but nonetheless appreciated his endeavors and replied in kind. "Indeed I do. I have not many opportunities for travel, and as much as I enjoy exploring new countryside, I find the sea air is also quite refreshing."

Mr. Darcy held her gaze for a moment before again taking up his coffee, seemingly content to gaze out the window as he nursed the warm contents of his cup. Not nearly as comfortable with their silence as the gentleman appeared to be, Elizabeth hurriedly ate a portion of her meal, and belatedly added, "As I said, I do enjoy the sea breeze, and it looks to be a beautiful morning. If you will excuse me, I am anxious to enjoy the fresh air."

As would any well-mannered gentleman, Mr. Darcy stood as Elizabeth rose from her seat, but surprised her with his response. "Yes, I believe I would enjoy the exercise myself, if you would not be averse to the company."

She could not politely refuse, and within a few moments, the two exited the house and selected a path circuiting the great wood along Ashingdon's border.

Their walk continued in a silence that was interpreted as companionable by one and awkward by the other until Elizabeth gathered her wits sufficiently to find a suitable topic for conversation.

"May I inquire after your sister, Mr. Darcy? I hope she was well when last you saw her."

"She is currently at Pemberley. I have not had the opportunity to join her these last weeks, but in her most recent letter she expressed that she is quite well, and enjoyed receiving a letter from Mrs. Bingley."

"I am glad to hear it. I know I can speak for my sister in that she took pleasure in making your sister's acquaintance as much as I, and is undoubtedly pleased by their correspondence as well."

"My sister enjoys hearing from any of her Hertfordshire friends." Mr. Darcy looked pointedly at Elizabeth, a gaze which she could not match for more than a moment before turning her eyes to the path at her feet.

"I would imagine so, as she is such an agreeable young lady," Elizabeth replied nervously, "though I would understand if you preferred her to correspond with certain acquaintances more than others."

Mr. Darcy had not removed his eyes from Elizabeth since he last spoke, but his expression had turned to one of confusion, and when she glanced up in anticipation of his response, she could not ignore the questioning nature of gaze. Elizabeth stopped suddenly, her distress apparent on her features as she drew in a sharp breath to collect herself.

"I am a very selfish creature, sir, in that I cannot go on without addressing a subject that may be equally discomfiting to you as it is humbling to me. I have long repined the abominable manner in which I treated you on our last meeting. I have never been one to easily control my tongue once my temper rises, but I spoke to you most cruelly, and no excuse shall justify my behavior, such that I dare not ask your forgiveness."

At this Mr. Darcy looked at her earnestly and replied in a solemn tone, "Miss Bennet, I would hope you do not believe my own temper so resentful that I would refuse forgiveness of those who ask."

Discomposed by the weight of his gaze, Elizabeth began walking again, glancing sideways at Mr. Darcy, her eyes beginning to sparkle with mischief as he followed suit and strode along beside her. "Oh but Mr. Darcy, I recall quite clearly you yourself stating a fault of yours to be that you might be termed resentful, and once your resentment was formed, it was implacable."

Mr. Darcy smiled as he confidently gazed out upon the horizon, "Yes, but do not forget madam, that on the same occasion you established that to be my propensity, I declared yours to be willful misunderstanding."

Mr. Darcy looked as though he might chuckle as he said the last, and Elizabeth could not but look upon his face in bemusement.

Meeting her eye, Mr. Darcy added, "I hope you will not misunderstand when I tell you that I am capable of forgiveness, and as you seem to have given yourself a great deal of reproach over the occurrence, I would ask that you consider yourself forgiven and think on the subject no more. We both of us have altered our opinions since that day."

Elizabeth looked down at her feet, "Yes, which is why I would understand your reasoning if you did not wish for a continued acquaintance between myself and your sister."

"Miss Bennet, I believe I may have to repeat my claim of your tendency towards misunderstanding. When I spoke of altered opinions I referred to my realizing that though I still do not accept blame for how my reticence in company is interpreted, there are other aspects of my conduct in Hertfordshire which I cannot look upon favorably. It is human nature to say things we do not mean when we find ourselves in stressful situations, and some of my own words from that particular conversation I now wish unspoken, though I will say that in light of that exchange, I believe I have a better understanding of your ill opinion of me."

"Mr. Darcy..." Elizabeth began shakily.

"No, Miss Bennet, I will not have you falsely deny it for the sake of politeness. I would much prefer that as I once expressed a wish that you not attempt to sketch my character at a moment in which the performance would reflect no credit on either of us, that you might take our time here in Hadleigh as an opportunity for a more faithful rendering of my disposition."

"Agreed, sir."

By this point, Ashingdon was within sight, and enough had been said between them for each to return to the house in silent introspection, parting shortly thereafter to seek other entertainments for the morning. Mr. Bingley was found in the study, tending his correspondence, and Mr. Darcy elected to do the same, while Elizabeth sought out her sister and hostess, joining the two ladies in more feminine pursuits.

ৡৡৡ

The following day brought clear skies and beautiful weather, such that Mrs. Beaumont suggested they might enjoy a picnic along the coast. She was well aware of her guests' desire to view the nearby shore, particularly Miss Elizabeth, and the day's weather seemed fine enough even to allow little Alexander and his nursemaid to join the party. The plan was unanimously approved, and within the hour an open carriage was loaded with sufficient supplies and refreshments for a leisurely day beside the sea.

The ladies of the house, with the addition of Alexander and his maid, traveled in the carriage, while the gentlemen rode alongside. After a few miles' drive, the marshes surrounding Hadleigh gave way to sandy beaches. Mr. Beaumont indicated towards a particular area where grassy clusters gave way to sand washed in by the sea, and the gentlemen dismounted their horses to assist in transporting their loaded goods to the water's edge. Once the necessary items had been delivered, the ladies set about arranging blankets and picnic baskets, while the gentlemen moved inland to find a suitable location for their horses and equipage.

With over an hour before their informal luncheon, Mr. Bingley suggested they might walk along the coast. Jane and Elizabeth readily assented, while Mrs. Beaumont demurred in favor of entertaining her infant son, a notion to which her husband agreed, leaving Mr. Darcy to fall into step with the walking party.

The group of four walked along the water's edge, Jane and Elizabeth linked arm in arm, their merry chatter sprinkled with the occasional pointing out of a sea bird or especially fine prospect. Neither paid particular attention to the one-sided conversation going on behind them until Mr. Bingley spoke loudly enough to address them.

"There certainly seems to be a fair amount of liveliness between you ladies, I hope you would not wish to exclude us from our share of the enjoyment."

"Not at all, Charles," his wife replied, extending her hand towards her husband.

Mr. Bingley came forward to claim his wife's hand, bestowing it with a kiss before tucking into its proper place on his arm.

"Forgive me, Elizabeth, for claiming the company of your sister for my own. Perhaps your levity will penetrate this gentleman's dour mood," he laughed as he indicated towards Mr. Darcy, "My attempts at rousing him have failed miserably."

Mr. Darcy faltered for the briefest of moments and looked sharply at his friend before falling into step with the rest of the party, gazing out over the water with feigned tranquility, seeming inattentive as Elizabeth moved to walk beside him.

"Do not concern yourself, Mr. Darcy, that I will pass judgment on you for your reticence at present. I believe we are both understanding of the Bingleys' desire for each other's company, and care for them enough to support the scheme."

Mr. Darcy had turned his attention to Elizabeth as she spoke, and offered a slight smile and a nod for her complaisance before returning his gaze to the coast.

"I was simply reflecting on my last occasion to visit the shore."

He seemed hesitant to say more, and Elizabeth feared that by her silence, he would think her awaiting further explanation.

"Do not think that I will press your confidence, sir."

"It is alright, Miss Bennet, I believe this is a subject on which my silence has reflected poorly on me in the past, though I assume information relayed to you by your father has relieved some of those misgivings, and I will explain to you its connection to my present frame of mind."

Elizabeth remained silent, struggling to make sense of his enigmatic statement, and failing to reduce her perplexity, replied, "I am afraid I do not comprehend your meaning, sir."

Mr. Darcy furrowed his brow and looked confusedly at the lady beside him. "Did not your father share with you the information I related to him regarding Mr. Wickham?"

"I was not aware that you had spoken to him on the subject."

"I did, a short time before Mr. Wickham left Meryton," Mr. Darcy clipped, a stern expression setting over his features.

Elizabeth blanched at the familiarity of his countenance, which in the context of their discourse she clearly understood as frustration over her father's silence, but had so frequently attributed to a less honorable source.

"Perhaps," Elizabeth replied timidly, "in light of that gentleman's absence from the neighborhood, my father did not feel the need to speak. I believe you are aware of his tendency towards leniency and indifference."

Mr. Darcy brought to mind a very prominent example of this inclination in her father, but as he could think of nothing appropriate to say regarding his distaste for his aunt's parson, he remained silent on the subject, and instead began to explain Mr. Wickham's connection to his family, divulging the information he had hoped Mr. Bennet would share with his daughters.

Elizabeth's shame was complete as she heard the gentleman she had spoken to in such abusive terms prove false the account which had greatly fueled her ill opinion of him. She began to apologize profusely, to which Mr. Darcy calmly replied that just as many before her, she had little reason to doubt Mr. Wickham's easy manners, but requested that she might hold any further remarks, as unfortunately there was more to relate.

"You may observe that I have yet to make any connection to our current surroundings, and while I did not relate this to your father, I believe your acquaintance with my sister will lead you towards compassion as well as discretion. Last summer Georgiana went to Ramsgate – do you see the land mass there on the horizon?" he halted his pace and took a step closer as he pointed south, "That is the northern coast of Kent, and if you follow it east," he said, moving his extended arm to the left, "it extends several more miles into the sea, and Ramsgate is situated on the southern side of its furthest point." He lowered his arm and cleared his throat, suddenly conscious of their proximity, and began to walk again.

"As I was saying, Georgiana traveled thither with her companion, Mrs. Younge..."

After Mr. Darcy had related the whole tale of Miss Darcy's calamitous visit to Ramsgate, Miss Elizabeth was appalled that any man who claimed himself a gentleman could behave in such a way, and expressed as much to Mr. Darcy. She enquired as to whether Miss Darcy's good spirits in the spring were truly indicative of ample recovery, and expressed her relief at hearing that while still subject to

A Noteworthy Courtship

the occasional painful remembrance, she was indeed much improved since the affair, though Mr. Darcy added that the experience had hardly been constructive towards her self-confidence.

Though Elizabeth had not provided the levity Mr. Bingley suggested to lighten Mr. Darcy's mood, by the time they returned to the Beaumonts, each was prepared to speak on happier subjects, and given the pleasant company, did so with relative ease. Soon all were situated comfortably on a large blanket, enjoying the contents of their picnic baskets and the gentle coastal breeze.

Chapter 21

The next morning when the party joined together to break their fast, Mrs. Bingley and her sister were the last to arrive, as Miss Elizabeth had become rather wary of entering the breakfast room early and alone.

"Beaumont, I believe it is time we got down to business," Mr. Darcy stated sincerely.

"I say, Darcy, does that not sound foreboding!" Mr. Beaumont replied, "Do enlighten me as to your meaning."

At this, Mr. Bingley laughed, Evelyn Beaumont seemed to be hiding a smile behind her napkin, and Mr. Darcy remained serious as ever.

"I believe you are well aware that in coming to Hadleigh I was more than just pleasure-bound, after all I did profess as much to Lady Catherine." Here he allowed himself a small smirk before he continued, "I have heard much of your growing 'hobby', which reportedly adds quite a sizeable income to your estate, and I had hoped you might propose a visit to your stables this morning."

"Aha!" cried Mr. Bingley, "I had wondered how long it would take you to ask after his horses. I requested the same myself when we arrived, but I will warn you, the best of them are already sold and will return with me to Hertfordshire."

"Well then gentlemen," said Mr. Beaumont, "If you are finished here, I suggest we adjourn to the stables."

Neither gentleman needed further encouragement to accept the invitation, and after taking their leave of the ladies, rose from the table and followed their host, collecting hats and gloves as they exited the house.

"Here we are Darcy," Mr. Beaumont said as the gentlemen approached the first of a series of small pastures before the stables, "My broodmares have given me two colts and a filly this past month, and we expect six more by the end of the season."

"The bay there seems a good size for so young a foal," commented Mr. Darcy.

"Not all of us breed Thoroughbreds, old friend. They may be all the rage amongst the ton, but the country gentlemen I do business with prefer a good draft horse for their fields. I have had much success breeding the Suffolk Punch so popular on the farms with a few Thoroughbreds even you would find impressive. The bay colt there looks to be a prime example of my efforts, and he will grow to make a fine hunter, though it will be well over a year before we break him, and I assume you would prefer a horse that is readily available."

The gentlemen continued into the stables where Mr. Beaumont proudly displayed the fruits of his labor, indicating which horses were best suited for hunting or riding. Amongst the riding mares was the chestnut Mr. Bingley had purchased for his wife, and Mr. Darcy spent a few minutes inspecting other mares he might select for Georgiana. Mr. Bingley then proudly led them to the stallion he had chosen for himself, his gleaming black coat and height of nearly seventeen hands giving every appearance of exactly the horse Mr. Darcy would expect his friend to choose. Mr. Darcy's attention was then drawn by a stallion of similar coloring to the colt he had inquired after, and Mr. Beaumont explained that he had been foaled by the same mare three years previous. A ride was suggested so that Mr. Darcy might put the horse through its paces, and Mr. Beaumont hailed a nearby groom, sending him off to retrieve the appropriate tack.

A Noteworthy Courtship

Over dinner, as Mrs. Bingley inquired whether any plans had yet been made for the following day, the gentlemen announced their mutual desire to ride a few of Beaumont's horses to Hadleigh Castle. The ruins lay an estimated five miles to the south of Ashingdon, and would make for a pleasant ride as well as an interesting locale.

Mr. Bingley and Mr. Darcy were of course eager for additional time in the saddles of the animals they intended to purchase, and Mr. Bingley suggested it to be an excellent opportunity for Jane to ride the chestnut mare and make sure the horse's temperament suited her. Mr. Darcy then made a suggestion of his own to Elizabeth.

"If I may, there is a dappled Connemara that struck my interest as a mount for Georgiana, and if you do not have a preferred horse in mind, I hoped you might ride it, Miss Bennet, that I might observe its gaits."

"I am afraid, Mr. Darcy, that I may do best to leave that task to more capable hands. I am capable of riding, but I am no horsewoman, and avoid the activity as often as I can."

"Have you seen the horse of which I speak?" pressed Mr. Darcy, "She is fairly small, in accordance with her breed, and Beaumont tells me that while she is quite agile and an excellent jumper, she is also very gentle."

Seeing Elizabeth's skepticism had not been reduced by his attempted assurances, and her expression verged on alarm at his mention of jumping, he asked Mr. Beaumont if the castle would be accessible by carriage. The gentleman in question masked a smirk at this evidence of his staid friend's malleability at the hands of a certain lady.

"The main path is wide and smooth enough to admit a curricle, but only comes within a mile of the place before it becomes rather uneven, and would be quite risky, so it would be necessary to walk beyond that point. I have a team that could use the exercise, if Miss Elizabeth can beguile one of us gentlemen into driving her," Mr. Beaumont replied, the last said with a wink towards Elizabeth.

"I will drive Miss Bennet," Mr. Darcy announced, "I would not be averse to walking the remaining length. I trust Miss Bennet would consider it no troublesome distance?"

The smile Mr. Darcy flashed in her direction as he finished his speech proved his unforeseen ability to tease, and at this pleasant surprise, Miss Elizabeth returned the gesture, and with a mischievous smile belying the self-important raise of her chin and tone of her voice, replied, "It would be no trouble at all, I am reputed to be an excellent walker, and a young lady must use such a trait to her advantage on occasion."

∾∾∾

The next morning, the gentlemen exited the house soon after breakfast as the two ladies planning to ride on horseback went above stairs to don their riding habits. Miss Elizabeth gathered her pelisse and waited in the parlor, where from her position at the window, she observed the gentlemen's return. The curricle arrived first, pulled by a smart pair of grays and driven by none other than Mr. Darcy, followed by Mr. Beaumont and Mr. Bingley, and a groom leading a pair of saddled horses. The voices of her sister and hostess were soon heard in the hall, and together they went to join the gentlemen.

Espying the ladies descending the steps, the married men approached their wives to assist them in mounting, while Mr. Darcy escorted Miss Elizabeth to the curricle before handing her in and walking around the horses to regain his seat.

"Andrew, I see you have selected Mr. Darcy's dappled beauty for me today," Mrs. Beaumont could be heard playfully commenting to her husband as she mounted her horse. She then rode closer to the afore mentioned gentleman and added, "Do not worry sir, I realize you have made no commitment to purchase this horse for your sister, but I believe you shall after we show you what this handsome creature is made of, and how she may tempt you." Seeing the other riders mounted and ready to proceed, she smiled humorously and with a light kick of her heel, cantered down the drive.

Though she had to admit the horse's unique coat was quite striking, Miss Elizabeth found a great deal of amusement in Mr. Darcy being addressed with such a particularly familiar phrase. Though she tried valiantly to restrain it, the clamped lips she concealed behind her gloved hand could no longer contain her smile, and a very faint chuckle escaped. Given their close proximity, this of course gained the attention of her driver, and unfortunately, as often occurs when one meets the source of their amusement, his blank expression as he turned towards her only increased her amusement and elicited a small involuntary giggle. Fearing she may need to pinch herself to regain her composure, Elizabeth calmly silenced her short-lived display, but as the gentleman beside her had neither averted his gaze nor softened his expression, she realized he was expecting some form of explanation. The reason behind her outburst was suddenly quite difficult to explain, and the many seemingly rational approaches she conjured seemed likely to confuse rather than clarify. At last she sighed, glanced up at Mr. Darcy, whose stony gaze had still remained fixed upon her, cleared her throat, and in a low, serious tone said, "She is tolerable I suppose, but not handsome enough to tempt me."

Mr. Darcy's eyes widened in horror, the whites of his eyes becoming further exposed with each word she spoke. Recollecting himself, he turned away, seeming very interested in the dirt and gravel covering the ground beside the curricle. After a few moments, his shoulders began to shake, and he glanced back at Miss Elizabeth, his gloved fist hiding tightly compressed lips that threatened to break into a grin.

"I believe I understand your source of humor, Miss Bennet," he finally said, with as much sincerity as he could muster, "That I could declare myself not tempted by such a beautiful woman, and then be challenged to resist the paltry charms of a good horse."

Elizabeth smiled, grateful for his lightheartedness, yet completely baffled by it at the same time, and not daring to reflect on his referring to her as a beautiful woman.

"I owe you a sincere apology Miss Bennet," Mr. Darcy continued, "I knew those words to be false the moment I spoke them, and I had not the slightest comprehension of your overhearing them, else I certainly would have said this sooner." He paused for a moment, and in a sullen tone added, "By your silence, I see you must truly hate me for it."

"On the contrary sir, I was simply bewildered by your reaction. It relieves me greatly that you react to my impertinence with equal humor rather than taking offense."

"Ha! The lady I degrade so carelessly is concerned that I might take offense to the manner in which I was reminded of my folly. You, madam, shall never cease to amaze me." The uncharacteristic levity and earnest smile from Mr. Darcy made Elizabeth feel so comfortable in his presence, such that she gathered the courage to broach a subject that had been impressed upon her from his first arriving at Ashingdon.

"You will most likely be appalled by my frankness, but I must tell you Mr. Darcy, at this moment I hardly recognize you as the gentleman who was introduced to me in Hertfordshire. I cannot imagine what has affected this change in your character."

"Can you not?" Mr. Darcy looked at her pointedly, flashing her a brilliant smile before turning towards the horses and flicking the reins, the well matched team jolting the conveyance to a quick start.

As the air of gaiety brought on by their exchange began to fade, the gravity of his last statement sunk in, creating an awkward silence that lasted for some time before Mr. Darcy felt the need to speak.

"Miss Bennet, though it was you who claimed to speak with frankness, I seem to have disconcerted you. While the damage is already done, I must tell you I was in earnest when I referred to you as a beautiful woman. I have long considered you one of the most handsome women of my acquaintance, though this must come as no surprise to you, for I am certain there are many who share my opinion of you."

"No Mr. Darcy, that will not do," Elizabeth teased with a nervous edge to her laugh, "I have lived these twenty years with my vanity in check, and with such phrases as these, you set out to inflate it terribly." She then added in a gently, "Though I should thank you for your compliments, as contrary to your supposition, such pretty words I do not often hear."

They rode on in silence for a short distance, Elizabeth noting a slight twitch of his hand as it rested on his knee, cradling the horses' reins.

"Miss Elizabeth...I," Mr. Darcy faltered and glanced at the path ahead, "I believe we must walk from here."

Chapter 22

Mr. Darcy busied himself with finding a proper place for the horses to rest while they proceeded on foot towards Hadleigh Castle. Miss Elizabeth observed the diligent manner in which Mr. Darcy approached his task, not meeting her gaze or so much as glancing in her direction as he tended the horses. He seemed to be settling into his former reserve, and she could only imagine that her liveliness in the curricle had agitated him. The conversation had gotten out of hand, even by her standards, and undoubtedly so by the standards of proper decorum, and while he had played along in the moment, she would not be entirely surprised if the scene reflected poorly in his retrospection. Mr. Darcy soon completed his task and walked in her direction, the two silently falling into step along the path. Miss Elizabeth found herself unequal to the task of initiating a conversation, and was relieved when at length, Mr. Darcy spoke.

"I understand your family at Longbourn is well, but I have yet to inquire after the Gardiners. I trust they are in good health?"

"Yes, to my knowledge they are in excellent health. I have not exchanged letters with my aunt since leaving Hertfordshire, but normally we are quite faithful correspondents, and the Gardiners were quite well after their return to London."

"I am glad to hear it. Mr. Gardiner seems a sensible gentleman, and Mrs. Gardiner showed a good deal of gentility in her conversations with Miss Bingley." Both suppressed a smile at his civil admission that by no means did the difference in station between the ladies indicate superior manners in the lady of higher standing, and they both knew the truth to be quite the opposite.

Miss Elizabeth and Mr. Darcy spoke of the Gardiners at length, and while Mr. Darcy admitted that he had not spoken much to them in the spring, he seemed genuinely interested in hearing about the relations Elizabeth held so dear to her heart. She offered a brief history of the Gardiners, from their marriage when she and Jane were quite young to the origins of her uncle's thriving business.

The largest impression was made by the knowledge that shortly after they were wed, and before her own children were born, Mrs. Gardiner frequently requested for her nieces Jane and Elizabeth come to visit her. At the time Mr. Gardiner was quite involved in his growing business, and while trips to Longbourn were infrequent and journeys to Lambton out of the question, Mr. Bennet took pity on his new sister and allowed his eldest daughters to visit. At the time, Mary was too young to be separated peacefully from her mother, and soon after, Mrs. Bennet went into confinement in expectation of Kitty's arrival. By the time Lydia was born, Mrs. Bennet's nervous condition began to develop, and as her whims frequently led her to desire her dear Jane at home, Mr. Bennet grew reluctant to antagonize her by disagreeing.

Fortunately for Jane and Elizabeth, their reduced frequency in traveling to London was soon answered by her uncle's business growing such that a foreman handled many day to day tasks, and frequent trips to Longbourn were inhibited only by Mrs. Gardiner's own confinements, at which times Jane and Elizabeth often came to entertain the elder of their cousins.

Not only did Mr. Darcy gain a much better understanding of the riddle that was the dynamics of the Bennet family by this discourse, but Elizabeth reflected that they had shared a pleasant conversation, and while the gentleman was not verbose, he was attentive and at times even amiable.

Such were her reflections that Elizabeth gladly introduced a favorite subject as she inquired of Mr. Darcy, "In recent years, my aunt and uncle can give us no greater reward than attending a play or an opera. Do you enjoy the theatre, Mr. Darcy?"

"That I do, Miss Bennet, though I prefer plays to musical performance."

"And does it follow that you have a particular favorite?"

Mr. Darcy hesitated before answering, "I have always enjoyed *Les Deux Amis*, though most are familiar with Beaumarchais for *The Marriage of Figaro*."

"An unlikely choice, though I admit I am vaguely familiar with it as there is another amongst my acquaintance with a similar preference." Mr. Darcy swallowed uncomfortably, clasping his hands behind his back, and as no response was forthcoming, Elizabeth added, "Though I suppose I cannot expect all men to prefer gruesome epics portraying the warriors of old."

"Yes," Mr. Darcy said with relief, "and by the same logic I shall not expect your favorite to be Romeo and Juliet."

"Nay, if I were to select a favorite to fulfill the romantic notions we ladies are to be so fixated upon, I would at least be sensible enough to choose a play with a more pleasant resolution."

"Which would you name then, when asked your favorite play?"

"I would have to say that all depends, as my preference for one over another sways with each play I read. Also, each play I have seen in the theatre seems to take on a new meaning beyond what I had interpreted through the written word, and I have not had the opportunity to visit the theatre often enough to see all of my favorites."

"For your enjoyment, I hope that may change in the future," he replied with a lighter air than he felt.

"So says my father, yet he has been forced to tolerate my vague answers and changing opinions for quite some time."

They continued towards the castle discussing the plays Elizabeth had seen and the merits of those she might enjoy. When the castle's tower came into view, both were content with having managed to pass the entire hour's walk pleasantly, and thought perhaps they could grow to get on famously when thrown into each other's company.

෴෴෴

"Miss Bennet, Darcy, there you are," Mr. Beaumont greeted upon their approach. "I hope Mr. Darcy was not too frightful a companion. I know he can pose quite the intimidating figure, though he has not shown it since coming to Essex."

"Indeed he has not," Elizabeth replied tentatively, offering a small smile towards the gentleman in question, hoping to mask her confusion on the subject, little knowing this gesture was the very one which Mr. Darcy had wished to see cast in his direction for some time.

"And who is my sister to be intimidated by anyone?" rejoined Mr. Bingley.

"Ha! Yes I believe she challenges even my Evelyn in terms of indomitable spirit!" laughed Mr. Beaumont, "In that case, I hope she allowed you some mercy in her thorough teasing."

Seeing Mr. Darcy's discomfiture, Miss Elizabeth commented, "We actually had quite a pleasant discussion about the theatre."

"Ah, so you are fond of the theatre as well, Miss Bennet?" Elizabeth nodded and Mr. Beaumont continued, "If it were not for that particular entertainment, I doubt we would have ever gotten Darcy here to mix in society, though he did often arrive moments before crowd dispersed to their seats, and leave immediately following the curtain's close."

As various opinions of plays were discussed, the small theatre in Southend was mentioned, and a suggestion that they attend was well received. Mr. Beaumont was vaguely familiar with the upcoming performance schedule, and a plan was made for the gentlemen to travel into Southend the following day to secure their attendance within the week. Conversation soon turned to their present location, and Mr. Beaumont asked if the assembled party would like to hear some of the history of the place.

Mr. Beaumont shared his knowledge of Hadleigh Castle as the group strolled leisurely about the ruins, which were situated on a large rolling hill and consisted predominately of a single round tower, partially in ruin itself. A small repast of fruits and cheeses had been packed in the saddlebags of Mr. Beaumont and Mr. Bingley's mounts, which the party settled down to partake after sufficient exploration of the castle. The view from their location atop the small mount was excellent, and some minutes were spent admiring the surrounding vistas as the Beaumonts indicated points of interest including Canvey Island, the various fishing boats at Leigh, and the more populated Southend just visible in the distance.

At last it was decided that the party best return to Ashingdon, those on horseback traveling leisurely with those on foot until the curricle was reached. Mr. Beaumont assisted Mr. Darcy in readying the horses, remounting his own horse as Mr. Darcy handed Elizabeth into their conveyance.

જન્ય

After riding for some minutes in silence, watching the mounted quartet ahead, Miss Elizabeth addressed the gentleman beside her. "I hope, Mr. Darcy, we have not extinguished your supply of conversation for the day. After all, you do have a reputation to uphold, lest you become as loquacious as your friends."

Mr. Darcy offered a curt nod in response, his solemnity untouched as he replied, "You have forbidden talk of books in a ball room, but what of a curricle?"

Miss Elizabeth smiled at his somber attempt at levity and stated cheekily, "Certainly in a carriage it would be appropriate, in a farm cart it would be absurd. In a gig is questionable, but I believe in a curricle, especially so fine a specimen as this, such refined conversation could be nothing but appropriate."

Mr. Darcy huffed out one light chuckle and shook his head at her remark as he complied, "Then by your own provision, madam, books it shall be, though I warn you I can be quite set in my opinions."

A Noteworthy Courtship

"Very well, I shall not to entice you into too heated a debate, lest you become so incensed that while you are engrossed in forming your rebuttals, you allow a spooked horse to run us into a ravine."

"I always drive with the utmost care, Miss Bennet," Mr. Darcy replied a bit defensively.

"Come Mr. Darcy, if we are to be on amiable terms, you must realize that I have a great fondness for teasing, which in combination with my flair for impertinence can be frightful if you are determined to always take me at my word."

"I shall endeavor to remember that Miss Bennet." Mr. Darcy answered seriously, keeping his attention on the road ahead.

Mr. Darcy then softened as he turned towards her, "Now tell me, what think you of Wordsworth? Surely your extensive reading has included his works, and if you enjoy them as much as I, you may know a line or two of his about the sea."

Miss Elizabeth expression brightened as she replied, "It is a beauteous evening, calm and free; The holy time is quiet as a nun, Breathless with adoration; the broad sun Is sinking down in its tranquility; The gentleness of heaven is on the Sea: Listen! the mighty being is awake, And doth with his eternal motion make, A sound like thunder—everlastingly."[1]

Mr. Darcy nodded his appreciation and countered, "With Ships the sea was sprinkled far and nigh, Like stars in heaven, and joyously it showed; Some lying fast at anchor in the road, Some veering up and down, one knew not why."[2]

Miss Elizabeth smiled playfully as she selected her rejoinder, "There is a pleasure in the pathless woods, There is a rapture on the lonely shore, There is society where none intrudes, By the deep sea, and music in its roar: I love not man the less, but nature more, From these our interviews, in which I steal From all I may be, or have been before, To mingle with the universe, and feel What I can ne'er express, yet cannot all conceal."[3]

"I see you are well versed in Lord Byron's works as well," Mr. Darcy said approvingly.

"That I am, though you have caught me at my game," Miss Elizabeth replied with an impish smile.

And so their conversation carried on, each taking in the sights much more attentively on their return than they had on their way out, all the while discussing poetry and various works of literature. Miss Elizabeth was surprised by the compatibility of their tastes, and Mr. Darcy began to realize she may not have been in earnest when declaring poetry not to be the food of love.

❧ ❧ ❧

That night, Miss Elizabeth reflected on the day's events and could not but focus her ruminations on the enigmatic man she was just beginning to understand. He was still far more serious than the other two gentlemen in residence at Ashingdon, but Mr. Darcy had actually complimented her, partaken in a conversation that even she considered to have been rather absurd, yet he had broken down into laughter – though he seemed embarrassed to display it. He even expressed a positive opinion of the Gardiners. She had not been aware of his speaking to them beyond an introduction, though she reluctantly admitted that with all the activity surrounding the wedding, she had never spoken to her aunt and uncle of him. Mr. Darcy's opinion of the theatre was strikingly similar to her correspondent's, and she found it quite unsettling that they both favored a play that was so little known. She considered the possibility that a particular interest in Beaumarchais' famous play would lead one to seek out his other works, yet the explanation her correspondent had given for his preference replayed at the forefront of her mind.

> *...Upon my father's first tour of the continent, he attended the Comédie-Française in Paris for the performance of Les Deux Amis. At the time, Pierre Beaumarchais was very little known, yet my father had greatly enjoyed that night at the theatre, and took pride in recognizing the talent that would later be so well renowned. The play is rarely performed and I have yet to see it – and have little belief that I ever shall – however the nostalgia of my father's reading the play and reminiscing created an impression that has yet to leave me.*

A small voice suggested that she ought reconsider the possibility that the two gentlemen could be one and the same, and often as she had pushed this voice aside, she began to consider whether the similarities outweighed the deterring factors. She knew not what to make of Mr.

Darcy's periods of absence, yet the biggest obstacle, his pride, she now saw in a different light, thinking of it more in terms of a reserve that needed little more than patience and understanding to overcome.

Chapter 23

Mr. Bennet was seated in his study at Longbourn attending his correspondence. One might assume that the increased time spent in his library due to the absence of his only sensible daughters might have inspired diligence in this pursuit, but the stack of letters was attended belatedly, as was his usual custom. However, it may have been considered fortunate that he did not delay any longer, as one letter contained information not entirely reassuring, and another particularly recent one proposed a plan he would have little time to thwart.

Mr. Bennet,

Be assured that our first days have passed amiably. Mr. Darcy has lately arrived here at Ashingdon, and bid me to pass on a message to you. He wishes to apologize for the lack of resolution in a matter of business discussed between you earlier this year, but offers his assurance that he continues to act in a manner suited towards the requirements of the other party. I will leave that enigmatic statement for you to decipher, and relate to you further details of my own business prospects with Mr. Beaumont...

Yours, etc.

Charles Bingley

Mr. Bennet was not surprised to hear Mr. Bingley's positive opinions regarding their stay, as he rarely heard the young gentleman express an opinion other than approval towards anything – and thus he rather wondered if the horses were quite as impressive as his daughter's husband would have him believe.

He was not pleased however, to hear of Mr. Darcy's residence in the same house as his favorite daughter. He had lost much of his esteem for Mr. Darcy when the gentleman left immediately following his eldest daughter's nuptials without so much as taking leave of those at Longbourn, and certainly hoped the young man intended to redeem himself. He was suddenly very grateful for Mr. Bingley's presence at Ashingdon, as he could not believe even Mr. Darcy capable of doing something untoward in the presence of the gentleman who was not only his closest friend, but also brother to the lady in question. He wished to know more of these "*requirements*" the gentleman was striving to accommodate, and how it was that he could have become knowledgeable of them.

Mr. Bennet sighed, resolved to do nothing at present but watch a little more faithfully for further news from Essex. He then reluctantly turned his attention to another letter from his cousin, its contents undoubtedly as ridiculous and unfounded as each letter before it. At least Mr. Collins had gradually written with less frequency.

Cousin Bennet,

Though I have made my sentiments known on many a previous occasion, allow me to again express my fond remembrance of your hospitality and the company of your amiable daughters. I consider it a great providence to have found the companion of my future life amongst the ladies of your household, and I flatter myself to profess that she must be as anxious for our union as I, as not only there is to be great comfort found in the securing of her mother and sisters, but until such time as she returns to Hertfordshire as mistress of Longbourn, she shall join me in receiving the enviable patronage of Lady Catherine deBourgh.

I digress, as my specific reason for writing to you on this occasion shall soon be made clear as I explain the counsel the honorable Lady Catherine deBourgh has so humbly condescended to give me. She has often stated that the marital felicity of a parson should be of no concern to his patroness, and the opinion on the matter she has so kindly bestowed upon me is most insightful, such that I felt the necessity of writing to you directly.

It is the opinion of my noble patroness, with which I most humbly concur, that there should be no further delay to the union between myself and dear Elizabeth. As I have mentioned in my previous letters, I have recently found a suitable curate, and as the Easter services have been completed these three weeks, Lady Catherine has impressed upon me the appropriateness of my absenting to your parish that the banns may be read and my marriage performed with utmost haste, that I return to her service with my new bride as soon as may be. 'Your parish, Mr. Collins.' Said she, 'has been without the benefit of a parson's wife for too long, and as she learns to perform her duty, I shall instruct her appropriately.' Consider yourself at leisure to share this expected pleasure with Elizabeth, and inform her that I shall arrive at Longbourn se'en-night hence that the aforementioned plan may take place.

Yours etc,

William Collins

Mr. Bennet was not at all pleased by his cousin's presumption, having never addressed him for his daughter's hand, and the additional assumption that a wedding would take place at his leisure – or rather the leisure dictated by his "*noble patroness*". Enflamed with indignation that should have consumed him long ago, Mr. Bennet wrote at once, his pen scratching forcefully across the page, outlining a message designed to end this farce once and for all.

His missive complete, he rang for Hill, and after requesting for an express rider to be hired, he reread the letter as the ink dried upon the parchment.

Mr. Collins,

Though you have frequently expressed your interest in my daughter, your petition comes much as a surprise to me, given that neither my daughter nor yourself have approached me for my consent regarding this matter.

I must inform you, however, that such a plan as you have outlined would be greatly hindered by the absence of my daughter Elizabeth, as she is currently in Essex, in company with Mr. and Mrs. Bingley, on the invitation of a friend of the latter. I do not take kindly to secret engagements, nor the false implication that my daughter has committed herself to you in any way, as I know her to be devoid of any motivation for such promises, and I certainly have provided no such commitment on her behalf. I highly suggest you consider the matter closed until you have a more appropriate manner of expressing your interest in one of my daughters, at which juncture I shall remind you of the convention that the express permission of the lady's father is required before a betrothal is formed, and I am not a man to give away his daughters lightly.

Sincerely,

Mr. Bennet

 formula

Once the rider had been sent on his way to Kent, Mr. Bennet wasted little time before penning a letter to the daughter so closely related to the subject of his express. So it was that just a few days after their outing to Hadleigh Castle, Miss Elizabeth was seated in the garden with Mrs. Beaumont when the post arrived, a letter from her father amongst its contents.

Dearest Lizzy,

You will undoubtedly be shocked by the letter I have just received, as by its contents I deemed an immediate response most prudent. Be not alarmed, we are all well; the letter was from our cousin, Mr. Collins, who has outdone himself in preposterousness – no small feat considering the precedent he has established.

Though I had thought him understanding of the state of these affairs long ago, it seems his patroness is unaware that he is in fact, not engaged. He related his plan for the final arrangements of his marriage to my daughter – which I shall not trouble you with as no such plan shall be acted upon – except to say that he was instructed in this proposal by Lady Catherine herself, fancy that! I had no notion of his taking such measures, but rest assured I have written him to make it exceedingly clear that engagements do not exist without paternal consent – which we both know he has yet to request and I have no intent of providing – and he should quit his delusional beliefs regarding the particular prospects of his marital status. I am sorry not to have taken this assertive approach sooner, you may not realize your brother Bingley advised me as much long ago, and I am glad to know you are now under his protection as well.

I hope you have been enjoying your time at Ashingdon, and will continue to do so until your return. I need not remind you that I have not heard two words of sense together since your departure, as I will simply hope that you shall forgive your father's imprudence by the time you arrive back at Longbourn.

With love,

Papa

Mr. Darcy had seated himself near a window in the library with his own correspondence, his attention caught by the movement outside of a servant bringing a letter to Elizabeth. He watched the concern written on her features fade as her eyes moved down the page, and she sighed with apparent relief as she folded the missive and approached her sister and Mr. Bingley.

As dusk fell and the evening's entertainments began, Miss Elizabeth sat down at the pianoforte, just as she had many evenings before. Mrs. Beaumont was quite a talented pianist, and the quality of her pianoforte provided sufficient inducement for Miss Elizabeth to practice more frequently. On this particular occasion, the party had adjourned to the drawing room after dinner, where Jane had requested that her sister play the piece she had been practicing earlier in the day. After her performance, her audience clapped and complimented appropriately, and requested she play again. Before she could choose another piece, however, a large shadow was cast across the various sheets of music as Mr. Darcy reached over to examine the selection.

"Mrs. Beaumont, you have quite a fine collection of sheet music here," Mr. Darcy commented before inclining his head towards Miss Elizabeth and adding in a much softer tone, "May I?"

"Of course, though I should warn you that as Mrs. Beaumont's talents exceed mine, so do some of these arrangements, and if you select one of the more difficult concertos, I may play it extremely ill."

"I believe you demure, Miss Bennet, for I have frequently overheard your playing as of late, and have rarely heard anything that gave me more pleasure."

"For shame, sir!" she dissembled, "I hope you are certain it was myself at this bench and not Mrs. Beaumont, else you may find yourself in need of redirecting your acclamations." The look she received in response caused her to add timidly, "I admit I have had the benefit of additional practice since Jane's marriage, and even more so since coming to Ashingdon. I hope I can honestly say my diligence has provided at least some small reward, else I shall be quite discouraged from continuing in such an industrious manner, for I have never played for more than my own amusement."

"We neither of us perform to strangers, Miss Bennet, but I believe with ample encouragement we have each applied ourselves to practice, and I only hope the effort in my case has been as productive as it has in yours."

He then paused in his thumbing through the sheet music, turned back a few selections, and looked inquisitively towards Miss Elizabeth. She was pleasantly surprised to see a familiar piece that she had played on occasion since coming to Ashingdon. She did not know it well, as it was not amongst the collection at Longbourn, but the movement of the score, with a recurring series of runs in the key of E minor was very conducive to her talents. Mr. Darcy's gaze questioning gaze was still upon her as she looked up and nodded as she whispered, "Yes, thank you."

Mr. Darcy then seated himself beside her on the piano bench, brushing his arm against her shoulder as he reached to position the sheets before her. Elizabeth subconsciously shifted in her seat, but if anything, Mr. Darcy only took this as an opportunity to move slightly closer. Fearing the whole room had noticed his movement, she was tempted to use her elbow to give him a gentle nudge in the ribs, but imagined the sniggering such action would elicit from Mr. Bingley, and perhaps the others as well. Instead she took a deep breath as she settled her fingers upon the keys of the opening chord, and began to play. She was soon very grateful for having at least a vague familiarity with the piece, as the first turn of the pages included a long but gentle brush of their shoulders, and though he seemed very conscious not to impose upon the range of motion she needed to play, he did seem to take rather longer than necessary to settle the page and return to an upright position.

After a few of these occurrences, she glanced at his face as he reached over in preparation to turn the page. He was doing an excellent job of leaning in with feigned focus on the lines of music, but all pretense was dissolved as his eyes darted to meet hers and an impish curl was set upon his lips. *Well played, Mr. Darcy.* Anyone aware of his fastidious nature might believe him desirous of turning at precisely the best moment, and his timing did vary with the movement of the score at each juncture. She intensified her efforts to focus on the task at hand, and to her flustered surprise, she realized that his closeness did not bother her as it ought, but that it was actually quite pleasant.

Chapter 24

The night of the theatre soon arrived, and after enjoying the early afternoon out of doors, the ladies retired to their rooms to assist each other in dressing. Mr. Beaumont joked about the exorbitant amount of time ladies took to prepare for such events, to which Mr. Bingley replied that his sisters had long since given him an understanding of the "*necessity*" of such things, and he found the ladies currently assembled at Ashingdon far more reasonable in their requirements. Mr. Darcy reflected that while he had enjoyed being in her company, if Miss Elizabeth's appearance at the wedding and the few balls he had attended in Hertfordshire were any indication, the inducement was well worth the wait. He was drawn out of his reverie as Mr. Beaumont clapped his friends on the back and suggested a few forms of mischief the men might use to occupy themselves while the ladies were otherwise engaged.

As the sun began to lower itself over the western horizon, the gentlemen could be seen galloping their horses up to the house, charging their mounts to the care of a groom as they went above stairs to conduct their own preparations for the evening. The gentlemen still preceded the ladies in descending to the foyer, and went about collecting hats and donning gloves. They were soon alerted to the ladies' proximity by the light and pleasing voices trickling down the stairs, and Mr. Darcy paused the straightening of his gloves, looking up to see Mrs. Beaumont and Mrs. Bingley descending the staircase, followed by an enchantingly adorned Miss Elizabeth. How long he stood transfixed he knew not, as he vaguely registered the sight of Mr. Beaumont and Mr. Bingley approaching their wives in his peripheral vision. As the lady of his rapt attention reached the foot of the staircase, Mr. Darcy stepped forward confidently, bowing formally over her hand as she curtsied in response.

"Your carriage awaits, Miss Bennet," Mr. Darcy stated as he offered his arm, his voice and posture exuding rigid formality, though Miss Elizabeth found she could not object to his strong and silent presence in comparison to Mr. Bingley and Mr. Beaumont's lenient affability.

The Beaumont party arrived promptly at the theatre, the crowd notably smaller than one might expect in London, though no less comprised of well-dressed ladies and gentlemen. Most had traveled hither for the fashionable purpose of summering by the sea, and were as desirous of displaying themselves to advantage as might be expected of any other members of the highest circles attending the theatre in London.

A Noteworthy Courtship

As they moved through the throng of attendees in the lobby, the Beaumonts were occasionally greeted by a neighbor or acquaintance, though the majority of attention towards their party was directed towards Mr. Darcy. The gentleman's curt responses gave the impression that he was not particularly well acquainted with any of those who wished to make their addresses, though this proved little hindrance to their fawning attentions and insipid remarks regarding the opera they were about to see. Miss Elizabeth was struck by the importance of his position in society, and with each minor acquaintance and wielding matron whose approaches bordered on the impertinent, her empathy towards his cold manners increased. However his civility towards her was not reduced, nor did he seem ashamed to escort her. With each affront by an unexpected party, he introduced her properly before she was uniformly ignored in response, though she did detect a sneer or two in her direction that would put Miss Bingley's darkest looks to shame amidst the whispers and subtle gestures that followed in her escort's wake.

As their party moved towards their box, Miss Elizabeth noticed the slight relaxation of his arm, leaving no doubt that her newly formed suppositions regarding Mr. Darcy's conduct were quite close to the mark. Though one of the best situated in the theatre, the box seemed larger than necessary for their party, as the group of six were seated comfortably in a single row along the railing.

Once they were settled comfortably in their seats, Mr. Darcy reached into the inner pocket of his coat, withdrawing a libretto bearing the same title as the evening's opera.

"Might I offer this for the translations, Miss Bennet?"

Miss Elizabeth's initial reaction was to be affronted by the presumption that she would require the English translation of the original Italian, yet she immediately chastised herself for so severe a reaction to his kind intentions and replied, "I thank you for the offer, sir, though I am well acquainted with the text in its original form."

"I am glad to hear it. My sister has been properly instructed in the modern languages, Italian included, yet often prefers to have the translation available, such that I have become accustomed to bringing such a volume whenever I am in attendance."

"Your sister appreciates your thoughtfulness, I am sure," she responded politely.

"Yes," he answered, looking down awkwardly at the libretto in his hands, "though I suppose being acquainted with your fondness for literature, I should have known you would be familiar with the original text and not require such a thing."

"Perhaps, but it does not follow that its availability must be unwelcome," Miss Elizabeth extended her hand, into which he placed the libretto, content to observe her casual perusal of the slender volume until the lights dimmed and the curtain rose.

Miss Elizabeth greatly enjoyed the performance, occasionally glancing at her companions, noting her sister and Mr. Bingley to be serene as always, and her own enthusiasm reflected in the face of Evelyn Beaumont. On the few occasions that she chanced a look in Mr. Darcy's direction, she found him equally attentive to the stage, with the faintest upturn at the corners of his mouth. She paused momentarily, observing that his subtle smile was actually quite becoming, until to her mortification his eyes darted to meet her own. She immediately returned her own gaze to the evening's entertainment, nearly positive that over the din of the crowd she could distinguish a few light chuckles emanating from the gentleman beside her as she flushed and raised her fan, rapidly flicking her wrist to cool her burning cheeks.

The first intermission soon arrived, and the remaining occupants of the box suggested they return to the hall for refreshments. Mrs. Beaumont noted that during the first act she had observed a few ladies of her acquaintance whom she had not had the pleasure of meeting since the birth of her son, and seeing them across the hall, politely excused herself and her husband to greet them. Jane took this opportunity to approach her sister, and as she inquired after her health, Elizabeth realized that her earlier discomposure had not gone unnoticed, and she suspected another late night chat would soon be in order.

She was relieved from further inquiry by the arrival of Mr. Darcy.

"I thought you might like some refreshment, Miss Bennet." He came to her side as he handed her the beverage, adding in a low tone, "You seemed a little flushed towards the end of the first act."

His address reflected nothing but seriousness, and considering the good humor expressed in his eyes, she wondered how he could speak so collectedly.

A Noteworthy Courtship

Her own speech contained a hint of playfulness as she replied, "You did not seem so solemn yourself Mr. Darcy, and I daresay there were at least a few moments where your enjoyment was perceptibly displayed."

Giving every appearance that he had not been ruffled by her reference to his amusement, he stated nonchalantly, "I will not deny that I take pleasure in a night at the opera, among other things."

As the crowd began to gravitate towards their seats, Mr. Darcy offered his arm to escort Miss Elizabeth back to their box, Mr. Bingley offering the same courtesy to his wife.

The remainder of the performance passed in much the same fashion as the previous act. Miss Elizabeth enjoyed every moment, though she did not dare to turn her head towards Mr. Darcy again, except to respond to his occasional comment or inquiry. The carriage was called promptly at the close of the last act, and while this limited Mrs. Beaumont's opportunities to mingle, she had already extended several invitations to tea, and their timely departure saved Mr. Darcy from being addressed by additional persons reminding him of their having been introduced in London.

The carriage ride to Ashingdon was filled with lively discussion of the evening's entertainment, and following a brief period of refreshment in the parlor, the ladies retired for the evening, while Mr. Beaumont invited the gentlemen to his study.

کی کی کی

"Well Darcy, I hope you no longer feel the need to deny your interest in my wife's sister," smirked Mr. Bingley, "though you proceed with an uncertainty I had not known possible for a man of your disposition."

Slightly confused, Mr. Beaumont added supportively, "Miss Bennet suits you well Darcy, I am surprised by your hesitation. Surely her father could not object to your courting his daughter."

Mr. Bingley chuckled, "Mr. Bennet is not the type to be impressed by social or financial standing, nor does he seem likely to accept or refuse a man's suit on any basis but the opinion of the daughter concerned. While Darcy here has sufficient redeeming qualities aside from his ten thousand a year," Mr. Bingley paused momentarily as he struggled with his composure, "he definitely made a mess of showing himself to advantage in Hertfordshire."

Mr. Darcy's dour mien expressed quite clearly that he was not pleased, at which Mr. Bingley sobered and added earnestly, "Forgive me, Darcy. It is simply that this is a side of you I have never seen, and now that you seem to have come to terms with your esteem for Miss Elizabeth, it is quite interesting to see you play the part of the attentive suitor. Though I do not suggest you reduce your efforts by any means, as your previous behavior has given her quite an impression to overcome."

"Now Bingley," interjected Mr. Beaumont, "Miss Bennet seems a sensible young lady, surely it is no great obstacle for her to understand his true character."

At this point Mr. Darcy was seriously displeased about being discussed as though he were not in the room, and in a manner not unlike two school masters discussing a difficult pupil nonetheless.

However the two genial men remained oblivious to their friend's indignation, and the conference continued as Mr. Bingley rejoined, "I would agree with you if he had not claimed in public that she was not handsome enough to tempt him, and I would not be surprised if the comment got back to her. After all, it is a small community, and particularly prone to gossip."

At this, both gentlemen looked quite amused, but before they could express their merriment, Mr. Darcy interjected dryly, "For your information, Bingley, the gossiping hens of Meryton were not required in this instance as she heard my ill-chosen words first hand."

Mr. Bingley's jaw dropped, his sympathetic nature impressing upon him that he had gone too far. After allowing his friend to wallow in a little well-deserved guilt, Mr. Darcy grinned most uncharacteristically and added, "Though I know quite well that she already finds the incident as humorous as you seem to, and I have corrected her understanding of my opinion on the subject of her looks."

"Well, well," Mr. Beaumont said thoughtfully, "there may be hope for you yet."

જ જ જ

Above stairs, Miss Elizabeth sat perched upon her bed, still dressed in the elegant gown she had worn to the theatre, having yet to even remove her full length gloves, her arms perched stiffly at her sides. She had been thinking over the details of the evening, as she had begun to

A Noteworthy Courtship

do quite frequently after being in Mr. Darcy's company, and was struck by the imminent conclusion hinted at by the circumstances that continued to add up. His reference to his sister, his tastes and opinions on a variety of subjects, his recently revealed wit and budding ability to tease – not to mention the disconcerting manner in which if she were not so convinced that she knew better, she might think he admired her.

She knew not whether to chastise herself for daring to hope, or for being blind to what seemed to be the obvious truth. If he were truly the man behind all of those notes, she knew not how to confront him regarding her epiphany or whether such action ought to be attempted. *Good heavens! The argument on that awful day... that would mean I affronted him as he was attempting to* – the thought was too humiliating to continue. She now fluctuated between wishing her correspondent to be him, and dreading the mortification if he truly were, for how on earth would they get on if all of this came to light?

Chapter 25

The next day at breakfast, conversation flowed easily between most assembled at the table, with the exception of two persons fighting the awkward sensations lingering from the night before which they fervently wished to conceal. As soon as would be considered polite, Miss Elizabeth excused herself, expressing her desire for a walk, and while Mr. Darcy frequently accompanied her on these morning rambles, he professed a need to attend his correspondence with Pemberley's steward and retreated to the library.

Over luncheon, the tension was eased as Mr. Beaumont, Mr. Bingley and Mr. Darcy reminisced about their Cambridge days, particularly their mutual interest in cricket.

"Say what you will, gentlemen, of your passing interest in the sport, but do not forget I was first bowler on the Cambridge team," said Mr. Beaumont proudly. "As a matter of fact, I still have the equipment," he added with a challenging look towards his former schoolmates.

"Don't be a braggart, Beaumont," retorted Mr. Darcy, "I could have beaten you left handed if I were not so caught up in my studies – which I will remind you were the primary reason for our attending Cambridge in the first place."

Such declarations could be followed by nothing less than an opportunity for the gentlemen to prove their assertions, and a few manservants were called to set up the wickets on the upper lawn. The ladies sought out a shady tree at a safe distance from the playing field, where a blanket was spread out for their comfort, as well as little Alexander and his nursemaid.

The gentlemen shed their restrictive jackets and sporting their more comfortable lawn shirts and waistcoats, went out onto the field. Mr. Beaumont bowled as Mr. Bingley and Mr. Darcy alternated between batman and fielder. Cheers and applause sprang from the ladies with each particularly fine hit or diving catch. Even Jane chuckled lightly behind her hand when Mr. Bingley inadvertently upset the wicket with his backswing in a failed attempt at hitting a fast pitch, and Mr. Darcy could not but laugh at his own folly when he tipped a ball just enough to pop it high into air, only to have it land within a yard of his feet.

As the gentlemen came over to the ladies to break for cold refreshment, Mr. Beaumont inquired if any of them were desirous of joining the game. This was said with a mischievous grin towards his wife who replied, "Andrew, you need not carry on with such pretenses before our guests, as you know very well I would like to join you, and I am not ashamed to relate that quite frequently during the course of our marriage have we spent our afternoons in just such an amusement."

Mrs. Beaumont then turned an inquisitive smile towards the other ladies, to which Elizabeth merrily assented, while Jane politely demurred, expressing a preference to keep little Alexander entertained. Mr. Bingley smiled at his wife and offered an extra cricket ball to entertain the baby. Meanwhile Mr. Beaumont extended his hand to assist his wife in rising, and seeing Mr. Bingley still seated in adoring conversation with Jane, Mr. Darcy offered his hand to Miss Bennet for the same purpose.

As the gentlemen and their two recruited players walked back to the cricket pitch, Mr. Darcy asked Miss Elizabeth if she would care for a brief explanation of the game.

Miss Elizabeth shook her head, and with a conspiratorial glance at Mr. Bingley, explained, "Jane may prefer that I not admit the truth of it, but our father was once an avid fan of the game, and as he had no sons, but five daughters, he would occasionally hold cricket matches for us in our younger years. Being a girl who had yet learned to restrain my curiosity, which I may as well admit is a vice that remains with me to this day, I could not be satisfied with only having our father bowl to me and begged him to instruct me. Perhaps even Jane, but most particularly my mother, would be scandalized to learn that I occasionally joined in matches with the neighborhood boys, though I am proud to say my superior skills earned me the position of bowler on more than one occasion."

As teams were selected, Miss Elizabeth and Mrs. Beaumont announced that they had no fear of being outplayed by the gentlemen, and would partner as batsmen while Mr. Beaumont continued as bowler. Though the ladies had no qualms against batting, they were at least civilized enough to declare themselves unsuited to fielding, and rather enjoyed racing between the wickets as the gentlemen ran and dove for their hits.

"Now Elizabeth," said Mrs. Beaumont, "do not think we can end our little tournament here without asking you to display your boasted bowling abilities for us."

"Here, here!" chimed Mr. Beaumont, "Evelyn, I will be your second while we allow Miss Bennet a few rounds, and once she has warmed up, I for one would like to see her challenge the self-reputed Mr. Darcy."

Mr. Bingley laughed and trotted off to the outfield while Mr. Darcy smirked and remained near the infield. After a few mediocre bowls, Elizabeth was fairly consistent, casting a variety of difficult bowls and even upsetting the wicket on a few occasions. Mrs. Beaumont laughingly declared defeat, and passed the bat to Mr. Darcy.

Mr. Darcy made an embellished show of a few practice swings before stepping into position, and nodded to indicate himself ready for the bowl. His first hit went sailing into air, landing cleanly beyond the established boundary, scoring six runs. Displaying more irritation than she felt over the smug look of satisfaction on his face, she bowled thrice more before attaining success. Mr. Darcy had apparently judged his hit would go over Mr. Bingley's head, yet as he turned to double back to the wicket at the batting end of the cricket pitch, Mr. Beaumont ran up behind and catching the ball on a single bounce, threw it expertly back to Elizabeth, who tossed the ball at the wicket, upsetting the bails before Mr. Darcy could score.

"Out!" called Mr. Beaumont as Mr. Darcy exaggeratedly slumped his shoulders in defeat.

"I believe you have been run out, Mr. Darcy," Miss Elizabeth teased impishly.

Alexander chose this moment to vocally express himself in need of his mother, and after a few minutes' attempt to settle the baby, Mrs. Beaumont related her intent to set him down for a nap. The Bingleys joined her in returning to the house while Mr. Beaumont set about having the cricket supplies put away.

"It is too bad, Mr. Darcy, that I did not get the opportunity to put your bowling skills to the test," said Miss Elizabeth.

"That can easily be changed Miss Bennet, with need for little more than bat and ball," Mr. Darcy replied, holding up the two indicated items in his hands.

Elizabeth accepted the bat, marching confidently to the bowling field as Mr. Darcy moved to prepare for his delivery. Mr. Beaumont glanced over his shoulder at the antics between the pair, chuckling softly as he continued on, opting to go to the stables and check in with his head groom before dispatching a man to collect the sporting equipment.

A pleasant half hour was spent with Mr. Darcy bowling several times to Elizabeth before retreating to field the balls and bowl again. He even went so far as to advise Elizabeth on her posture as she swung, the slightly awkward experience having a positive impact on her performance, greatly increasing the distance Mr. Darcy jogged across the lawn to retrieve her subsequent hits.

When it was agreed they ought to return to the house for tea, Mr. Darcy gathered their equipment neatly and offered his arm to escort Miss Elizabeth back to the house. He hoped she would not object to the fact that he had neglected to replace his coat, and smiled to himself as she took his arm without calling attention to his continued state of informal dress.

Choosing a circuitous route through the garden, the two had yet to approach the house when a loud voice could be heard making demands of the Beaumonts' housekeeper. Miss Elizabeth looked puzzled while

Mr. Darcy's countenance went cold as he recognized the unmistakable voice.

"I demand that you take me to my nephew at once! Do you know who I am? Have you no shame over employing yourself in a household where such infamous behavior is taking place?" Finally, the lady's tirade was ended as she rounded the corner of the garden and came face to face with the solemn mien of the very nephew whose presence she required.

"Aunt Catherine," Mr. Darcy greeted evenly.

Lady Catherine's shock was evident, and as she delayed her response, Miss Elizabeth was left to wonder whether the great lady was most disturbed by her nephew's casual attire or her own presence on his arm. Though Mr. Darcy may have found the continuation of her silence preferable, it was but a moment before Lady Catherine regained her powers of speech.

"Darcy, there you are. What on earth possessed you to visit these people I cannot imagine, and though I have expressed such sentiments to you previously, I had not the slightest idea of the objectionable company they dare to keep while you are in residence here." She sneered, turning disdainfully towards Miss Elizabeth and commanded, "You *will* release my nephew."

Mr. Darcy's free hand rose from his side, but before he could place it protectively over Miss Elizabeth's, the young lady tactfully removed her arm from his. Knowing her presence to be superfluous to an impending conversation that was certain to be rather unpleasant, Elizabeth distanced herself from the gentleman and his relation.

Mr. Darcy sighed, and recognizing the wisdom of Miss Elizabeth's actions, responded to the lesser offensive of his aunt's presumptions. "Mr. Beaumont and I attended Cambridge together, as I am sure you are aware."

"Regardless I am shocked to see you wasting your time here, and when I heard of the company you are keeping in this house I resolved to come immediately and bring you to your senses. Now that I have seen with my own eyes that you have come to no serious harm, I insist that you join me in resolving the matter at hand. Am I to understand that Mr. Collins' fiancée is also in residence here at present?"

Miss Elizabeth blanched, grateful to be facing away from the conversation she could not help overhearing, but Mr. Darcy answered calmly, "I was not aware that Mr. Collins is engaged."

"Do not play me for a fool, nephew! It has come to my attention that you have been here under the same roof as that infamous Miss Bennet! I demand that she be brought to my attention at once."

At this, Miss Elizabeth – who had been all but ignored as Lady Catherine addressed her nephew – cleared her throat and approached the formidable lady with her head held high as Mr. Darcy performed the introduction.

"Aunt Catherine, may I present Miss Elizabeth Bennet?"

"Ah, so *you* are Elizabeth Bennet. I must inform you that I am most seriously displeased to find that you would attempt to ingratiate yourself with my nephew in such a manner. Your conduct is made all the more disgraceful by the fact that you yourself are engaged to Mr. Collins."

"Forgive me, your ladyship," Miss Elizabeth interjected with strained civility, "but I must inform you that I am in no way promised to Mr. Collins."

"Nonsense! All of Hunsford is aware of your engagement, and I understand from Mr. Collins that it is widely known near your father's estate in Hertfordshire as well. You should be ashamed of yourself for the manner in which you and your family have led him on. Your father has yet to invite your fiancé to return to your home and finalize the arrangements for your marriage, and I believe you are taking gross advantage of him in light of the entail upon your family's estate. I demand that you explain yourself to me."

Mr. Darcy clenched his fists as his indignation on Miss Elizabeth's behalf grew with each word spoken by his aunt, but before he could satisfy himself with any response, Miss Elizabeth spoke.

"Lady Catherine, your concern for your parson would be admirable if it were not so misguided. I have already stated that Mr. Collins and I are not engaged, and I am under no obligation to discuss the detailed affairs of myself or those of my family with a person so wholly unconnected with me."

Lady Catherine gasped dramatically and narrowed her eyes as she replied sharply, "Never before have I been exposed to such obstinate, disobliging behavior. When you have the good fortune of becoming

Mrs. Collins, an honor which I see you do not deserve, I suggest you reconsider your conduct, and if you atone yourself appropriately, I may deem to acknowledge you."

Greatly aware that any reply she might consider suitable would only add to the hostility of their conversation, Miss Elizabeth dropped a stiff curtsey and retreated towards the house. Without acknowledging the young lady's departure, Lady Catherine turned to address Mr. Darcy.

"Nephew, this has been a difficult journey and I insist that you escort me back to Rosings. While we are there, your engagement to Anne can finally be settled."

"I shall do no such thing," Mr. Darcy replied firmly, "Anne and I have mutually agreed that we are not amenable to the idea of a marriage between ourselves, and might I suggest that you should be perfectly able to return to Rosings Park the same way you arrived – without me."

"Nonsense. You cannot expect me to travel unaccompanied, and I have already given leave for Mr. Collins to join Miss Bennet and her relations on their journey back to Hertfordshire, that their wedding ceremony may be performed with no further delay. Before we leave, I must speak to that Mr. Bingley to ensure he understands his duty to support his future brother. He may need to assist Mr. Collins in procuring a marriage license, as well as seeing that the bride is instructed as to her proper place. As you see, I am excessively attentive to all these things, and even under such unusual circumstances, I have devised a suitable plan," Lady Catherine decreed.

Mr. Darcy furrowed his brow in consternation as he replied, "I fail to see what would be accomplished by Mr. Bingley's support when Miss Bennet's father is alive and well, but do you mean to say that Mr. Collins is here?"

At that moment, a loud slap was heard, and both Mr. Darcy and Lady Catherine turned their attention towards the scene unfolding across the lawn. Miss Elizabeth's posture was stiff as she glared indignantly at Mr. Collins, whose eyes were round with shock as he held a palm over his reddened cheek. Mr. Darcy immediately moved in their direction as a heated conversation began between two, rapidly increasing his pace as he saw Mr. Collins grabbing Miss Elizabeth firmly by the shoulders, seemingly ignorant to her protests as he simpered and smiled, his words indiscernible to the approaching gentleman.

As Mr. Darcy stormed up to the scene, two shocked faces turned towards him, though one looked rather confused and the other helpless. Mr. Darcy removed the offending hands, placing himself between Mr. Collins and Miss Elizabeth as he bellowed. "Mr. Collins! By what twist of your imagination do you dare think it appropriate to lay your hands upon this lady?"

Torn between showing deference to Lady Catherine's nephew and explaining his arrival to his supposed fiancée, Mr. Collins chose to proceed with a combination of the two. Bowing deeply to Mr. Darcy, he explained, "She is my betrothed, sir, and while I have gently attempted to increase her understanding of these matters, she is reluctant to further our courtship. It was my intent to provide to her those delicate displays of affection which are always reassuring to young ladies, that she might be comforted by introducing her sensibilities to the earnest nature of my desire for us to be wed. I flatter myself that you may already have been informed of my intentions to marry with utmost haste by the means your esteemed aunt has so generously provided."

"Are you convinced as to the veracity of your assertions, Mr. Collins?" Mr. Darcy inquired hotly, "As to your proclaimed engagement, conversations with the lady's father would lead me to believe otherwise."

Miss Elizabeth looked strangely at Mr. Darcy, wondering at the conversations to which he referred, however she was quick to confirm the gentleman's statement as she added, "Yes, I understand my father has even written to you to clarify any misapprehensions you may have been holding."

Mr. Collins looked smilingly at Miss Elizabeth, as though he were imploring her to grasp that the situation was beyond her understanding. He then turned to Mr. Darcy, and seemed to shift nervously at the prospect of disagreeing with so esteemed a personage. "Indeed sir, it is unfortunate that you seem to have been misinformed. The arrangement between Miss Elizabeth and myself is of long standing, its only hindrance being Mr. Bennet's failure to announce it publicly. I fear my cousin Bennet's health and soundness of mind must be declining more rapidly than we realize, as in light of the honor of my proposal, he cannot in good conscience mean to refuse me his daughter's hand. Under such circumstances, it is to my benefit that the eldest Miss Bennet has lately married, that Mr. Bingley might take on the expected role and set the situation between myself and Miss Elizabeth to rights. I cannot but express my felicity on our reunion, as is my privilege."

"How dare you–" Elizabeth's exclamation in defense of her father halted abruptly as to her horror, Mr. Collins again moved to embrace her – at which point Mr. Darcy punched him soundly in the face, his last ounce of restraint having been ripped to shreds, sending the stunned clergyman reeling backwards a few steps.

After staring icily at Mr. Collins to ensure that he had been properly understood, Mr. Darcy turned to Elizabeth, and speaking in as calm a voice as he could muster, said, "I believe my aunt and Mr. Collins have no further business at Ashingdon and will now be returning to Kent. Might I escort you to the house, Miss Bennet?"

Taking his offered arm with a small smile, Elizabeth replied, "Yes, Mr. Darcy, I believe I should like that."

The pair walked into the house without a backward glance.

Chapter 26

Upon returning to the house, Mr. Darcy and Miss Elizabeth were confronted with concerned and questioning gazes from the Beaumonts and the Bingleys. After establishing the identity of the mysterious guests, and learning that they had departed as quickly as they had arrived, the truth of the matter was pieced together with the aid of the housekeeper.

The master and mistress had both been unavailable when the formidable lady made her presence known, and even twenty years of service had left poor Mrs. Nicholls at a loss for how to handle the unprecedented insistence of the unexpected guest. Her polite inquiries and obliging suggestions were rebuffed almost before they were spoken, and within minutes she found herself trailing the fuming dowager instead of leading the guest as convention required.

Mrs. Nicholls apologized thoroughly and sincerely to both Miss Elizabeth and Mr. Darcy, the latter of whom assured her she had performed her duty well, as he had yet to come across another soul besides his uncle with the aptitude to influence his aunt, and even the Earl's abilities were limited, and primarily based on his role as head of the family.

After some minutes of relating the basic elements of their conversations, Miss Elizabeth added little to the conversation and seemed to drift into reverie. Observing this, Mr. Darcy turned his attention towards her, "May I enquire after your health Miss Bennet? I must say I am impressed by your fortitude, as I would expect anyone to be more shaken by this afternoon's events than you seem to be. I hope you are not suffering under any false belief that you need hide your distress."

Miss Elizabeth came back to attention at the sound of his voice, and was struck by the tender expression in his eyes as he made his earnest inquiry. Until this moment, she had never realized how much she truly esteemed and cared for the gentleman, despite her efforts to suppress the sentiments.

"Believe me, sir, I am well. If anything I need but a few moments to absorb the reality of such an unexpected event. Though your hand, Mr. Darcy," she said, looking pointedly at the red and swollen knuckles resting gingerly in the palm of his left hand, "allow me to send for some cool bandages to ease the swelling. Mrs. Nicholls?"

The housekeeper nodding understandingly and excused herself, returning a short time later to inform Mr. Darcy that his valet would be ready to attend him at his convenience. As Mr. Darcy rose to excuse himself, the conversation lulled, and Mrs. Bingley offered to escort her sister upstairs, under the pretense of dressing for dinner. In truth, she wished to provide support and comfort by allowing Elizabeth to speak of any details she preferred not to address in company. However Elizabeth had little to express that had not already been said, as there were many particulars of Mr. Collins' ludicrous behavior that would only distress her sister. She had many more concerns besides, but they were related to a much more proper gentleman, and she dared not speak of them to anyone.

A Noteworthy Courtship

None too soon for Elizabeth's preference, the party gathered for dinner; Elizabeth making a genuine effort to buoy her spirits and Mr. Darcy exuding a small amount of embarrassment over the bandaged hand he attempted to conceal. After a few moments of silence, Miss Elizabeth impertinently declared that no somber atmosphere was required on her account. She would much rather discuss their plans for the upcoming days, and she reminded them that they had yet to speak of the day's cricket match. The forced nature of her speech was not lost on anyone, though understanding her desire to put the unchangeable past behind her, they complied. Jane smirked at her sister and stated that she was rather surprised by the *interesting* knowledge her husband seemed to have obtained during the course of the afternoon, to which Elizabeth replied that Jane should consider herself fortunate that the subject was not addressed when she shared childhood stories at the engagement dinner at Netherfield. Mr. Bingley declared how scandalized his sisters would have been to hear such a thing, and Miss Elizabeth performed a skillful impression of her mother expressing her conviction that Mr. Bingley would be driven away by such shameful anecdotes. These remarks drew laughing responses from all, and the party settled into their typical joviality, discussing potential activities for their remaining days together.

Miss Elizabeth's continued attempts at levity could only go so far as the evening went on. After dinner, the party adjourned to the drawing room, where it was requested that Elizabeth perform at the pianoforte. After playing a few songs from memory, Miss Elizabeth demurred and suggested that Mrs. Beaumont provide the remainder of the evening's entertainment. She then seated herself near the Bingleys and Mr. Beaumont, making a half-hearted effort at joining the conversation as her gaze periodically drifted to the severe gentleman seated slightly away from the group, alternating between scowling in no direction in particular and feigning attention to a book. If only Miss Elizabeth had known how much her subdued demeanor contributed to his foul mood, she would have greatly increased her efforts to engage the others in her typical lively manner.

A few minutes later, Mr. Darcy placed his unattended book on a side table, and gaining Mr. Beaumont's attention, requesting that the company might excuse them for a private conference. Assuming his friend to be desirous of finalizing the purchase of his stallion and a few other horses, Mr. Bingley shrugged, and smilingly announced to the ladies that he would gladly keep them entertained until the other gentlemen returned.

The ladies did not see Mr. Darcy again that evening, excepting his brief appearance in the drawing room to bid the party good night. As the hour grew late, Elizabeth and Jane expressed their wish to retire for the evening, and after a quick assurance that she was well, Elizabeth parted her sister's company in the hall, entering her room for a long period of mulling over the day's diverse events.

೭೭೭

The next morning, Miss Elizabeth rose early, as was her custom, and though she had come to fondly anticipate his company, she was relieved to find Mr. Darcy absent. She was anxious to enjoy a solitary walk, allowing nature's tranquility to calm her jumbled thoughts without the hindrance of making polite conversation. After walking the meadows and groves she had come to know quite well, Miss Elizabeth turned back towards the house. As Ashingdon came into view, she espied none other than Mr. Darcy walking towards her across the drive, the gravel crunching beneath his boots and the morning sun silhouetting his figure as he emerged from the shadow of the house. Elizabeth offered a friendly smile, which he returned as he addressed her.

"Miss Bennet, we are all just assembling in the breakfast room if you would care to join us for refreshment from your morning walk."

Miss Elizabeth accepted his arm and looked up at him curiously. He knew very well that she took a light repast before walking out that she might return in time to dine with the rest of the household, as he had frequently joined her in just such a pursuit. She wondered at his seemingly having ventured out for the sole purpose of escorting her back in, but he seemed silently contented as usual, and she gave the matter no further scrutiny as they continued on into the house.

The pair exchanged fond good mornings with the Beaumonts and the Bingleys before moving to the sideboard. Mr. Darcy poured himself a cup of coffee and stood beside the table, taking Elizabeth's plate and assisting her with her chair before returning to the sideboard to fill his own plate with a warm and hearty breakfast.

A Noteworthy Courtship

"I am glad you have joined us, Mr. Darcy," said Mrs. Beaumont, "for I understand there is some great secret in our plans for the day. Andrew was kind enough to tell me that you had made a suggestion yesterday evening, but refused to tell me any further details."

"It is nothing so grand or unusual," replied Mr. Darcy, "I merely wished to discover if it were feasible before announcing it at large. Yesterday's cricket match put me in mind of another hobby we enjoyed at Cambridge, though I hope the ladies will not be unsettled by the prospect."

"If you are suggesting steeplechase, I am not sure it would be advisable for any of the ladies to participate," laughed Mr. Bingley, "though for Elizabeth's sake, I ought to hope there is no riding involved whatsoever."

"No Bingley," Mr. Darcy replied, "I'll leave the fox and hound chases for another day, and though we will need to travel a few miles, whether we do so by carriage or on horseback is of little consequence, as I understand from Beaumont the surrounding lanes provide a route that is not particularly circuitous."

"What say you Mrs. Bingley, Evelyn, shall I call for the carriage or the curricle?" inquired Mr. Beaumont with a smile.

"I believe this has gone far enough!" Miss Elizabeth cried teasingly, "By this description, you would all think me deathly afraid of horses instead of merely lacking the fondness for riding you all possess. I have never been one to allow myself to be intimidated, and it is no great sacrifice for me to ride simply because it is not my preference."

"Forgive me, Miss Elizabeth, you are correct. I should not have presumed so," said Mr. Beaumont, "And are the other ladies determined to ride as well?"

Mrs. Bingley nodded her acquiescence, and Mr. Darcy finally became aware of the grin that had spread across his face when Miss Elizabeth declared her intention to ride.

"Bravo, Elizabeth!" cheered Mrs. Beaumont, "I am glad I am not the only one whose courage rises when others make such assumptions. I gather I would be correct in assuming that you did not travel here with suitable riding attire, however we are of similar height and I should be able to outfit you accordingly, if you would accompany me after the meal."

Conversation then turned to the details of the day's activities, at which Mr. Darcy primarily remained silent and Mr. Beaumont rebuffed all inquiries.

The ladies then rose to don their riding habits, owned and borrowed, assuring the gentlemen that with any luck they would return within the hour. Mr. Darcy was pleased to see no sign of the distress he expected to appear on Elizabeth's face at the prospect of riding on horseback to their destination. *Perhaps it shall be her Connemara after all.*

Chapter 27

Properly attired, the group of six, most of whom would consider themselves more accurately described as three couples, walked towards the stables. Mr. Darcy wondered if it would be inadvisable to ask Miss Elizabeth when she last rode, and instead asked if she had occasioned to visit the stables at Ashingdon and set her eye on a particular horse. After hearing her negative response, he suggested she look at a few suitable horses, as Mr. Beaumont could advise her of their temperaments. Miss Elizabeth laughingly stated her only requirement was that she not be seated on a twin of Mr. Bingley's black beast, who flicked his head impatiently as a groom approached his stall. Mr. Bingley laughed at the ominous description of his stallion, while Mr. Darcy smiled understandingly, and along with Mrs. Bingley, they walked towards the mares and ponies.

Mrs. Bingley's mare was first, and as she reached to stroke its soft muzzle, a gray head emerged from the next stall, belonging to none other than the dappled Connemara whose coat Mrs. Beaumont had teasingly admired. Miss Elizabeth shrugged, and seeing that the horse seemed friendly enough, considered one unfamiliar horse not greatly different from another. She informed Mr. Darcy that while she still lacked the skill to show a horse to its advantage, he would see her mounted on the horse he intended for his sister after all.

Once each horse had been saddled and the riders mounted, the group was only able to ascertain from Mr. Beaumont that they would be riding approximately seven miles, and would be traveling south. Mrs. Beaumont smiled knowingly, and suggesting they may as well proceed, moved to ride beside her husband as they crossed the fields.

Miss Elizabeth was the last to move, as her horse seemed content to placidly follow the movement of the other horses. Jane momentarily held back, but with a reassuring smile from Elizabeth and a nod from Mr. Darcy, she visibly relaxed and shared her attention between her husband and her sister.

Elizabeth released her stiffness in the saddle as she became accustomed to the horse's rhythmic movement. Glancing over at Mr. Darcy who was riding nearby, she noted the lighter coloring of his horse and asked if he were riding his usual mount. The gentleman smiled lightly in appreciation of her having taken notice, and explained that he had indeed chosen a different horse for this ride, as geldings are by nature more docile and better suited to riding in a large group. He then pointed to Mr. Bingley's stallion, which proved his point with perfect timing as it skitted away from Jane's mare. Mr. Darcy then allowed his horse to fall into step with Elizabeth's, and she smiled appreciatively at his thoughtfulness.

As the group traveled across the lush fields, Elizabeth realized that the leisurely pace and refreshing sea breeze made the ride more enjoyable than she had expected, though if directly questioned she would have admitted to prefer traveling afoot, despite the lengthier amount of time needed to cover the same distance. Soon the grassy fields gave way to marshes and sand bars, and Mr. Darcy came alongside to inform her that they were near their destination.

A small village came into view, which the Beaumont's indicated to be Benfleet. As Benfleet consisted of no more than a few shops, it was not long before they reached the outskirts of the far side of the village heading in the direction of a wide placid creek, near which was situated a small building with a sign reading "Boat Hire" at the foot of a short pier. Mr. Bingley laughed merrily at the sight of it, making a few comments to his wife, and continued to smile at the idea as the group approached the establishment and dismounted.

As the proprietor spoke to the gentlemen of his available services and vessels for hire, Miss Elizabeth was surprised that rather than a larger touring vessel suitable for the entire group, their attention seemed focused on a series of rowboats. After a few minutes, the gentlemen returned to the ladies to discuss their plans.

"As you may have already guessed," Mr. Beaumont smiled, "our grand scheme for the day is a small boating excursion about Canvey Island – that is, if you ladies do not object to such conveyance."

"I think the idea is quite charming," Mrs. Bingley reassured.

"I am surprised by your choice, Mr. Darcy," said Elizabeth, "though I suppose the proprietor has gone to fetch his boatmen."

"Indeed not, Miss Elizabeth. Though the Boat Club at Cambridge had not been officially formed at the time of our attendance, rowing was a sport we three quite enjoyed, often without boatmen to do the rowing."

"And as much as Beaumont here will boast of his skills on the cricket pitch, it was rowing for which Mr. Darcy garnished the most attention." Added Mr. Bingley.

"Well it cannot be helped, considering his extraordinarily height! We should have shortened his paddles as a handicap," laughed Mr. Beaumont, "But enough of our reminiscence, what say you ladies to a tour about the island? We gentlemen, of course, will allow you to peacefully take in the scenery as we transport you."

"It will be most practical to pair ourselves in three separate vessels," Mr. Darcy added hesitantly, his eyes darting towards Miss Elizabeth.

Charmed by his uncertainty, Elizabeth replied with a smile, "Never fear, Mr. Darcy, I recognize the pairings that would be most preferable to the other members of our party, and my brother need not fear entrusting me to your company."

"I appreciate your faith in me, Miss Elizabeth," Mr. Darcy replied, meeting her gaze intently as he offered his arm to follow the other couples down the dock.

"After all," Miss Elizabeth baited playfully, attempting to ease the impression of his earnest remark, "I should have no reason to suspect any untoward behavior from a gentleman I am not handsome enough to tempt."

Miss Elizabeth tried desperately to restrain her soft giggles as Mr. Darcy struggled to keep the firm set of his jaw, while her sister Jane had no success in her similar endeavor and gaped at her in a rather unladylike fashion.

"Forgive me, Mr. Darcy," Elizabeth said lightly, "I believe I warned you of my tendency towards impertinence, though I hope you realize I would not jest so if we had not settled this matter between us."

Mr. Darcy seemed to relax and made a faint attempt to smile. Miss Elizabeth observed the questioning gaze from Mr. Beaumont and the responding nod from Mr. Darcy, wondering if there was only person present who was not privy to his remark, and the lady would soon be informed.

The proprietor could then be seen coming up the dock with a young boatman, and Mr. Darcy offered Miss Elizabeth his hand to steady herself as she stepped into the boat, waiting until she was firmly seated before stepping in himself. The wooden boat swayed gently from side to side as Mr. Darcy moved towards the bow, setting the oars to rights before the boatman untied the rope securing them to the dock and gave them a push towards the open water.

"Do not get yourself too far ahead of us, Darcy!" called Mr. Bingley.

Mr. Darcy's response to his friend's gaiety was more negligible than usual, and with a few long strokes, they began to glide swiftly across the peaceful water. After a few minutes of silence, Mr. Darcy's expression was particularly pensive, and he seemed to be applying more concentration than necessary into rowing, as his eyes had yet to turn towards the surrounding scenery. Miss Elizabeth watched him fixedly, wondering if her teasing was the subject of his reflections. Moments later, Mr. Darcy realized the attention he had drawn as he caught the intent gaze of the lady facing him.

"How our acquaintance might have been different had I not insulted you." He said wistfully as he turned his attention back to the oars.

Elizabeth offered a gentle smile as she said good-naturedly, "Oh, but that would have deprived us of criticizing stares met with incivility, heated debates and dancing in silence, all brought to a climax of scathing remarks." The expression of her voice was light and teasing, though understanding was portrayed in her eyes.

"I am glad you can think so lightly of past offences, Miss Bennet."

"I would not have you think that I do, however to understand this, you must learn some of my philosophy. Think only of the past as its remembrance gives you pleasure. It is much easier to move forward when one puts this theory into practice."

"I imagine so," Mr. Darcy then smiled as he added, "There are plenty of fond remembrances I have from my time in Hertfordshire."

"The shooting must have been rather fine then, or perhaps your bent is more in favor of riding across the countryside."

"I do enjoy a shooting party and a good ride, though the fond memories I have of each are from Derbyshire," he said, his intent gaze leaving her not entirely composed.

The implication of his words was not lost on Miss Elizabeth, but whether he intended to flatter her, was attempting to reveal himself as her correspondent, or she was severely unhinged for drawing such conclusions, she could not gather.

"Miss Elizabeth, surely you..."

"Well this is a fine way to go about rowing!" Mr. Bingley called amiably, "It is as though Miss Elizabeth has forbid you from touching the oars to the water."

"Bingley, you spend entirely too much time with Mr. Hurst. Even I recognize his mode of expression in that statement." laughed Mr. Beaumont.

For a fleeting moment, Mr. Darcy seemed to be gathering his composure before managing to regain his stoic façade. Miss Elizabeth smiled nervously, and Mr. Darcy shrugged as he grabbed the oars and said, "Well, I suppose I cannot let him get away now, can I?"

The gentlemen exhausted themselves sufficiently in a display which they all termed a good-spirited race for old time's sake, though in reality it may have been more an effort to outdo one another and impress the ladies bearing witness to their exertions. Afterwards, they allowed their momentum to gently fade, leisurely floating along the creek as their proximity allowed for pleasant conversation. Mrs. Beaumont spoke of their first excursion to Canvey Island, which occurred while she was still Miss Howard. Mr. Beaumont explained that the far end of the creek reached the River Thames and in a larger vessel they might use the river to circle the island as it extended into the bay. Soon a turning point was suggested, and the gentlemen set about turning the boats with their oars before heading back in the direction from which they came.

Miss Elizabeth noticed Mr. Darcy's decidedly slower pace and wondered if he would continue their earlier conversation which had ended so abruptly.

"It is hard to recall that such tumultuous events occurred only yesterday when in surroundings such as this," he offered hesitantly.

"I believe I owe you many thanks for your assistance, sir," Elizabeth replied.

"Do not trouble yourself. If my aunt had not brought him here, the scene would never have taken place."

"I must admit your aunt is a bit more formidable than Mr. Collins' descriptions would lead one to believe."

Mr. Darcy let out one short chuckle at so restrained a description of his aunt. "Yes I dare say she is, and she has never been one to apologize for her frankness. I, however, hope I did not offend you with my ungentlemanly display."

Elizabeth smiled impishly, "Fear not, Mr. Darcy, for your conduct puts me in mind of my own similar behavior just minutes before."

Mr. Darcy grinned. He could not but be proud of her literally striking out in self-defense, and given what he knew of her character, knew he should have expected nothing less. "I only hope his eye heals before Sunday. I should not have acted so rashly."

"Do not overly concern yourself, I am grateful for your interference, and it seems Mr. Collins had already enlisted a suitable curate in anticipation of his absence, though for a different reason to be sure." Elizabeth shuddered slightly at the thought. "I had no idea my cousin would be so obtusely persistent."

When Elizabeth looked towards Mr. Darcy, she saw his eyes gleaming mischievously and his shoulders begin to quake with mirth. With a raised brow her only demand for explanation, he said humorously, "I am afraid, Miss Elizabeth, you may have to get yourself engaged just to fend the man off!"

The words were spoken before Mr. Darcy could regret the implication of them, and he laughed more strongly than was his wont to emphasize the levity of his remark, an action which Miss Elizabeth graciously mimicked – albeit with less enthusiasm. Neither wished to acknowledge the awkwardness of his possible suggestion that she become engaged to himself, as they both wished for just that and were convinced the other could not possibly be in agreement.

Conversation between the two floundered as each made stilted attempts at introducing a new topic, though as is often the case when avoiding a certain subject, most all topics they could think of were loosely related to the cause of their awkwardness, and rejected before they were spoken. Mr. Darcy's frustration grew such that he considered telling her all, as he could not imagine the situation getting any worse than it already was, and he had already come quite close to speaking of it. However the possibility of rejection followed by a long ride to Ashingdon did not appeal to him. Thankfully, it did not take much effort for Mr. Darcy to catch up with the others, and before long, the dock at Benfleet came into view.

Their feet once again firmly planted on dry land, a general consensus for refreshment was made, and the group walked into the small village of Benfleet for a late luncheon. The meal was not prolonged as several were anxious to return to Ashingdon, particularly Mrs. Beaumont, who expressed her anxiety over such a long separation from her son. The gentlemen went to retrieve the horses, and soon all members of the party were mounted and headed towards Hadleigh.

వచచచ

After the pleasant outing to Canvey Island, any uneasiness caused by the fiasco the day before had dissipated, and the renewed sense of merriment continued over the next few days. Miss Elizabeth settled back into a routine of early morning walks with Mr. Darcy and days spent in company with her sister and hostess, typically joined by the gentlemen for tea. A few more picnics and trips to the coast were enjoyed when the weather was particularly fine. It was on just such a day that Miss Elizabeth found herself casually perusing the beach for shells, her sister sitting on a blanket beside a lounging Mr. Bingley, and Mr. Darcy walking by her side.

After reaching to pick up another shell, Elizabeth looked out across the salty waters and remarked on how quickly such environs had grown on her since arriving in Essex, shyly adding that such pleasant company had only added to the positive experience.

"I shall be sorry not to continue in your company then, as I will be returning to London shortly," said Mr. Darcy.

"Such things are inevitable for any gentleman who does not live a life of idleness, though I am sure we shall all be sorry to see you go," Elizabeth replied, "When must you depart?"

"The day following the morrow would be best. I have a few matters to address in London before I must journey to Derbyshire," Mr. Darcy smiled ever so slightly as he added, "I am afraid there was more truth to my aunt's words than I would like to admit."

"I see."

Mr. Darcy realized her misinterpretation of his ill-phrased remark, teasing though it may have been. "Miss Bennet, I can see the turn your mind is taking, and no, it is not what you think. The only truth to my aunt's statements is simply that it is time for me to leave Ashingdon. I shall not be long in my own home before traveling again, though not in the direction she would prefer. Mr. and Mrs. Bingley have invited me to Netherfield, and I will travel to Derbyshire that Georgiana might join me in accepting the Bingleys' hospitality. I must remain in the north at least a week or perhaps two in order to tend my estate business. I have been away from Pemberley for far too long, though I am sure you can imagine why." He met her eye with a meaningful expression as he said the last.

Miss Elizabeth looked away embarrassedly as she said, "I am anxious to renew my acquaintance with your sister. Though I have not had the pleasure of knowing her long, I hope to soon think of her as a dear friend."

"I imagine there is more than one friendship you will be able to strengthen when you return to Hertfordshire."

Elizabeth was again left to wonder whether he alluded to a possible attachment on his part, or perhaps a friendship founded in his potential identity as her correspondent, a confusion she felt all too frequently of late.

Mr. Darcy was not afforded the opportunity to walk out with Miss Elizabeth the following morning, as the business of purchasing a few of Beaumont's horses and arranging their transport to his own stables took much of the morning. When his carriage pulled up before the house the day of his departure, it felt as though he had scarce been able to enjoy her company since their last beach excursion. As the Beaumonts and their remaining guests gathered outside to bid their farewells, Mr. Darcy was grateful for his last conversation with Miss

Elizabeth, as the present company afforded him no more than a lingering kiss on the hand as he bid his beloved a formal adieu.

Chapter 28

Upon her return to Hertfordshire, Miss Elizabeth became more unsure of her new impression of Mr. Darcy with each day that passed without bringing his return. The gross impropriety of Mr. Collins' arrival at Ashingdon had been shocking at best, and she could not imagine any gentleman maintaining an interest in the face of such relations – except that the presumptuous scheme seemed to have been orchestrated by his own aunt. She feared the scandal that would develop from her cousin's misconceptions, but fortunately news of it had yet to reach her mother, as none of their acquaintance resided in Kent, aside from the gentleman in question. If he had been so bold as to have written of his folly to her father, Mr. Bennet had not spoken of it.

Their recent holiday was frequently discussed when the Bennets and the Bingleys sought each other's company, and aside from uninvited visitors and perhaps an improprietous sporting match, most all details of their time in Essex were discussed. Mr. Bennet was visibly displeased upon hearing of Mr. Darcy's presence at Ashingdon, and though Mr. Bingley reminded his wife's father that he had told him as much in the first of many letters sent during their stay, he soon learned that any references to Mr. Darcy's friendship with Elizabeth were not well received, and he would do best to remain silent on the subject.

Equally inadvisable, in terms of conversation with Mr. Bennet, would be raising the subject of her correspondent, and with little desire to raise her father's suspicions and incite such a conversation, Miss Elizabeth thought it best to delay her excursion to the bookshop, despite her anticipation of returning to her most enjoyable mode of communication. So it was that three days passed before she allowed her rambles to lead her into the bookshop.

Upon entering the establishment, Miss Elizabeth observed Mr. Awdry's nephew standing behind the counter, and greeted him cheerfully as he indicated the location of several books recently arrived from London. She was courteous enough to peruse them before setting about her original intent, however as she carefully removed a folded note from her reticule, she found its hiding place mysteriously absent. She furrowed her brow, wondering how she could have forgotten its exact location, gradually becoming more concerned as closer examination of the surrounding shelves did not reveal the title she sought. Her search eventually came to the attention of the young man behind the counter, who good-naturedly came to offer his assistance.

"Is there something in particular I might help you with, Miss Elizabeth? My uncle is away at present, and though I have yet to become as knowledgeable regarding his inventory as he, I hope I may be of assistance."

"Thank you," Miss Elizabeth smiled weakly as she tried to calm the frantic edge to her voice. "I was... looking for a particular title I know my father might enjoy, and had thought I remembered seeing it in this section previously."

Matthew Awdry hesitated, furrowing his brow ever so slightly as though debating whether or not to speak on the subject. "There was a gentleman who came in a few weeks ago. I believe I had seen him previously on occasion, and he did make a purchase which I believe came from these shelves." Noting the lady's rapt attention, he added, "As I recall it was by Storne or..."

"Sterne?"

"Yes, that was it."

Miss Elizabeth could not restrain the eager inquiry in her expression and young Mr. Awdry added, "I am not aware of the gentleman's identity, as we have never been properly introduced and I had not previously seen him above twice, though he is of light build, perhaps my uncle's height, fair hair, and I gathered he came from at least some distance as his coat was equally brown with road dust as with natural color. Perhaps he is in your father's employ?"

"I do not believe my father employs a man by that description, though I appreciate your information. I shall simply continue to browse for another of my father's favorites. Though I know he would enjoy that particular author, he would enjoy many others as well, so it is of little consequence."

Matthew Awdry nodded his head and left her to the pretense of browsing, not observing the petite figure that left the shop almost the very moment he retreated to the back room.

As she walked along the familiar paths back to Longbourn, Elizabeth's feelings of surprise and confusion over the missing book turned to disappointment and frustration. Any hopes she had of continuing the exchange of notes had disappeared with Sterne's title. While she was not certain that the book had been purchased by her correspondent, she admitted that seemed the most likely possibility. She was bothered by a twinge of disappointment that the man described bore no resemblance to Mr. Darcy. She admitted that as much as she had always anticipated reading *his* notes, she had returned from Essex hoping to find additional support in the notes for the notion of Mr. Darcy having written them. She now deemed her suspicions of Mr. Darcy to have been completely irrational. She knew Mr. Darcy had been absent, and it was not until she saw him in a more favorable light that she began to consider him, despite the facts that discredited the possibility. Yet her mind had latched on to the favorable prospect of the two men she most esteemed being one and the same – *how terribly convenient*.

Upon returning to Hertfordshire, Mr. Bingley could no longer avoid inviting his sisters to Netherfield, and though Miss Bingley would no longer be mistress of the house, the invitation was one that could not be politely refused. So it was that within a week of the Bingleys' return, Netherfield was occupied much as it had been since Mr. Bingley's first having taken possession of the house, with one unmistakable addition. Mrs. Bennet gloried in her status of mother to the mistress of Netherfield, just as she had before the trip to Essex, which at least one member of the traveling party began to believe had not been long enough. Mrs. Bennet astounded her second daughter with her ability to ignore the subtly hostile comments made by Miss Bingley and Mrs.

Hurst, though they gave every appearance of civility in their brother's presence.

One morning, after the Hursts and Miss Bingley had been in residence at Netherfield Park just less than a week, Elizabeth was approached by Mrs. Hill, who slipped a note into her hand as Elizabeth smiled in appreciation. It had become a frequent occurrence since Jane's marriage for the sisters to exchange notes by way of servants, as their mother's tenacity scarcely allowed for private conversations, and any letters delivered by less covert means may as well be addressed to the family at large. This particular note had been written the evening before, and in it Jane related that Mr. and Miss Darcy had arrived that afternoon, and would certainly be agreeable to Elizabeth's company at her earliest convenience. Elizabeth dressed quickly, stopping in the kitchen for a few breakfast rolls before heading out with the intent of taking a leisurely walk across the blooming countryside that she might arrive at her sister's house when an appropriate hour for making calls was reached. Upon reaching Netherfield, the housekeeper directed her to an antechamber where she might refresh herself before joining the ladies in the morning room. Elizabeth greeted Miss Darcy warmly, and tolerated Miss Bingley and Mrs. Hurst as best she could. Soon the ladies were joined by the gentlemen, and just as expected, Mr. Bingley's sisters improved their demeanor in their brother's presence.

Another of the gentlemen was more surprising however. After having been accustomed to relaxed greetings and occasional smiles, Miss Elizabeth was struck by the stiff formality of Mr. Darcy's curt bow and short address. Her only comfort was that he showed little more warmth to the other ladies present, save his sister. He did seat himself in a chair near the sofa where Elizabeth and his sister were seated, making occasional attempts at contributing to the conversation, though he was just as frequently addressed by Miss Bingley. As the hour for luncheon drew near, Elizabeth politely refused an invitation to remain, as she had not notified anyone besides Hill of her departure, but did accept Mr. Bingley's insistence that she make use of his carriage for her return to Longbourn.

Upon returning home, Elizabeth was scolded for her disappearance as well as her neglecting to inform her mother that the Darcy's had returned. Mrs. Bennet then announced her intention of calling the next day, in such a manner as to deny that she had every intention of visiting

Netherfield more days than not without any regard to what guests her daughter had in residence.

Thankfully the call the next morning did not last particularly long, as Jane regretfully informed her mother that she would be meeting with her housekeeper immediately following luncheon. At Miss Darcy's particular request, Miss Elizabeth was permitted to stay at Netherfield, though Mrs. Bennet's inability to extract a similar invitation for Kitty was quite vexing, as said daughter would have no opportunity to converse with Mr. Darcy.

After the meal, Mrs. Bingley withdrew as planned to meet with her housekeeper while Mr. Bingley saw the departing Bennets to their carriage. Mr. Darcy excused himself immediately after, shortly followed by Miss Bingley, who Elizabeth could not but suspect of intending to canvas the house in pursuit of the gentleman. Miss Darcy and Miss Elizabeth adjourned to the music room, as they were both eager for the opportunity to play together. At length they exhausted their fingers, and took a welcome respite from the pianoforte in favor of conversation. Miss Elizabeth mentioned a letter she had recently received from Mrs. Gardiner, and as she related a particular story regarding the antics of her young cousins, she was surprised to hear Georgiana gasp. The younger girl sheepishly admitted that the story reminded her of a letter from her Aunt Matlock, which related tales of her aunt's young grandchildren, and that with her recent traveling, she had yet to reply. Elizabeth insisted that it would be no inconvenience for her to find other entertainment as she would be perfectly content to wander the gardens while Georgiana attended to her letter.

"I have yet to give proper attention to the improvements Jane has been making to the gardens," Elizabeth explained, "and it would not do for me to compliment my sister on her efforts without having had the opportunity to fully appreciate them."

Mr. Darcy had been sulking – though he would never refer to his behavior as such – in his bedchamber, frustrated with this being his second occasion in two days to see Miss Elizabeth, and yet any attempt at private conversation seemed impossible. Elizabeth's sparkling conversation, which he had enjoyed so greatly in Hadleigh, seemed directed towards his sister rather than himself, and with every attempt to break the awkwardness that had developed between he and Elizabeth, Miss Bingley uniformly interrupted on some ridiculous pretense or other. On more than one occasion, he wished he had simply kept Sterne's book in his pocket that he might entice her into joining him in the hall under a ridiculous pretense of his own and let it be done with. He sighed; after so many months of delaying his disclosure, there was little sense in making a hasty business of it now.

With a determined huff, he rose, intent on devising an unshakable plan for revealing himself. As he reached the window, however, he was arrested by the blessed sight of Miss Elizabeth walking out towards the gardens, and as he stood transfixed, he confirmed that she was quite alone. Whether he reacted sedately as a proper gentleman ought or with the excitement of a schoolboy going out to play in the winter's first snow, no one bore witness, though a passing maid noted the purpose in his stride as he walked briskly down the hallway, tucking something into his pocket as he moved.

❧❧❧

"Miss Bennet," Mr. Darcy called out as he approached her.

His address reflected neither the coldness of his former manners that had reappeared with his return to Netherfield nor the ease she had come to expect in Hadleigh, such that she knew not quite what to make of him and replied cautiously, "Mr. Darcy."

"Miss Bennet, Elizabeth, I…there is something I must tell you before another word is spoken, for I fear I have delayed too long as it is."

Elizabeth had watched confusedly during his speech, all expression fading from her features as he reached to pull a leather-bound item from his coat pocket, extending it towards her.

Her breath caught her in her throat as she reached to accept the familiar book, her lips parting unknowingly as she ran her fingers across the familiar title stamped into the leather. *A Political Romance by Laurence Sterne.*

"All this time," she said earnestly, in barely more than a whisper, before looking up at Mr. Darcy with a small smile, "it was you."

"Yes," he answered, a hint of nervous hesitancy breaking the serious tone of his voice.

Elizabeth returned her eyes to the book resting in her hands, the truth taking root as she recalled bits and pieces of the letters she treasured, in her reverie the words now being spoken in his voice.

"You are not angry with me for concealing this from you?" he asked, concerned that she had not met his eye for some time.

"Nay, forgive me if I was momentarily lost in reflection. At present I feel a great sense of relief for finally knowing. Not long after our first meeting at Ashingdon, I wanted it to be you, and at times I thought it might be, but I dared not hope."

"And all the while, I have dared not hope to be well received," Mr. Darcy smiled widely, a gesture Elizabeth had come to anticipate since their curricle ride to Hadleigh Castle, and was greatly pleased to receive for the first time since their stay at Ashingdon.

A subtle awkwardness inevitably followed the imparting of information so monumental to the feelings of both parties, and Elizabeth anxiously explained how she had been exploring the gardens that she might appreciate the work her sister had commissioned over the spring. Mr. Darcy offered her his arm that he might join her in completing the tour. As they walked through the garden, conversation gradually warmed to the subject of their correspondence, as each party navigated the delicate task of meshing their written exchanges with the reality of their acquaintance. As Elizabeth saw more and more glimmers of the Mr. Darcy she had known at Ashingdon, she gave mention to his reverted behavior.

"Miss Elizabeth, you must forgive me if my conduct since returning to Netherfield gave you the impression that I no longer desired your good opinion."

"I suppose I should be more understanding, Mr. Darcy. Though your behavior is different than at Ashingdon, it is not new to me."

"You do realize the cause of that change, do you not?"

Elizabeth looked down, any reason she could surmise was either a slight to her family and general acquaintance, a disappointment to her own hopes, or both.

Mr. Darcy cleared his throat, "There are those in residence at Netherfield who hold opinions with which I no longer concur, and I have often realized silence is the best method of preventing a further onslaught."

"Is that your polite way of saying that the Great Mr. Darcy is afraid of Miss Bingley?" Elizabeth inquired impishly.

"Erm, I do not know about Great..."

Elizabeth laughed, "I will take that as a reply to the affirmative, though I will admit to a similar feeling towards some of the opinions expressed in my sister's house, and I shall have to take advantage of your method of dissuading them."

"I should warn you that an imposing figure is an integral part of my tactic. I hope that does not prevent your effective use of it."

"Nonsense," Elizabeth declared haughtily, her head held high and her features stern, "As an accomplished lady of good breeding, I can be perfectly imposing when I see fit."

The pair laughed companionably, and Elizabeth waited until their mirth had subsided to inquire further.

"I do hope you will not find it troublesome to remain at Netherfield." Realizing the forwardness that could be interpreted into her statement she stumblingly added, "I am greatly enjoying Georgiana's company, and I would not wish her to leave the country too soon."

"I would not be overly concerned. Though their plans are not entirely fixed, I have it on good authority that the Hursts will soon be returning to London, and Miss Bingley with them."

"Is that so? Oddly, I had been given quite a different impression by the ladies in question."

Mr. Darcy glanced around mischievously to ensure their privacy before leaning in to say, "It is amazing what the promise of a case of fine brandy and mention of upcoming card tournaments at his club in London can accomplish with respect to Mr. Hurst."

Elizabeth was left to her own opinion of whether the brandy was supplied from the cellar of Netherfield or of Pemberley, but smiled at the idea of it being a conjoined effort by the masters of both.

"Well then, with that information in mind, I shall be sure to wish them a pleasant journey when their plans are settled."

Chapter 29

Within a few days, the Hursts and Miss Bingley paid a call at Longbourn to take their leave of the Bennets. The call was rather short as they intended to travel London directly, but all was not lost as joining them in visiting Longbourn were the Bingleys and the Darcys. After the travelers departed, Elizabeth approached Georgiana and entered into conversation about their respective gardens and the many blooms brought by the changing of seasons since last they met. As a stroll in the gardens was suggested and accepted, Mr. Darcy watched his sister and his beloved exit the room, not knowing that this would provide an opportunity for a gentleman most desirous of a private audience.

"Mr. Darcy," Mr. Bennet greeted with bare civility, "how kind of you to join us this morning."

"The pleasure is all mine, sir," Mr. Darcy replied warily.

"Well sir, I am sure that Mrs. Bennet has plenty of things to discuss with Jane, and while I shall not tear Mr. Bingley from her side, I imagine you may find yourself more agreeably engaged amongst the books in my library."

Mr. Darcy accepted the subtle command gracefully, and motioned for Mr. Bennet to precede him out of the drawing room. Upon reaching the library and firmly closing the door, Mr. Bennet wasted little time in making his paternal sentiments known.

A Noteworthy Courtship

"Mr. Darcy, it is apparent that I did not sufficiently clarify the course of action I expected when last we met. Given your sudden departure following the wedding of my eldest daughter, I supposed myself to be with little option for recourse but to wash my hands of you, and considered that to be in the best interest of my second daughter, lest she find herself connected to a dishonorable gentleman. Yet I come to find that you have been in my daughter's company these six weeks at least during her stay in Essex, and now I find you present under my very roof."

"I had requested of Mr. Bingley that he communicate my intentions to you immediately upon my arrival at Ashingdon."

"Yes, and that garbled explanation was equally vague as it was illegible. Allow me to inform you sir, that you find me at my leisure this morning should you be inclined to explain yourself properly."

Mr. Darcy sighed. As much as he abhorred discussing his private matters, there was no gentleman to whom it would be more appropriate to relate these details than Elizabeth's father.

"I should begin, sir, by explaining that I have come to a much greater understanding of your daughter since last we spoke. While I believe her opinion to have undergone no small amount of change during that time, it would have been beneficial for me to heed your warning regarding her former opinion of me. I would not have you think my failure to approach you soon after our last conversation to be indicative of a lack of action on my part."

Mr. Bennet smirked. He dared not laugh in the face of the gentleman who – in his own round-about way – admitted to having received some form of rejection from his daughter, at least not until he had heard the rest of his story. He doubted Mr. Darcy would be so forthcoming if he knew himself to be a source of amusement.

Mr. Darcy cleared his throat and continued, "Having established the nature of the *difficulties* between Miss Elizabeth and myself, I endeavored to present myself more openly during our time in Hadleigh, such that I hope any information she may have related to you regarding my conduct there would show a marked improvement in her opinion."

"I admit, Mr. Darcy, my daughter has told me little of her trip that did not relate to Mrs. Beaumont or her young child. I did hear one particularly interesting story from Mr. Bingley involving a distant relation of mine, though from what I have heard, you were more directly involved in the event than Bingley himself."

Mr. Darcy reddened slightly, whether in anger or embarrassment Mr. Bennet could not tell, until the younger gentleman dropped his eyes to the floor momentarily before looking up and saying, "I suppose I ought to apologize for striking your cousin, sir. I hope you have not been offended by my actions."

"On the contrary, given the circumstances, I could not have handled it better myself. As a matter of fact, I understand my Lizzy quite agreed with such a course of action as well."

"That she did," Mr. Darcy could not help but smile proudly at the remembrance of the determined look on his Elizabeth's face as she stood proudly after slapping Mr. Collins soundly across the face.

"On a more serious note, however, I would have your word that you will bring this situation to a timely close, and to be certain that I will not be misunderstood, I shall clarify that the expected resolution would be your making an offer of marriage."

"I give you every assurance that my intent is to do exactly that, and if it were not for my respect of your daughter's opinion, I would have made such an offer some time ago."

"You might start by relating to her the purpose of your frequent trips to Mr. Awdry's establishment in Meryton, that she might form an honest opinion of you."

"I already have, sir."

Not wishing to reveal his surprise over this information, Mr. Bennet merely nodded his head. "Then I shall be expecting your request for a private audience before your next departure."

"You have my word, sir."

All necessities having been addressed, Mr. Darcy was more than happy to excuse himself from Mr. Bennet's presence. Upon gaining the hall, he required not a moment's deliberation to direct his course to the garden in hopes of locating Miss Elizabeth and his sister. He soon found the ladies seated on a garden bench while the youngest Bennet sisters could be seen laughing on the swing hanging from a large oak tree on the other side of the green.

The mutual enjoyment of the discourse between the two ladies of his highest esteem was evident as he approached, and Mr. Darcy was warmly welcomed into their conversation. Before long, the appropriate time for even a lengthy call had expired, and the party returned to the house, the Darcys thanking Mrs. Bennet for her hospitality as they joined Mr. and Mrs. Bingley in returning to Netherfield.

Chapter 30

The friendship between Miss Elizabeth and the Darcy siblings allowed her frequent reason for venturing to Netherfield to repay the courtesy of calls paid at Longbourn. Rare was the occasion that Mrs. Bennet did not conspire to send Kitty along with her elder sister; however, Mrs. Bennet was none the wiser that once she arrived at Netherfield, Kitty was most likely to be found in conversation with Jane and rarely spoke to Mr. Darcy beyond the necessary civilities. Jane did attempt to forward conversations between all of her guests, as any good hostess would be expected to do, and found little difficulty in initiating pleasant discussions between Kitty and Miss Darcy.

On one such occasion, Mr. Darcy realized he and Miss Elizabeth had been left to converse amongst themselves, and suggested a walk along the circuit path bordering the woods. Mr. Bingley offered to accompany them as a proper chaperone, but within a few yards of the front door, excused himself to the stables with a knowing smile. The remaining two paid him little attention, as their time at Ashingdon had accustomed them to the notion of walking together alone, and both gladly embraced the opportunity to discuss subjects which could not be addressed in company – namely their correspondence.

"You must think me a fool for not knowing it was you writing those notes," Miss Elizabeth said, once they had gained a safe distance from the house.

"There were times when I was convinced you must know, or at least feared you would perceive my behavior as a reflection of my good information."

"Such as?"

"The Yuletide Ball," he replied a bit sheepishly.

Miss Elizabeth could not hide her astonishment at his reference to an event so early in their correspondence. "I am beginning to wonder if you knew it was me from the very beginning."

"On the contrary, initially I was intrigued as you, though you may remember a certain exchange on the merits of accomplished women?"

"And I all but quoted Miss Bingley," Miss Elizabeth laughed embarrassedly.

Mr. Darcy smiled in return, "Yes, the number of people in the room at the time those words were first spoken greatly decreased the ambiguity of your identity."

"At the time I did not consider any likelihood of my words being written to you," Elizabeth replied, "and that was before you absented yourself from Netherfield, which only strengthened my convictions! I now wonder how your end of our diligent correspondence was accomplished. Were you secretly ensconced at Netherfield throughout the winter, or did Mr. Awdry assist you?"

"A man of *'ten thousand a year'* has his resources, and may occasionally be inclined to use them quite frivolously."

Mr. Darcy expected nothing less than silence and a raised eyebrow in response to such a statement, and Elizabeth did not disappoint.

"Thompson had already been dispatched to and from London on occasional errands by the time I first left Netherfield," explained Mr. Darcy, "Let us say that during my time in London, he journeyed to and from Netherfield rather more frequently than my continued assistance to Mr. Bingley would require, and in the process became quite familiar with a certain shop in Meryton."

"That would explain Matthew Awdry's description..." Elizabeth mumbled, trailing off with embarrassment.

"I beg your pardon? I did not catch that," Mr. Darcy inquired, his innocent tone contradicted by the impish curl of his lips.

"I believe I may safely assume that Thompson is a man of light build and coloring, with perhaps a preference for a brown coat?"

Surprised by the accurate description of his trusted courier, Mr. Darcy asked how she came to discover such information.

"When I discovered the book was missing," Elizabeth replied sheepishly.

"And all this time you have been wondering what had occurred, who this man was and why he had not returned your last note – forgive me. There were many times in Hadleigh that I found myself wishing to tell you the truth, and I see now that I should have."

"Not at all, sir. As much as I may have liked to know, our time at Ashingdon remains idyllic in my memory, and I can completely understand your reluctance to speak, as my former misconduct must have given you a great deal of pause. In fact, I rather wonder at your courage to speak at all. Many a man would not have given himself the trouble."

"Your assessment does not allow for sufficient inducement," Mr. Darcy gazed intently at Elizabeth as he spoke, and after a few moments' deliberation, stopped and turned towards her before he spoke again, his eyes never leaving hers.

"You may have noticed the book was missing something when I presented it to you. I can go no longer without giving you this."

He reached into his pocket and withdrew a crisply folded sheet of paper, extending it towards her.

Elizabeth cautiously accepted the note, and looking up to see him nodding for her to open it, she carefully opened the folded parchment.

Dearest Elizabeth,

You must allow me to tell you how ardently I admire and love you.

Yours,
Fitzwilliam Darcy

Tears formed in her eyes, threatening to reveal her emotions while Elizabeth marveled at the note as she reread its contents, at length lifting her eyes to behold Mr. Darcy watching her earnestly with an equally tender expression.

Taking her free hand, Mr. Darcy spoke sincerely, though in a soft tone Elizabeth had not previously heard, "I thought you deserved a note that finally acknowledged the identity of its author."

Though unequal to verbal response, Elizabeth could not tear her eyes from his, watching while his expression took on a hint of determination as he cleared his throat and spoke again, indicating towards his note.

"The sentiments expressed therein are entirely true. I can go no longer without conveying to you how I truly do admire and love you in a most ardent fashion. To own the truth, I have held these feelings for you for quite some time, and while I cannot point to the exact time of their origin, I hope you were aware of my regard, at least to some extent during our time together at Ashingdon."

Amidst her delight at hearing these words from the gentleman who had come to mean so much, she realized the imploring nature of his expression, and dropping her embarrassed gaze to their joined hands, willed herself to respond.

"Your manners were so charitable and considerate in Essex that I could not but appreciate your kindness. For any sentiment beyond that, I dared not hope."

"And now that you have reason to hope, dare I hope for the same?"

The happy truth revealing itself through their discourse could no longer be restrained, and with a brilliant smile, Elizabeth said playfully, "In all good conscience sir, I believe you must."

Mr. Darcy laughed as he returned her smile, "Then please, dearest Elizabeth, say you will restrain your delightful teasing until I have made one further request of you, after which you will find me at leisure to be teased mercilessly to your heart's content."

Elizabeth sobered as she nodded her assent, watching amazedly as the master of Pemberley lowered himself to one knee, pressing her hand with both of his.

"I have long known that you, Elizabeth, shall be in sole possession of my love and affection for the rest of my days, and it is impossible for me to be content without you by my side. If you find yourself able to return my affections, I beg you relieve my suffering and consent to be my wife."

Her radiant smile was enough to draw him to his feet, to which she replied by looking up to his face and answering softly, "Yes...yes, Fitzwilliam Darcy, I will marry you."

It was but a moment before Elizabeth found herself the recipient of an eager embrace and a very tender first kiss.

"Forgive me, Elizabeth. It seems I will be forever exposing you to my assertive behavior."

Placing a reassuring hand on his arm, she said, "It is alright, ...Fitzwilliam. I have long realized that your behavior is not so officious as I once believed."

"Though you are undoubtedly shocked by my forward behavior."

"Surprised perhaps, though as we were both witness to Mr. Bingley's courting of my sister, I believe you are entitled to at least one spontaneous display of affection, despite your strength of character."

Mr. Darcy grinned, and took her good humor as inducement to allow himself a second impulsive display of affection with a kiss upon her cheek before tucking her arm neatly into his and continuing their walk.

Elizabeth smiled widely in response before adding impishly, "I should warn you perhaps, that while I might not object to so devoted a fiancé, Mr. Bingley's behavior led my father to humorously refer to him as Jane's barnacle, and if he believes you half as besotted as that poor gentleman, he may invent an amusing appellation for you as well."

Elizabeth knew Mr. Darcy's current good humor to be unprecedented as he laughed deeply in response. "Well then, perhaps I should warn him not to be alarmed if his most beautiful daughter is frequently trailed by the largest puppy he has ever seen, as puppies from the northern wilds of Derbyshire are as persistent as they are committed, and can be quite unshakable."

Mr. Darcy could not but follow this remark with a display of his commitment, and pulled her arm closer to his as he pressed his free hand over hers. Elizabeth, however, felt quite a different response to be necessary, and with a mischievous grin, removed herself from his arm, skipping ahead down the path and looking back to see if she could goad her new "puppy" into running in pursuit – and he did.

❧ ❧ ❧

Upon their return to Netherfield, it was but a few moments' work for the Bingleys to discern the particular event likely to have taken place during the course of Mr. Darcy and Miss Elizabeth's walk, and not many moments longer before their suspicions were confirmed. Fond congratulations were offered by all, Miss Darcy could not contain her excitement at gaining such a compassionate sister, and Miss Catherine Bennet seemed a mix of well wishes and relief that with Mr. Darcy's engagement to her sister, her mother could no longer pressure a match between said gentleman and herself.

The hour for the Miss Bennets' departure soon arrived, and after a brief discussion, it was decided that Mr. Darcy would accompany them in returning to Longbourn, that he might address Mr. Bennet for his consent. As the carriage rolled towards Longbourn, Mr. Darcy followed on horseback and began to wonder if Mr. Bennet's good information regarding the bookshop ought to have been discussed between himself and Elizabeth before approaching the gentleman, but there was nothing to be done for it now.

Miss Elizabeth knocked on the library door and at her father's bidding, entered the room and informed her father that Mr. Darcy had escorted them home in hopes of discussing a matter of some importance. Mr. Bennet observed his daughter's serene smile and responded in kind before he requested that she see the gentleman in, and as she made to exit the library, he motioned for her to remain and seat herself in a nearby chair, as there could be nothing to discuss that she should not hear.

"Mr. Bennet," Mr. Darcy began formally as he seated himself before the elder gentleman's desk, "your daughter Miss Elizabeth has accepted my offer of marriage, and I have come to seek your consent and blessing to my request for her hand."

"Well sir, as I know you to be an honorable gentleman and you have gained my daughter's approval, I see no reason to deny your request. Although," Mr. Bennet turned his eyes towards his daughter, "not long ago, I would have expected some degree of hesitancy on her part due to a particular *friendship* she would not wish to forsake."

"Papa," Elizabeth protested embarrassedly, "I should have informed you sooner. The *friend* you refer to and the gentleman seated before you are one and the same."

"I know," Mr. Bennet answered, struggling to control his merriment.

A Noteworthy Courtship

"You...you do?" Elizabeth stumbled incredulously.

"Yes, I rather wonder that you did not suspect him sooner, though through the eyes of an impartial observer, perhaps these things can be seen more clearly. I always say many a person does not conceal their inner struggles as effectively as they believe." Mr. Bennet cast Mr. Darcy a pointed glance as he said the last, causing the younger gentleman to see his "odd" behavior at a certain engagement dinner in a different light. Mr. Bennet's strange looks over dinner and request that Mr. Darcy turn the pages for his daughter quickly became a source of consternation for the younger gentleman.

Amused by his success at ruffling the feathers of his future son, Mr. Bennet turned his attention back to his daughter, "I am certain, my Lizzy, that the interesting series of events leading to this juncture are of little consequence now that the two of you have finally come to an understanding, though your noteworthy courtship has given me no little entertainment, and I am glad to have played an active part in it."

Elizabeth looked at her father confusedly, while Mr. Darcy realized he may have made a grievous error in addressing Mr. Bennet before providing certain details to Elizabeth. He may have escaped being called onto the carpet by Mr. Bennet only to place himself in the same position at the hands of Miss Elizabeth Bennet.

"If I might ask you to excuse us, Mr. Bennet, there is a small matter I would like to address with your daughter."

The anxiety he had inspired in the young gentleman provided Mr. Bennet with sufficient amusement for him to forgive the concern he had been caused by Mr. Darcy's last departure from Hertfordshire, and he cordially excused himself.

కౖకౖకౖ

After Mr. Bennet departed, it was a moment before Mr. Darcy began to speak. "Elizabeth, I imagine you are curious as to the 'active role' which your father mentioned, and let me assure you while it is nothing dreadful, I fear my having neglected to tell you previously may make you very cross with me."

Mr. Darcy glanced up at Elizabeth as he continued, "There was a point when it was brought to my attention that your father knew of my identity, and his knowledge of my regard for you – which apparently dates back to your sister's engagement dinner, and explains his motivation for asking you to play while I turned the pages." Elizabeth chuckled at this, and Mr. Darcy joined silently as he shook his head, neither of them surprised that Mr. Bennet would act in such a way. "Your father confronted me not long before the Bingley's wedding. You may imagine my surprise at entering the bookshop to leave you a note, and finding your father waiting for my arrival."

Elizabeth gasped. "Dare I ask what he said to you?"

"His duty as your father to protect you was exercised well, and I thought he would escort me to Longbourn directly if not for his belief that his daughter 'would not take kindly to an obligatory offer of marriage in the aftermath of her suitor being called onto the carpet by her father.' He tried to warn me of your ill opinion..."

"...and the result of his pressuring was our terrible confrontation after the wedding," Elizabeth said dismally.

"Not at all. I informed him that I had already resolved to reveal myself to you. In fact, the note I left for you that day was the very one in which I suggested that we meet, and it had already been written before I left Netherfield for the bookshop. Your father's presence had little impact on my resolve, and confident as I was, I did not heed your father's warning."

"I believe my conduct that fateful day was more than sufficient punishment in and of itself."

"My intent in discussing this was not to distress you. I might remind you of your own philosophy to think of the past only as its remembrance brings your pleasure, or suggest my own that forgiveness is not to be given lightly, as with it comes the implication that in accepting it, all is to be forgotten. We have long since agreed to forget that day, and if you can forgive me of my secrecy, we shall forget this day as well."

"That, I am afraid, we cannot do," Elizabeth replied seriously.

"No?"

The penitent expression on his face led Elizabeth to envision him as a schoolboy, complete with messy hair and tattered breeches, offering a switch for the administration of his punishment, no small feat considering that the gentleman stood no less than a foot taller than she.

"No," she smiled, "For I shall always remember this day as the happiest, the day you professed your admiration and gifted me your proposal of marriage, and it is ludicrous for you to suggest I forget it."

Mr. Darcy returned her smile, and given the warmth of her expression, could not but offer her a light kiss on the cheek as he thanked her for such kind understanding.

"Now if we are careful, I believe we may be able to steal away into the gardens before my mother discovers you and keeps you for tea."

"Your suggestion of the gardens is an excellent one, though contrary to your belief, I think tea to be a fine idea."

Chapter 31

Now that an engagement had been formed and officially announced between Mr. Darcy and Miss Elizabeth, certain privileges were enjoyed which would not have been allowed under previous circumstances. Scarcely a day passed in which Mr. Darcy did not journey to Longbourn with his sister and remain well into the afternoon, or arrive shortly after breakfast with a curricle to whisk his fiancée off to Netherfield for the day.

It was on just such an occasion that Mr. Darcy drove Miss Elizabeth towards her sister's home, though to her surprise, instead of passing through the gates to approach the great house, he drove on, stopping their conveyance before the stables.

Mr. Darcy wordlessly descended from the curricle, and came around the horses to assist Miss Elizabeth, still without explanation as he offered his arm to escort her.

"Am I not to learn why today's visit begins with the stables?"

Mr. Darcy smiled innocently, "We great men must keep some secrets, lest the ladies always hold us at a disadvantage."

No further explanation was offered as Mr. Darcy guided Miss Elizabeth into the stables, where she was surprised to see a familiar dappled head poke out as they approached the horse's stall. She was even further surprised to hear Mr. Darcy refer to the horse as her own.

"I have never seen you mounted upon one of your father's horses, and thought you might prefer the horse that suited you so well in Hadleigh."

"Though I do appreciate the docile nature of this horse with which you have so thoughtfully gifted me, perhaps it would be better said that the company suited me well. I find I am not so indifferent to riding as I once was, and though I may never have the passion for it that some do, accompanying the gentleman who holds my affections in one of his favorite pastimes can never be so trying an experience."

Mr. Darcy smile fondly at his beloved, clasping her hands in his. "Then I am glad you shall enjoy riding with me, my love."

Elizabeth smiled broadly as she replied, "And here I thought this horse was intended for Georgiana."

"Do not worry," he said, gesturing to the next stall, "I have made adequate provision for her as well."

Mr. Darcy then showed Elizabeth the white pony he had purchased for Georgiana, indicating that the two Connemaras had been foaled the same year, and would likely be glad not to be separated. He then suggested they inform the Bingleys of their arrival, and offered his arm to escort her to the house.

"I do appreciate your thoughtfulness, Fitzwilliam."

"I am glad to hear it, though I intend to give you many more appropriate gifts as well. I realize a horse may not have been your ideal, and while I wish to always stable a horse you would feel comfortable riding, do not feel obligated to indulge in the pastime any more frequently than you desire."

Elizabeth laid her free hand upon his arm and looked sincerely into his eyes. "I was in earnest when I said the experience is more enjoyable when accompanied by the man I love."

"Elizabeth," he breathed, reaching to brush his finger across her cheek, "I do love you so."

"As I love you, William."

Her first declaration of love coupled with so familiar an appellation could not but encourage him to express himself as sensibly and as warmly as a man violently in love can be supposed to do, such that it was some minutes before the couple approached the house.

A Noteworthy Courtship

As much as the betrothed couple may have wished to spend each day of their engagement in such a way, detailed planning of the wedding soon placed its requirements on their time together. Miss Elizabeth and her mother handled the majority of the arrangements, while Mr. Darcy took up what few tasks he could, such as the settlement papers and meeting with the rector of Longbourn's parish.

After such tasks had been completed, Mr. Darcy dutifully reported his success to the ladies concerned, not neglecting the opportunity to steal his fiancée away that they might converse in the garden.

"I have just come from securing Mr. Martin's services for the ceremony. I am glad your mother did not suggest your cousin for the office, as more than one circumstance would have been cause for discomfort."

"Yes, and it is quite providential that only one deterrent was sufficient for my mother, as she is not knowledgeable of all of them. What would people think to know we have assaulted a man of the cloth in such a way? We should be grateful it happened so far from home, else we might have trouble finding a rector willing to perform a wedding ceremony for so infamous a pair," Elizabeth teased.

"I must admit I was tempted to lay hands on him long before that day at Ashingdon," Mr. Darcy asserted.

"Is that so? And when might that have been?"

"The day he coerced you into taking his arm as we walked to Thompson's pond," Mr. Darcy answered brusquely.

"It certainly would have made things easier for me if you had. Is that why you walked back with me?"

"When I offered you my hand, I believe I acted before I had the chance to give it much thought – after all, I was still foolishly fighting my attraction to you. But even then I knew I could not bear to see you suffering that odious man's company. At the time I was under the false impression that you truly were to be his wedded wife, and I cannot tell you of the revulsion I felt at the idea of your being tied to that man for the rest of your days."

"Well I am glad you have been disabused of that notion, as I believe you now know my father well enough to recognize that he would not have forced such a match, regardless of Mr. Collins' position as heir to the estate. Though imagine my mother's shock at seeing Mr. Collins return without me that day. We are fortunate she did not see you in his place, as it would have only added to my crimes."

Mr. Darcy's lack of understanding was evident upon his face.

"After all," Elizabeth clarified impishly, "you were intended to walk with Kitty."

༒ ༒ ༒

It was with great pleasure that Mr. and Mrs. Bingley hosted a dinner in honor of Mr. Darcy and Miss Elizabeth, and though such a gathering was by no means an unusual way to celebrate an engagement, the married couple could not but be overjoyed by the impeding union of their sister and close friend.

Mr. Bingley had no need to trouble himself over the seating arrangements at dinner, as he and his wife were in complete agreement as to the positioning of their guests. Mr. Darcy and Miss Elizabeth were allowed the pleasure of being seated side by side, surrounded by Miss Darcy, Mr. Bennet, and Mr. Bingley, and with little effort from the liveliest members of their group, conversation was steady and rarely allowed interjection by those at the opposite end of the table.

As the meal came to an end, Mr. Bennet teasingly waved off the convention of separating from the ladies, as he was becoming quite familiar with the besotted preferences of his daughters' admirers. It was with a great deal of amusement that Mr. Bennet suggested that the betrothed couple repeat their previous actions by entertaining the company with his daughter at the pianoforte and Mr. Darcy to turn the pages. The couple was happy to comply, and remained at the piano through several pieces, both finally able to enjoy the other's proximity in anticipation of having the scene repeated many an evening at Pemberley. Shoulder brushes were no longer discomfiting as they were admittedly enjoyable, and the degree of contact between thighs and calves was neither here nor there as to the rest of the party it was not discernable behind the large instrument.

Alas propriety did require that Miss Elizabeth allow the other ladies present adequate time to display their own talents, and at length she acquiesced to its demands. Miss Darcy was entreated to take her future sister's place, and at her brother's hesitation, insisted that she would be playing a few selections from memory, and would have no need of his *'superior talents at page turning'* as Mr. Bennet had termed them.

Mr. Darcy escorted Miss Elizabeth to a comfortable sofa where they might enjoy his sister's playing, and following her performance, enjoy their being situated slightly away from the rest of those assembled. With such a degree of relative privacy, Elizabeth asked Mr. Darcy to tell her of Pemberley, as while she had heard much of the place, she believed the most trustworthy assessment would come from the master himself.

As Mr. Darcy described the size of the park, and detailed the additions and renovations of previous generations which made up the current state of the house, Elizabeth was stuck by the thought that to be mistress of so grand a house, in the tradition of many great Mrs. Darcy's before her, must truly be something. To assume that such thoughts would inhibit her desire to tease, however, would be ill-judged indeed.

"Does it compare to the modern splendor of Rosings Park?" she asked impertinently.

"Perhaps in terms of the cost of fireplaces and number of staircases, though in essentials I have always found Rosings to be very formal, where as for Pemberley, I do not think nature could have done more."

"But does it have excellent glazing upon the windows or shelves specifically designed for practicality in the closets?"

Mr. Darcy smirked in her direction, "Miss Elizabeth, I believe you tease."

"Indeed, sir," Miss Elizabeth smiled back, "I see you begin to understand me."

Elizabeth rested her fingertips lightly upon his knee as she added sincerely, "By what you have described, and with the addition of your own residence there, I am sure I will like Pemberley very much."

ಶಿಶಿಶಿ

The next six weeks saw a flurry of activity within the walls of Longbourn as wedding plans were amended and revised as soon as they were completed. On more than one occasion was Mrs. Bennet convinced that were it not for Mr. Darcy's ten thousand a year, she would insist upon an additional month at least, despite his expressed desire to return to his estate before the harvest. Elizabeth's entreaties that a small wedding would be better suited to their time constraints were uniformly ignored by her mother. Mr. Darcy's supportive requests along the same vein were accepted courteously, though they too had little effect on the end result. Nothing short of an act of God would deter Mrs. Bennet from providing a wedding ceremony and breakfast appropriate for the future Mrs. Darcy, and aside from the untimely withering of a dozen rose bushes ordered from London, nothing did.

Lady Catherine was of course livid once news of the engagement reached her. While the letter written soon after was as angry and abusive as one might expect from so imperious a lady, it's language was not greatly different from the letter she sent her nephew after he supported and contributed to such a scandal at Ashingdon. Those family members of greater importance to the groom were in attendance on the occasion of his wedding, and as Mr. Darcy's breath caught in his chest while he watched his beloved bride walk down the aisle towards him, he knew he could have no cause to repine.

Epilogue

So it was that the unsurpassable joy Mrs. Bennet felt on the wedding day of her dearest Jane was equaled the day her second daughter married a man of ten thousand a year. Whether or not Mr. Collins eventually married or bore a son to inherit Longbourn became less of a concern to the Bennets, as they found themselves secure in the good fortune of their connection to the Darcys and the Bingleys. Whether or not this had a significant effect on Mrs. Bennet's nerves was another matter.

For the two happy couples, interaction with relations close and distant, pleasant and unpleasant could not be entirely avoided, though the length of the journey to Derbyshire proved quite effective for the Darcys and in time for the Bingleys as well, when they purchased an estate not thirty miles from Pemberley. Though the level of improvement in the remaining Miss Bennets' comportment varied from sister to sister – and the opinion of the person relating the information – each did eventually marry, much to their mother's relief and satisfaction.

As for the Darcys and the Bingleys, no two sisters could have found more devoted husbands, nor two friends be more pleased to become brothers by marriage. It became common practice for the two young families to visit their friends at Ashingdon each spring, excepting the occasional season of confinement for one of the three ladies, causing the reunion to be delayed or relocated. Many years later, Mr. and Mrs. Darcy would watch their children chasing Edward and Emma Bingley down the beach or joining in a game of cricket where an aging Mr. Beaumont happily bowled to his children, all the while reflecting on the many years they had spent in just such activities, all starting with their first journey to Hadleigh so many years before.

It must also be said of Mr. and Mrs. Fitzwilliam Darcy that Mr. Bennet always understood why when either received a book from the other as a gift, as by nature of their dispositions they frequently did, the widest smiles and fondest looks were reserved for the loose unmarked sheet to be found tucked within the book's pages.

The End

And now a series of added and alternate scenes, giving further insight and alternate endings to the original story.

Mr. Darcy Fears Discovery

The door of the bookshop could be heard creaking open and Mr. Darcy glanced discreetly over his shoulder to see who had entered. Just as he espied none other than Lydia Bennet, his eyes went wide as he noticed she stood on tiptoes, her eyes taking survey of the shop and moving perilously close to his direction. He cursed under his breath as he ducked his head behind the shelf. He was certain that if he were a boy of ten he would have hunched down and run to the other side of the shop, but he was a gentleman, and he moved discreetly *but quickly!* Across the wooden floor, thinking the section devoted to agricultural reference least likely to attract her attention. A burst of giggles embellished by a snort caught his attention, and he rolled his eyes as he observed her purpose in entering the bookshop. The young man in the shop, of some relation to Mr. Awdry if he had heard correctly, rested a crate upon the counter as the young *"lady"* placed a hand on his arm flirtatiously, jabbering about some nonsense Mr. Darcy did not bother to attend.

With a huff, he exited the shop; his errand would just have to wait. Perhaps he could invent some business at the tailor's. It certainly would not be the quality he was used to, but after all, Miss Bingley had complimented how fine he appeared in the waistcoat he had worn out riding the day before, saying the tawny hue was quite her favorite – *there's an article of clothing I am never wearing again.*

A Noteworthy Courtship

Bennet Ladies and Interfering Carpeting

Mr. Darcy and Mr. Bingley are in the Netherfield library, discussing the upcoming engagement dinner in honor of Charles Bingley and Jane Bennet.

"So the Bennets shall be dining at Netherfield," commented Mr. Darcy once the gentlemen had gained the privacy of the library. "One might wonder if you will be able to keep yourself from Longbourn's door long enough for the family to prepare for the evening."

Mr. Bingley chuckled as he poured a glass for each of them. "Come, Darcy. You know as well as I it is only appropriate for me to invite them to dine, particularly in light of my sisters' reluctance to pay a congratulatory call on Miss Bennet. I recognize your distaste for her family, but I am confident even you can survive their company for one evening."

"And have you invited the riveting Mr.....gah!" Mr. Darcy began to pace the room, his reply halting abruptly when the toe of his shoe caught on the rug, nearly causing him to spill his drink as he fought to keep his balance. Turning his eye to the offensive carpet, he looked agitatedly at the awkward edging of the ostentatious design. *Singular choice for a library*, he muttered.

"What is this style of rug called, Bingley? I do not recall it being present the last time I attempted to walk across this room without losing my dignity."

"Money."

Mr. Darcy raised his brow, entreating his friend to continue, which he did.

"Its name is money. Caroline had it ordered from London, insisting that it is of the latest fashion and apparently believed my library would be an embarrassment without it. Exactly who she thinks to impress when she disdains the local society, I have not the slightest idea." Mr. Bingley cast a mischievous glance at Mr. Darcy, "Then again, perhaps I do. However I really should rein in her spending habits regardless."

"Here," he gestured for Mr. Darcy's assistance as he reached down to grab the offending rug, "let us roll it up and ask a servant to place it in the attic before the effect of this port settles in and one of us impales himself in attempt to walk over this atrocity."

"Indeed, remove it we shall, however if you are amenable, the attics shan't be necessary. Tell me the number of pounds this monstrosity has cost you and I shall purchase it from you." Mr. Darcy smiled impishly as he moved to assist his friend, "It is exceedingly difficult to find gifts for my Aunt Catherine, and apparently I should have thought to solicit your sister's similar taste long ago."

The Indigenous and Migrant Toad Populations of Thompson's Pond

We start our scene on a crisp December morning, when a walking party was dispatched from Longbourn, consisting of a thoroughly besotted Mr. Bingley, his future wife (though not yet betrothed) Jane, Elizabeth, unfortunately escorted by Mr. Collins, and Mr. Darcy, who in Mrs. Bennet's mind was escorting Kitty, though his attention was perhaps drawn to another of the lady's daughters. We join the group as they reach their destination overlooking Thompson's pond.

Finally the walking party reached a knoll overlooking the pond, and seeing the small bench situated at its crest, Mr. Bingley offered Jane the opportunity to sit and rest. Mr. Bingley then turned to converse with Mr. Darcy while Mr. Collins rambled on to no one in particular about the surrounding flora and how such specimens would thrive at his parsonage under the advice of Lady Catherine. Elizabeth gladly took the opportunity to quit her cousin's company and seated herself beside Jane. Unfortunately, upon witnessing her movement, Mr. Collins moved to stand beside her, and his comments alternated between courting his cousin and displaying reverence to the nephew of his patroness.

As Mr. Collins' monologue continued, Mr. Darcy turned his head away from the rest of the party and stared into the horizon. Elizabeth grew angry that he would willingly arrive at Longbourn only to stalk off as though they were unworthy of his attention. He was under no obligation to mix with Meryton society if he found their company insufferable. If only she could have read his thoughts, she would have known it was only Mr. Collins he found insufferable, and on that subject, they were in perfect agreement.

It was greatly providential then, that at that precise moment, Mr. Darcy turned to glance in Miss Elizabeth's direction, and caught the exaggerated rolling of her eyes aimed at the back of her rambling cousin. She looked as though she knew not whether to flee in any given direction or entertain a hope that steadfast glowering might inspire his spontaneous combustion. Mr. Darcy watched a multitude of less than polite but highly understandable expressions passed across her features while Mr. Collins' speech on the superior natural waters to be found near Rosings Park continued. At length, he met her eye as she let out an animated though silent huff. She immediately froze, embarrassed to be caught indulging in such child-like behavior, and by Mr. Darcy of all people. Before she could turn her discomfited gaze to the ground, however, Mr. Darcy winked at her, and his eyes darted in Mr. Collins' direction. Elizabeth rolled her eyes slightly as she shrugged understandingly, offering a small smile in appreciation of his good humor. Her expression quickly changed to surprise as Mr. Darcy strode decidedly towards her.

"...as I was instructed by Lady Catherine deBourgh, there is no more suitable a remedy than..." Mr. Collins halted his speech abruptly upon observing the decided movements of his revered audience. It was with a great haste that surprised even himself that he rushed to Miss Elizabeth's side before the distinguished gentleman could reach her, hoping to smooth over whatever offences she might have caused.

"Mr. Darcy, sir, I beg you would forgive my young cousin. She has rarely had the good fortune of being in company with esteemed persons such as yourself, and I assure you she shall quickly learn to curb whatever behavior offends you when she becomes Mrs. Collins. Your noble aunt is excessively attentive to all these things, and has assured me she will instruct my wife as to whatever manners would be conducive to the parish's needs should her education be found lacking."

"Mr. Collins…" Elizabeth cut in sharply, though her voice was quickly spoken over by her cousin.

"Do not trouble yourself, dear cousin, that our arrangement has not been formally announced. A gentleman of Mr. Darcy's standing…"

"…finds it terribly rude to interrupt a lady," Mr. Darcy finished sternly. Turning towards Elizabeth he added, "You were saying, Miss Bennet?"

Elizabeth was astounded by the strength of his address, and even more so that he seemed to have spoken in her defense. Realizing the attention of the entire party had turned towards them, she observed the shock on Jane's face, the glare on Mr. Bingley's, and tried to ignore the appall on Mr. Collins'. Mr. Darcy's eye was turned to her intently, and as he raised a brow she nodded in acknowledgement and said, "I was attempting to express that while it is true no formal announcement has been made, Mr. Collins, it would be misleading indeed to suggest that such an announcement is forthcoming, as I have not entered into any 'arrangement' with you, nor do I expect that I shall do so in the near future."

Always master of his countenance, Mr. Darcy was certain he kept a stern façade in light of this pleasing revelation, though the gleeful look on Mr. Bingley's face and wink in his direction was troubling. Little time for reflection was allowed however, as Mr. Collins gathered the proper words to address his…well, apparently just his cousin.

"Cousin Elizabeth, surely you understand the marked attentions I have bestowed upon you. However if I am incorrect in this presumption, your innocence only adds to your feminine charms, and I shall happily make my intentions known to you."

"That will not be necessary, sir, as your intentions have long been understood by myself. The clarity of your intentions, however, does not infer that they must then be welcomed."

"Cousin Elizabeth, I fear you misunderstand…"

"ENOUGH!"

The resounding sharpness of Mr. Darcy's outburst surprised even the gentleman who verbalized it, and he soon found himself placed firmly beside Elizabeth.

"Mr. Darcy, I must apologize. If I could simply remove my fiancée from your presence I am certain she will apolo…"

"The lady has stated that she is NOT betrothed to you."

"But her mother…"

"Oh, BLOODY HELL!"

And with one great shove from the Master of Pemberley, Mr. Collins found himself reeling down the muddy bank of Thompson's pond, arms flailing uselessly as he careened into the water with a great splash.

Jane gasped.

Mr. Bingley restrained the urge to cheer and nearly settled for lobbing any loose object he could find in the parson's general direction. However, a nearby log seemed too large to be worth the effort, and he was rather fond of his walking stick.

A third member of the group did finally find her voice.

"Mr. Darcy!" Elizabeth cried, her tone exuding more a sense of astonishment than displeasure.

The gentleman turned towards the lady who had addressed him, as any proper gentleman should, and smoothing his coat, glanced at the cumbersome gentleman who seemed rather well situated amongst the cattail reeds and the toads.

"I suppose I should apologize for that," he commented nonchalantly as he straightened his gloves, "though I have the distinct impression it was bound to happen eventually."

He then looked up at the lady whose own glove was making a valiant effort at disguising a most becoming smile and offered his arm, "Miss Bennet, might I escort you home?"

A More Assertive Elizabeth (Elizabeth the Daring)

A week before the Yuletide Ball, Elizabeth, deciding she's had enough of caution and patience, takes matters into her own hands.

Elizabeth had greatly enjoyed the secrecy of her correspondence, and rather enjoyed toying with whatever young man in the neighborhood thought himself so particularly clever. What said man had not anticipated, however, was that Elizabeth would soon lose patience with her efforts to reason out his identity on her own. While the pattern to the days she had determined would bring his delivering a note was no great secret, her accurate speculation as to the time at which he might arrive on this particular day was as shocking to her as it would eventually be to him.

Elizabeth had chosen her location carefully, being fully aware of the unknown gentleman's particular destination, and therefore also aware of the best location for discreetly observing any movements in the vicinity without being discovered. The borrowed bonnet from her sister Mary worked quite well at masking any distinctly recognizable evidences of her identity, should the gentleman happen to be conscious of such particulars. After all, she could not be too cautious in supposing that her odd questions at recent social gatherings had not gone unnoticed. Her musings over the potential outcome of her plan were interrupted as heavy footsteps moved in her direction, each step further indicating her probable success. As the footsteps paused in the predicted location, she rose lightly from her seat, moving to return the book she held to its shelf, just one row behind the aisle which contained her primary interest. With the briefest of upward glances over the shelf as she replaced the book, she was afforded a clear view of the gentleman's profile.

Only intense fear of discovery kept Elizabeth silent as she felt the shock of seeing Mr. Darcy handling her book just a few feet away. She silently moved back to the chair she had vacated, gently seating herself with complete disregard for the pretense of reading another book. Her breath caught in her throat as the heavy footsteps began again, each contact of riding boot to wooden floorboard pounding in her ears with more magnitude than the last. She held her breath as the rhythm of the fading steps gradually increased and sighed with relief as she heard the door open and close. Not daring to approach the note, which in all likelihood was still warm from its author's hold, Elizabeth waited restlessly for a quarter hour to pass before exiting the shop herself.

That evening, Elizabeth pored over each of the notes she had received, vainly attempting to reconcile the impression she had drawn to the man she now knew to be behind them. As difficult as it was to consider that her impression of Mr. Darcy was false, believing that she had misinterpreted her correspondent was inconceivable. In her

A Noteworthy Courtship

efforts, she did not get on at all, her every confidence in her discernment questioned by the conflicting conclusions she had drawn. *Until this moment,* she sighed, *I never knew myself.*

The following day, on which she intended to pick up the note, though she had witnessed its being placed; Mr. Bennet called his favorite daughter into the library, suggesting a ride into Meryton for a little holiday shopping. He noted that his Lizzy still seemed rather preoccupied, just as she had when she returned from her walk the previous day before disappearing into her room.

Mr. Bennet was increasingly puzzled by his daughter's apprehension as their carriage departed for Meryton, as was about to inquire as to its cause when Elizabeth hastily spoke.

"Papa, forgive me the impertinence, for I can longer restrain my curiosity. Of what did you and Mr. Darcy speak at Netherfield when Mr. Bingley invited us to dine? I could not help noticing that you joined us several minutes after the other gentlemen."

Mr. Bennet sighed, "I had hoped I would not need to relate this information as the gentleman it pertains is no longer in the area. However since you have inquired directly, I see little harm in sharing with you that the subject of our discourse was Mr. Wickham, and I believe we were all misled as to the true state of affairs between the two gentlemen."

Mr. Bennet proceeded to relate the knowledge he had gained of the history between Mr. Darcy and Mr. Wickham, which of course included the matter of 3,000 pounds given in exchange of the living at Kympton and the depletion of said funds which implied an undesirable shade to Mr. Wickham's character. The narrative did not, however, include the more recent particulars of Mr. Darcy's acquaintance with Mr. Wickham, which the more respectable gentleman would wish to forget; as such information had not been related to Mr. Bennet.

To say that this information increased Elizabeth's confusion would be a rather modest portrayal of her state of emotion. Upon returning to Longbourn and reading Mr. Darcy's note, however, she was thankful that she had discovered his identity when she did, else his reference to accomplished ladies may have inspired her to make references which would certainly reveal her identity to him.

ৰেৰেৰে

As the Bennets arrived at the Yuletide Ball, Elizabeth's feelings were very little clearer than they had been over the past several days. Of one thing she was certain – for better or for worse, her correspondence with Mr. Darcy needed to end before any damage could be done to her reputation by its accidental discovery. The severity of the impropriety committed could no longer be ignored when the identity of her correspondent was revealed to be not a young local boy, but the eligible master of a great estate. While her examination of his notes and the information from her father had greatly deflated her ill opinion, she still could not imagine an obligatory marriage would be amenable to either party.

Elizabeth could no longer reflect on how to best handle her predicament, as at that moment, the gentleman in question entered the room. Mr. Bingley had arrived at the ball in company with the Bennets, as he had offered use of his carriage for their conveyance, and it was of little surprise to Elizabeth that the remainder of the Netherfield party would arrive at an hour considered fashionably late. Neither was she surprised by the haughty air that graced Miss Bingley's countenance as she was escorted into the ballroom by Mr. Darcy. As expected, her expression was matched in the face of said gentleman. Upon further observation, however, Elizabeth noticed that Mr. Darcy cast a somewhat wistful glance at Mr. Bingley as he led Jane to join the first set, and he sighed as Miss Bingley used a rather forcible manner to lead him into conversation with some of the local ladies and the Hursts. Elizabeth quickly averted her eyes as Mr. Darcy made his escape from Mr. Bingley's sisters, only to join the gentleman himself as he led her sister away from the dance floor and the trio came towards her.

"Bingley, Miss Bennet." Mr. Darcy bowed as he greeted the couple, "As this is the first public event in honor of your engagement, allow me to again offer my congratulations."

"No need for formalities, old man," Mr. Bingley laughed, "I know you have long recognized Jane for the angel that she is."

Mr. Darcy gave a slight nod to Mr. Bingley and turned to Miss Bennet as she thanked him politely.

"Miss Bennet, would you allow me to deprive your fiancé of your company by dancing the next with me?"

"Certainly, Mr. Darcy."

Upon her positive reply, Mr. Darcy offered his hand to escort Miss Bennet to the floor, leaving a shocked Elizabeth in their wake.

"I see you are surprised by Mr. Darcy's inviting your sister to dance, Miss Elizabeth, but he is ever conscious of paying respect where it is due, and he is a very loyal friend," Mr. Bingley smiled and indicated towards the dancing area as he extended his hand, "Would you do me the honor?"

"Why yes, Mr. Bingley. Propriety calls for nothing less, and our dancing now will keep you from the necessity of giving up a later dance with our dear Jane." Elizabeth returned Mr. Bingley's smile, belying the sterile nature of her words.

Mr. Bingley was quick to reunite with Jane after her dance with Mr. Darcy, and offered to bring her refreshment. Mr. Darcy joined him without a word, and upon their return, Bingley offered a glass of punch to Jane as Darcy did the same for Elizabeth.

"Thank you, Mr. Darcy," Elizabeth struggled to keep a curious expression from her features as she reached to accept the refreshment she had not requested, though she was most disconcerted by her confusion over how to interact with the gentleman in light of the knowledge she had recently obtained.

Elizabeth took a sip of punch, tensing as she observed the excited approach of her mother and younger sister, fearing the mortification to come much more acutely than she had on previous occasions.

"There you are Jane! Oh, what a wonderful affair this has turned out to be, and all in the honor of yourself and Mr. Bingley."

"Yes mama, we are all glad to gather together and celebrate the season with our friends and neighbors."

Ignoring the majority of her daughter's demure response, Mrs. Bennet turned an eager eye upon the eligible gentleman in the group, who then realized with horror that he was the primary reason for her approach. "Mr. Darcy sir, I noticed you dancing with Jane, how kind of you to compliment her thus."

"It is expected that I honor the intended bride of so close a friend."

"Why yes, being such a good friend as you are to Mr. Bingley, we shall all be nearly family once he is married to Jane. And gentlemanly as you are, I am sure you would enjoy giving a dance to one of his future sisters as well." If Mr. Darcy had not deduced meaning of her words,

Mrs. Bennet made all clear with a nod and pointed look towards Miss Catherine, before turning back to him expectantly.

Mr. Darcy cleared his throat in futile attempt to break the matron's gaze before replying. "Indeed Mrs. Bennet, I was just about to ask Miss Elizabeth if she might dance the next with me."

Turning to Elizabeth, he asked sedately, "Would you do me the honor?"

Not unconscious of the glare being sent her direction by her mother, Elizabeth assented. She was greatly appreciative of the polite manner in which Mr. Darcy had thwarted her mother's schemes, though not convinced he was entirely pleased by the prospect of dancing with one Bennet sister over another. The gentleman offered his hand to escort her, and without another word, led her to their place in the next set.

Ever skillful at diffusing social tension, Mr. Bingley promptly addressed his future sister, "Miss Catherine, I would be delighted if you might dance the next with me."

Mr. Bingley then escorted her to the floor as well, leaving Mrs. Bennet and her eldest daughter to each other's company.

"Well Jane, can you believe the nerve of her!" Mrs. Bennet huffed. "First, Lizzy allows her fiancé to leave for Kent without so much as a formal announcement to the neighborhood, and now she is dancing with Mr. Darcy, who we all know finds her only tolerable. I dare say I cannot blame him, what with the impertinent remarks always flying from her mouth, but how is Kitty to catch his eye if Elizabeth wastes his time so?"

As the dance began, Elizabeth addressed Mr. Darcy.

"It seems I am to apologize for my mother's behavior Mr. Darcy, as she goaded you into this dance."

"Do not apologize for conduct that is not your own."

The emotionless tone of his voice convinced Elizabeth that Mr. Darcy had spoken with more politeness than sincerity, though she could not blame him for the sentiment in face of her mother's impropriety. The weight of her present situation inhibited her skills at conversation and she was glad when at length, Mr. Darcy spoke.

"Do you have any particular plans for the holiday season?"

"Mr. Bingley has been kind enough to invite us to spend Christmas Day at Netherfield."

"I see."

Elizabeth fought back her frustration as the movement of the dance turned her away from Mr. Darcy. His meager attempt at forwarding the conversation was hardly encouraging, considering the revelation she needed to make.

"And yourself, sir?"

"I shall be leaving shortly to spend the holiday with my sister."

Elizabeth smiled, "I wish you and your sister a merry holiday then, sir. I understand that she is rather shy, and would imagine she prefers a quiet holiday with her brother to a house full of acquaintances."

"She does," Mr. Darcy replied cautiously, searching his memory for an instance when Georgiana's reserved nature had been mentioned in Miss Bennet's presence.

Rallying her courage, Elizabeth added, "I imagine she also anticipates the enjoyment of your company, as the discussion of many subjects, such as recently published books for example, are better served by direct conversation than written correspondence."

Mr. Darcy nodded in agreement, and the remainder of the dance was spent in silence, a circumstance which was not particularly objectionable to either party. The gentleman still bore an impassive expression as he led Elizabeth off the floor, though rather than silently turning away, he hastily requested the supper set, which she could not politely refuse.

Mr. Darcy then retreated in search of a less crowded room, or preferably an empty hallway, where he might attempt to order his thoughts.

The supper set commenced with no little amount of apprehension on the part of Mr. Darcy and Miss Elizabeth, thus conversation during the set was stilted at best. The earnest looks cast in her direction left Elizabeth in no doubt that upon reflection, the gentleman had deduced the correct meaning of her words during their previous set, though the responding sentiment behind said looks was not as easy to discern.

Mr. Darcy offered his arm to escort Elizabeth to supper, and given the silence that primarily reigned over their repast, each finished rather quickly. Elizabeth flicked her fan, attempting to dispel the nervous agitation she felt seated beside the gentleman to whom she wished to say so much, though little of the subject matter could be addressed in company.

"Miss Bennet," Mr. Darcy addressed her with practiced calm, "I fear the dining room has become rather warm for your taste. Might I offer you additional refreshment, and perhaps to escort you out for some fresh air?"

"Yes," Elizabeth smiled slightly, anxious to relieve the tension between them, "I believe that would be quite welcome, sir."

Mr. Darcy offered a small smile in return before setting upon his face the same stern countenance he had so frequently worn. Offering his arm, he led Miss Elizabeth from the dining room, collecting a glass for each of them from a nearby servant as they followed the small contingent of guests beginning to return to the ballroom.

Upon gaining the hall, however, Mr. Darcy took an abrupt turn down a partially lit corridor which opened upon the far end of the balcony. After reaching the location he deemed most appropriate for private conversation without the outward appearance of an overt attempt at seclusion, he looked out into the darkened sky as he addressed Elizabeth in a collected manner which few men could achieve.

"Miss Bennet, I gather the conversation during our first dance this evening was of greater import than the subject matter would normally imply."

"I confess that such communication was my intent, sir," Elizabeth replied nervously, turning to rest her hands upon the railing. The tender hesitance which overtook his features would have been plainly visible to the lady, had she dared to look upon his countenance.

"Then you mean to say...that is...Have you become rather fond of the bookshop in Meryton as of late?" Mr. Darcy inquired.

Elizabeth smiled delicately, turning her eyes up to his as she spoke. "It seems we have both become rather diligent patrons of the bookshop in Meryton, yes."

Any irritation Mr. Darcy felt in discovering her to be the lady behind the notes began to dissipate, as a certain part of him insisted he could not imagine a more pleasing end to his clandestine correspondence. He could not prevent a slight upturn of his lips, knowing that his suspicions were correct. With such an expression continuing on his face, containing neither smugness nor disdain, Mr. Darcy rested his elbows against the railing beside Elizabeth, turning his face to hers as he addressed her. "I admit myself rather curious regarding how you came into such information. I had not thought my words to be that transparent."

"Indeed they were not," Elizabeth smiled impishly, considering that perhaps his honest expression and casual stance were indicative of his true nature, "but a girl does what she can, sir. I believe you know enough of me to realize I do not have the timidity that would keep me from discovering you by covert means, when simple conjecture from your written words was insufficient."

"In that case, I can at least take some comfort in knowing that a well-strategized scheme was required to discover me, as Bingley was quite correct when he accused me of putting a great deal of study into choosing my words carefully."

"I admit I am well aware of the truth in that statement. Your fastidious style leaves little room for improvement." Elizabeth chuckled lightly, earning a soft response from her companion. However he soon moved his head ever so slightly closer to hers, his tone becoming slightly more serious as he spoke.

"Your manners towards me seem to have softened since discovering this information."

"I might say the same of you, sir."

At this moment, the musicians could be heard from the ballroom, breaking the hazy spell that had cast itself upon them, and reminding the pair that while relatively private, their location was not far from prying eyes.

"Miss Bennet, I believe the dancing is about to resume."

Mr. Darcy extended his hand, and with no further communication between the two, escorted her to the ballroom and into the dance. Though neither party was particularly more verbose than they had been during their previous dances, the easy manners and congenial smiles of both made for pleasant conversation, a circumstance which did not go unnoticed by several parties in the room. Miss Bingley had yet to dance with Mr. Darcy, and while her feelings towards the present pairing in the dance were highly predictable, a certain gentleman's were not.

Mr. Bennet had never found more than a passing amusement in the possibility of Mr. Darcy taking an interest in his daughter, but by his count, and apparently many other attendees of the ball were in accord, Mr. Darcy's requesting a third set gave statement to a very particular interest in his Elizabeth. All the more surprising was the pleasant nature of Elizabeth's response to the gentleman, which gave Mr. Bennet to certain suspicions regarding the identity of her correspondent and her good information regarding the same. The dance soon ended, and after Mr. Darcy had delivered Elizabeth to Miss Lucas' company, Mr. Bennet took the opportunity to seek the young gentleman out.

"Mr. Darcy, I see you have developed quite a fondness for dancing, and with my Elizabeth in particular. I hope you realize your recent partiality has established a certain expectation, and leads me to inform you that many gentleman in the neighborhood frequently call at Longbourn, finding me at leisure for a game of chess, or otherwise if necessary."

"With your permission, sir, I believe I may avail myself of your hospitality in the morning."

"In that case, sir, I believe my daughter may find herself in need of a partner for the last set, as while she had originally attempted to coerce me into the activity, I believe there are others more suitable to the task."

The grin on Mr. Darcy's face left Mr. Bennet in no doubt of the accuracy of his supposition, nor the wisdom of his suggestion. He had never been a man to pay great mind to the gossiping hens of the neighborhood, and if harmless circumstances that were highly agreeable to his daughter and her suitor would set the ladies talking, then so be it.

"Miss Elizabeth, might I request your hand for the final set?" Mr. Darcy inquired.

"I regret sir, that my dance card is full for the remainder of the evening."

"I see. I should tell you that have it on good authority – in fact from the gentleman himself – that your partner for the last set finds himself unequal to the task, and has graciously requested that I take his place."

"For no purpose other than his own inability I am sure," Elizabeth smiled impishly, "How gracious of you to intercede."

"The honor is all mine, I assure you." Mr. Darcy returned her smile, a slight chuckle on his lips as he extended his hand to escort her.

Though the looks exchanged by Mr. Darcy and Miss Elizabeth during their dance could never rival those that passed between Mr. Bingley and Miss Bennet, it was no less a heady experience for either party. His drastic transformation was so different from what Elizabeth had imagined would be the result of her reveal. She would have though it unbelievable were she not bearing direct witness to it.

"I believe we must have some conversation, Mr. Darcy, and though I have said as much on a previous occasion, it is no less true during the fourth half-hour of each other's company than the first."

"Indeed you are correct, and I hope you understand I only mean to impress one particular occupant of the room when I say your appearance is even more stunning this evening than it was on the occasion to which you refer."

Elizabeth blushed lightly, glancing down before she replied, "Your compliments inspire me to respond in kind, and say that you are turned out rather handsomely yourself this evening, sir."

"And yet with no reference to my previous appearance, I may assume that at the last ball I was rather frightful."

Elizabeth laughed, "You jest, sir. And to think you claimed that *I* was prone to the twisting of other's words, I believe *you* are now twisting mine."

"Perhaps it is so, in which case I may claim you to have had a very mischievous influence on me, Miss Bennet."

"Very well then, if nothing more than an influence, I can rest assured that as the instructor of your emerging teasing abilities, I may yet find myself victorious."

"An experience I shall look forward to having repeated frequently in the future."

Elizabeth found herself unequal to anything more than a modest smile in response.

"I hope it will not bother you that I intend to call at Longbourn tomorrow morning, and said as much to your father this evening."

"He has invited you to play at chess then," she replied archly.

"That he has, though my primary incentive for visiting Longbourn lies elsewhere." His tone turned from playful to sincere as he added, "I hope you would not object to my calling at Longbourn, Miss Bennet."

"Not at all, sir. I confess I shall be looking forward to it."

Mr. Darcy's eyes darted over her shoulder, and Elizabeth turned her head to follow his line of sight, finding the Hursts and Miss Bingley across the room, searching the diminishing crowd as they retrieved their cloaks.

"The weather earlier today looked promising that its mildness might continue into the morrow," Elizabeth offered tentatively.

Mr. Darcy studied her face as he replied, "That it did, in which case we might indulge in a short walk before I meet with your father."

"I would enjoy that, Mr. Darcy," Elizabeth said softly as she boldly met his gaze, wishing to communicate her understanding.

Mr. Darcy met her gaze, raising her hand in his, "As would I, Miss Elizabeth," he answered huskily before placing a lingering kiss upon her fingertips and turning to rejoin his party for their departure.

ৎৎৎ

The following morning brought Mr. Bingley and Mr. Darcy to Longbourn at an hour deemed appropriate in consideration of the late hour of the ball the night before, though that is not to say it met the preference of one gentleman in particular who could have easily been prepared to leave at dawn.

Upon arriving at Longbourn, the gentlemen were led to the parlor where the ladies of the house were assembled. Mr. Bingley greeted Jane warmly, and suggested they might walk out into the gardens and enjoy what remained of the unseasonably pleasant weather. Mr. Darcy looked at Miss Elizabeth in askance, to which she supplied the information that her father was occupied at present, but would join the party for luncheon. Mr. Darcy responded with a smile, and offered his arm to escort her out of doors, following Mr. Bingley and Miss Bennet.

Upon leaving the house, however, Mr. Darcy showed little interest in joining the others as he led her towards the little wilderness on the outskirts of the garden and continued on through it down a path towards the nearby wood. As the gentleman seemed determined to remain silent, Elizabeth resolved to enjoy the companionable silence until he chose to speak, which at length, he did.

"I hope you found the festivities last evening to your enjoyment."

"Indeed I did, sir. For fear of expressing myself in a manner more expected from my sister Jane, I must say I cannot recall when I last had a more pleasant time nor enjoyed more pleasant company."

"I am glad to hear it," Mr. Darcy smiled. He then cleared his throat and stated, "There is a decision I made last evening, Miss Bennet, and I

A Noteworthy Courtship

admit I have been able to think of little else but your opinion on the subject."

Mr. Darcy then stopped abruptly and turned towards Elizabeth. She looked up at him, her eyes entreating him to continue.

"Miss Elizabeth, I hope you would not object to my frequent presence at Longbourn, for I would be very pleased if you were amenable to my calling here. Would allow me to court you?"

"I would, sir. I look forward to your calls."

Mr. Darcy reached for her hand, and placed the lightest of kisses upon it. "Thank you, Elizabeth, I shall look forward to this as well."

He placed another lingering kiss upon her hand before intertwining her arm tightly in his and returning to others gathered in the garden.

It was not long before all assembled agreed they ought return to the house, as Mrs. Bennet had prepared for a late luncheon to be served for her guests. Mr. Bennet joined the family for the meal, which passed pleasantly with conversation centering on the previous evening, and of course Mr. Bingley and Miss Bennet's engagement, as Mrs. Bennet could speak of little else. As the meal drew to a close, Mr. Bennet patted his napkin on his lips, clearing his throat with a pointed glance towards Mr. Darcy as he rose from the table. The younger gentleman soon excused himself to join Mr. Bennet in the library under the pretext of challenging him to a game of chess.

Mr. Darcy rejoined the party in the drawing room just as Mrs. Bennet insisted the gentlemen must stay for tea. Each accepted the invitation politely before they were once again ushered out of doors that the matron might make the appropriate preparations. Mr. Bingley and Jane seated themselves comfortably on a stone bench where they might converse quietly, while the newly courting couple chose to ramble about the garden. Miss Elizabeth engaged Mr. Darcy in many pleasant topics of conversation, the former laughing delightedly as the latter exhibited his wit and new-found ability to tease. After some time, the gentleman found himself entirely spellbound. The lady's confidence in herself and ease in the gentleman's presence were such that her melodious laughter and delightful conversation continued, despite his increasingly hazy replies. So might their conversation have continued until tea had Mr. Darcy not suddenly pulled her aside and led her into a small copse beside the garden.

Just a few moments after his swift movement had interrupted her laughter, Elizabeth found herself standing directly before Mr. Darcy, his earnest gaze upon her and her hands clasped in his. How she had ever mistaken his intense look for dislike she could no longer understand. She swallowed sharply as at length, the gentleman spoke.

"You will think me positively rash, I am sure of it, though I beg you not to refuse me and turn me away outright if I need exercise a greater amount of patience."

Elizabeth was overwhelmed by the fervently passionate expression dancing in his eyes as he inclined his head ever so slightly closer to hers. *Goodness, he wants to kiss me.*

"Though we have only just discovered the true depths of our acquaintance, I have long known you to be the most enchanting and remarkable woman I have ever met. I can no longer deny how ardently I admire and love you, and I can only hope that you might return some portion of my feelings and will consent to be my wife."

"Yes." Elizabeth smiled widely, amazed at how simply and clearly she had known her answer to his unexpected question.

"Yes?"

"Yes, I will marry you, and yes, you may hope that your feelings shall be returned. Though I confess the feelings I have for you at present may not be as strong as your own, I cannot but anticipate that they soon shall be."

"Elizabeth," Mr. Darcy smiled brightly, unable to keep a grin from reappearing inbetween his words as he spoke, "You have made me so happy. For a moment I feared your reaction, you looked apprehensive when I first began to address you."

Embarrassed, Elizabeth blushed and turned her eyes to the grass beneath her feet. "I was simply imagining you had a different request to make of me."

Amused by the thought of *his* Elizabeth – *oh, the glory of being truly able to think of her as such* – displaying any form of timidity he inquired playfully, "And what request might that be?"

"Nothing." Elizabeth replied, striving for a semblance of her typical good humor, "It was quite silly, and it was not what you had in mind in any case."

"You need not fear telling me," he said earnestly, compelling her to meet his gaze.

"I thought you were wanted to...I thought you were asking to... kiss me," she admitted, her eyes still trained on the nearby foliage.

Mr. Darcy smiled and stepped closer, raising their joined hands between then, "Well in that case, you were not entirely wrong, as while we both know that is not the particular request I made, I would very much like to kiss you."

At last Elizabeth raised her eyes to his, and inhaled sharply when she realized the closeness of his face to hers. The expression in her eyes answering the question in his, she closed her eyes as she felt his lips brush gently against her own.

Her eyes fluttering open to meet his same intense gaze, she nervously thought to lighten the atmosphere surrounding them, "You must think me rather brazen for suggesting such a thing."

"Not at all, you merely save me the trouble of asking directly by anticipating my next request."

Each shared a tender smile with the other which, in combination with the loving gazes so fixed between them, could not but result in another, longer, display of his love for her, and her mutual regard. It was but a moment's work before Elizabeth found herself wrapped in Mr. Darcy's gentle embrace, relishing in the comfort brought by the gentleman of her affections, and the joy of knowing that he returned her feelings in kind.

An Unfortunate Mishap at Rosings Park

For those who felt the previous alternate ending was sloshed in superfluous mush, rest assured that while portions of this next scene are sloshed in an equally sticky substance, the result is quite the opposite.

Colonel Fitzwilliam was taking his tour of the Park as he did each year upon his visit to Rosings, this year venturing forth rather earlier than usual on account of his cousin Darcy's imminent departure. He had rather enjoyed the scene in the drawing room as Darcy tried to justify his reason for visiting an old acquaintance. Fitzwilliam did remember rather well the friendship between his cousin and Andrew Beaumont, but to resume the acquaintance now, after having heard nothing of the gentleman during the years since his marriage, was puzzling. If he had not known his serious cousin's disposition so well, he would have suspected a young lady to be involved – that would certainly be motivation enough for the Colonel to resume a tedious acquaintance from his own Cambridge days. Chuckling over the idea of Darcy secretly being in love, he failed to notice the streak of black headed towards Rosings along a nearby path. When his dog, Brinkley, eagerly ran off towards the same path, he thought little of it as he assumed the dog to be chasing a squirrel or perhaps a rabbit. Good riddance, as his aunt's grounds seemed to be riddled with a superfluous population of unsavory vermin.

It was not until Brinkley's ferocious barking was answered by a piercing shriek followed by muffled and indiscernible sounds that Fitzwilliam became concerned, his alarm mounting as the cries ceased but the growling of his large canine was still audible. By the time the colonel reached the other side of a large hedgerow, he gasped, making the stark realization that he had arrived too late, and nothing could be done but notify his aunt of the unfortunate event that had taken place.

ঙঙঙ

"Darcy!" Colonel Fitzwilliam shouted as he approached the gates of Rosings Park.

Mr. Darcy nodded in acknowledgement of his cousin, thankful that his escape was interrupted by the only person of the household who would not have been sent by his aunt's bidding to summon him back to the house like an escaped pig.

"Darcy!" Colonel Fitzwilliam called out again, his urgency now evidenced not only by his tone of voice but by the quickening of his step.

"Fitzwilliam?" Mr. Darcy answered tentatively.

"Darcy, I am afraid there are tidings I must share with our aunt that are equally unpleasant as they are bizarre."

Mr. Darcy looked at his cousin in askance, bidding him to continue.

"Brinkley and I had set out into the park, as is our usual habit...oh, I never once conceived a single thought that such a thing could occur."

"Fitzwilliam, you are making about as much sense as our great-uncle Milton when he used to mutter that the French were after his boiled potatoes."

"It seems I neglected to inquire with my man as to whether or not Brinkley had been fed before leaving for our walk."

"I hardly see a reason to be so distressed, Fitzwilliam, Brinkley has always been skilled at hunting."

"You need not remind me, cousin, as I have always been one to encourage that trait in him! A fact which only makes it worse, though I have never known him capable of attacking a man! But what was the reason he had to have all that damnable ham on his person? I wonder if all of this could have been prevented."

"Damnable ham? Do you mean to say that Brinkley has attacked someone?"

"I am afraid he has done more than attacked him. I begin to regret any jests I made at the expense of the man. I would never have wished such an end on our aunt's parson."

"....Mr. Collins? You mean to tell me that Brinkley....and now he is...?"

"Yes. Satchel full of ham and all."

"Well, there is nothing for it but to inform our aunt I suppose, after which we shall commission ourselves to the parsonage to relate the sad truth to the staff there as well. Through my acquaintance with the gentleman in Hertfordshire, I am aware of his only living relations, and I will take upon myself the task of informing them of the unfortunate incident."

‹‹‹‹

The next morning an express rider made a delivery a Longbourn, and much to the chagrin of Mrs. Bennet, Mr. Bennet refused to reveal the contents of the letter, insisting that he must write to Mr. Gardiner in London and Mr. Bingley at Ashingdon with utmost haste. He hardly knew how to explain the bizarre events to his family, though he assumed as little detail as possible would be the most prudent approach with his wife and youngest daughters. As to composing his letters, it seemed vulgar to discuss the ramifications his cousin's fatality would have upon the estate, which both Mr. Gardiner and Mr. Bingley would realize by their own conjecture, so he resolved that a quotation of Mr. Darcy's own letter would best suit his brother and son. After all, there could not be more than one way to explain that Mr. Collins had instructed his cook to slosh excessive amounts of extracts from his beehives over a large ham, and sought to impress his patroness with a large sample of the honey-baked concoction.

It was not until supper that Mr. Bennet left his study, seating himself at the table with a feigned air of nonchalance and began to eat his dinner. With a huff, Mrs. Bennet resigned her efforts of extracting the news and turned her attention to her remaining daughters, such that she was taken quite by surprise when her husband spoke.

"Well my dear, it seems the entail on Longbourn has been broken, as Mr. Collins has been eaten."

"Eaten?" Mrs. Bennet asked incredulously.

"Yes....eaten."

After sufficient pause for the ladies at the table to realize he was in earnest, the sentiment acknowledged by the gaping of their mouths and widening of their eyes, Mr. Bennet added, "It seems there was an unfortunate incident involving an overly aggressive canine that had missed its breakfast."

Christmas in London

Mr. Darcy paced back and forth in his study, interrupting his motion only to occasionally poke at the fire, glancing wistfully at the shaggy mop of his dog Jemma as she lounged beside the fire, sprawled on the generously sized stuffed bed Georgiana had commissioned for their canine companion. He was not entirely surprised at Georgiana's bringing the animal to town when she traveled from Pemberley, he only reflected on the irony that for all the times Jemma begged for attention and unsettled his paperwork with her rambunctious behavior, now –

when he would most appreciate the distraction – she would not trouble herself to be roused from her lethargy. With a last vengeful poke at the fire, he let out a large sigh and decided to seek out his sister's company in the drawing room. As much as he anticipated Thompson's return, that he might know his note had been delivered safely, the earliest he might be expected to arrive was still over an hour away, and there was a good chance he would not have a return note from *her* so close to Christmastide.

"Brother, I am glad you have come to join me," Georgiana greeted cheerfully as her brother entered the room.

"Yes, I was just about to drag you out of your study," Colonel Fitzwilliam added jovially, "Great estate or not, every master deserves his fair share of leisure to enjoy the festivities."

"Fitzwilliam, how kind of you to join us," said Mr. Darcy, "I hope you have been keeping Georgiana entertained."

"Oh, I think we managed tolerably well, even without the addition of your enrapturing conversational skills." His cousin jested.

"I have just received a letter from Caroline Bingley," Georgiana added kindly, "she asks that I extend to you her fondest holiday wishes."

"How kind of her," Mr. Darcy replied. His attempt at a civil reply for the sake of his sister was somewhat effective, though the sarcasm he attempted to disguise was not entirely lost on his cousin.

"She gave brief mention of her brother's engagement to Miss Bennet," Georgiana continued, "Can you tell me of her? Miss Bingley declares Miss Bennet to be a sweet girl, though she fears the manners of her many sisters may overwhelm me."

"Mr. Bingley is quite satisfied with his choice of wife, and though another match could have been an improvement in terms of fortune and connection, I admit I can find no fault in the lady herself. Her sisters however..." Mr. Darcy trailed off, reminding himself of the old adage that if one could not say something nice, one should not speak at all.

"Let me guess," Fitzwilliam chuckled, "since you are Bingley's friend, the next eldest must by default try to make a catch of you too, eh Darcy?"

"Not to any large degree, as Miss Elizabeth's penchant runs more towards the argumentative and impertinent."

"A bluestocking then? I suppose she must not be very pretty if she lacks the confidence to garnish your attention with her charms."

"Oh, she is quite beautiful," Mr. Darcy retorted a bit too quickly before adding, "though definitely quite a handful."

That explains Miss Bingley's comment on her 'fine eyes'. Georgiana thought amusedly, the slightest of smirks forming upon her lips as she observed her brother. She startled as she noticed her brother scrutinizing her with an inquisitive expression, and excused herself before he might ask her to explain.

"Tell me Fitzwilliam, how long have you been in town?" Mr. Darcy asked his cousin.

"This past fortnight," the gentleman replied.

"And this is the first I have seen of you? I suppose I should not be surprised, considering there are plenty of young ladies to entertain you during your leave."

"That there are, and though I may not be able to entice them into matrimony with so little fortune to accompany my share of the Fitzwilliam name, finding an enjoyable young lady to flatter at a ball is easy enough."

"Yes," Mr. Darcy scoffed, "I suppose it is a simple business to walk into a ballroom and single out the one lady in all of England whose lively nature fills your heart with joy."

"Ha! I doubt I have ever met a lady of that description amongst the peerage or gentry who make up our insipid society – have you?"

The wan smile Mr. Darcy offered in response did little to communicate his opinion on the subject, though his mind quickly turned to a certain lady in Hertfordshire who was certainly capable of filling that description, and when he might avail himself of Bingley's hospitality once again.

A Noteworthy Courtship

An Unexpected Meeting

Having arrived at Netherfield the night before for Mr. Bingley's wedding three weeks hence, Mr. Darcy had anxiously ridden to the Meryton bookseller's and relished in her light-hearted note, discussing their mutual appreciation for the outdoors and the written word. He had already determined to return to Hertfordshire to court his Elizabeth, and reading these words only increased his confidence in his decision to pursue the woman who already owned his heart. Little did he know that a slight detour on the way back to Netherfield would bring him face to face with the object of his affections.

Elizabeth walked out into the sunshine, enjoying the gradually warming weather and the opportunity to escape the house before her mother confined her along with her sisters in preparation for the evening's festivities. A simple dinner at the Philips' it may be, her mother still would not allow any of her daughters to go out into society without displaying themselves to advantage, particularly as her eldest would soon gain the prestigious title of Mrs. Bingley.

Having removed her bonnet, Elizabeth continued to walk along the wooded path until a sudden gust of wind stripped the article from her fingers' loose and inattentive grasp. She sighed, reflecting on the irony that *of course* her wayward bonnet would settle into the nearby stream. Fruitlessly attempting to retrieve the lost item before it drifted out of reach, Elizabeth huffed and searched the surrounding bank for a means of fishing it out. Little did she know what a charming picture she created for the approaching horse and rider as with a triumphant "Aha!" she picked up a long stick, bending slightly forwards as she stretched to hook her prize upon the branch's end.

"Miss Bennet, might I be of assistance?"

The sound of Mr. Darcy's voice startled her from her concentration, a drenched bonnet then slipping from the end of her stick as she jerked into an upright position.

"I *was* getting on well enough, sir," Elizabeth replied, unsure of how to proceed, for she dared not continue her improvised fishing in the gentleman's presence.

"Allow me, Miss Bennet."

Elizabeth stared awkwardly and loosened her fingers as Mr. Darcy took the stick from her hands, only to place it on the ground beside him as he moved down the bank. Within a few moments he reached the bonnet, his tall riding boots partially submerged as he lifted the item and flashed her a cheeky grin.

"We gentleman must have some advantage." He said smugly as he extended the dripping bonnet towards her, its saturated ribbons dangling perilously close to her skirts.

Elizabeth placed her hands upon her hips, and was preparing a retort suitable for the occasion. Noticing her rising indignation, Mr. Darcy wondered if perhaps he had been to rash in teasing her. He spoke hastily before the inevitable remark escaped her lips.

"Excuse the interruption, Miss Bennet, but please allow me to stop you from saying something you will only come to regret for the rest of our lives."

His steady gaze was finally broken as he looked down at drenched article in his hands, the continuing flow of droplets being absorbed into the grass between them. "I can hardly expect you to accept this in its current state."

Mr. Darcy then gently wrung out as much of the remaining water as possible before again offering the retrieved bonnet to her.

"Will you be in attendance at the Philips' this evening?" he asked hesitantly.

"Yes, my family and I shall attend the dinner party."

"I am glad to hear it," Mr. Darcy smiled politely as he spoke before turning to mount his horse.

"Until this evening, Miss Bennet."

Elizabeth responded in kind, and with a tip of his hat, Mr. Darcy departed, leaving her to wonder at his uncharacteristic ease of manners, and at least one of his statements in particular. He had referred to the rest of *their* lives. From any other man, she might have freely acknowledged the implication. As impossible as it was to credit such implications to Mr. Darcy, assuming that he had spoken in reference to frequently being in each other's company through the Bingleys was not entirely plausible either. And what did he mean by the boyish grin as he fished out her bonnet? A gallant Mr. Darcy? Implausible, indeed.

A Noteworthy Courtship

Mr. Bingley's Revenge (or Bingley the Hun)

We return to a warm spring afternoon, at a modest estate just off the coast of Essex, where a merry party consisting of the Beaumonts, the Bingleys, Mr. Darcy and Miss Bennet had gathered on the lawn for a game of cricket.

Just as the informal cricket match came to a close, little Alexander Beaumont had begun to fuss, and after a few moments of failed attempts to sooth him through various entertainments and changed positions, Mrs. Beaumont relented and expressed that she would be returning him to the house for a nap. Mr. and Mrs. Bingley shared a smile, and announced their intent to return to the house as well. Mr. Bingley rose from his partially reclined position at his wife's side, and offered his hands to pull her up as well, gleefully stealing a quick kiss once she gained her feet. Arm in arm, they walked towards the house, Mr. Bingley suggesting that while he would first gain a fresh change of clothes, he would enjoy escorting his wife on a quick tour of the gardens before dinner. They had just crossed the foyer and nearly reached the stairs when a carriage was heard approaching. Mr. and Mrs. Bingley paid it little mind until the front doors of Ashingdon House opened rapidly, immediately followed by an imperious voice demanding to see Mr. Darcy.

Espying the last swish of Mrs. Beaumont's skirts disappear down an upper hallway as she rushed her fussing babe towards the nursery, Mr. Bingley turned and descended the few stairs he had gained, hoping to be of assistance.

"If you would allow me, madam, may I inform you that Mr. Darcy is expected to return to the house momentarily. Might I be of assistance?"

"You, sir, may be of great assistance by locating my nephew."

"If you please, ma'am," interjected Mrs. Nicholls, the Beaumont's housekeeper, "might I offer to escort you to the drawing room for refreshment while we anticipate the gentleman's return from the afternoon's sport?"

"A fine idea, Mrs. Nicholls," Mr. Bingley enthused, "My wife, Mrs. Bingley and I, would be happy to offer our company..."

"Mr. Bingley," greeted Mr. Collins with a solemn bow, having just entered the house in his patronesses' wake, "forgive me when I suggest that you assist us in locating Mr. Darcy directly, as Lady Catherine has urgent business with the gentleman."

"*You* are Mr. Bingley?" Lady Catherine sniffed, "In that case, Collins – you shall stay with your future relations that you might sort out your own affairs, and *you*," she gestured to Mrs. Nicholls, "shall direct me to my nephew, immediately."

Shocked expressions graced the faces of Mr. and Mrs. Bingley as they witnessed the great Lady exit the house as quickly and deliberately as she had entered it, though their attention was quickly drawn back to Mrs. Bingley's cousin as he returned from escorting his patroness to the door.

"Mr. Bingley, Mrs. Bingley, allow me to greet you properly now that my revered patroness' needs are being attended."

"You are very welcome, Mr. Collins," Mr. Bingley greeted, baffled in no small degree, "I believe Mr. and Mrs. Beaumont will forgive us the presumption of retiring to their drawing room in their absence."

"Indeed. I shall call for some refreshment." Jane curtsied as headed towards the kitchen, considering it most prudent to inform the kitchen staff personally, as Mrs. Nicholls was otherwise engaged.

ﹲﹲﹲ

"Mr. Bingley, I flatter myself that the day I may call you 'brother' approaches at an ever increasing pace. It is with great honor that I have received the assistance of Lady Catherine deBourgh in securing my future happiness, and with your blessing, I hope to secure an audience with Miss Elizabeth directly that I may relate to her the considerations that have been so generously provided to us."

"I beg your pardon, sir." Mr. Bingley said with some concern, "Do you mean to say that your arrival here is not for the assistance of Mr. Darcy's aunt, but rather your intent is to locate Elizabeth?"

"Indeed, sir."

Mr. Bingley stared confusedly at Mr. Collins. How the gentleman had come to know Elizabeth's present location was puzzling, though the particular outcome he expected to result from his traveling hither was less discernable. "I fail to understand your request for my blessing, both in the specific action you wish me to approve and your reason for approaching me, her brother, as opposed to the lady's father, Mr. Bennet."

"Indeed, it is most troubling, sir – Mr. Bennet's condition, that is. It is most providential that you have recently married, as you may now fulfill the duties of head of the family. Though I suppose considering my age and future inheritance of Longbourn, I might fill such an office for my wife's sisters once Elizabeth and I are married."

Mr. Bingley stared and sputtered, completely taken aback by Mr. Collins' presumptuous remarks, not knowing which portions he found most offensive and most disturbing, though he assumed each word he had the misfortune of hearing fit into both categories. Unfortunately for Mr. Bingley, his silence was interpreted by Mr. Collins as encouragement to continue his speech.

"Lady Catherine so kindly provided my transportation into Essex, that I might request your blessing, though I suppose it is merely a formality, as Mrs. Bennet has thoroughly supported the match, and though Mr. Bennet has attempted to dissuade me, none of his family can truly mean to refuse me, considering my status as heir to the estate. Now sir, nothing remains but for Elizabeth to join me at my side. I confess Lady Catherine was seriously displeased to hear of my dearest's unconventional behavior, but given Mr. Bennet's infirmity, I cannot blame her for the confusion. I assured Lady Catherine that Elizabeth will quickly learn to submit, as a wife ought to her husband, and a parson's wife ought to her patroness, and as soon as we are married I will set about making sure she…"

"Why you…" Mr. Bingley barked forcefully before his powers of speech failed him, though his interruption was successful in silencing the abhorrent man before him, and the immense reddening of his complexion related his sentiments more clearly – and far more civilly – than any of the words forming in his mind.

A barbaric shout resonated into entrance hall of Ashingdon, and Mrs. Bingley burst into the drawing room just in time to see her husband throw himself at Mr. Collins, leaping enragedly from his current position, the sofa between them only offering further leverage for his vengeful descent upon the odious man.

What havoc Mr. Bingley might have then wreaked upon Mr. Collins' person will unfortunately never be known, as at that moment, a sharp voice cried out.

"Bingley!"

"Darcy?" Mr. Bingley questioned innocently, popping his head up above the overturned sofa in search of his friend, heedless of the repulsive gentleman whose chest was now firmly pinned between Bingley's knee and the floor.

Upon observing that the room now contained many more spectators than he had anticipated – namely Mr. Darcy, Lady Catherine, Mr. and Mrs. Beaumont, Miss Elizabeth, and of course, his own wife – Mr. Bingley cleared his throat and stood, removing himself from Mr. Collins person, though neglecting to offer him any assistance before moving to stand beside his wife.

"Mr. Bingley," Lady Catherine stated icily. "I have already borne sufficient shocks today over the appalling behavior conducted in this house, and have no need of witnessing such wild displays as you have just forced upon me. Let it be known that though you shall become a brother to Mr. Collins, you shall never be welcome at Rosings Park."

"Never fear, madam. I doubt you shall be exposed to my outlandish and offensive behavior again, as under no circumstances will Mr. Collins become any closer relation to me than a cousin by marriage."

"But..." Mr. Collins sputtered sheepishly, not entirely fond of the idea of further upsetting the gentleman who had recently tackled him like Attila the Hun.

"Mr. Collins, not only have you insulted the good name of my wife's father, but you have also greatly trespassed upon the reputation of my sister. I speak confidently of Mr. Bennet's opinion in saying that you will never receive his daughter's hand in marriage should you approach him to request it, a sentiment of which you would be aware had you troubled yourself to solicit his consent." At this Lady Catherine turned her steely gaze from Mr. Bingley, and raised a formidable eyebrow in her parson's direction.

"As for you soliciting my blessing," Mr. Bingley continued stalwartly, "Miss Bennet's father is of sound mind and body, and therefore my opinion of the matter is of no consequence to your suit, though I believe I have made my sentiments known. I am also quite knowledgeable of the fact that the lady in question has repeatedly expressed her sentiments along the same vein. At this juncture you can have nothing further to say, and as Miss Bennet's brother, I demand that you leave this house at once."

Mr. Bingley had stepped forward during this speech, placing himself protectively before his wife and sister. He then turned to the ladies and offered an arm to each of them, silently passing the remaining occupants of the room as he guided the ladies through the open doors and up the staircase, safely depositing them into Mrs. Bingley's room. Whether or not he immediately retired to Mr. Beaumont's study for a stiff brandy to steady himself after such an uncharacteristic display of bravado is neither here nor there, as is whether or not he overheard a rather heated conversation from the window of said study, which soundly distinctly like Mr. Darcy addressing his aunt with a speech not dissimilar from the one he had just addressed towards Mr. Collins.

An Interlude at Ashingdon

I have been kindly informed of the capital offense committed by naming the Bingley's children in my epilogue and failing to provide a similar service for the Darcys' children. As reparation, I gladly offer a little further insight into one of the many holidays spent at Ashingdon, in particular the spring of 1820, eight years following the first gathering of this particular group of family and dear friends.

The carriage ride from Pemberley to Ashingdon started much as it had in years previous, save the addition of a third darling child traveling on the lap of his mother. The Darcy's had only traveled as far as the Bingleys' estate the previous year due to Mrs. Bingley's confinement, a circumstance which was not too grievous as at the time Mrs. Darcy must preferred the shorter journey with her own toddler being so young. The fresh salty air signaled the nearness of their destination, and Elizabeth smiled in remembrance of her first occasion to experience the sensation of the sea breeze.

Once the carriage finally lurched to a halt in the drive, a tall boy the age of seven leapt from the open door, his excitement matched by the tousle-headed lad making a similar escape from the house. With a brief nod from his father, the taller of the boys ran off towards the gardens, his friend hard upon his heels. At a much more genteel pace, the remaining occupants of the carriage descended, the gentleman first, assisting his five year old daughter Margaret before cradling his sleepy two year old Matthew in one arm as he handed down his wife with the other. Mr. Darcy looked in the direction of his long disappeared son and shook his head, knowing full well that once his William was reunited with Nathaniel Beaumont, the two were thick as thieves, and lord knew what mischief they would invent – a trait he universally claimed could only stem from his mother.

"I recognize that look, Fitzwilliam, and I would advise you not suggest that our son's mischievous nature is my doing, lest I be required to solicit your cousin for tales of your own childhood exploits."

"Touché, my dear. Though should you make good on your threat, I may be forced to remind you that your father has long since provided stories from your younger years, several of which bear a striking resemblance the tales of my own."

Elizabeth Darcy laughed. "Well in that case, I have often said it is best we not argue over who carries the greater blame, and I suggest we apply such wisdom to our present circumstances. I would not wish dear Evelyn to think we have traveled across a half-dozen counties simply to stage a debate in her drive."

"Darcy! There you are," Mr. Beaumont called jovially as he descended the front steps of his home, bowing properly to Elizabeth as he approached.

"Mrs. Darcy, it is a pleasure as always to welcome you to Ashingdon." After taking a brief survey of the family noting one missing from its number, he added slyly, "I gather by the absence of your eldest that my Nathaniel has anticipated your arrival, and the two have already run off to see what trouble they might drum up."

"Your supposition could not be closer to the truth," replied Mr. Darcy, "I thought it an excellent idea that the boys practice their writing skills by corresponding with each other, and while I admit it has inspired William to be rather attentive to his penmanship, I fear the two shall be inseparable as I have heard of little else these last weeks but the sand crabs and garden snakes to be found near your estate."

Mr. Beaumont laughed, "I cannot say that surprises me in the least. Well, let us get the remaining members of your party indoors. I am sure you would appreciate a good rest." He smiled fondly at young Matthew resting his weary head on the broad shoulder of his papa. "The Bingleys arrived yesterday afternoon, and are eager to see you as well, I am sure."

Margaret Darcy obediently held her mother's hand as Mrs. Nicholls lead the young family to their suite of rooms. Mr. Darcy gently lowered Matthew onto his bed, handing him a very worn and well loved stuffed animal, aptly named "Puppy", assuring the little boy that his nursemaid Hannah would come in and check on him shortly with a glass of milk from the kitchens to soothe him to sleep.

As Mr. and Mrs. Darcy quietly left the room, young Margaret's patience had been expended and she eagerly asked if she might be excused to seek out her cousin Emma. In a house occupied by two brothers, female companionship was important to her, even at the age of five, particularly as she knew her cousin Emma Bingley to be as enthusiastically fond of dolls as she. The fact that Margaret was equally fond of playing with the dogs or climbing trees – where Emma most definitely was not – was of no great importance, as there would be ample time for such activities when she returned to Pemberley, a home decidedly overrun with brothers.

Fortunately for Margaret, her Aunt Jane was met in the hall, and after fond greetings were exchanged, she learned that while ten month old Elizabeth Bingley was sleeping soundly, her cousin Emma could be found in the small drawing room downstairs. Aunt Jane quietly admonished her for the squeals of delight that might awake the young ones as a result of her offer to escort her niece downstairs.

Mr. Bingley was found keeping company with his daughter, slightly embarrassed to be caught playing tea as he intoned an *interesting* falsetto for the voice of Mrs. Perifeathers, as his daughter's doll had been named. Margaret was quick to intercede, however, leaving the adults to converse amiably as six year old Edward Bingley proudly told his Uncle Darcy of his recent accomplishments and insisted that this year they would not play checkers, but chess.

In the weeks that followed, Nathaniel Beaumont and William Darcy canvassed every conceivable aspect of their mutual penchant for mischief. Thankfully, each boy was well-bred enough to target only each other with respect to their antics. Each evening commenced with the boy's eager tales of exploit, giving every impression that a frog in one's wash basin or a garden snake slithering beneath the door gave delights that rivaled those to be expected on Christmas morning. After being dutifully scolded by their mothers that the maid did not appreciate the occasional honor of being the first to discover such prizes, the theme of their evening tales shifted to the likes of slingshot contests and pirates' battles.

Edward Bingley frequently joined his cousin and friend at play, until he discovered Alexander Bingley's mutual interest in games – chess in particular – despite their three year age difference. The ladies could not but smile at the singular picture painted by the pair of chess tables set up in the library, and the equally studious expressions of the young lads at one, and the grown men at the other.

It was not long before Margaret Darcy and Emma Bingley announced that there would be a ladies afternoon tea held in the gardens. It was with some persuasion that they agreed to allow the men and boys of the house to join them, and only on the condition that the ladies would still meet in the gardens, albeit a half hour before tea time, and the gentlemen could meet them for refreshments on the green. Alexander and Nathaniel requested that their father arrange for the cricket pitch to be set up for the early afternoon, but Mr. Beaumont suggest croquet might be more suitable to the *refined* party the young ladies had in mind. Delighted giggles divulged the girls' opinion of the scheme, and after wagering a stash of sweet drops on whether Nathaniel Beaumont or William Darcy could hit the ball farther, the boys agreed as well.

That afternoon, the ladies of the house did enjoy each other's company, little Elizabeth Bingley included. Mrs. Darcy commented on how much her namesake had grown since Christmas, and Mrs. Beaumont marveled that they could not have chosen a more appropriate namesake, as the little girl's hair was a striking auburn, in tone with her aunt and a great contrast to the pale blonde of her elder siblings and parents.

The ladies soon prepared to move to the lawn, and were joined by two husbands eager to escort them. Mr. Bingley joyfully scooped his little Lizzybeth off of her mother's lap, alternately tickling her feet and making a good display of rapt attention to her mumbled attempts at speech. With a bit of concern, Mrs. Darcy looked in askance at Mr. Darcy, who explained that two year old Matthew had been eager to remain with his brother and the other boys, a sentiment which greatly pleased him when coming from his shy little boy.

Thus the party gathered on the lawn, enjoying their refreshments under the shade of a large oak. The older children were quick to finish their tea and start a game of croquet, the adults remaining to enjoy the repast, which always took a little longer when assisting the younger children with their refreshments. Lizzybeth gripped tightly to her mother's hands as she took a few steps, laughingly dropping to crawl to her papa and take another slice of fruit from his plate.

Mr. Darcy asked young Matthew if he would like to play, and as he grinned in response to his son's eager jumps and shouts, led him to the grass and showed him how to hold the croquet mallet. As two year old boys are wont to do, he took a few swings as his father instructed, but soon found himself content to swing the mallet sidearm, shouting triumphantly with each hit as the ball tumbled across the grass. Laughingly enjoying their son's antics, Mr. and Mrs. Darcy gave him an extra ball to play with at a safe distance from the playing field and innocent bystanders, and decided to play a match between themselves instead. Mr. Darcy always admired the sparkle in his wife's eyes when they entered into competition, as much as her desire to win might be concealed beneath her merriment and laughter.

Neither the Darcys nor the Bingleys dwelled greatly on the subject of their daughters' eventual marriages, as they strongly desired all of their children to one day marry for love. However the thought did occasionally cross their minds that should the children grow to have such an inclination, they would gladly welcome Alexander or Nathaniel Beaumont as a son, that by extension their dear friends Andrew and Evelyn Beaumont would be family in truth, just as they would always be in spirit.

The End *(again)*

References

Terms:

Curricle: A two-wheeled, lightweight open carriage, pulled by one or often two horses.

the Ton: the more elite circles of London society.

Connemara: A large breed of pony named after the region of Ireland it originates from. Known for its good temperament as well as its agility and versatility.

Suffolk Punch: A breed of draft horse suitable for heavy farm work.

Hands: A unit of measure (based on the width of a human hand) commonly used to measure a horse's height. At 17 hands, Bingley's horse would have been quite tall. The Connemara selected for Elizabeth would have been no more than 14 hands.

Locations:

Essex: County in southeastern England, covers the northern coast of the inlet to the Thames River. Kent is on the southern coast of the inlet.

Hadleigh: inland town a few miles west of Southend and north of Canvey Island.

Hadleigh Castle: the ruins of the castle are still intact today, located approximately 1 mile south of Hadleigh.

Southend (Southend-on-Sea): a small sea-side resort town that gained popularity during Regency times.

Southend Theatre: opened in Southend-on-Sea in the 1790's.

Canvey Island/Benfleet: Canvey Island is located south of Hadleigh, just beyond Hadleigh Castle. Its sandy marshes are bordered by Benfleet creek.

Works:

***A Political Romance* by Laurence Sterne**: A satirical work originally published in 1759.

The Marriage of Figaro: an opera by Mozart based on the original play by Pierre Beaumarchais. *Les Deux Amis* is another of Beaumarchais' works. *Les Deux Amis* premiered at *Comédie-Française* in 1770. *Voi Che Sepete*, as used in the 1995 adaptation of Pride and Prejudice, is from *The Marriage of Figaro*.

[1] Wordsworth's "By the Sea."
[2] Wordsworth's "With Ships the Sea was Sprinkled Far and Nigh."
[3] Lord Byron's "There is a Pleasure in the Pathless Woods."

Further details regarding these references and corresponding images can be found at www.anoteworthycourtship.com

Made in the USA
Lexington, KY
07 February 2011